Praise for Edgar Award-winner

WILLIAM HEFFERNAN

and

RED ANGEL

"Heffernan knows how to create characters through sharp and distinctive dialogue; his pacing is fast and fluid, and his plotting is superb."

NELSON DEMILLE

"[A] strong new entry in his series featuring New York City detective Paul Devlin . . . . [a] complex plot weaving together the Mafia with greedy U.S. and Cuban government officials . . . . The Cuban characters are well-drawn and attractive, even when slippery. Heffernan does a superb job explaining the varieties of Cuban religious experience, the Cuban sensibility, and the ominous shadows of a rigid police state."

Publishers Weekly

"The suspense is fine, and the pace of writing makes one look out for the next jiggery-pokery to jump out of the nganga (caldron)."

Los Angeles Times Book Review

"Heffernan can write a mean page and create a living character in a few words."

Stuart M. Kaminsky

"A real attention grabber . . . deeply involving, expertly detailed, and strategically plotted . . . highly recommended."

Library Journal

Books by William Heffernan

CITYSIDE
THE DINOSAUR CLUB
BRODERICK
CAGING THE RAVEN
THE CORSICAN
ACTS OF CONTRITION
RITUAL
BLOOD ROSE
CORSICAN HONOR
SCARRED
TARNISHED BLUE
WINTER'S GOLD

WILLIAM HEFFERNAN

RED ANGEL

A PAUL DEVLIN MYSTERY

AVON BOOKS
An Imprint of HarperCollins*Publishers*

AVON BOOKS
An Imprint of HarperCollins*Publishers*
10 East 53rd Street
New York, New York 10022-5299

ISBN: 0-380-81881-7
www.avonbooks.com

First Avon Books paperback printing: December 2001
First William Morrow hardcover printing: December 2000

Printed in the U.S.A.

10 9 8 7 6 5 4 3 2 1

This book is for Ellen and Mimi;

and for Tom and Dona, wonderful in-laws

and even better grandparents to my sons.

ACKNOWLEDGMENTS

I would like to thank my editor, Zachary Schisgal, and my agent, Gloria Loomis, for their unwavering enthusiasm for this book. Also, a special thanks to my Cuban friends and fellow writers Luis Adrián Bentancourt, Ignacio Cárdinas, Daniel Chavarria, Justo Vasco, José Latour, and especially Arnaldo Correa, all of whom taught me about their country and the great love they have for it. I would also like to acknowledge the memory of Plante Firme, Cuba's great Palo Monte *palero,* who before his death generously shared the mysteries of his faith with me.

It should also be noted that the political views in this book are those of my imagined characters (and in some cases my own) and should not be attributed to any individual mentioned here.

PROLOGUE

SANTIAGO DE CUBA

The priest stood in the center of the clearing, naked to the waist, his stomach protruding over white cotton trousers that billowed about his legs. His shaved head, a gleaming brown, rocked from side to side; eyes rolled back, mouth open, almost as if in pain. Bare feet began to stamp the ground, raising small puffs of dust. Then his eyes snapped forward, wide and glaring, fixed on the badly burned corpse that lay before him on the ground.

"BabaluAye erikunde. BabaluAye obiapa. Bindome."

The sound of drums filled the clearing, low and sonorous, the resonant beat intensifying as the higher pitch of basket rattles and beating sticks joined the rhythm. Now the chanting voices came, repeating the priest's words, over and over, the bodies of the worshipers moving in a circle about the corpse, swaying to the drums, heads rocking wildly as if unsupported by bone.

The priest's hands shot into the air, his grizzled, aging face resolute, eyes intent on the body. The arms caught the light of torches that illuminated the circle and cast wavering shadows that made it appear he, too, was dancing. Drums and chanting ceased. Worshipers stood frozen in place, bodies tense with anticipation.

"BabaluAye nfumbe. BabaluAye nkise."

Behind the priest the circle parted and the first of the gods appeared. The drums started again as Chango began to sway, bright red robes flashing with the movement, a gleaming ax swinging in a wide arc above his head. Next came the god Oggun, machete held high, body gyrating to the drums, green robes flowing as his torso spun and dipped. Now Ochun, dressed in yellow, goddess of love, her body long and supple, each motion sensuous, seductive. Then Yemaya, blue-robed goddess of the sea, conch shell held high, her movements large and powerful like the ocean's ebb and flow. Next Oy, encased in flowing white, goddess of wind and lightning, face rigid, eyes wide and staring, ruler of the cemetery.

The gods spun about the corpse; each form caught in the beat of the drums. Brown and black faces glistened with sweat, then suddenly froze in place, all attention now drawn to the far end of the circle. The priest turned, raised his eyes to the distant moon.

"BabaluAye nfumbe."

Again the worshipers parted, and the god all awaited entered the circle, body slithering across the ground, snakelike, arms and legs covered by festering sores. Slowly, laboriously, BabaluAye crawled toward the blackened corpse, his head twisted with pain and suffering. Again, the drums, the chanting. Bodies of worshipers swayed in the circle; voices rose to a frenzy. The one they had awaited—the god of death and sickness—was here. Tongue flicking, mouth distorted, BabaluAye moved on the corpse.

"Angel Roja. Angel Roja. Mendez nfumbe. Mendez nfumbe. Mendez, Mendez, Mendez."

In the shadows, as the chanting voices rose, a figure dressed in the uniform of Cuba's State Security Forces watched. A smile played at the corners of his mouth as Oggun passed his machete to the waiting priest. The circle fell to a hush as the priest raised the blade, paused, then sent the gleaming edge down toward the corpse. Sparks flew as the blade struck stone beneath the neck. The head rolled away. Again, drums and chanting filled the circle. Again, the gods renewed their dance.

1

NEW YORK CITY

Vinnie "Big Head" Tedesco stood on the sidewalk, one hand pulling at the tight crotch of his trousers. His eyes roamed the street, as if searching for someone or something he wanted to avoid. Both were nervous affectations, which if recognized, Vinnie would have preferred to hide. Even so, there was an underlying cockiness about the man. His black silk shirt was open to mid-chest, allowing sunlight to reflect the glimmer of a heavy gold chain, and he occupied the sidewalk as if it were his private domain, forcing passersby to move around him. He was a large man, not exceptionally tall, but put together like a block of cement. His hair was long and dark and thickly curled, and it made his already large head seem enormous, almost a caricature: thus his street name, Vinnie Big Head. He was thirty-six years old, an up-and-coming member in the Rossi crime family, and in less than two minutes he would be dead.

* * *

Ollie Pitts stared at the body, already outlined in chalk. He made a sucking sound as he tried to remove a bit of food from his teeth. Then he belched.

"How do you see it?" Paul Devlin asked.

Pitts gave an almost imperceptible shrug. "The one witness we got saw him about five minutes before it went down. Says our boy was standing here, takin' up half the sidewalk like he was waitin' for somebody." A small grin flickered across his lips. "Of course it coulda been just bad luck for Vinnie. A couple of shooters from another family drivin' around lookin' for a target, and Vinnie just happens to be standing there scratching his ass." Pitts paused and belched again. "But I don't buy it. To me it smells more like a setup. Our boy here gets a call and somebody he knows says, Hey, Vinnie, meet us on the corner and we'll go get some scungilli, or a blow job, or whatever Vinnie happens to be up for today. Then the car pulls up and Vinnie Big Head gets two in the chest before he knows what hit him." He raised his chin, indicating the sunburst splatter of blood and bone and tissue that surrounded Vinnie's head on the sidewalk. "Then the shooter gets out and pumps two in his head, just to make sure. Typical mob heart-and-head stuff." He paused, thinking about that. "Looks like a heavy-caliber, though, not the twenty-two peashooters they usually use for this kind of thing." Another shrug. "But Vinnie was a big guy with a nasty rep. Maybe they wanted to make sure the first ones knocked him down. They also didn't have to worry about noise. Not in this fuckin' neighborhood."

Devlin studied the surrounding buildings. The body lay on Broome Street, just off Mulberry in Manhattan's Little Italy. It was one of the city's landmark districts, an area forged more than a century ago by a continuous flow of Italian immigrants and the Mafia goons who lived in their shadow. Today, only a few Italians remained. Over the last twenty years nearby Chinatown had gradually spread across

Canal Street, taking over the once fabled neighborhood so noted for its reticence with police. But that attitude of silence had not changed with the ethnicity. Pitts was right. This was still a see-no-evil kind of place, and not a single neighborhood denizen could be found among the tourists who stood gaping at Vinnie Big Head's blood-soaked body. Those who lived and worked here knew better than to stand around where they might be asked questions they did not want to answer.

Devlin smiled at the thought. The one "witness" they had found was a tourist, a man from Iowa who had been inside a nearby shop when the shooting took place. He had been a good citizen and had waited to tell police the little he knew, excited about a story he would now have for his friends back home. Had he known anything at all, he might have returned to those friends in a box.

"This is number five," Devlin said. "All of them Rossi's people. And, so far, no retaliation. I'm starting to think John the Boss is really sick this time."

"It should only be cancer of the throat." Pitts grinned at his boss. He knew Devlin shared the sentiment.

Giovanni "John the Boss" Rossi had plagued police for more than thirty years, the last twenty as head of a Mafia family whose criminal enterprises stretched from New York, to Miami, to Las Vegas. It was a fact disputed by his doctors, and one very suspect Catholic priest, all of whom swore that Rossi had developed Alzheimer's disease more than a decade ago and was little more than a sick old man, barely capable of finding the bathroom in his Ocean Parkway home. In short, Rossi was an enigma who had kept police at bay by feigning mental enfeeblement, as he regularly went about the city, conducting mob business, dressed in pajamas, bathrobe, and slippers, his retinue of accompanying thugs acting more like keepers than the bodyguards they were. Police attempts to question him were often met with blank, drooling stares. The media, of course, loved the act, and had even dubbed him "the Bathrobe Don."

Devlin had gone after Rossi on his last high-profile case, the death of socialite Natasha Winter. But the don had again proved too elusive. He had entered a private sanitarium, and had managed to wiggle free of the various crimes surrounding that death, including a near-successful attempt on Devlin's life.

Now Rossi seemed to be at the center of the storm. Five of his underlings had been gunned down in the past two months, all supposed victims of a gang war between Rossi and the rival Columbo crime family. The media had beaten those war drums with uncontrolled gusto, until the mayor had ordered Devlin to take over the investigation and, hopefully, calm public concern. But there was little Devlin could do. It was a one-sided war, with Rossi allegedly hiding out in his Brooklyn home, under the personal protection of his top enforcer, Mattie "the Knife" Ippolito, the don, himself, said to be too ill to direct an effective counterattack.

If true, it was a plus as far as Devlin was concerned. In the past Rossi would have had the backing of the powerful Gambino crime family, headed by his nephew, Donatello Torelli. This time, however, the Gambino soldiers had remained on the sidelines, either unwilling or unable to help. Devlin took personal satisfaction in Rossi's "family" problems. Two years ago he had put Rossi's nephew behind bars, helping to weaken the ties between the Rossi and Gambino factions. At the time Rossi had sworn vengeance for that arrest, and Devlin was certain the attempt on his life had been the result of that oath. Now, despite Mayor Howie Silver's interest in ending the war, Devlin was privately rooting for the Columbo family, hoping its thugs would find a way to send the Bathrobe Don to that great cannoli factory in the sky.

"Don't count Rossi out yet," Pitts said.

Devlin wondered if Pitts was reading his mind. He took

Pitts by the arm and led him away from the body. "It's been a long time since we paid John the Boss a call," he said.

Pitts nodded. "Not very respectful of us. You thinking about a ride out to Brooklyn?"

Devlin looked back at the body of Vinnie Big Head and pursed his lips. "This thing isn't going anywhere. Not unless we find ourselves a suicidal witness who can ID the shooters." He turned back to Pitts. "Tell the other guys to canvas the area, just in case. Then you and I will make a little house call on the Bathrobe Don."

"Maybe we should take an enema bottle in case the old fuck really is sick." Pitts grinned at him. "Besides, it's a lovely day to visit Brooklyn, and there's nothing I like better than an afternoon drive to a grease factory." He watched Devlin narrow one eye at the ethnic slur and laughed. "Hey, I'll be good. I promise. I just wanna detect and solve, just like Hizzoner told us."

Devlin looked away and shook his head. Pitts was incorrigible. And the mayor was living a pipe dream. Detect and solve—the actual words the mayor had used at his press conference announcing that Devlin's special unit would investigate the latest mob bloodbath. It sounded wonderful. In newsprint. But right now the mayor would have to settle for half a loaf. Detection was the best Devlin could offer. The solution the mayor wanted—or the resolution—wouldn't come for another month or two . . . when the wiseguys got tired of killing each other. He jerked a thumb toward their unmarked car.

"Let's go detect," he said.

Giovanni "John the Boss" Rossi's home was a stately, three-story pile of bricks situated behind a high, thick hedge on Brooklyn's Ocean Parkway. The house was only three miles from Coney Island, and Pitts had already put in a request that they drive to Nathan's and "scarf down a couple of hot dogs" before returning to Manhattan.

Pitts was an enormous man who ate like there were two of him. He was six-two, and an easy two hundred and thirty pounds, and despite a protruding gut, everything about him was solid and formidable. He had a bristling crew cut and a square, flat street fighter's face, and the largest pair of hands Devlin had ever seen. They were the kind of hands that would look comfortable holding nothing less than a leg of lamb.

He also had one of the worst personnel jackets Devlin had ever read. A twenty-seven-year man who had specialized in homicide most of his career, Pitts had a long list of brutality complaints—none ever proven—to go with an equally impressive record of arrests and convictions. He was forty-eight years old, three years shy of a three-quarter-pay pension, and most of the other bosses in the department believed he would be bounced off the force before he ever reached it. Devlin thought he was the best working street detective on his squad.

Pitts parked their unmarked car in front of Rossi's driveway, effectively blocking any exit, and smiled at the two goons guarding the entrance. They were both in their early thirties, and despite the July heat, each of their wide bodies was covered by a windbreaker. Pitts had no doubt about what the jackets were concealing.

One of the goons took two steps forward. "Move the fuckin' car," he snapped.

Pitts turned to Devlin and shook his head. "Do you believe this shit? Every fucking garbanzo street punk in this city can spot an unmarked car three blocks away. These two 'Mafia killers' "—he made quotes in the air to surround the words—"they think we're here to visit our fucking guinea aunt, who lives across the street."

"Disabuse them of the notion," Devlin said.

Pitts displayed his detective's shield from the breast

pocket of his suit coat, then pushed open the door. He emerged from the car like a bull entering a Spanish bullring, took three quick steps to the man who had spoken, grabbed him with one ham-sized hand, and propelled him toward the trunk of the car.

"Spread 'em, asshole," he growled. He turned to the second man. "Join him, you piece of dog shit, before I put my foot halfway up your ass."

When Devlin reached the back of the car, Pitts had already relieved the pair of matching Browning nine-millimeter automatics. Devlin handed Pitts his pair of cuffs and inclined his head toward the center of the car. Pitts grinned and quickly lowered the driver and passenger windows, then used his cuffs and Devlin's to manacle the men hand to hand so their arms were encircling the centerpost of the car.

"We got fuckin' licenses for them pieces," one of the men shouted.

Pitts reached out and pinched his cheek. "That's good, Cheech. You show 'em to us when we come out."

"Hey, you can't leave us here like sittin' fuckin' ducks." It was the second man. His voice sounded like gravel rolling around in a dryer.

Pitts gave him a cold grin. "Quack, quack," he said.

Rossi's front door was opened by a woman so frail and ancient that her skin seemed nearly transparent. There was no smile or hint of welcome on her weathered face, and her soft brown eyes turned hard and glaring as she took in the inspector's shield that Devlin held out to her.

"Don Giovanni is sick. Go away," she snapped.

Devlin tried a smile, but it only caused the woman to step forward, further blocking their way. "I can't just go away," he said softly. "Please tell Mr. Rossi that Inspector Devlin and Detective Pitts are here to see him."

"It's all right, Anna."

The voice came from behind the woman. Devlin looked

past her into the foyer and saw Mattie "the Knife" Ippolito standing in the doorway of an adjoining room.

Ippolito didn't look like a mob enforcer, especially one whose personal body count would supposedly fill a small warehouse. He was tall and slender, with thin, ascetic features, and Devlin had always thought he could pass for a Catholic priest if you dressed him in a Roman collar. Only his weasel's eyes gave him away. He'd be a priest who'd happily steal the congregation's bingo money.

Devlin approached the man and found that he was now blocking the way to the next room. At six-one, Ippolito stood fairly even with Devlin, but gave away a good twenty pounds.

"You want to take us to the Bathrobe, Mattie?" Devlin made the suggestion with a small, hard-eyed smile. "Or should I just toss you out of the way and find him myself?"

Ippolito shook his head with mock sadness. "Hey, we could be nice about this, you know? Don Giovanni, he's sick, just like the old lady tol' you. All I'm asking here is a little respect."

"Hey, Mattie, we could respectfully drag his ass down to headquarters. How about that?" Pitts had come up beside Devlin, hovering like some intimidating specter ready to be unleashed.

"All right. All right. Let them in. We'll have the place fumigated later."

Devlin smiled at the sound of Rossi's crackling, rasping voice. Pitts's suggestion that they drag him down to headquarters had momentary merit. It would be a waste of time, of course. It would prove useful only if Columbo-family hit men were waiting when he left One Police Plaza. But the mayor would not be amused by a mob shoot-out one block away from City Hall.

Rossi was seated in a wingback chair when they entered the room. His small, frail body was covered by a silk bathrobe over silk pajamas, his rattier, moth-eaten attire being reserved for public appearances. His feet were clad in slippers, revealing bony, painfully white ankles.

"So, the New York Police Department's inspector of detectives. Such an honor." Rossi's chin was elevated and seemed to point at Devlin. The pose was a replica of the portrait that hung above the mantel behind him—Rossi's hero, Il Duce, at the height of his power, when all the trains in Italy ran on time.

"How old are you now, Devlin?" he continued. "Thirty-eight?" He shook his head. "Amazing. I never thought you'd live past thirty-six. God has been good to you."

Devlin glared at him. It was two years ago that Rossi tried to have him killed. "You did your best, Bathrobe. It just wasn't good enough."

Rossi wagged a finger. "Hey, that's an ugly rumor. I'm seventy-three, a sick old man. The doctors say I'm dying." A small smile toyed at the corners of his mouth. "Besides, if I wanted you dead, the worms would already be eating your eyes." He let out a theatrical sigh. "But, instead, you'll probably go to *my* funeral."

In spite of himself, Devlin smiled at the man's chutzpah. He raised his eyes to the portrait of Mussolini. "They tell me that back in forty-five, when you saw the newspaper pictures of Il Duce hanging by his feet, you wept."

Rossi nodded. "I even sent flowers to Italy."

Devlin stared at him, unmoved. "I'll send flowers for you, too, Rossi. But I think I'll skip the wake."

Rossi let out a low cackle. "See, that's the difference between us. Me? I'd come to *your* wake. And I'd *piss* in your coffin."

Rossi's laughter grew, then he turned to Ippolito. "This is a hard man, Mattie. Don't let him fool you. You see that scar on his cheek?" He waited while Ippolito looked. "A crazy cop gave him that, five, maybe six years ago. And, after he did, Devlin blew that cop away." He widened his eyes, feigning surprise. "That's right, the man's a cop killer, just ask him."

"Shut up, Rossi." It was Pitts, and the words came with a growl.

Rossi ignored him. "This crazy cop, he cut the inspector's arm, too—cut it so bad Devlin retired on disability. Took a job as chief of police in some shithole town in Vermont." He glanced back at Devlin. "You didn't think I knew so much about you, eh?" He turned back to Ippolito and regretfully shook his head. "But then he came back. Seems one of those crazy serial killers was out to get an old girlfriend of his. So Devlin here, he comes back, and this killer ends up dead, too, and now his old girlfriend is his new girlfriend again. Just like fucking Hollywood. They live together with Devlin's daughter in some hotsy-totsy loft down in SoHo. It's a beautiful story."

Rossi's eyes went back to Devlin and the two men glared at each other. The scar on Devlin's cheek had turned white, a telltale sign that anger had reached the edge of control. Devlin's lover, Adrianna, and his daughter, Phillipa, had been with him two years ago when Rossi's killers had come. The threat that it could happen again was clear.

Hatred fled Rossi's eyes as quickly as it had come, and he turned back to Ippolito. "But the story's not over, Mattie. There's more. Devlin gets the killer, and he gets the girl. It's all beautiful, like I said. But then the mayor comes to him"—he raised a finger—"the mayor, no less. You got that?"

"I got it," Ippolito said.

"And the mayor asks him to come back to work for the city. But not just as some shitheel detective, like he was before—but to come back as *inspector of detectives*. And working exclusively for the mayor, himself." He paused for effect. "You know what that means, Mattie?"

"No. I don't know what that means."

Rossi wagged another educating finger. "That, my friend, means that Devlin, here, can supersede *anybody* in the police department—even the *chiefs*." He shook his head. "Can you imagine what it would mean if the crooks did something like that? Chaos, my friend. Chaos." He waved his hand in a circle. "Soldiers superseding capos. Capos superseding bosses. It would be crazy. Everybody would be at everybody's throats."

"Crazy," Ippolito said.

Rossi's finger shot up again. "Maybe that's why the other cop bosses don't like Inspector Devlin." He turned back to Devlin, his eyes brimming hatred again. "You think maybe those other bosses wouldn't go to your funeral, Devlin?"

Devlin returned the stare. "I'll be happy as long as you're there, Bathrobe. Pissing in my coffin."

Rossi threw back his head and laughed. "I don't like you, Devlin. But I like you." The hatred returned. "So why the fuck are you here? Tell me quick. I feel an attack coming on. And then I won't be able to talk to you no more."

"I'm here to tell you it's time to retire, Bathrobe. To go someplace nice and sunny, and let all the killing stop."

"Retire from what, Devlin? I'm already retired. I even get Social Security from the government." He cackled again.

"Keep laughing, Bathrobe. They got another one of your boys, today." It was Pitts. He was grinning. "Vinnie Big Head. All that's left is a big grease spot on Broome Street."

Rossi's jaw tightened. "Makes you happy, huh? So you come out here, and you handcuff my people to your car. Oh, yeah, I saw that *shit*. You're hoping, maybe, some shooters come by and kill them, too. Well, fuck you." Rossi jabbed a finger into his cadaverous chest. His hawklike nose and jutting chin pushed forward. "I'll be here when all of you are fucking dead. You tell that to the fucking mayor. Tell *him* to fucking retire."

"So your doctors are wrong, huh?"

Rossi's head snapped back to Devlin. He was smiling again, and his eyes glittered with a touch of madness. "I got a new doctor. A kind of doctor you never heard of." His smile widened, revealing ancient, crooked, yellow teeth. "But you will, Devlin. I promise you. And you'll be amazed at the miracles this doctor can do."

"I don't think he fucking likes you."

Pitts was driving toward Nathan's, his hotdog request having been approved. Devlin stared out the passenger window, watching the neighborhood become rougher and more battered as they headed south.

"The man's crazy as a bedbug. I never recognized that before. Now I'm sure of it."

Pitts had pulled up at a stoplight. He turned in his seat. "Don't fucking believe it for a minute. Old Bathrobe is the best fucking dago actor since Robert De Niro."

Devlin thought about the not-so-veiled threat Rossi had made against his family. It was stupid, and Rossi wasn't a stupid man. Maybe it was because he was dying, and felt he had nothing to lose. If so, it would make him even more dangerous.

"Too bad those two bodyguards had carry permits for their weapons," Devlin said. "It would have been nice to lock their asses up, then drop a dime to the Columbo family that the Bathrobe was sitting there with only the Knife protecting him."

Pitts let out a little cackle. He enjoyed that idea. Then he turned serious. "Hey, that's another thing. I wanna know the name of the judge who approved those permits, and the name of the scumbag boss on The Job who let them slip through unchallenged. We find that out, we got two probables for Rossi's pad."

"It's already on my list," Devlin said. "I'll have Stan Samuels digging into it before the day's out." He pointed a finger at Pitts. "And no cracks about Stan," he warned.

Pitts called Samuels "the Mole," because of his love of burrowing into long-forgotten records, a denigration of the very talent that made him an essential part of Devlin's five-man team. Everyone on the squad had a nickname—the more derogatory of which had been coined by Pitts. Ramon Rivera, a self-proclaimed Latin love machine and Devlin's computer expert, was called "Boom Boom." Red Cunningham, a three-hundred-pound, baby-faced hulk who could plant a bug anywhere Devlin wanted one, was "Elephant Ass." And Sharon Levy, a beautiful, redheaded lesbian sergeant, who was Devlin's second in command and who ran the squad like a marine drill instructor, had become "Sergeant Muffdiver"—although even Pitts lacked the guts to say it to her face.

Pitts pulled up in front of the original Nathan's Hot Dog Stand—still a Coney Island landmark—and glanced hungrily at the take-out counter. "You want something. A couple of dogs, maybe a knish?" he asked.

He watched Devlin shake his head. The man was tense; pissed off, Pitts thought. You could always tell when the scar on his cheek—the old knife wound Rossi had ragged him about—turned that warning shade of white. Except for the scar, he was a good-looking guy in a rugged sort of way, even more so now that a touch of gray had come to the temples of his wavy dark hair. There was also an easy gentleness about the guy. Nothing prissy, or namby-pamby, but definitely a feel that you could talk to the man. Except now it wasn't there. Now his normally soft, blue eyes were simmering.

"The old bastard really got to you, didn't he?"

Devlin continued to stare straight ahead. Then he drew a long breath and let it out slowly. "You turning into a shrink, Ollie?"

"Yeah, that's me." Pitts reached out and gave Devlin's arm a squeeze. He left his hand there. It wasn't cop-to-boss talk now. It was friend to friend. "He ain't gonna do nothin' to your family, Paul. I don't think he'd even let anybody go after *you* if they were around. And I don't think he'll even try to have you whacked again. Remember, last time he had somebody else he could lay the blame on, and the way it turned out, he gotta know even that was a mistake." Another squeeze. "Hey, maybe he is crazy, like you said, but he's not *that* crazy. He went after your lady or your kid, it would bring so much heat down on all the families, they'd never fucking forgive him. Hell, the trouble he has now would seem like a fucking picnic. The other four families, they'd get together and kill his miserable old ass, and then they'd blow up his fucking grave."

Devlin smiled in spite of himself, the tension broken. What Pitts was talking about had actually happened. Frank Costello, one of the mob's more notorious bosses, had died peacefully in his sleep. But the enemies Costello had left behind were still unforgiving, and almost a year after his death a dynamite charge had leveled his tomb.

He gave Pitts an appreciative nod, his eyes softer now. "You're not half-bad, Ollie. A pain in the ass as a cop, but not too shabby a shrink."

"I'll send you a bill."

"Just go stuff your face so we can get back to the office sometime today."

Devlin's office was on Broadway, around the corner from City Hall and two blocks from One Police Plaza, a brick-cubed headquarters building that overlooked the East River. Street cops, aware of the endless political machinations that went on inside, called the building the Puzzle Palace.

When the mayor had cajoled him back to the department,

Devlin had insisted his new squad be housed outside headquarters or any police precinct. Howie Silver had understood. Politics ruled the department, and anyone who trod on the very private fiefdom of the police brass was quickly ground underfoot. And even the mayor—though treated with greater subtlety—was not immune. During his first year in office, Silver had found himself repeatedly boxed out of high-profile cases when the police brass had felt threatened. It was the reason he had opted for a special squad—one that would handle those cases at his direction and report only to him.

Back in his office, Devlin went through the phone messages that littered his desk. There were four from the chief of detectives and three each from the chief of organized crime and the commander of the Fifth Precinct, where the latest mob hit had taken place—all the bosses his squad had cut out of the investigation. There was also a message from the mayor. It was the only one that would get a response.

Sharon Levy sat across from Devlin, a tall, shapely, beautiful redhead who made men's heads turn when she entered a room, and whose sexual orientation had made her anathema to the bosses of the Puzzle Palace. She was also a gutsy, no-nonsense cop, and Devlin had made her his second in command despite howls of protest from One Police Plaza.

"We've got zip," Levy said. "Little Italy is loaded with monkeys, all doing a hear-no-evil, see-no-evil, speak-no-evil bit. This thing won't end until the Columbo family nails Rossi, or until the price gets too high to keep trying."

"So let's up the ante," Devlin said. "Pull in a half-dozen gold shields from the Fifth, and a half dozen from the Seven-eight. Use the mayor as your authority. You know the drill. I want the Fifth Precinct guys to work Little Italy. The Seven-eight Precinct dicks will handle Brooklyn. Their only job will be to roust every Columbo and Rossi hood who sticks his nose out of his cave. I want every bookie, every numbers runner, every strong-arm punk dragged in. We find a betting slip, we bust everybody in sight. We find a weapon, we lock up every wiseguy within fifty yards of it. We find stolen furs in a back room, the whole building goes to jail. And I *don't* care if every arrest we make gets thrown out of court, because as soon as they walk out the door, we'll bust them again."

"Hit 'em in their wallets."

"Until the pigskin squeals."

"I like it. It'll get their attention."

"Yes, it will."

Devlin noted the skepticism on her face. "I see a *but* in your eyes."

"It's more an *unless*." She gave him a small shrug. "Unless they want Rossi so bad, they don't care what it costs."

Devlin thought that over. It was possible. It could also explain why the Gambino family, still run from prison by Rossi's nephew, was standing on the sidelines. He gave Sharon a quizzical look. "What the hell could that old bastard have done?"

The telephone interrupted them before Levy could answer. Devlin expected to hear Howie Silver's growling baritone, demanding to know why his call hadn't been returned. Instead, the anguished voice of his lover, Adrianna Mendez, came across awash in sobs. Rossi's threats immediately returned, pushed away only after he was certain that neither she nor his daughter, Phillipa, had been hurt.

After five minutes of soothing assurances, he returned the phone to its cradle and stared across at Sharon Levy. "I'm going to be leaving you with this whole Rossi bag for at least a week," he said. "Providing I can get the mayor to pull some political strings."

"What's wrong, Paul?" There was genuine concern in Levy's voice.

"Adrianna's aunt has been in a serious accident." He

shook his head and offered up a weak, uncertain smile. "Now I have to find a way to get us both into Cuba."

The SoHo loft that Devlin shared with Adrianna Mendez was located on Spring Street, amid a collection of iron-fronted buildings that decades earlier had been home to glove manufacturers and tanning merchants. Later, rising costs had forced those companies to flee the city, and the architecturally unique district had been abandoned to the bums and vagrants who wandered in from the Bowery. Then struggling artists in search of large and inexpensive work areas had discovered the loft-warehouses that made up a part of each building. Within a few years the artists were followed by real-estate speculators, who sniffed the aroma of financial gain. Touting the area as the "new bohemia," they sold the battered lofts to young stockbrokers and commodity traders and other upwardly mobile denizens of fashion. Soon the artists were driven away, save the few successful enough to afford the now pricey lofts. But the artists were no longer necessary. They were replaced by a collection of galleries and restaurants and boutiques, which seemed to sprout unbidden like wildflowers in an abandoned field, and the area, which had once seen animal hides stacked on sidewalks, became the city's newest attraction for well-heeled tourists.

Adrianna had been one of the artists able to remain. She had moved to the area as a struggling painter, and the birth of the "new bohemia" had coincided with her sudden recognition as a major talent. The only other "old residents" were the bums and vagrants who had refused to leave. They were the city's crabgrass, constantly reappearing despite all efforts at eradication. To Devlin they were the only mark of humanity the real-estate moguls had failed to devour, and much to the chagrin of neighboring merchants, he kept a ready supply of dollar bills stuffed in his pocket to encourage their continued presence.

Devlin found Adrianna packing when he entered the loft. She glanced up at him over a half-filled suitcase. "I can get into Cuba from Canada, Mexico, or the Bahamas," she said. "I have a travel agent checking flights for me."

"If the U.S. government finds out, it's ten years, or up to a quarter of a million in fines."

"They won't find out. The travel agent told me the Cubans don't stamp your passport. It's their way of helping U.S. citizens beat the embargo. So there's no record of you ever having been there."

Devlin crossed the room, lifted her to him, and slipped his arms around her waist. "I'm sorry about your aunt," he said. "And you don't have to sneak in the back way. Howie Silver made some calls. Your license from the Treasury Department and your Cuban visa will be ready tomorrow morning. Mine, too."

"Yours?"

"You didn't think I was going to turn you loose in Cuba all alone, did you? The place is supposed to be overrun with sexy male salsa dancers."

Adrianna's head fell against his chest. "Thank God," she said. "I was terrified. I just didn't want to tell you. All the stories I grew up with, the stories about Castro's storm troopers, have been playing in my mind all day. And the phone calls to the hospital in Havana haven't helped."

"What did the hospital tell you?"

She shook her head against his chest, her long, raven-black hair swinging slightly. "When I got the first call, telling me my aunt María had been in a car accident, I called the hospital right away. At first they couldn't be more helpful. Then her doctor got on the line, and suddenly everything changed. He acted like I wasn't supposed to know.

Like someone calling from the United States was somehow suspicious."

He stroked her head. "You told me she was a respected doctor—even worked a bit for the government. That's probably why." He ran his hand down her back, trying to comfort her. "You know what hospitals and doctors are like when it comes to their own. They're like cops."

She shook her head again, then stepped back and looked up at him. Her light brown eyes were weary, and her normally smiling mouth was now tight and narrow. "It was more than that, Paul. The doctor was acting like I might find out something I wasn't supposed to. I was sure he was lying to me."

"What did he say about her condition?"

"He said it was *grave*." She pronounced the word in Spanish—graa-VEY.

Devlin stroked her arm. "I put in a call to the American Interests Section at the Swiss embassy in Havana. The congressman Howie got to expedite the U.S. license and the Cuban visa recommended we do that. No one was available, but I left our number here. The congressman told Howie he'd make sure someone got back to us."

"Thank God you have friends in high places," she said. "When I called the State Department for help, the person I spoke with acted like I was crazy. He said I needed this idiotic license from Treasury, because everything involving Cuba falls under something called the Trading with the Enemy Act." She shook her head again as if none of it made sense. "So I was transferred to the Treasury Department, something called the Office of Foreign Assets Control."

"What did they say?"

"They told me it could take as long as six months to get a license. Apparently it's a policy thing to try and discourage people from going there."

"You told them it was a family emergency?"

"Paul, they couldn't have cared less. The woman I spoke with was more concerned about throwing regulations and restrictions at me. Like, if I got a license and visa and everything, I still couldn't spend more than a hundred dollars a day while I was there."

Devlin grinned at her. "So, what's the problem? You get a good hotel room, and you don't eat. Or you can sleep on a park bench and have all the rice and beans you want. Makes sense to me."

Adrianna leaned against him again. "I wish stupid government regulations were the only part of this that seems so wrong." She fought back a sob, hardened herself against it. "But it's more than that. Maybe I'm just being paranoid because I'm so upset. But somehow nothing about this seems right. The second person who called to tell me about the car accident acted so odd. When I asked who he was, all he'd say was that he was a friend. He wouldn't even give me his name."

"Wait a minute, what do you mean, the second person who called about the accident? There were two?"

Adrianna nodded, then seemed to think about what she had just said. "Yes, there were two calls. That is strange. I was so upset I didn't even think about it. First this—" She stopped and rummaged around on a table until she found a piece of paper with a name on it. "This Colonel Cabrera called. He sounded very official, and said my aunt had been in a serious accident, and I should come at once if I wanted to see her. He said to call him back and he'd have me met at the airport." She stared into his eyes and shook her head, as if trying to make sense of what she was saying. "Then, after I talked with the hospital, the second man called. He said he was a friend of my aunt's. And he was, I'm sure of it, because he knew about you."

"What do you mean?"

"He asked if Señor Devlin was coming with me. He said he'd make hotel reservations for a double room, if you were."

"How'd he know about me?"

"I asked him that. He said my aunt told him. And if he was a friend, she would have, Paul. I wrote to her about you all the time, and she even wrote back asking questions about your job, your daughter, everything."

"But this guy, he wouldn't give you his name?"

"No, he said it was unwise to do that on the telephone. He said he'd meet us at the airport. When I told him this Colonel Cabrera was sending a car, he said it would be unwise to let the colonel know when I was arriving. He said the colonel worked for State Security, and was no friend of my aunt." She stared at him, hoping he'd say something comforting. "It *is* strange, isn't it?"

"Yeah, it is. I think we should just go, ourselves, and avoid both of these characters. At least for now."

Something didn't smell right, but Devlin didn't want to say it. Not now. Not until she calmed down. He took her to their large, overstuffed sofa and drew her down next to him.

"Tell me about your aunt. All you've ever said was that she was a doctor who worked for the Cuban government, and that she and your dad didn't get along."

Adrianna looked at him as though confused by the question. Her features softened with thought, and Devlin realized, as he had so often before, how much he enjoyed looking at her. Adrianna's nose was slightly too large; her mouth just a bit too wide; her light brown eyes too much in contrast with her raven-black hair, and all together it made her the most strikingly beautiful woman he had ever known.

"There really isn't a lot I do know about her," she said at length. "I know that sounds strange, but it's true. My father always refused to talk about her, and when I finally got to meet her after he died, she was always very reticent about what she did. All she really ever told me was that she was a doctor who specialized in children's problems. I do know her government sent her to several conferences at the UN and the World Health Organization, because we'd see each other during those trips. She was here eight or nine times like that, and she always stayed a week or two, so we saw a lot of each other when she was here. But that's really all I know about her life. That, and the fact that she hated Batista, and was a fierce supporter of Fidel Castro, and everything she thought he'd done for Cuba."

"You must know more than that," Devlin said.

"Paul, I don't. After my father died, she sort of adopted me from afar. I was an adult by then—" She stopped, as if considering her own words. "I guess I never recognized it before, but all our interactions were about me—her hopes for me and my work, whatever problems there were in my life. That's all that seemed to interest her. *My* life. *My* welfare. Everything. All of it centered around me. Whenever I asked about her, she just dismissed herself as some country doctor who took care of children. All she ever wanted to talk about was me, and my problems, my hopes, my needs. I guess you could say she was more mentor than aunt." She closed her eyes and fought back tears. "She was wonderful, Paul. She was the first *real* intellectual friend I ever had. The first person who ever took me seriously."

The call from the U.S. Interests Section in Havana came as they were completing their packing. Devlin spent twenty minutes on the phone, making notes about the arrangements that had been made and listening to a detailed explanation of what they could expect to find when they arrived.

When he replaced the receiver he stood quietly, digesting what he had been told.

"What is it, Paul?"

He shook his head, a look of mild disbelief in his eyes. "I just found out a little more about your aunt," he said.

"What did they say?"

He shook his head again. "Honey, María Mendez is no country doctor who just works with little kids." He blew out a stream of air. "Up until a few months ago she was the top medical official in the Cuban government." He paused, still digesting it all. "Adrianna, she's one of the original heroes of the Cuban Revolution. She fought in the mountains with Castro in the fifties, and since then she's been the closest thing they've had to a living saint. The people down there call her *Angel Rojo,* the Red Angel."

2

HAVANA, CUBA

The international arrivals terminal at José Martí Airport is a sprawling, modern edifice that would befit any major city in the world. Completed in 1998, it replaced a small, dark, musty building that made arriving visitors feel they had just entered an oppressive banana republic. It is a carefully stated message, a clear abandonment of the old workers' state, all part of a new Cuban image, intended to make tourists and foreign businesspeople believe that their much-sought-after dollars will be well spent in this former bastion of Soviet-sponsored communism.

Devlin felt slightly overwhelmed by the unexpected glitter of glass and steel, and the complete absence of expected threat left him mildly disoriented. He had telephoned his daughter—who had been left behind with his sister in Queens—just to tell her they had arrived safely in Castro's Cuba.

"Are there guys with long beards and guns?" she had asked, her nine-year-old mind a victim of U.S. television.

"Not yet, sweetie," Devlin had replied. "Most of the people working here are young, and the airport reminds me of the new terminals at La Guardia. Only it's cleaner."

His daughter had sounded disappointed.

As he and Adrianna waited for their bags to be disgorged onto a gleaming carousel, they watched other travelers unload dozens of large corrugated boxes. A fellow passenger had explained the practice. It was all part of the new dollar economy born of the U.S. embargo. Each week traveling "Samaritans" would bring in money and goods sent to Cuban nationals by relatives in the U.S. It was all done for a hefty fee—20 percent of the money and five dollars a pound for the goods, and only a few years ago it would have put everyone involved behind bars. Now, for many, it was a full-time business, which a financially strapped and desperate Cuban government chose to ignore.

When the bags arrived, Devlin loaded them on a cart and headed for a rapidly moving customs line. They had gone through passport control with only a cursory check of their documents. Devlin had expected hard-eyed inspectors who would view Americans with suspicion. Instead he had found smiling men and women, all dressed in crisp khaki uniforms, all eager to make processing as painless as possible.

Customs proved the same, a few terse questions from a pleasant young woman. It was like entering Canada from the U.S., and far less challenging than returning to the States from anywhere in the world. All U.S. customs officials, Devlin decided, should be turned over to Fidel Castro for training. If nothing else, they would learn how to manage an occasional smile.

"I'm still waiting for the storm troopers," Devlin said as they made their way through the packed lobby toward ranks of cabs and buses that lay beyond sliding-glass doors.

"So am I." Adrianna raised her eyebrows at the chaotic, nonthreatening scene that surrounded them. It could have been any airport in any U.S. city. "This is so strange. It's the opposite of everything I expected. And somehow it doesn't seem real. It's making me feel like Dorothy after she woke up in Oz."

"Señorita Mendez. Un minuto, por favor."

They were stopped by a short, stocky, mustachioed man somewhere in his mid-fifties. He spoke softly behind sad, weary, gentle eyes that still managed to display authority. Very much a cop's eyes, Devlin decided.

He felt a familiar tension as the man reached into a pocket. Normally, the appearance of a badge would have relieved that tension. This time it remained as the man displayed the credentials of a major in the national police. The first storm trooper? Devlin gave the man a quick once-over. He had thinning hair and a deeply weathered face that seemed as worn and weary as his eyes. Yet the badge he carried looked almost new. It glittered in the fluorescent light, in sharp contrast to the man's aging suit coat and slightly frayed sport shirt.

"My name is Martínez. Major Arnaldo Martínez. And I would very much like to speak with you." The major directed his words at Adrianna, offering Devlin only a faint smile. "Perhaps I could drive you both to your hotel, and we could speak on the way." The smile became stronger. "It is much cheaper than a taxi."

"I recognize your voice," Adrianna said.

Martínez nodded. "We spoke yesterday. Forgive me for not identifying myself." He offered Adrianna a small shrug. "As I said then, sometimes it is not wise to do so on our telephones. If you'll wait until we are in my car, I will explain."

"Do we have a choice about going with you?" Devlin asked.

"Of course you have a choice, Inspector Devlin."

"You know my rank, I see."

"Yes, Inspector Devlin. I know who you are."

The major's car was a battered 1957 Chevrolet. Devlin had last ridden in one in high school. That car had been a ten-year-old relic owned by a teenage friend. This one was an ancient, rusting hulk that only a collector could love. Definitely not a police car.

"This your personal car, Major?"

Martínez smiled. "Yes, it is."

"Are you restoring it?" Devlin asked.

"Restoring?" Martínez seemed puzzled at first, then began to laugh. "Señor, I have been restoring this car for thirty years. Every week it needs some new restoration."

As Martínez opened the rear door, Devlin placed a hand on his arm. "Major, that tin you flashed back there, it looked a little shiny. You mind if I take another look at it?"

Martínez seemed confused. "Tin? Shiny?" The lightbulb went on and he smiled again. He took out his credential case and handed it to Devlin. "You are right, Señor Devlin. The badge is new. I was just recently promoted." He retrieved the credential case and returned it to his pocket. "You see, in Cuba, until just a few years ago there were no ranks above captain. Fidel was commandante—which is equivalent to a major—and everyone else held a rank below that. Now"—he shrugged—"things have changed. Now we even have generals. Luckily, the new promotions finally made their way down to me. Here in Cuba, these things come more slowly for people who are not high in the government."

They drove out of the airport and onto a main thoroughfare which seemed to have more people hitchhiking or riding bicycles, than cars. It was nine P.M., when traffic in any large city would still be moderately heavy. Yet cars were scarce, and most were not unlike the antiquated wreck Martínez drove.

"Lot of old cars here," Devlin said.

Martínez nodded. "Yes, many. Your country's embargo has been in place since 1963, señor. The only new cars you will see all belong to car rental companies. Only the tourists drive them. Oh, you will see some newer than mine, of course—some that are only ten years old—but they are mostly Russian, and they are garbage. They break down more than the old cars do." He patted the steering wheel as if assuring his own car that the words were intended as a compliment. "But we can't get parts for the old ones, or even the not-so-old ones, so it doesn't make much difference. It is why Cubans are the best mechanics in the world. It is a gift of the embargo. Give a Cuban some chewing gum and wire and he can make anything run—at least for a day or two."

Adrianna leaned forward from the rear seat. "Major, you said you'd explain the phone call. I don't mean to be rude, but I'm very worried about my aunt."

From his place in the front, Devlin could see Martínez's jaw tighten.

"Yes, of course," he said.

He pulled the car to the side of the road. They were next to a park that overflowed with people, all out searching for relief from the tropical July heat.

Martínez turned in his seat; his eyes were more sad and weary than normal. Devlin could sense what was coming.

"I'm afraid I must tell you very bad news, Señorita Mendez. The automobile accident in which your aunt was involved left her very badly burned. The hospital informed my office this morning that your aunt died of her injuries." He heard Adrianna gasp, and hesitated a moment before going on. "The news, I'm afraid, is even worse. The funeral home where her corpse was taken reported that her body disappeared shortly after it arrived there."

Devlin had moved into the rear of the car, and now held Adrianna in his arms. Martínez was driving more rapidly, hurrying to get Adrianna to their hotel in Old Havana.

"What have you found out about the body being taken?" Devlin asked.

"Only that it disappeared three days ago—only a few hours after she died."

"Three days ago? What the hell are you talking about? You said your office just got the call this morning, and Adrianna spoke to the hospital yesterday."

"The death was not reported," Martínez said. "At least not to us, as it should have been."

"Who . . . was it . . . reported . . . to?" It was Adrianna this time, her voice broken by sobs.

"It was reported to State Security," Martínez said. "Both the death and, later, the theft."

"The secret police?" Devlin's voice was incredulous.

"No, the secret police are different. I will explain later."

"Why would anyone want to steal her body?" Adrianna asked.

Martínez let out a long breath. "Are you familiar with Regla Mayombe, señorita?"

"What the hell is that?" Devlin snapped.

"It is one of the Cuban-African religions. Very primitive and very feared. Also very widespread in our country."

Devlin's voice was still snappish and angry. "For chrissake, what are you trying to say? That we're dealing with some kind of voodoo?"

"Yes, señor," Martínez said. "That is exactly what I am telling you."

The Hotel Inglaterra is located on the Paseo Martí, a name personally created by Fidel. To the people the street is known as the Paseo del Prado, the name it carried for more than two hundred years. The hotel is directly across from a small park and flanked by the Gran Teatro de la Habana, a baroque architectural masterpiece that would rival anything in Europe. The exterior of the Inglaterra rises four stories, its neoclassical facade marked by high French windows that lead to small, individual terraces outside each room so guests can view the nightly chaos that rules the street and the park beyond. Inside, the mood harkens back to the 1870s when the hotel was part of La Acera del Louvre, a meeting place for Creole revolutionaries. Here it changes to a mixture of Sevillian and Moorish designs. Mosaic tiles and a massive gate of twisted ironwork accent the lobby, mixed together with stained glass and ancient heraldic symbols, all rising to an intricately ornate, gold-leaf ceiling. It is like stepping into Bizet's *Carmen,* or—to Devlin's eye—a comfortable, old Humphrey Bogart film.

Major Martínez waited at a table in the Sevillana Bar while Devlin took Adrianna to their room. He seemed decidedly out of place, his well-worn jacket and frayed shirt standing out among the designer labels worn by the tourists and the sleek, sensual clothing that decorated the prostitutes gathered at the bar. Behind him a gold statue of a woman dancing with castanets added to the contrast. It glittered almost as brightly as his shiny new badge.

Devlin made his way to the table, his eyes taking in every corner of the room. A small smile played across Martínez's lips. Police, he thought, were the same everywhere.

"Sorry to keep you waiting," Devlin said. "I wanted to make sure Adrianna was asleep. This little surprise you laid on us has hit her pretty hard." He adjusted his chair so it faced the entrance to the bar. It produced another small smile from Martínez.

"It is better she is sleeping," Martínez said. "What I have to tell you would only be more upsetting for her."

Across the room, two prostitutes, no more than eighteen, offered up welcoming smiles. "I thought Castro did away with all the hookers," Devlin said.

"Yes, it is true. There is no prostitution in Cuba." Martínez glanced at the two young women. "There are only thousands of friendly children, each one looking for romance." He shrugged. "And dollars to feed their families." He paused to light a cigarette and sent a stream of smoke across the table. "Great mechanics are not the only thing your embargo has given us."

Devlin ignored the political gibe. He needed Martínez on their side—if possible—at least for now. "Tell me about María Mendez," he said.

Martínez flicked the ash of his cigarette. "She was my friend. My very dear friend." He drew on the cigarette again, then put it out. "Did you know the people of Cuba called her the Red Angel?"

"Someone in the U.S. Interests Section told me that."

Martínez nodded. "Yes, they would know about her. She was a very powerful figure. Until recently, she was even powerful politically."

"Why until recently?"

"She had a falling-out with Fidel."

"With Castro, himself?" Devlin's voice sounded incredulous, even to his own ears.

Martínez nodded again. "She and Fidel were very close for many years. It is even said they were lovers many years ago." He smiled. "But Fidel is known to have had many lovers. Along with several wives. *And* children. Some say he doesn't remember most of their names."

"But María Mendez was not one of those." Devlin spoke the words for Martínez.

"No. She was very important in the government. And very important to the people. She was one of the few who could tell Fidel he was wrong."

"Are you implying she did that once too often? That Fidel bounced her out of the government?"

"Fidel would never be that foolish. For the people, there

are some heroes who must never be tarnished. Fidel, of course, is one. Then Che Guevara. And there is also the Red Angel."

"How did she come to be . . . so revered?"

The major's eyes became a wistful mix of pleasure and pain. "Ah, that is both a beautiful and a sad story. In the early years María Mendez became a symbol of everything that was good in our revolution. And in recent years she became a symbol of everything about it that has failed."

A waiter brought them cups of strong Cuban coffee that Martínez had ordered. Devlin pushed his aside and leaned forward. "Tell me about her."

Martínez lit another cigarette and sat back in his chair.

"In 1957, María Mendez had just graduated from the medical school at Havana University. She was young, younger than the other graduates. She was a brilliant child. She graduated from high school at fifteen. And from university at eighteen. Now, at twenty-two, she had completed her medical studies, and was an intern at the Infantil Hospital.

"You must understand those times, my friend. Batista ruled our country with an iron fist, and his secret police crushed anyone who opposed him. Fidel had already attempted one insurrection and had failed. The Mafia controlled Havana, and it had become a playground for the rich, a city filled with gambling and drugs and prostitution.

"But for the people it was hell. Batista had become rich selling off the land to foreign corporations and a handful of cronies. Cuba was an oligarchy. The peasants owned nothing, and were paid almost nothing for the work they did. Only the rich received medical care, and education was available only to the sons and daughters of the privileged class.

"María Mendez was one of those privileged children, as was Fidel, himself. She was the daughter of a successful physician, but unlike her father, her heart was with the people.

"María was not political. She was certainly not a revolutionary. She knew Fidel because he was at the university law school when she began her studies, and he was a respected figure among the students. But violence of the kind that Fidel and many other students preached was something alien to her. She told me this many times. She wanted a political solution. She simply believed in the people, and the desperate need to ease their suffering."

Martínez paused and smiled. "An idealist, eh? Like so many young people everywhere."

He took a sip of his coffee and glanced again at the young women at the bar. Devlin thought he was perhaps wishing idealism would find its way to them.

"But there were others, students who realized that idealistic goals were impossible as long as Batista lived. They formed a plan to kill him. They believed the peasants in the countryside would rise up once he was dead.

"The plan involved an assault on the Presidential Palace in March of 1957, where Batista would be assassinated. But the students knew that many of them would be killed or wounded in the attack. They needed secret hospitals where the wounded could be taken, where the secret police who would be hunting them would not think to look. María was one of the young doctors they went to for help.

"It was foolishness, of course. The students were untrained and poorly armed. The attack failed, and the police easily followed the wounded back to their secret hospitals."

"And María?" Devlin asked.

"She was arrested, of course. She had refused to leave the dying student she was trying to save." Martínez closed his eyes momentarily. When he opened them they were filled with a deep sadness.

"She was tortured, asked to give the names of others who had escaped. When she refused, she was turned over to her guards. She was raped so many times that her organs were badly damaged. She was never able to have children because of this." He paused again, his entire face now marked by the sadness of his eyes. "Perhaps that is why she chose to work with children. Perhaps that is why your lovely Adrianna became so important in her life."

Martínez seemed to push the speculation aside. He lit another cigarette and finished his coffee.

"She was saved by her father. It took several months, and many bribes, but she was finally released from prison. By that time Fidel's second invasion in Oriente Province was well under way, and his troops had established bases in the Sierra Maestra Mountains.

"María joined him there, not only as a doctor, but fighting at his side. She became a fierce warrior, it is said, leading other men and women into battle against Batista's troops. She had come to understand, you see, that brutality such as Batista's could only be fought with guns."

A wan smile came to Martínez's lips. "Of course, the revolution succeeded. And when Fidel entered Havana in 1959, María was with him. She, like Che Guevara, was one of the great heroes. And like Guevara, who was also a physician, she knew that the health of the people—especially its children—was the first task the revolution had to address.

"It is said that she and Guevara went to Fidel and convinced him of this need. He put her in charge. Guevara was needed elsewhere in the government. And so it fell to María Mendez to bring health to the people."

"That sounds like quite a job," Devlin said.

"Even more than you think." Martínez spread his arms, as if taking in the entire room, perhaps the entire country. "Cuba is a difficult place. Even more difficult in 1959."

He leaned forward and lowered his voice. "You recall that I asked Señorita Mendez if she was familiar with our Cuban-African religions?" He waited while Devlin nodded. "Well, in Cuba, even today, the people will consult the priests of these religions about their illnesses. Some will even go to a priest first, to see if they really need a doctor. And even the more sophisticated people—those who believe in the powers of *scientific* medicine—will still consult these priests *after* they see a doctor." He smiled. "Just to be certain the doctor was right." He wagged his head from side to side. "Even Fidel does this. In fact, he once had a personal physician who was also a *babalau,* which is the highest rank among these priests."

Martínez seemed to fight back a smile, as if he were enjoying the look of surprise on Devlin's face.

He nodded vigorously. "Yes, it is so. These beliefs are very widespread. They are at every level of our society. And among the poor and less educated they are even more strongly held." He raised his hands, indicating futility. "So from the start, as you can imagine, María Mendez had this obstacle to overcome. But she was not only an intelligent woman, she was also a wise one. She formed very strong alliances with these priests. And she seduced them into helping her. And it worked, you see. Within a few years all the children of our island had been inoculated against the great diseases that had always killed so many of our people. All pregnant women were receiving prenatal care, and the doors to the hospitals—once closed to everyone but the rich—were now flooded by people seeking care. And today everyone receives this care. Today Cuba has more than sixty thousand doctors serving the people, all of it her doing. And it has the lowest infant mortality rate in Latin America—the same rate they have in France and Italy and Israel." He raised his hands, then let them fall back to the table. "So now, perhaps, you can see why the people love her, why they think of her as their Angel Rojo. Their Red Angel."

Devlin was about to reply, when he noticed Martínez's eyes snap toward the entrance of the bar. He turned and found a tall, uniformed officer approaching their table. When he reached them, Martínez was already standing.

"Colonel Cabrera, I am at your orders," Martínez said.

A small smirk formed on the colonel's lips. He was tall and angular, with a carefully trimmed beard as black as his eyes. His tan uniform was crisply starched, as though it had just come off a hanger. "You address me in English now, Major?" There was a cutting edge to the words.

"In deference to our guest, Colonel."

Devlin noticed that Martínez's eyes were hard, almost defiant. They remained that way as he turned abruptly and extended a hand toward Devlin.

"Colonel Antonio Cabrera, may I introduce Señor Paul Devlin of the United States. He is here—"

"I know why he is here," Cabrera said, cutting him off.

Devlin stood and offered his hand. "Everyone seems to know who I am. Are the Cuban police always this well informed?"

Cabrera inclined his head, as if accepting an undeserved compliment. "Had I known you were arriving today, I would have met you at the airport, señor. Unfortunately, I was not informed until you had checked into this hotel." His gaze hardened on Martínez. "Obviously, the major's information was superior to mine." The colonel's features softened. "I was hoping to offer my condolences to Señorita Mendez."

"I'm afraid she's asleep," Devlin said. "The news about her aunt's death, and the theft of the body, came as quite a shock."

Cabrera nodded. "Understandable, of course." He had put as much sympathy in his words as possible. Yet his demeanor showed none of it. He remained erect and formal and intimidating, as if those were things he could never quite shed.

"Has there been any progress in the investigation?" Devlin asked. "Anything I could pass on to her?"

Cabrera shot Martínez a look. Devlin could not tell if it

was a warning to remain silent, or simply because their dislike was mutual.

"I'm afraid there is not much I can tell you. We believe enemies of the revolution stole the body. The plan may even have come from Miami. There are Cubans there, as you know, who are always seeking ways to undermine the government. It is why the matter has been turned over to State Security."

"You have suspects?"

"Yes. That I can tell you. There are suspects presently under investigation."

Devlin nodded. He had used the same line of bullshit more times than he cared to remember. If this were New York, it would mean the investigation had hit a brick wall.

"Then I expect we'll have a body to bury shortly," Devlin said.

"It is our hope, señor." Cabrera let his eyes fall hard on Devlin. "You plan to remain, then?"

"I don't see that we have any choice," Devlin said. "I don't believe Señorita Mendez will want to leave with her aunt's body still missing."

Cabrera seemed to grow another inch or two. "Then I would like you both to come to my headquarters tomorrow to discuss certain matters."

"When?"

"Would late afternoon be convenient?"

"I'm sure we'll make it convenient," Devlin said. "How do we get there?"

Cabrera's eyes shot to Martínez, cold and hard and filled with contempt. "Perhaps the major would be kind enough to bring you."

"I am at your orders, Colonel," Martínez snapped.

"Yes, I know you are," Cabrera said. There was a small smile on his lips, but it held nothing but disdain.

When Cabrera had left, Devlin noticed that the hookers had all disappeared from the bar. One glimpse of the colonel's crisply starched uniform had sent them scurrying into the night.

"So now you have met our Technical Department of Investigation, our secret police," Martínez said as he reclaimed his chair.

"I thought you said State Security *wasn't* the secret police," Devlin said.

Martínez held out one hand and wiggled it back and forth. "It is more complicated than that. But I will explain tomorrow. For now, I would like you to agree to go some places with me in the morning. Both of you, if possible."

"Where?"

"I would like to invite you to meet a very close friend of the Red Angel. He is a man who may have some interesting things to tell you. Then I would like to take you to meet the Red Angel's sister, your lovely Adrianna's *other* aunt. And finally, I want you to accompany me to the home of Plante Firme, one of the most revered priests of the Regla Mayombe."

"A witch doctor?"

"Much more than a witch doctor, my friend."

Devlin sat back and shook his head. "And why are we doing all this?"

"I assure you it will be necessary if we are to find the body of the Red Angel."

"We?" Devlin stared across the table, incredulous. "I thought State Security was doing that."

Martínez shook his head. "No, señor. *We* will find the body. Provided you are willing."

Cabrera's car was parked half a block away, with a clear view of the hotel's front entrance. He sat in the rear and watched Martínez leave. Two young men sat in front, both dressed completely in white. One turned to look at him, as if anticipating an order.

"It will not be necessary to follow the major," Cabrera said. "That is already being done. I want you to concentrate on our two visitors. I want the names of everyone they contact. And I want those names quickly."

"Should we take action if—"

Cabrera waved a hand impatiently, cutting the man off. "First I want to know who is helping them. We do not want just one or two vipers. We want the entire nest. But do not underestimate the man. He is a trained detective, so you must assume he is a danger to us."

"If he finds—"

Again, Cabrera waved away the man's words. "If our visitors become dangerous, we will see to it that they disappear."

"Permanently?"

"I know of no other way to disappear." Cabrera raised a cautioning hand. "But only on my order."

"And Martínez?"

"If he interferes . . ." He paused as if considering the wisdom of his words. It was a dangerous decision, but there really was no choice. The fact that he despised the scruffy little major made it easier. "If he interferes, we will see to it that he disappears as well."

3

But why, Paul? What does he think we can do?"

Devlin considered the question. They were seated in the hotel dining room, where a breakfast buffet had been set out for guests, made up mostly of fruits and rolls and some type of processed ham that Adrianna had dubbed "Cuban mystery meat."

All about them vacationers stumbled from buffet to table, all recovering from the delights of Cuban nightlife. They were a mix of Spaniards, Brits, Italians, Canadians, Mexicans, and Germans, part of the steady flow of foreigners that filled hotels each week. Many were men vacationing alone—here to sample the island's newfound position on the world sex-tour circuit—many bringing last night's "catch" to breakfast with them, slender and lithe women, mostly mulatto and black (Negroes in the Cuban terminology), all still dressed in the blatantly short skirts, revealing tops, or brightly colored body stockings they had worn the night before. Devlin studied the parade, then turned back to Adrianna.

"I have no idea what Martínez is thinking, but right now he may be our only shot at finding out what really happened."

"But you don't trust him."

"I sure as hell don't. And I trust Cabrera even less. Between the two of them, I feel like we're being hung out to dry, and there's nobody even watching our backs." He shook his head. He had been in the country for less than twelve hours and already felt thoroughly mystified. He glanced around the dining room again, studying the parade. And this was certainly a first, he thought: Here less than twelve hours, and you're having breakfast in a whorehouse.

"What did Martínez tell you about my aunt?"

Adrianna's words drew him back. Her eyes seemed both eager and fearful, and Devlin wondered just how much of it she could handle. In the end, he told her all of it. There was nothing Adrianna liked less than being protected by "a big strong man."

When he finished, she just sat and stared at him for several moments. She had handled the ugly news well, concentrating instead on the new things she was learning about her aunt's life.

"My God. I had no idea. She was really a hero." She stared at Devlin. "I mean, *really*."

"Yes, she was," Devlin said.

The waiter arrived at their table and he had to ask a second time if Adrianna wanted coffee.

She looked at him as though he had arrived from another planet, then shook her head as if freeing it of cobwebs.

"*Sí, gracias,*" she said. The shake of her head and affirmative answer seemed to confuse the waiter even more. She looked back at Devlin and shook her head again.

"She never told me any of that, Paul. Not the attempt to kill Batista. Not her arrest. The torture. The rapes?" She closed her eyes momentarily. "Oh, God." She stared into her freshly poured coffee as if wondering how it got there. "She never even told me about the two years she spent in the mountains with Castro, or the work she did after the revolution was won. All she ever talked about was her work with children, and how she had been given a government position that involved making sure they were all immunized."

"Didn't your father ever tell you the rest of it? He must have known."

Adrianna shook her head again. "He would never talk about her. He said she was a communist, and a disgrace to the family." She clasped her hands, the fingers intertwined, and held them in front of her face. "My father was very young when he left Cuba. He was ten years younger than María, only about twelve when she was arrested. Two years later, when Castro took power, he and my grandfather fled to Miami, and then to New York. My grandfather had disowned my aunt for what she had done. He refused to have her name spoken in their home. When he died, eight years later, my father said his last words were a curse on her name."

Tears formed in the corners of Adrianna's eyes and she brushed them away. "When my grandfather died, my father was forced to leave college. That's when he joined the New York Police Department." She gave her head another small, sad shake. "My dad was very much like his own father—a very hard, very unforgiving man." She folded her hands again and stared across the table at Devlin. "In all the time before he was killed, he honored his own father by never speaking my aunt's name in our home." She paused, started to pick up her coffee cup, then stopped and let out a long, tired sigh. "Even when she wrote to him when my mother died, he refused to answer the letter. He did write to his other sister, who had stayed behind with her husband. But he always said *she* was crazy." She leaned in closer to the table, as if it would give emphasis to her words. "That's really all he ever said. That he had two sisters in Cuba. One of them crazy and the other a communist."

Devlin had been a newly made detective, working in the same squad, when street punks in a Harlem tenement had gunned down Rudolfo "Rudy" Mendez. Adrianna's father had been a homicide detective on his way to make a fairly routine arrest, when he and his partner had stumbled on a drug buy. Both detectives had been killed without ever having a chance to draw their weapons.

Devlin had known Adrianna years before. They had been lovers then, he a young cop, she a graduate student and aspiring painter. But the relationship ended abruptly. Adrianna had given Devlin the news simply and directly. She wanted a different life—different from everything she had known as a child. And that life did not include living with a cop.

Years later Devlin had met Mary, the woman who would become his wife, and he was finally able to push Adrianna from his mind. Then a drunk driver had killed Mary, leaving him with their small daughter. Adrianna had come to his wife's funeral, and when Phillipa, still a toddler, had begun to fuss, she had taken the child outside. Devlin had found them sitting on the grass, searching for four-leaf clovers. Phillipa had already found two, and the smile on her face had softened all the grief and misery of the day.

A year later Devlin found himself at Rudy Mendez's funeral. Unable to find a baby-sitter, he brought Phillipa with him, and when the services ended, Adrianna had sought the child out. It was as though her new status as an orphan had required her to hold a child in her arms—perhaps just to give the kind of comfort she would never again know.

Still, despite obvious mutual attraction, Devlin and Adrianna's own relationship had not rekindled, and several years passed before the vagaries of fate—and the madness of a serial killer—brought them together again.

Devlin's reverie was broken by the appearance of Arnaldo Martínez. The major was again dressed as he had been the night before—rumpled and threadbare, a perfect match to his world-weary face and mournful eyes.

Today Martínez had opted for a pale blue shirt, missing one button and hanging outside brown trousers that Ollie Pitts would have described as "shit-colored." Devlin studied the untucked shirt. He wondered if it was used here as it would be by a New York cop—to conceal a weapon. There was no way to tell. If Martínez was carrying, it was probably an automatic, stuck into his trousers flat against his lower back. He gestured to a chair and offered Martínez coffee.

The major accepted with obvious gratitude, then smiled in turn at Adrianna and Devlin. "I am pleased you have both decided to assist me," he began.

Devlin cut him off. "We haven't decided anything. Not until you've explained some things."

"Of course. That is understood." Martínez held his sad smile.

"Number one." He paused to emphasize that more than one explanation was needed, then leaned toward Martínez and softened his tone. "First, we need to know your involvement in this. Your official involvement. And we need to know Cabrera's involvement. *And* I want some clarification on these confusing statements you keep making about him. Does he work for State Security, or not. For the secret police, or not. And what the hell is the difference between the two."

A waiter brought coffee, and Martínez sat smiling and silent until he had left.

"Let me explain our police structure first. When you understand this, you will understand who Cabrera is. And who I am. Perhaps then you will better understand what I am doing, and why it must be so." He leaned forward and lowered his voice. "First, you must understand that there are many police agencies in Cuba—nine that are known to the people, and one more that officially does not exist. All come under the Ministry of Interior."

He raised a finger, then clasped it with his other hand. "First is the national police, in which I serve. We have a simple duty. We are to protect our citizens against crime." He released his finger and waved his hand in dismissal. "Next are several police agencies that do not concern us. The coast guard, fire protection, the immigration police, all of whose functions are explained by their names. Then there are political police. They deal in propaganda and in making sure the attitudes of the government personnel do not become antirevolutionary or revisionist." He shrugged. "The mind police." He laughed at the term. "Most Cubans today listen to what they say, and then ignore them."

He leaned even closer to the table. "Now we come to the more serious and more secret agencies. First is the intelligence service." Another shrug. "Our spies. Next is the counterintelligence service. Our spy catchers. And finally is our Office of Internal Security, or State Security. These are the people who watch everything that goes on inside Cuba, and who are responsible for serious crimes against the government. And it is this organization in which Colonel Antonio Cabrera serves as number two in command."

"And the unofficial police agency?" Devlin asked.

"This is the Departamento Técnico de Investigación, the DTI, more commonly known as our secret police." Martínez smiled across the table. "The DTI have no offices, but work out of ordinary-looking houses in utmost secrecy. No one, except their own officers, knows who is a member. Those who are, are drawn from other police agencies and each of the various ministries, where they all continue to work, supposedly undetected. It is their job to watch the people who are watching everyone else. And they answer to no one except the highest people in the government. It is said that evidence presented against you by the DTI assures that you are doomed."

"Sounds like the man in charge pretty much holds the fate of everyone in his hands," Devlin said.

Martínez inclined his head. "If he has done what I believe he has, even he is vulnerable."

"So, who is he?"

Martínez smiled. "It is a secret, of course. One that only the highest people in our government are supposed to know."

"But you know."

"Yes," Martínez said. "I know. The head of our secret police is Colonel Antonio Cabrera."

"And *how* do you know?" Especially as a freshly minted major with a shiny new badge, Devlin added to himself.

"I was told several years ago, by someone high in our government. Someone who trusted me, and who believed that certain things were happening in our government that could destroy the revolution." He turned to Adrianna. "I was told by your aunt. María Mendez."

Adrianna seemed at a loss for words. "She would know something like that?" she finally asked.

Martínez let out a long sigh. "There was very little that our Red Angel did not know."

"And what was she afraid was happening?" Devlin asked.

Martínez gave him a regretful look. "That, my friend, I cannot tell you. Let us just say it is something that could jeopardize the security of my country. So, in this matter, I will have to ask you to trust me."

Devlin sat back and stared at this small, sad, middle-aged man. Trust you, he thought. I don't even know you. "And why should we trust you?" he asked.

Martínez made a helpless gesture with his hands. Devlin suspected that his helplessness was as phony as his rumpled clothing and mournful eyes. "I believe you should trust me, because in this matter we have a common interest. Finding the body of María Mendez."

"Do you believe she died as a result of a car accident?" Devlin held his gaze, searching for a lie.

Martínez shook his head. "But I cannot prove this. Not yet."

"Who would have wanted her dead?"

A sly look came to Martínez's eyes. It seemed so out of character it was almost comical. "Perhaps the same person who is now charged with finding her corpse."

"Cabrera," Adrianna said.

"This is what the investigation by the national police has found?" Devlin asked.

"There has been no investigation by the national police," Martínez said. "The matter was taken from us before any investigation could begin. It was given to State Security. The explanation we received is the same one Cabrera gave last night. That the theft of the Red Angel's body is somehow an act against the government."

"Have you gone to anyone with your suspicions?" Adrianna asked.

"Ah, señorita. And who would I go to? Someone that I know for certain is not a member of Cabrera's secret police? And who would that be?"

"So who's working with you?" Devlin asked.

"I am hoping you and Señorita Mendez will be working with me," Martínez said.

"Just us? That's it?" Devlin's tone was pure incredulity.

"The gentleman we will see this morning may also help."

"Who is he?"

"He is a well-known Cuban mystery writer, who, before he retired, also worked as a propagandist with our political police."

"That's it?" Devlin snapped. "One Cuban cop, a retired mystery writer, and a pair of tourists? And against us we've got the Cuban secret police?"

"You are much more than a tourist, my friend."

Devlin shook his head emphatically. "No, I am not, my friend. Here, I am definitely just a tourist."

"I am also hoping that Plante Firme will assist us," Martínez said.

"The witch doctor?" Devlin stared at him, wide-eyed.

"Please, señor. The term 'witch doctor' would be an offense to him. He is called a *palero*, a priest of the Palo Monte sect, a follower of the Regla Mayombe."

"Great," Devlin snapped. "One Cuban cop, one retired writer, two tourists, and a goddamn *palero*."

"A powerful mix, my friend. If used well, a very powerful mix."

Devlin leaned forward, eyes hard on Martínez's mournful face. "Well, not quite powerful enough for me, Major." He held up a hand, stopping the words Martínez seemed about to speak. "I'll help you," he said. "Because I damned well want to know what happened to this woman's body. But there's a condition."

"A condition?" Martínez blinked several times.

"I bring one of *my* people from New York to help us."

"Who, Paul?" It was Adrianna.

"Ollie Pitts."

"God, Paul. No. Not Ollie."

"Who is this Ollie?" Martínez asked. He pronounced the name Oily.

"One of my detectives. The best damned street detective I have."

Martínez turned to Adrianna. "You do not seem to like this man," he said. "Why is that?"

"No one likes him." Adrianna looked sharply at Devlin.

"I like him," Devlin said. "I especially like him watching my back."

"No one likes him except Paul," Adrianna said.

"And why is that?"

"It's simple." Adrianna threw another sharp look at Devlin. "Ollie Pitts is a beast."

Martínez sat back in his chair and nodded. "Ah, a beast," he said. "Yes, that is definitely what we will need. A beast."

Robert Cipriani sat in his brightly lit cell, the day's edition of *Granma* propped on his lap. He glared at the newsprint, his face twisted in a sneer. He despised everything about Cuba's daily newspaper. Even the fact that it was named after the battered ship that Fidel and eighty-six followers had used for their 1956 invasion at Alegría de Pio. It was so like these goddamned Cubans, he thought. Deifying some leaky tub, just because the fucking "Comandante" and his band of bearded greasers had once puked in its head. Naming their one fucking national newspaper after it. His jaw tightened. Christ, they had even put up a monument to the boat right behind Batista's old Presidential Palace.

Cipriani tossed the newspaper aside. It was useless. The only financial news it carried was so laden with propaganda, all the facts became skewed. Fidel's view of world finance. Like tits on a bull.

He pulled himself out of his leather easy chair, walked the three steps it took to cross his cell, and punched the button that would boot up the mainframe of his IBM computer. At least they had given him this—a way to communicate with the still-sane world. He moved to the cell's one barred window while Windows 98 performed its magic. Outside, across the wide, green parade ground of the State Security compound, he could see an occasional car move past the barbed-wire-topped gate that opened onto Canuco Street. Most Cubans avoided the street. The high, wire-topped wall with its watchtowers and heavily armed guards, the mounted video cameras that tracked each car and pedestrian, made the entire two-block area inhospitable.

He snorted over the final word, then turned to take in his own "hospitable" surroundings. A ten-by-eight-foot cell, closed off by a solid iron door. A single bed, not even adequate for the weekly whore they provided. A leather reading chair. And the goddamned computer they had confiscated from his own house.

He closed his eyes and raised his hands to his face. He could feel the changes that had taken place in the five years he had been locked away. His hair was thinner now, the former widow's peak now reaching back to the middle of his head. His face felt skeletal under his fingers, the cheeks sunken, the lines deeper across his forehead and around his eyes. He had kept his mustache, still too vain about the harelip it hid to cut it away. Christ, he was only fifty-five, but he looked ten years older, all of it coming since they had stuffed him in this cell. The bastards were killing him.

Cipriani's eyes snapped open with the sound of the key in the lock. He watched as the door swung away and *that prick* Cabrera stepped into the cell.

"Hola, my friend. Have you come to free me at last." He had forced a wide smile that Cabrera did not return.

"We have a problem." Cabrera spoke to him in English, as he always did to protect their conversations from any eavesdropping guards. The colonel had taken care to make certain all the guards on the cellblock were not fluent in the language. It had only added to Cipriani's miseries.

"We?" he said. "Why is it that *we* have problems, while only *you* enjoy the occasional success?"

"Spare me your philosophical observations." Cabrera perched on the very edge of Cipriani's bed, worried, as always, about damaging the knife-edge crease in his trousers. He was dressed in a business suit—his normal attire. Like all officers of State Security, he wore his uniform only for ceremonial occasions, or when he wanted to intimidate someone.

Cipriani returned to his leather armchair and became as attentive as possible. There was no point in irritating the man. The first two years of his incarceration had been spent in serious prisons. First, here at the State Security detention facility, the Villa Marista, but in a regular cellblock where he lived with four other men in a cell half the size of the one he now occupied. Next he went to a general prison, at Combinado del Este. There it was eight men to a cell, sleeping in tiered bunks one atop the other, the food so meager that doctors classified their level of undernourishment as moderate, severe, or critical, and it was not uncommon for prisoners to kill each other over food brought in by relatives. No, he thought, there was no point in irritating the colonel. He had saved him, brought him back to the Villa Marista, and put him in this well-appointed hellhole. And the price of redemption for his "financial crimes" was at least interesting.

It was a strange turn of fate. Robert Cipriani was a fugitive from the United States. There, he had done what other financiers do daily. He had taken money from fools. He, however, had been caught, and had fled—twenty million dollars in hand—to one of the world's few havens from extradition. Here, the Cubans had accepted him, and his money, allowing him to live well for more than a decade. Then they had come in the night and dragged him away, convicted him of financial crimes against the government, which to this day were vague at best. All of it to one purpose. To put him where he was now, serving the interests of State Security.

But at least there was decent food, and the weekly teenage whore. There was his computer, which allowed him to work again, and over the past five years he had accumulated another five million. And that was the best game there was. Better even than anything the teenage whore could offer.

"Tell me your troubles," Cipriani said. He studied the colonel's dour expression. He was a tall man—six-foot-two, a full six inches taller than Cipriani—and when dejected, his tall, hard, angular body curved like a great, bony question mark. He was hatless today, and it pleased Cipriani to see his balding head glistening above his dark beard. The man was only forty, at best, and he already had less hair than the prisoner he pissed on at will. He also had a big nose that ruined any chance of being handsome. *You* were handsome once, Cipriani told himself. But that was before. Before they turned you into a walking skeleton.

Cabrera told him about Devlin and Adrianna Mendez. "I did not know María Mendez had any relatives, other than her lunatic sister. I only learned of her after the old man told me what he wanted done."

"Look, you agreed to what the old man wanted. That's a fait accompli. And I still don't see the problem." Cipriani shrugged away concern. "This is Cuba. They are in a maze with only one exit, the airport."

"I told you the problem. This woman, this niece of María's, her lover is a detective."

"But he's a detective walking in the same maze."

"But he has a guide." Cabrera told him about Martínez. "I had no idea they would have this kind of help. If they begin to inquire too deeply . . ."

Cipriani shook his head. "You have the ability to stop all of them. I'm still missing the problem."

Cabrera glared at him. "The problem is María Mendez, a hero of the revolution. Everyone above me is shitting their pants that the people will learn, not only that she has died, but that her body has been stolen. If they learn this, and then learn that her only surviving relative is raising questions about her death . . ." He lowered his eyes and ground his teeth. "It could become serious—serious enough to put our plan in jeopardy."

Cipriani rubbed his face, feeling again its cadaverlike transformation. *We,* he thought. It's always *we* when things don't work out. "I still don't know why you chose the Red Angel." He waved a hand in the air. "Oh, I know we needed her dead anyway, that it was necessary to keep her from putting the screws to our overall plan. But then to give that crazy old man what *he* thought he needed? Just so he'd finally give his support?" He shook his head. "That, my friend was a mistake. You should have thought about the effect, the disgrace it might bring on Fidel and his cronies. Christ, we'd already gotten Fidel to accept what we wanted." He shook his head. "If you recall, I told you this Palo Monte–Red Angel nonsense was dangerous. There were other ways to keep the old man happy. Christ, we could have found *any* doctor. The old man never would have known the difference."

Cabrera jumped up from the bed, furious. "He wanted *her*."

Cipriani drew a breath, buying time. He kept his voice soft, free of accusation. "Yes, he did. And now, from what you tell me, there are people who want *him* dead."

Cabrera spun away and stared at the cell door. "That is not the reason. They wanted him dead before this happened. Because he at first opposed the plan."

"Yes, but only because they thought he wanted a bigger share. But that was a matter that could be negotiated. Resolved." Cipriani raised his hands. "Since he's coming here, maybe it already has been resolved." He shook his head. "But now, because of the Red Angel, there may be no share for anyone. This, they will not forgive. And they will blame him. Perhaps even you."

Cabrera spun back, eyes glaring. "Is that all you have to offer? I could get more from some crazy *palero,* rolling coconut shells on the floor to divine my future."

"What do you want me to tell you? Finding the body now is impossible, unless you want to produce a corpse with its head and hands and feet missing."

"That may be my only choice."

"Then you will have to have arrests. Arrests that could lead back to you."

"Not if the people responsible are dead."

Cipriani shrugged. "That's always a solution." He tapped a finger against his lips. "And for more than just your fellow conspirators."

"What are you talking about?"

Cipriani stroked his chin, as if ready to impart a unique wisdom. "Tell me something first. Does Mickey D know about any of this?"

"He knows about the ritual that will be performed," Cabrera said.

"But not about these problems?"

Cabrera shook his head. "No, he knows nothing. He is due to arrive here in a few days. I am hoping to have it resolved by then."

Cipriani nodded. "I think that's wise. In fact, I think it's imperative that it *is* resolved by then. Unless you want to see this whole deal blow up in your face."

Cabrera stared at him. "And what do you suggest?"

"I think you need another accident. I'm talking about María Mendez's niece. *And* her detective lover. *And* Martínez." He gave Cabrera a regretful smile. "There are billions of dollars at stake, my friend. You've already gotten rid of two people who threatened our little deal—that Pineiro guy, and the Red Angel. So, do what you did the other times our plan was threatened. Arrange another automobile accident."

Cabrera's jawline hardened. "I have considered this, and already I have people in place." He let out a long breath. "But, of course, you are right. There is no choice now. It is something that must be done quickly."

Before they left the hotel, Devlin got a list of available flights from Cubana Airlines, then placed a call to New

York. Ollie Pitts mumbled something about grave-robbing communists when Devlin explained the problem. He grunted when Devlin told him what he wanted. Then he cackled when Devlin said he would personally cover the cost of the flight, the hotel, and all the detective's meals and expenses. When Pitts started to negotiate beer money as an expense, Devlin gave him two choices. He could arrive in Havana later that night via a connecting flight from the Bahamas, or he could spend the rest of his career wondering what "new shit assignment" HIS BOSS would have for him each and every day.

That done, Devlin changed Martínez's plan. Putting together their collection of misfits could wait, he said. The first stop he wanted to make was the funeral home that had managed to lose María Mendez's body.

As the ancient Chevrolet made its way toward the Vedado section of Havana, Devlin lowered his window to gain some relief from the lack of air-conditioning. Music blared from open louvered doors and windows, and somewhere in the distance he heard a cock crowing. It was his first look at the morning madness of Cuban traffic. Bicycles and aging motorcycles dominated the streets, all with at least two riders. Many of the motorcycles were equipped with sidecars and carried two or three more—all of it, Martínez explained, a tribute to the fuel shortages that plagued the island. As they turned a corner, Martínez pointed out two enormous buses, the likes of which Devlin had never seen, each one disgorging its passengers into plumes of diesel smoke. The buses were tractor-trailer trucks converted to transport people. They had arrived on the island in exchange for Cuban sugar and citrus, part of a deal with the now defunct Soviet empire. The trailer section, which Martínez described as "a tribute to Cuban insanity," had then been converted by Cuban engineers, fitted with cheap plastic seats and a row of narrow windows that seldom worked. The engineers also created a large dip in the center to accommodate a second door, and it made the entire vehicle appear to have two enormous humps. "The people call the buses 'camels,' " Martínez said. "They also call them many other things when the windows fail to work. Especially on steamy July days, like the one we are now enduring."

Devlin stared out the window. The surrounding buildings looked battered and beaten, the absence of paint and repair leaving exterior walls pitted like decayed teeth. Sections of sidewalk had crumbled away, and holes in the roadway had been haphazardly filled with sand and stone.

In many ways, Havana had the look of a city that had endured a recent war. Except for the inhabitants. He had never seen people in a large city seem more relaxed or at ease with each other. Pedestrians wandered into the streets, unconcerned about oncoming traffic. And drivers simply stopped and waited for them to pass. There were no blaring horns, no shouted curses, threatening mayhem. It was as though everyone had the right to move about as they pleased, as if every inch of territory was shared equally. And, God, they were beautiful people, Devlin thought—almost uniformly beautiful, in every shade of white and tan and brown and black. Adrianna came by it naturally, he told himself. It was in her genes.

The funeral home was located on Calzada and K streets, and the sign out front identified it simply as FUNERARIA CALZADA Y K.

"Why was the body sent here?" Devlin asked as he stepped from the car onto another crumbling sidewalk.

They were standing on the edge of a small park, two blocks away from the U.S. Interests Section office. In the distance Devlin could see a long line of people, all waiting for a chance at a U.S. visa.

Martínez waved his arm, taking in the exterior of the funeral home. It was a shabby, three-story poured-concrete structure, dotted with small casement windows and fake marble trim. "This is considered the finest funeral home in Havana," he said. "It is where the bodies of all high government officials are taken."

Adrianna slipped her arm in Devlin's. She was staring at the covered stone staircase that led to the second level. The interior beyond seemed forbidding, and her normally calm brown eyes were suddenly nervous.

"Do you want to go in?" Devlin asked. "I want to use Martínez to get into the areas the public doesn't normally see. So we might end up in places—"

Adrianna shook her head, cutting him off. "No, I think I'll wait here in the park. I brought a sketch pad with me. I'll just find a place to sit and draw. I don't need this to be any grimmer than it already is."

The floor and walls of the lobby were covered with stark pink marble that had not been polished in a long time, and it gave off a dull, flat, lifeless look that offered little hope of comfort. From the lobby Martínez and Devlin entered a long, wide room where the marble gave way to stone. Here a line of identical wooden rocking chairs ran down the room's center. Freestanding ashtrays had been placed between the chairs, all of which were now empty. Smaller rooms opened off the larger one. Devlin entered one and found an old man lying in an open coffin, its lid standing on end against a nearby wall. There was an elderly woman seated in a chair beside the old man's bier. Devlin nodded a condolence, or an apology, he wasn't certain which, then turned away. A stained-glass window at the far end of the room drew his eye. It offered the only natural light in this otherwise dimly lighted space, and it depicted a scene of a sailing ship out at sea. Devlin wondered if it was meant to imply some final journey now under way.

"How long do bodies stay here?" he asked.

"Normally, only one day. Burials are done quickly here, because of the heat."

"Is there any security when the place is empty?"

"It is never empty," Martínez said. "It is our custom to have a family member remain with the body until it is buried the next day."

"But that didn't happen in this case."

Martínez shook his head. "The Red Angel's body never reached this room."

"Let's go see the room it did reach."

The office was off the lobby. There were four people inside—a middle-aged woman seated behind a cluttered metal desk and four men lounging about, drinking coffee. All wore lab coats and bored faces.

Martínez flashed his badge and asked several questions in Spanish, the words coming too rapidly for Devlin to make even a stab at interpretation.

The woman nodded and signaled to one of the men, who immediately opened a rear door, beckoning them to follow. The man, who was tall and slender and somewhere in his mid-thirties, led them down a dark, narrow staircase that opened into a large, dingy room. Several carts were lined up along one wall, two of which held bodies covered with graying, white sheets. There was a hole in one of the sheets, through which the nose of one corpse protruded as if getting a final whiff of life. To the left was an open bay with two hearses parked in tandem, the hood of one jutting out into the street. An old man sat in a chair beside the open door.

Devlin raised his chin toward the old man. "Is he the only guard?"

Martínez relayed the question to their guide.

He answered with a terse *"Sí. Solo."*

Martínez walked to the first of two other doors and opened it. Beyond, Devlin could see a refrigerated room that held more carts and bodies. He closed it and opened the second door, revealing the naked body of a young woman on a mortician's table. Two men dressed in lab coats looked up quickly. The older of the pair stared at Martínez with annoyance. His younger assistant simply looked startled, as though he had been caught doing something illicit. Martínez displayed his badge and apologized, then turned back to Devlin and shrugged.

"What time did the body disappear?" Devlin asked.

Martínez glanced at his watch. "It was about this time of day."

"Let's find out if the old man was working then."

The old man stared up at them, a slightly amused look spread across a weathered face.

Martínez loosed a string of questions, which the old man answered with a nod, a raised eyebrow, and a rapid flow of Spanish that Devlin could not follow.

"He was working here when the body disappeared," Martínez said. A small smile played across his lips. "He is very defensive. He says he had to relieve himself and went to the *baño*—um, the bathroom. He says the body must have been taken then."

"Where was the body?"

Martínez raised his chin toward one of the interior doors. "It was in the refrigerated room. He said the body still had bandages on it when it came from the hospital, and it is his job to remove them. He did this, and saw that the body had been badly burned about the face and arms. He feared decomposition would come quickly, so he placed it inside the room so it would remain cool."

"Does he know who it was?"

Martínez asked the question, then turned back to Devlin

and shook his head. "He said the paperwork did not have a name. The driver told him he had not been given any, that it would be sent later in the day."

"And he didn't recognize who it was?"

Martínez relayed the question. "He says the face was badly burned and swollen, that it could have been his mother and he would not have known."

The old man smiled at Devlin. He had only four teeth in the front of his head. He reached into his shirt pocket and removed a black feather, then began babbling in rapid Spanish. His final words were the only thing Devlin could understand. They were "Palo Monte."

"Did I hear him right?" Devlin asked.

Martínez took the feather and nodded. "He says he found the feather inside the refrigerated room. I have seen these feathers before. They are from a scavenger bird called the *aura tinosa,* and are considered sacred by the followers of Palo Monte, who call the bird *mayimbe*. The feather is always used as a part of their *mpaca,* which is a type of charm made from an animal horn that must always be worn by a Palo Monte priest."

"Did the old man tell anyone else about this feather?"

Martínez asked, then shook his head. "He says the young officer who was here treated him like an old fool, so he didn't offer the information. He says he decided to save the feather so he could give it to the *palero,* the Palo Monte priest, when he returned for it."

"Is that likely? That the *palero* will come back for it?"

Martínez shrugged. "I do not think so. There will be other feathers in the *palero*'s *nganga*."

"His what?"

Martínez smiled and took Devlin's arm. "Come. I think we have found everything we can here. If Palo Monte is involved in this, there is much that you must learn. And I can tell you only a small part of it."

4

Two men are watching us," Adrianna said. She handed Martínez her sketch pad. "I drew this. It only shows their faces in profile. It was the best I could do without them knowing."

Martínez nodded. "Yes, the two men dressed in white. They have been following us since we left the hotel. I suspect they will continue to follow us, so this picture of their faces may be useful." He tore off the top sheet, folded it, and put it in his pocket.

"Cabrera's men?" Devlin asked.

"They are Abakua." He pronounced the word *Ahh-bah-quah*. "This particular sect is unusual. They dress all in white and are known to work for State Security, which in itself is unusual. Normally, the Abakua shun the police and the government. Fortunately for us, these Abakua are not very good at their jobs."

"What the hell is an Abakua?" Devlin asked.

"It is a secret society with many sects. Very violent and dangerous, and much feared by the people. They consider themselves part of Palo Monte, yet apart from it. Most *paleros* wish they were even more apart."

"Great. We're being followed by *lunatic* voodoo worshipers, who also happen to work for the secret police." He reached out and placed a hand on Martínez's shoulder. "You have any good news?"

Martínez offered up one of his mournful smiles. "Soon, my friend. Soon we will have good news. I promise you."

They drove a dozen blocks before Martínez pulled to the curb in front of a large, crumbling house that would easily qualify as a small mansion.

He turned to face Adrianna. "This is your ancestral home," he said. "It was the home of your grandfather before he left Cuba. It was also the home of his father before him."

Adrianna turned to look at the house. It was two stories of stone, covered with stucco that had fallen away in places. There were two balconies visible from the front, with ornately carved stone balustrades and curved floor-to-ceiling windows. The small front yard was closed off by a low stone wall and iron gates, and behind it thick tropical vegetation hid much of the house from view. There was a long driveway that led back to a large detached carriage house, with long-disused servants' quarters above. It was one of those houses that years before must have seemed impervious to any changes that might come.

On either side stood equally once elegant homes, homes that now spoke of the new Cuba of the past forty years. To the left was a brightly painted and well-tended mansion that served as the headquarters of the Cuban Olympic Committee. To the right was an even larger, but fast-crumbling house that had been converted into apartments. A large Cuban flag hung from one window of the second house, while another held freshly washed clothing set out to dry.

"It's like seeing a world that doesn't exist anymore," Adrianna said. "I'm trying to imagine what all this was like when my grandfather lived here."

"It was an elegant neighborhood," Martínez offered. "People like your grandfather lived in great splendor, while others barely lived at all." He shrugged, as if apologizing for that regretful truth. "Your aunt returned to the house after the revolution. She lived here with her sister, Amelia, and her sister's husband. But apparently the two women did not get along, and later Fidel gave her another house in Miramar, where many of the leaders of the revolution still live."

"Fidel *gave* her a house? *Himself?*"

"Oh yes. All the houses given to heroes of the revolution were selected by Fidel, or at least personally approved by him. It is the same today. He is—how do you say it?—a micromanager?" Martínez seemed pleased with his use of the word. "Anyway, your tía Amelia lives here alone now. Her husband died several years ago. But certainly you knew that."

Adrianna shook her head. "No, I didn't. I never even met my aunt Amelia." Her hands tightened in her lap. "I guess it's time I did."

A small, agitated woman with the darting eyes of an angry bird opened the door. Amelia Mendez de Pedroso glared at Adrianna, then at the two men. Her hair was pulled back in a tight gray bun. Strands had pulled free on either side, and it gave her a wild, slightly mad look. She was frail, almost shrunken, and well into her seventies. Yet there was an intimidating quality about her that caused Adrianna to hesitate.

"Auntie . . . it is I. Adrianna . . . your niece. Your brother Rudolfo's daughter."

The old woman stared at her, horrified. "Rudolfo is dead. Don't talk to me about the dead. It is bad luck."

Adrianna turned to Martínez, momentarily confused. She switched to English. "What do I say to her? Does she even know about my aunt María?"

"I understand what you are saying," the old woman snapped. "Don't think you can fool me by speaking in English. Why are you talking about my communist sister, may God forgive her treacherous soul. And who are these men? They smell like Castro's police."

Martínez stepped forward. "Ah, your nose is good, señora. At least for me."

The old woman let out a grunt. "Even an old woman can smell swine. Why are you bringing my niece here? Has she been arrested?"

"No, I assure you, señora. No one has been arrested. I have brought your niece here to speak to you about your sister's death." Martínez spoke to the woman in Spanish.

The old woman snorted and looked at Martínez with contempt. "I can speak English, you know. You think I am not educated, but I am. And do not try to fool me. My sister is not dead." She waved a dismissive hand. "You communists are not clever enough to kill her."

"Señora . . ."

Another wave. "I saw her only yesterday." Her eyes narrowed with suspicion. "I had just awakened from a dream, and she was standing there in the room. Ochun was with her. It is how I know the *paleros* have her." There was a sly smile, then her eyes turned hostile again. "It is all Juanita's fault, may her cursed heathen soul burn in hell."

Adrianna stepped forward and took her aunt's hand. "Tía Amelia, may we come in? I so much want to speak with you."

The old woman's eyes remained suspicious. Then she seemed to surrender to the inevitable. "You may come into my house. But you remember. Nothing in here is yours. My father gave me this house when he and Rudolfo left Cuba. It is all mine, even though my communist sister will tell you differently."

They followed her into the dark interior, down a long hall

absent of any light, passing several closed doors as they moved toward the rear of the house. The hallway was narrow and confining, the heat trapped inside it oppressive. Whatever paint was left on the walls was peeling badly, mostly from areas where pictures had once hung. A heavy odor of mildew and decay seemed to permeate everything, to come from deep within the structure itself, almost as if the house was mourning what it once had been.

They passed through a final door and entered a large kitchen. It had the look of a place heavily lived in. There was an ancient wooden table with six sturdy chairs, set apart from the cooking area. A pedal-operated sewing machine sat before a tall, wide window that looked into an overgrown garden, behind which stood the carriage house and servants' quarters.

Amelia waved at the chairs, waited for them to be seated, then stared at the one empty seat beside her niece before reluctantly sitting herself.

Adrianna reached out and took her hand again. "Tía Amelia, tell me about this Juanita you spoke about. Was she the nana you and Tía María and my father had as children?"

Amelia pulled her hand away, then pushed herself up and went to a small bookcase next to the door they had entered. She returned with a photo album and began turning the pages.

She let out a long, somewhat nervous breath when she reached the photo she wanted, and jabbed a finger at it. "Here," she said, pointing to three small children gathered around a large black woman, a bandanna around her head, a cigar protruding from her mouth. "Juanita Asparu," Amelia said. "A daughter of Obatala."

Adrianna looked at Martínez. The major gave her a helpless shrug.

"Obatala is one of the *orishas,* the African gods," he explained. "There are two hundred and thirty-six gods and goddesses, about thirty who are very important. Obatala is among the most powerful. All children belong to her. As a daughter of Obatala, this Juanita would be able to give a child to another god."

"Yes, yes." Amelia's voice had grown insistent. "When she was just a child, María was given to Ochun by Juanita." She gave her niece a cunning smile. "This is why the communists could never kill my sister."

Devlin leaned forward, bringing the old woman's eyes to his. "This Ochun, this is the person who was with your sister?"

Amelia gave Devlin a look of contempt. "Ochun is not a person," she snapped. "It is like this policeman says. She is one of the *orishas*." Her eyes flicked to Martínez, as if asking why he had brought such a fool into her home.

Devlin refused to give up. "What did this Ochun look like?" he asked.

The old woman snorted. "As she always looks," she snapped. "Like the Virgin of Caridad, very saintly and black as the night. Protector of all the whores and deviants."

Martínez placed a hand on Devlin's arm. "Ochun is one of our most popular *orishas.* You will see many women dressed in yellow to honor her. She is very powerful. Also very vindictive. She can give twenty-five blessings, or twenty-five curses. And if you should ever harm a daughter of Ochun . . ." He ended the sentence with a shrug.

"Yes, yes." Amelia echoed Martínez's warning with a vigorous nod. "It is why María is safe from them." She gave Martínez a contemptuous look, as if he was one of her sister's enemies.

"Do you believe in these gods?" Devlin asked.

She gave Devlin a sly look. "You are my niece's lover, eh? I saw your picture. My niece sent it to my sister and she showed it to me." She nodded as if coming to a decision.

"You are very handsome. But you are also from the police. I know about you."

"Do you believe in these gods, Aunt Amelia?" Devlin asked again.

The old woman stared at him. "I am not your aunt. Do not try and fool me. And I believe in nothing." She turned her glare on Martínez and elevated her chin defiantly. "And, especially, I do not believe in that communist fool Fidel. The Negroes believe in him, just as they believe in their gods." She made a slicing gesture with one bony hand, as if wielding a knife. "Fidel cut off their tails and let them down from the trees, and now I have them living next door to me. And now their gods even enter my home with my sister." She reached out and slammed the album shut, as if closing away her childhood. "It is all the communists' doing. All of it."

"I am afraid she will be of little help to us," Martínez said. They were driving back toward the old city, headed to the apartment of José Tamayo, the mystery writer–cum–political cop whom Martínez wanted to enlist in their small army.

"You think she's . . ." Devlin finished the sentence by tapping the side of his head.

Martínez shrugged. It was the major's habitual response to any question. But it wasn't just Martínez. Devlin had gotten it from bellmen and waiters, and just about everyone he had met. It seemed to be the Cuban national answer to any question.

"She is old," Martínez said. "But I suspect she is also very clever. She also likes to say things that are not acceptable. Perhaps she feels it is safer to act"—he glanced regretfully at Adrianna—"shall we say, somewhat mentally infirm."

"Do you think she believes in these . . . these *orishas*?"

Martínez kept his eyes straight ahead. Devlin could see he was smiling. "Did you notice the bracelet she wore on her wrist. The one made of blue and white beads."

"I noticed it," Adrianna said.

"It is a symbol that marks her as a daughter of Yemaya, the goddess of the sea and the home and motherhood. Sailors worship her and seek her protection. She is also Ochun's older sister, and the one who gave Ochun her powers. And Yemaya, herself, is very powerful, her dark side very capable of vengeance."

Adrianna gave Martínez a sharp look. His words had seemed sly to her, almost condescending. "I don't care what she believes, or doesn't believe. I think she was frightened." She held the major's gaze, defying him to contradict her. "I want to go back and see her again. But next time I'll go alone."

"I'm not sure that's—" Another sharp look from Adrianna killed Devlin's objection in mid-sentence. "Maybe Ollie could go with you," he said instead.

"God, no."

"He could stay outside," Devlin offered.

"He'd scare the entire neighborhood." Adrianna shook her head, letting him know further discussion was useless. "I want to see her again, and I don't want her to feel her home is being invaded. I want her to talk to me, and I don't think that will happen unless I go alone."

Before heading to their next stop, Martínez stopped at a public phone to check with his office. When he returned to the car, his face was masked by uncertainty.

"It seems Colonel Cabrera has postponed your appointment."

"Until when?" Devlin asked.

"Tomorrow morning at ten."

"Do you think that means he's found something?" There was a hint of hope in Adrianna's voice.

Martínez inclined his head slightly as if considering the possibility. "I think it is more likely he wants to await a report from his Abakua henchmen and see what we are up to. But we can be hopeful."

"Maybe we should ask him why the Abakua are following us," Adrianna suggested.

Martínez and Devlin exchanged a quick look.

"Perhaps it would be better to let the chicken sit on the nest undisturbed," Martínez said. "But on our way to José Tamayo's apartment, perhaps we also could give the chicken something to think about."

"What would that be?" Devlin asked.

Martínez offered up his Cuban shrug. "Perhaps I can come up with something," he said.

José Tamayo's apartment was in a battered block of tenements off the Plaza de Armas, a small square dominated by a statue of Carlos Manuel de Cespedes, who led the fight to free Cuba from Spanish domination.

Martínez parked his ancient Chevrolet in front of what appeared to be a diminutive church that sat behind a spiked iron gate and an ancient tree with wide-spreading branches.

"Come," he said. "Let me play tour guide for the benefit of the Abakua."

Martínez stood before the gate. Fifty yards away, the two Abakua who were tailing them sat in their car on the other side of the plaza.

"Those clowns certainly stand out in a crowd," Devlin said.

"Yes. They are not very good at surveillance, but they are persistent." Martínez raised one hand toward the small church hidden behind the massive tree. "So, I will play tour guide for a few minutes. Then we will lose our Abakua friends before we go to José Tamayo's home. And, who can say, you may even enjoy my instructions."

Martínez waved his hand in a circle. "Here, under this sacred ceiba tree, on November sixteenth, 1511, was held the first mass to celebrate the founding of the city. The small church behind the tree, the Templete, was built later, in 1828, and it holds paintings commemorating that day."

"It can't be the same tree," Adrianna said.

Martínez raised and lowered his bushy eyebrows. "It is unlikely. Some say succeeding trees were grown from shoots of the original. But, according to legend, it is the same tree. I suspect the tree has been replaced several times, possibly from these shoots, but many prefer to believe the original tree has endured." He smiled. "Like Cuba itself."

Martínez took each of their arms and started to walk toward the small park at the center of the plaza. "The ceiba tree is also very important in Palo Monte. The *paleros* believe the god Iroko lives in the tree. If a *palero* must leave his home, he will bury his *nganga* under a ceiba tree and Iroko will protect it. Then, when the *palero* returns he must leave money for the god in order to retrieve his possessions." A broad smile creased Martínez's face. "The gods, the *orishas,* do nothing for free, you see. If they are not paid, they will do no work, either for good *or* for evil."

The major led them into the small park, the surrounding sidewalks of which were filled with used-book stalls. "We will buy one of Tamayo's books," he said. "He will be very honored if you present it for him to sign." He let out a small laugh. "Like the *orishas,* Cubans also do not like to work for free."

"What kind of books does he write?" Adrianna asked.

"He is a great follower of your American writers Raymond Chandler and Dashiell Hammett. I do not know the work of these men, but it is said that Tamayo's is very similar."

"They were very good," Adrianna said. "What we call 'hard-boiled' fiction."

"Ah, yes," Martínez said. "That is Tamayo. Very hard-boiled. But only in his writing."

After buying a copy of one of Tamayo's books, they made their way through the plaza and into a government building that housed offices for the Ministry of the Army. Once inside, they immediately moved to a side door that opened onto an adjacent street. Three entryways down, they turned into a dark, narrow hall covered in ancient mosaic tiles.

"This is Tamayo's building," Martínez said as he led them to a narrow staircase that had frayed electric wires hanging from the ceiling. "The Abakua will be staring at the government building we first entered, wondering who in the army is giving us aid and comfort." He laughed. "It will also give Colonel Cabrera great concern when they tell him where we went."

Devlin glanced at the ceiling of the battered building they had entered. "He won't have anything to worry about if we don't get out of this firetrap alive."

Martínez followed Devlin's gaze. "Do not worry," he said. "Tamayo is a son of Chango, the god of thunder and fire—a very powerful rascal—and he will not allow flames to touch the home of his follower. Besides, Tamayo also keeps a statue of Eleggua behind his door, which he feeds every day."

"Feeds?" Devlin asked.

Martínez nodded. "Yes, feeds, my friend. From his mouth he sprays it with aguardiente, a cheap Cuban rum. This way he gives Eleggua his *ache,* his spirit, and this assures the god is content and that Tamayo has nothing to fear inside these walls."

"Jesus Christ," Devlin said. "Is there anybody in Cuba who doesn't believe in these gods?"

"Oh yes," Martínez said. "There are many. You will know them by the misery in their lives."

They climbed the battered staircase, past crumbling walls and metal doors, many of which had more than one lock. Martínez had told them that Tamayo was one of Cuba's most revered and successful writers. Now he had also told him that the man practiced a form of voodoo that was beyond Devlin's comprehension. And that those who didn't practice voodoo could be known by the misery in their lives? He glanced about him as he climbed the steamy, battered staircase to the fourth floor of this hellhole firetrap of a building. If this was viewed as the absence of misery, he wondered what life in Cuba was for those who rejected these two hundred and thirty-six African gods. And what had it been before the arrival of Comandante Fidel. Perhaps that was it, he thought. Like Castro, perhaps these strange religious beliefs simply offered hope in a country where hope had always been the one elusive commodity of life.

A tall, slender, coffee-colored man with short, tightly curled gray hair opened the door of the apartment. He was well into his sixties, but his face was spread into a smile that made him seem far younger, a smile so genuine that Devlin had the inexplicable feeling they had known each other for years.

The man bubbled forth in perfect, if somewhat formal English. "I am José Tamayo. Welcome. Welcome. I am honored to have you visit my home."

Over Tamayo's shoulder Devlin glimpsed a small, sparsely furnished apartment. There was a main room, consisting of four dinette-type chairs covered in plastic, set in a line before an old black-and-white television set. A small table sat next to one of the chairs, holding only a telephone and a single ashtray in which a large cigar smoldered. Off that room was a galley kitchen, giving off a rich aroma of Cuban coffee, and a long, narrow terrace overlooking an interior courtyard. Two open louvered doors on the terrace led to small, cramped bedrooms. Martínez had told them that Tamayo's son and daughter-in-law lived there as well, but that both were now at work.

Tamayo ushered them into the main room and seated them on the dinette chairs with all the formality of someone offering the comfort of a plushly furnished room. He then hurried to the kitchen, returning with steaming cups of coffee. When Adrianna presented the battered book they had purchased, his face again burst into youthful radiance, and he quickly signed it with the exuberance of a child opening gifts on Christmas morning.

As he handed back the book, Tamayo's expressive face filled with unabashed regret. "My wife, who is away working this morning, asked me to add her condolences to my own," he said. He reached out and took Adrianna's hand. "Your aunt was a great woman, and a great hero of our revolution, and my wife and I were greatly honored by her friendship."

For the first time since she learned of her aunt's death, Devlin saw tears form in Adrianna's eyes. He leaned forward, drawing the writer's attention.

"The major tells me you once worked with the political police," he said. "We are hoping you can use your knowledge to help us find the body of María Mendez."

Tamayo nodded, then made a small wave with one hand, as if brushing aside his past activities.

"I was merely a propagandist, señor. My job was to put forth my government's views on political matters." He wagged his head from side to side. "Sometimes they were accurate expressions, sometimes merely views my government wished others to share. So, my police abilities, I'm afraid, are really limited to my fictional writings." He leaned forward, his face filling with more sincerity than Devlin had ever seen crammed in the face of one man.

He nodded toward Martínez. "Arnaldo has explained, however, that Palo Monte may be involved. In this I can help you. I have written extensively about Palo Monte in my fiction, and I am also a believer in its powers."

Martínez interrupted, explaining what they had discovered at the funeral home. He handed Tamayo the black feather the ancient security guard had given them.

Tamayo held the feather up to the light and nodded. "There is no question this is from the *aura tinosa*." He looked at Devlin. "This is the scavenger bird we call *maybimbe*, very sacred to the Palo Monte, and very integral to their rituals."

"We are also under surveillance by two Abakua," Martínez added.

Tamayo's eyes hardened into a look of true hatred. He turned to Adrianna. "First, I must tell you that I have grave doubts that your aunt's death was the result of any accident."

Adrianna's eyes widened and she seemed ready to speak, but Tamayo hurried on. "I have no proof of this." He brought his hand to his chest. "But from here I believe this is true."

"What makes you believe it?" Devlin asked.

Tamayo shook his head, his eyes still severe. "Something sinister is going on in my country, Señor Devlin. I do not know what it is, but I do know that two people high in our government also held this belief. And now both are dead." He looked back at Adrianna. "Regrettably, one of those people was your beloved aunt."

"Who was the other?" Adrianna asked.

Tamayo drew a deep breath. "Are you familiar with the name Manuel Pineiro?"

Adrianna shook her head. Tamayo turned to Devlin and received the same response.

Tamayo picked up his cigar, noted that it had gone out, and returned it to the ashtray. "Manuel Pineiro was known as *Barba Roja* to the people—or Red Beard. For twenty years he was the head of our intelligence apparatus, our spymaster as my fellow novelist John le Carré would say, and someone equally as respected in the intelligence community as the famous East German Markus Wolf, who le Carré used as the model for his great villain. In short, he was very good at his job—a man who knew all the secrets."

"And he was also killed?" Devlin asked.

Tamayo nodded. "Also in a car crash earlier this year."

"Was his body stolen?"

"No," Tamayo said. "But there were reports that several men dressed all in white were seen near the site of the crash. I believe they were members of a particular sect of the Abakua."

Devlin turned to Martínez.

"This is true." Martínez glanced at Adrianna, his eyes filled with regret. "Police also saw these Abakua near the scene of your aunt's accident. The Abakua fled when they arrived, and I am ashamed to say the police did not pursue them. There were only two police officers, and at least five Abakua. As I explained, they are much feared by the people." He hesitated, then added: "And some of our less courageous police."

"And it is known that these Abakua—the ones who dress in white—are often the tools of State Security," Tamayo added.

Devlin sat back and digested what he had been told. He let out a long breath. "Tell me how Palo Monte fits into this."

Tamayo took time to relight his cigar, sending a stream of thick smoke up toward the high ceiling. "Before you can grasp what I am about to tell you, you must first understand something about our Afro-Cuban religions." He raised two fingers of one hand, then one of the other hand. "There are two of these religions, and one false religion. First is Regla de Osha, which is also known as Santeria. It is the most gentle of the religions in its divination rites, and it is very closely tied to Catholicism. It was brought to Cuba by highly educated African slaves from Nigeria. Next is Regla Mayombe, also known as Palo Monte. This is a much darker and more primitive religion, which performs its divinations through contact with the dead. It originates from very primitive Bantu slaves brought here from the Congo. And finally there is the Abakua, which is not a true religion, but rather a secret society that believes in solving all problems through violence. These Abakua originally came from West Africa's Calabar River basin, where they were part of the leopard society of the Negbe people. Here in Cuba, they have formed their own sects, which are tied to Palo Monte through the use of corrupt *paleros* who seek to use the power of the Abakua."

"And you think one of these corrupt *paleros* was behind the theft of María Mendez's body?"

Tamayo nodded.

"Why?" Devlin asked.

"To make a *nganga* to the god BabaluAye."

Devlin let out another long breath and held up his hands. "You are losing me again. First, I keep hearing about all this *nganga* business, but I can't seem to find out what the hell it is."

Tamayo smiled. "I will explain." He turned to Adrianna and his face filled with regret. "Some of the things I will tell you will sound unreasonable, perhaps even cruel and barbaric. I ask you to be indulgent, and to remember that the followers of Palo Monte hold these beliefs as strongly as those who believe deeply in the teachings of Judaism or Christianity or any other religion."

He turned back to Devlin. "The *nganga* is at the center of all Palo Monte ritual. It is basically a large pot"—he made a circle with his arms, indicating something two and a half to three feet in diameter—"into which various sacred items are placed. The *nganga* is dedicated to one of the gods, but its purpose is to speak to the dead, and get the dead to answer questions about the future, and to perform certain acts for its owner—acts of both good and evil. But the main purpose of the *nganga* is to protect the owner from harm.

"Central to the *nganga* are the bones of a dead one—man or woman—with whom the owner can drive a bargain by feeding the *nganga* his own blood at least once each year. In addition, the owner must give the *nganga* whatever it asks for, which is usually money or some offering, but in some rare cases it has been known to involve the life of another—even someone very dear to the owner.

"So first we start with the bones of a dead one—the skull so it can think and speak; fingers so it can do what it must; feet so it can travel wherever necessary. There also may be the bones of other dead ones, but the first bones—the oldest—rule the *nganga,* and the other dead are there only to assist."

Tamayo glanced at Adrianna to assure himself that his words were not causing her distress.

"The bones that are selected for the *nganga* determine the type of power it will possess. If, for example, the owner wants to do harm to his enemies, he will use the bones of a killer, or a person who was evil in life. If, on the other hand, he wishes to cure an illness, or protect against illness, he will choose the bones of a great healer." Again he glanced at Adrianna.

"Where do they get these bones?" Devlin asked.

Tamayo gave him a somewhat sheepish half smile. "Usually, they are stolen from cemeteries."

"Is this common?" Adrianna asked.

Another half smile. "Let us say it is more common than the government would like it to be known. Let me give an example. For some reason that I have never been able to understand, Palo Monte believes that the bones of a Chinese are very lucky, and can be used to bring good fortune." He shrugged away his lack of understanding. "For this reason many Cubans have *paleros* make *ngangas* with Chinese bones, or have them include Chinese bones in *ngangas* made for other purposes." He leaned forward. "Here in Cuba, the Chinese have their own cemeteries, and the theft of Chinese bodies is so prevalent that most of the graves in these cemeteries have been protected by alarms."

"Burglar alarms?" Devlin sounded incredulous.

"I am afraid that is so," Tamayo said. "To the Chinese, we are viewed as a nation of grave robbers."

"What else goes into these *ngangas*?" Adrianna asked.

"Ah, many things. First there is earth from the four sides of the grave from which the body was taken, or where it was to be buried. Then there is the hide of a snake, which was the origin of the religion, and which consolidates the *nganga*'s power. Then the skeleton of a dog to go and fetch things for the dead one. Also the skeleton and feathers of *mayimbe*—the scavenger bird I told you about. There will also be the bones and feathers of a night bird to allow the dead one to see in the dark. Then there are many sacred woods from the forest—*palo monte* actually means 'sticks of the forest.' These are woods that can do either good or evil. One of the most powerful of the sticks is from a tree called the *jaquey*. Another is from the *rompezaraguey,* a very evil forest wood. Then, of course, there are things needed by the dead one to perform his duties—herbs for healing, if that is the purpose. A knife or gun for killing, perhaps. And then there are the things needed by the god to whom the *nganga* is dedicated. If that god were BabaluAye, there would be items related to illness and death and healing. If it were to the great warrior Oggun, it would be filled with objects of metal, over which Oggun holds all power."

"But once you have all these things, how does it work?" Adrianna asked.

"Everything is based on the three principles of magic,"

Tamayo said. He raised three fingers. "First, that the same produces the same. Next, that things that have been in contact influence each other. And, finally, that everything—man, animal, object—has a soul." He folded his hands in front of him as if preparing to pray. His voice became solemn. "Using these principles, the *palero* questions the dead one—or asks its assistance in certain matters. He does this through prayers, chanted in a mixture of Bantu and Spanish, and by throwing the coconuts—special religious shells that the *palero* has made from pieces of the coconut shell, each about the size of a large coin. The dead one answers the questions and requests put to it by means of the shells. Let me show you."

Tamayo left for a moment and returned with some paper and a pencil. He began drawing and writing rapidly.

"Now, the coconut shells have both a concave and convex side, and how they end up when they are thrown by the *palero* determines the answer of the dead one." He pointed to the first drawing, which showed all the shells with the concave sides turned up. "This answer is *Alafia*. It means yes, good news, but is not conclusive. More questions need to be asked, or offerings made if it involved a request.

"Next is two shells up, two down. This is *Eyife.* It is a definite yes, a conclusive answer."

He pointed to the third drawing—three shells with the convex side up and one down. "Here the answer is *Otawe*. This means that the answer could be yes, but there is an obstacle to overcome.

"Next is three shells down and one up—*Ocana*. This is a definite no to the question or request. It tells us that something is wrong, or has happened, or was done by some enemy. To overcome this there must be an *Ebbo,* an offering to the god of the *nganga*.

"And finally is *Oyekun,* which is all shells facing down.

This means that the dead one wants to speak, and you must question him."

Devlin stared at Tamayo. The man seemed sincere in all he had said, like a Christian explaining the equally unfathomable resurrection of Christ.

"And you believe all of this?" he asked. "You believe that it works?"

"I have seen it work, my friend." He gave Devlin a small smile that seemed a mixture of patience and tolerance. "And tonight, at midnight, when you visit the great *palero* Plante Firme, I believe you also will see it work." He turned to Adrianna. "And it will be you who will make this magic happen. Because tonight, with Plante Firme's help, *you* will speak to the dead man."

5

Ollie Pitts sat on the terrace that ran the entire length of the Inglaterra Hotel. It was ten-thirty in the evening. Devlin and Martínez had picked him up at José Martí Airport two hours before, and Pitts had simply dumped his bags in his room and retreated to the terrace to have the first of the many beers he planned to add to Devlin's tab.

Martínez sat on the other side of the small tile-covered table, a cup of strong Cuban coffee before him. He had offered to keep Pitts company while Devlin returned to his room to give Adrianna whatever comfort he could before her meeting with the dead man, now only an hour and a half away.

Pitts had only rolled his eyes when told of their midnight séance with the Palo Monte witch doctor. Now those same cop's eyes roamed the sidewalk, taking in the array of beautiful young prostitutes who strolled by, smiles flashing at the tourists who crowded the terrace. Pitts let out a small snort and brought his attention back to the sad-eyed major.

"So, listen, Martínez. We pull this thing off, and find this old broad's body, I figure Fidel owes me a big one. Am I right?"

Martínez fought off a smile. "I am sure the Comandante will be very grateful."

"Yeah, well, gratitude don't quite cut it. You know what I mean?"

"What is it you would wish in payment for your services, Detective?"

Pitts smirked and again fixed his gaze on the young prostitutes parading along the sidewalk. "I want the Lycra concession for the whole island." He let out a louder snort. "Hell, I'll be a fucking millionaire overnight." He shook his head and turned his gaze back on the major. "Where do these broads get their clothes, Martínez? You got a store down here called Whores 'R' Us?"

Martínez closed his eyes momentarily. "It is more simple than that, my friend. They see these clothes in American movies and on American television, and they think this is how they must look to be desirable."

Pitts was now staring at a young woman with dark hair and garish makeup. She was no more than eighteen, and she was wearing a jersey-style top, tight about her neck but with a hole cut in its center large enough to allow half of each breast to protrude lasciviously. "I must be seeing the wrong fucking movies," Pitts said.

The young woman seemed to sense that Pitts was speaking about her. She stopped at the row of plants that created a barrier between the terrace and the street. Slowly, she withdrew a cigarette from her purse and indicated she wanted Pitts to light it.

"You are being offered one of the few capitalist delights of Cuba," Martínez said. There was a hint of regret in his voice.

"I've been here for two hours. It's about fucking time," Pitts said.

Pitts pushed himself up from the table. He was dressed in

a flamboyant Hawaiian shirt over khaki slacks, but his feet were still clad in the black iron-toed cop brogans he had worn since his first day as a patrolman. He clomped over to the woman, grinning at the sizable breasts protruding from her blouse.

"You need a light, sweetheart?" Pitts raised his eyes, then glanced quickly over her shoulder toward the street.

The young woman gave him a coy look, drawing his eyes back, then placed the cigarette between suggestively puckered lips. When Pitts had applied flame from an oversized Zippo lighter, she tilted her head back and sent a stream of smoke into the air. Then she thanked him and rattled off a stream of Spanish in a soft, suggestive voice.

"You speakee the English?" Pitts asked.

The woman shook her head and offered up another soft phrase. It required no translation.

"Sex?" Pitts asked.

"*Sí.* Sex," the woman said. She smiled at his sudden comprehension.

"Fuck?" Pitts asked.

"*Sí*. Fuck," the woman said. She was still smiling.

Pitts shook his head in mock regret. "I'm sorry, sweetheart, but I promised my old mom that I'd never ball a chick who didn't speak English." He grinned again and started back to the table.

"You are a cruel man," Martínez said as Pitts reclaimed his chair.

"So I'm told," Pitts said. "By the way, there are two assholes standing next to a car over by that little park. They're both dressed in white. Are these the two voodoo boys we got tailing us?"

"Is there anyone else near them?" Martínez asked.

"Not within fifty feet."

Martínez nodded. "They will be our Abakua. No one will get very close to them."

Pitts leaned forward and lowered his voice. "These guys are dangerous? Armed?"

Martínez nodded again. "With knives, only. But they are—how do you say?—very proficient with these implements."

The detective's eyes glittered. "Listen, Martínez. Since we got these armed scumbags—these known fucking killers—shadowing us, what are the chances of you getting me some heat?"

"Heat?"

Pitts rolled his eyes, "A *pistolero*. Boom, boom."

Martínez shook his head. "Ah, a *pistola*. No, my friend. Not here in Cuba. It is not allowed for citizens, and certainly not for tourists. Besides, if Colonel Cabrera were to learn of it, it would give him an excuse to lock you away in one of our very unpleasant prisons for many, many years."

"You carry one?" Pitts asked.

The major dropped a hand to the waistband of his trousers, which was covered by the tail of a pale blue shirt. "*Sí,* my friend. I carry one."

Pitts sneered at him. "If it gets too heavy, I'll relieve you of the burden."

"Thank you, Detective," Martínez said. "But it is very light, this *pistola*."

Colonel Antonio Cabrera climbed out of the rear of his car and glanced casually over his shoulder. The large truck that had followed him had pulled to the curb on the opposite side of the park. Cabrera was dressed in civilian clothes and walked casually now to one of the benches that faced the Inglaterra Hotel. He beckoned to the two Abakua, and watched with satisfaction as people nearby scattered as the two white-clad men approached.

"Your truck is on the other side of the park," he said. "If

they leave the hotel, take care of this matter tonight. If not, do so in the morning."

One of the Abakua, a tall, lean, hard-eyed man somewhere in his thirties, stared down at Cabrera. There was no fear in his eyes as he confronted the colonel.

"It will be easier to make it seem an accident if they are driving."

"They will definitely be driving in the morning," Cabrera said. "They have an appointment at State Security at ten. But tonight, if possible. It will be better in darkness. And an evening stroll could put them in your headlights."

"And if the major is with them?" the second Abakua asked.

"As I told you once before, I have little concern for the major's safety," Cabrera said.

Devlin and Adrianna arrived on the terrace at eleven-thirty. Adrianna was dressed in khaki slacks and a scoopneck, sleeveless yellow jersey. Despite efforts to appear outwardly calm, she could not hide the hint of nervousness in her eyes.

"You are dressed in the color of Ochun," Martínez said. "Plante Firme's *nganga* is dedicated to Oggun, who has always favored this goddess of beauty. It is a good omen." He turned to Devlin, taking in his green, short-sleeved shirt. "And green is the color of Oggun," he said. "Another favorable omen."

"What about me?" Pitts asked, pulling at the front of his flamboyant Hawaiian shirt.

Martínez smiled. "The gods are tolerant," he said.

Devlin glanced at Pitts, noting that his shirt was not tucked into his trousers—the street cop's method of concealing a weapon when going jacketless. He knew Ollie was not carrying, had made sure of it when he arrived at the airport, and he wondered if he had chosen to wear his shirt this way out of habit or to give himself the comfort of at least pretending he had a weapon.

Devlin had no such need. He hated guns, a hatred that stemmed from the times he had been forced to use one lethally. He still dreamed about those times, especially the first, when he had been forced to take the life of a fellow cop gone mad. *That's right, the man's a cop killer.* John the Boss Rossi's words flooded back at him. He shuddered inwardly. Never again, he thought. Please, God, never again.

"I think we must be going," Martínez said. "Plante Firme's home is in the Lawton district, and it will take us twenty minutes, or more, to get there. And I want to go carefully, to see if we are followed."

Martínez drove his old Chevrolet along the Avenida de Maceo, which fronted the coast. Like the streets of Old Havana, here the sidewalk promenade was awash with people, many with small children, all escaping the heat-filled confines of small apartments. At the National Hotel, which stood on a high bluff overlooking the sea, Martínez cut back inland, then headed south on the Avenida de los Presidentes. As they entered a large traffic circle with a fountain at its center, he pointed to a tall, stark building on his right.

"That is the Hospital Infantil," he said. "It is where your aunt worked as a young intern before the revolution." He gave a small shrug. "But then it was only for the children of the rich. Later your aunt changed that, and it was at this hospital that most of Havana's children received their inoculations. To this day many people still call it the Hospital of the Red Angel."

As he had done since they started out, Martínez kept a constant watch in the rearview mirror. From the rear seat, where he sat with Adrianna, Devlin glanced out the back window.

"I don't see our Abakua friends," he said.

"No," Martínez said. "Just the same truck that has remained fifty meters behind since we began."

Devlin gave the truck greater attention. As he did, the truck pulled out and accelerated. It seemed to leap ahead, coming quickly alongside their rear quarter panel. Now, under the streetlights, Devlin could see two white-clad men behind the windshield.

"Watch it," he shouted. "They're in the truck."

"I see them," Martínez shouted back. He hit the accelerator and the old Chevy's big V-eight threw the car forward.

Devlin watched as the truck also jumped forward, quickly coming even with the Chevy's rear bumper. Before he could warn Martínez, the truck cut sharply to the right, and he felt the jolt and the simultaneous thump as the truck struck the rear fender. Instinctively, he threw his arm around Adrianna and pulled her toward him, hoping his body would serve as a buffer to any heavier impact.

The truck pulled out, preparing to swerve into them again. They were headed down a steep incline, a large rock formation on their right, a sharp right-hand curve rapidly approaching.

As the truck started to jerk toward them again, Martínez hit the brakes, allowing the truck to slide past. Then he cut the wheel left, pressed the accelerator to the floor, and began a quick passing maneuver before the truck could respond.

"Give me your piece," Pitts growled from the passenger seat. "I'll pump a few in their door."

"No," Martínez snapped.

The Chevy leaped forward, and Martínez took it into the sharp right-hand turn at full speed. The car fishtailed, then straightened, racing along Avenida Rancho Boyeros, then into another sharp turn onto Avenida 20 de Mayo.

To their right, as they made the turn, the large marble monument to José Martí loomed above them. Opposite the statue, the wall of the Ministry of the Interior displayed an illuminated silhouette of Che Guevara.

"Back there, in the heavily treed area behind José Martí's statue, is where Fidel's office is," Martínez said.

Devlin noted there was no hint of fear in his voice. "Never mind the tourist crap, Martínez," Devlin snapped. "Just get us the hell out of here." He tightened his arm around Adrianna. He could feel her tremble under his touch.

"Hey, maybe we should drop in and pay a social call," Pitts said. "Maybe Fidel's got some boys with Uzis who can discourage these fucking voodoo assholes." He jabbed a finger toward Martínez. "You know, you really pissed me off, not giving me your piece back there."

"I will try to remember next time," Martínez said. "For now, I must concentrate on losing our pursuers."

Martínez cut off the main thoroughfare and into a rabbit warren of small streets, turning right, then left at every third or fourth intersection, gradually weaving his way through clusters of small houses, past scattered residential shops, the streets growing darker, the houses poorer with each turn.

The old Chevy, with its large engine and more maneuverable chassis, quickly left the truck behind. Now the streetlights vanished, the houses became even smaller and more squalid. Here the occasional faces staring out from the sidewalks and front porches were entirely black, the quiet broken only by the sporadic strains of Latin music drifting out from open windows.

Five minutes later Martínez pulled the car to a stop in front of a small blue cinderblock house, with a matching high wall that enclosed a small courtyard.

The major let out a long breath. "We are here," he said as he climbed out and walked to the rear of the car. Devlin heard him utter a curse as he viewed the damage to his left rear fender.

"We are here," Pitts mimicked. His eyes roamed the darkened street, taking in a small group of black youths gathered a short distance down the street. "We're in fucking Harlem and Señor Major's got the only heat, which, if you ask me, he probably forgot to load."

"Shut up, Ollie," Devlin snapped. "In case you didn't notice, Señor Major kept us from being roadkill back there. So cut him some slack."

Pitts pushed open his door and heaved his bulk onto the sidewalk. "I hope that's the only thing that gets cut around here." He walked to the rear of the car. "Hey, Major, nice neighborhood. You got any baseball bats in the trunk."

Martínez ignored him. He was still staring at the crumpled rear fender. Even with the lack of light, Pitts could see his face was glowing with rage.

"I'm sorry about your car," Devlin said as he and Adrianna joined him. "It seems the colonel wants our visit postponed a little longer than he said."

Martínez nodded. "So it would seem." He looked up at Pitts, his eyes still angry. "And you do not have to fear our Negroes, Detective. Here in Cuba, they have no need to attack an oppressor. Here we all share misery together."

Martínez took a bottle of rum from the Chevy's oversized glove box and led them to a solid iron gate set in the high blue wall. He pulled a chain that rang a small bell inside. Moments later the gate was opened by a thirtyish brown-skinned man, dressed only in a pair of shorts and rubber shower sandals. He greeted Martínez in rapid Spanish, then led them into the small courtyard.

"This is Plante Firme's son," Martínez explained. "He asks that we be seated while he gets his father." The major turned to Devlin and Pitts. "The *palero* speaks only Spanish and Bantu. If you will permit me, I will translate for you. Señorita Adrianna, of course, will be able to converse with the *palero* in Spanish."

The courtyard was small and sparsely furnished. There were four kitchen chairs arranged in a line so they faced a larger, solitary chair that sat with its back to the house. A small pen stood off in one corner, and they could see a half-grown pig snuffling about in the dirt. Martínez pointed to two cast-iron pots off to one side, one slightly larger than the other.

"These are *ngangas* being prepared for believers," he said. "Please do not touch them."

"They got the bones of some stiff in them?" Pitts asked.

Martínez nodded. "Among other things."

They seated themselves in the four chairs. Devlin noticed bunches of feathers hanging from an arbor, along with bundles of sticks. The skull of what he thought was a dog sat on a small table off to his right, and, inexplicably, there were posters of American cowboys hanging on the exterior wall of the house.

A large black man came around a corner of the house and entered the courtyard. He stopped at the pen that housed the pig, picked up a bucket, and threw feed to the grunting animal. Finished, he walked slowly—majestically, Devlin thought—to where they were seated. He was naked to the waist, ballooning pants hanging from surprisingly narrow hips. From the waist up he was immense, with a wide chest, thick arms, and a protruding belly; well over six feet and easily two hundred and forty pounds. He was in his late sixties, or early seventies, but still gave off a sense of physical power. The only hair on his head was a closely cropped gray beard. He wore a necklace of green beads around his neck, and a length of rope surrounded his waist, from which hung a woven straw pouch.

Martínez leaned into Devlin and nodded toward the

pouch. "His *macuto,*" he whispered. "Inside is his *mpaca,* the horn which contains all the elements of his *nganga*."

"Including . . . ?" Devlin whispered.

"Yes. Inside are small parts of the dead man."

They all stood as Plante Firme stopped in front of them. His eyes were curious, but not in any way threatening. He extended a massive hand to each of them. He was the only man Devlin had ever met with hands even larger than those of Ollie Pitts.

"Npele nganga vamo cota. Npelo nganga ndele que cota."

"He welcomes us to speak with and to consult his *nganga*," Martínez said.

With that, Plante Firme turned and walked to the large chair opposite. He sat, placing his massive hands on his knees. Equally large feet, with gnarled, twisted toes protruded from well-worn shower sandals. Everything about the man looked impoverished. Everything except his demeanor, Devlin thought. There was an aura of power about the man, and it was reflected in his son's eyes as he took a subservient position behind the *palero*'s thronelike chair.

Plante Firme uttered a stream of Spanish in a low, soft, rumbling voice.

"He says he has consulted his *nganga* before we arrive," Martínez said. "So he can know about us."

Plante Firme's eyes fixed on Adrianna. He shook his head as he spoke again. *"No es amarillo. No es Oshun. Yemaya. Madre de la vida. Madre de todos los orishas. Es la dueña de las aguas y representa el mar, fuente fundamental de la vida. Le gusta casar, chapear y manejar el machete. Es indomable y astuta. Sus castigos son duros y su cólera es temible pero justiciera. Sus colores son azul y blanco."*

Adrianna turned to Devlin. "He says I'm wearing the

wrong color. That I am not a daughter of Oshun. He says I must wear blue and white for Yemaya. He explained why, and who Yemaya is."

Plante Firme turned to Devlin, and again his voice rumbled forth. *"Oggun. Sí, Oggun."* He continued rapidly, in what to Devlin became a jumble of words.

Martínez leaned in again. "He says you are a son of Oggun, which pleases him, because he is also Oggun's son, and has dedicated his *nganga* to him. But he also says you are in conflict. Oggun is a warrior who fears nothing. He says you fear your own power, and wish to avoid violence. This, he says, is because you have been forced to kill, and this has caused peace to flee your heart. He says this is wrong for you, that you lose Oggun's power by believing this way." Martínez hesitated as Plante Firme spoke again, then quickly translated. "He also says you have a child who is very self-willed. That you must care for this child around water, which is a danger for her. He says Adrianna, a daughter of Yemaya, can help you in this."

Devlin sat stunned as Plante Firme turned to Pitts. The *palero*'s face hardened.

"*Chango.*" The word came from his mouth in a low growl. He shook his head and turned quickly away.

Martínez fought back a smile as he turned to Pitts. "I am afraid you will receive no help here," he said. "The *nganga,* which is dedicated to Oggun, has identified you as a true son of Chango, the great enemy of Oggun. The *nganga* would not speak of you."

"I'm fucking crushed," Pitts said.

Devlin stared at the voodoo priest. He turned to Martínez. "How did he know those things about me? You have a dossier on me, Martínez?"

Martínez nodded. "I know much about you, my friend. It is part of my job. But I assure you I have not shared my knowledge. This is the first time I have met with Plante Firme. But, as I have told you, he is a great *palero*. Perhaps the greatest in all Cuba."

Adrianna had ignored them, and was now speaking to Plante Firme in rapid Spanish. Martínez leaned in close again, his voice just above a whisper.

"The señorita is telling the *palero* about her aunt, and her need to find the Red Angel's body so it can be buried and give peace to her family."

Devlin heard Adrianna say the word "Abakua," and saw Plante Firme's body stiffen. The old witch doctor's eyes became hard and he leaned farther forward as if preparing to leap from his thronelike chair. He began to speak, and Martínez translated again.

"Plante Firme says we must go to the cemetery where the Red Angel was to be buried, and look for earth taken from the four corners where her body was to rest. He says if Palo Monte is involved, it is the work of a *palero* he knows well, a man of great evil who has joined with the Abakua. He says if this is true, we must go to this man, for only through him will we find the bones of the dead one who was once María Mendez."

Devlin listened to the rumble of Plante Firme's voice. Standing beside him, the man's son seemed to shiver uncontrollably. "What's he saying now?" Devlin asked.

"He is warning us about the danger ahead," Martínez said. "He says we must be cautious if parts of María Mendez's body have already been placed in a *nganga*. We must not just try to take them back. He says we must now consult his *nganga* to see if we should abandon our efforts, or if seeking her body is the right path to follow."

Plante Firme rose from his chair and started back toward the house. Martínez beckoned the others to follow. As they passed the pigsty, the animal began to snort and squeal. The *palero* stopped and snapped out a string of Spanish epithets, then reached down and removed one of his shower sandals and gave the pig several slaps on its snout.

Out of the corner of his eye, Devlin saw Ollie Pitts take an angry step forward, and he reached out and grabbed his arm. As brutal as Pitts could be to fellow humans, he had an inexplicable affection for dumb animals, to the point of keeping five stray cats in his three-room Manhattan apartment. Devlin's second in command, Sharon Levy, claimed Pitts liked animals because they bit people.

"Leave it," Devlin whispered. "We need the man's help. And remember, this guy makes a living laying curses on people."

Pitts started to say something, then stopped himself, and Devlin wondered if it was the threat of a voodoo curse that silenced him. He momentarily considered asking Plante Firme for some mojo that would keep Pitts under control for the remainder of his cop career.

They followed the *palero* into a small room. A cast-iron pot stood near its center, this one at least three feet in diameter, and rising from it was an aggregation of items so vast that the entire mass stood over six feet high.

"This is said to be the most powerful *nganga* in all Cuba," Martínez whispered as they followed the *palero*'s instructions and sat on four small stools placed before it.

Devlin couldn't quite grasp what he was looking at. An assortment of small bones had been hung around the rim of the pot. They could be animal, or human—there was no way to be certain. Rising from within the pot and its necklace of bones was a collection of objects so eclectic it seemed overwhelming. Spears, swords, and axes mixed together with chains of various lengths and thicknesses, military medals, an old revolver, several religious crosses and medallions. There were numerous lengths of wood, and from deep within, Devlin could see the skull of what appeared to be a goat, horns still attached. Hanging beneath the skull, just barely visible, were the skeletal remains of what could only be human fingers, each joint held together by small wires. Sitting on top of the entire mass was a cloth, black-faced doll, dressed in a brightly patterned shirt and wearing a straw hat. An unlit candle in a long metal holder stood before the *nganga,* its base surrounded by small statues and vases, an ornate, cast-iron bell, and a large wooden bowl filled with water.

Hanging on a wall next to the *nganga* was a portrait depicting in profile a white-haired black man dressed in a white shirt. Martínez leaned in close to Devlin and nodded toward the picture.

"It is a picture of Plante Firme's teacher," he whispered. "Before Plante Firme he was the greatest *palero* ever to have lived, a holder of great magical power. It is said that his bones are the dead one in Plante Firme's *nganga,* and that when he dies, Plante Firme has decreed that his own bones will join those of his teacher to create the most powerful *nganga* that has ever existed."

Using a long taper, Plante Firme ignited the candle, then took up a seven-foot stick, forked at the top into five branches, each at least a foot long. He placed a straw hat, festooned with green feathers, on his bald head, so he now resembled the cloth doll atop the *nganga.* Slowly, he lowered his bulky body onto a wide stool, wooden staff in hand, like some primitive potentate.

Martínez handed Adrianna the bottle of rum he had taken from his car. "This is an offering to Oggun, the god of the *nganga,*" he whispered.

Adrianna seemed momentarily confused, then bent forward and placed the bottle before the candle.

Plante Firme pointed to the cast-iron bell.

"You must ring the bell to awaken Oggun," Martínez whispered.

Adrianna did so, the loud clanging sound almost deafening in the small room.

Plante Firme's voice rumbled, low and sonorous, in a mixture of Spanish and Bantu.

"Vamo a hacer un registro con los obis. Y creo que le oi a Planta Firme también decir parte do esto a continuacíon."

"He is informing us that he wishes to make a *consulta* with the coconuts," Martínez explained. "But first he must pray to the god Eleggua, because nothing can happen unless you first ask Eleggua, who opens and closes all roads."

The *palero* ignited a second, smaller candle, set on a white saucer before a statue of the god Eleggua, and his voice rumbled forth again.

"Omi tutu Eleggua." He dipped a hand into the bowl of water and sprinkled the statue.

"He gives fresh water to Eleggua," Martínez whispered.

"Ana tutu. Tutu Alaroye."

"In his *moyurbaciones,* his prayers, he asks for fresh relations with the dead one, if Eleggua will remove all disagreements."

"Eleggua, ile mo ku e o."

" 'In your care I leave my home.' Señorita Mendez must now say *'A kue e ye,'* which means, 'We greet you.' "

Adrianna repeated the chant.

"Eleggua, mo du e o," Plante Firme said, resuming his chant, and instructing Adrianna to again chant her response.

"They are telling Eleggua that they trust him completely," Martínez whispered.

"Ariku, baba wa." Plante Firme's voice rumbled out the words.

"He says, 'Health, Father, come,' " Martínez whispered. "Now Señorita Mendez must say *'Akuana.'* This is like saying amen to the prayer."

Plante Firme raised one arm, holding it high above his head. *"Yu soro mo bi."* He lowered his arm.

"He says, 'Come in.' Now we will ask the dead one."

Plante Firme's voice bellowed out into the room. *"La fo!"*

Martínez lowered his eyes. "He is casting out the last of all unexpected evil," Martínez whispered. "Now we may begin."

Plante Firme turned to Adrianna, telling her that she could now consult the *nganga,* but only with questions that could be answered with a yes or a no. As Martínez translated, she asked if they would be able to find her aunt.

Plante Firme picked up a leather pouch and withdrew seven coin-shaped pieces of coconut shell, the concave portions painted white, the convex stained with a black dye. Again, he chanted in a low, rumbling voice, then cast four of the shells on the floor. When they rolled to a stop, all four came to rest with the white, concave sides facing up.

"Alafia," Plante Firme said, nodding.

"This means the answer is yes, good news," Martínez said. "But not conclusive. More must be asked."

Adrianna lowered her eyes. Devlin could see her lip tremble.

"Has my aunt's body been placed in a *nganga*?" Her voice was barely audible, as if she did not want to hear the question as well as the answer.

Again, Plante Firme cast the shells. This time all four black convex sides pointed up. The *palero* stared at the shells and drew a deep breath.

"Oyekun," Martínez said. "It means the dead man wants to speak. Now Plante Firme must ask the questions. Only he can speak directly when the dead one asks to talk."

Plante Firme rumbled forth with a heavy mix of Bantu.

Martínez shook his head. "It is too complex. I do not understand the question," he whispered.

Again the shells were thrown. When they stopped rolling, three convex sides faced up.

Now Martínez drew a long breath. "*Ocana,*" he whispered. "The answer from the dead man is no. Something is wrong, or has happened, or was done. It is needed some *ebbo,* some offerings."

Plante Firme opened the bottle of rum that had been given to the god Oggun, drank deeply, then sprayed the rum onto the *nganga*. Then he spoke again to the dead man, a long, rambling question, almost exclusively in Bantu. Only the word *Santiago* was in Spanish. Again he cast the coconuts. This time two of each side faced up.

"*Eyife,*" Martínez said, his voice excited. "This is a conclusive yes. The dead one has told the *palero* what must be done."

The *palero* lowered his eyes, then slowly picked up the shells and returned them to the pouch. When he raised his eyes, his face seemed heavy with concern. Martínez translated as he spoke.

"He says it is as he feared. The *palero* of the Abakua has the body you seek. You must go to Santiago de Cuba and confront him. But before you go there, you must go to the cemetery where María Mendez was to be buried. There, if the words of the dead one are true, you will find that earth has been removed from the four corners of the grave. You must take handfuls of dirt from each of these places, and carry it with you. Only this will protect you from the *palero,* and the dead one he has created. Only in this way will you learn the truth. The *palero* you seek is called Baba Briyumbe."

The *palero* reached out to the *nganga* and withdrew a red feather attached to a gnarled stick and handed it to Adrianna. He spoke again.

"The feather must be placed with the earth and carried at

all times," Martínez translated. "It will create a charm that comes from the dead one, and from a power greater than Baba Briyumbe. Only this will protect against the evil of Baba Briyumbe."

Plante Firme rose, leaned his staff against the wall, and removed his feathered hat.

"You should make an offering," Martínez said.

Devlin was momentarily confused, his mind filled with visions of earth from a grave and bright red feathers.

"Money," Martínez said. "An offering to the *palero* for his work."

Devlin reached into his pocket and withdrew some folded currency. He took a twenty-dollar bill from the top and glanced at Martínez for some indication it was enough. Martínez nodded.

"Place it on the floor, before the *nganga*," the major instructed.

Devlin did so.

"Now you must ring the bell."

Devlin's jaw tightened. He felt like a fool, but did as he was told. Again, the sound of the iron bell filled the room. When Devlin stood, Plante Firme placed a meaty hand on his shoulder, nodded his approval, and spoke again in his mixture of Spanish and Bantu.

"He likes you," Martínez said. "But he says you must put aside your fears and follow Oggun."

"For a picture of Andrew Jackson, he should give him a kiss," Pitts said.

Adrianna threw Pitts a disapproving look. The big detective gave her a shrug and an impish smile.

Out in the courtyard, Pitts held up his hand. "Let me check the street before we go out," he said.

He opened the gate, stepped out, then returned smiling. "There's a big truck parked about three quarters of the way down the block," he said. He turned to Martínez. "Ask the man if there's a way to get into the backyard next door so I can work my way down the street and check it out."

Martínez relayed the question to Plante Firme. The *palero* nodded and answered in rapid Spanish.

"There is a rear gate that leads to an alley and into the next property," Martínez said.

Pitts glanced around and saw a piece of lead pipe lying on the ground near the rear wall. He pointed to it. "Ask the *palero* if I can borrow that."

When told he could, Pitts turned to Devlin. "Give me five minutes, then you and the major step outside, okay? Just keep their attention on you while I see if it's our boys in white."

"How far away is the truck?" Devlin asked.

"About fifty yards," Pitts said. "Close enough for you to get there if it looks like I need help." He glanced at Martínez. "You still got your peashooter?"

"*Sí,* I have my peashooter," Martínez said.

Pitts entered the alley and moved into the next yard. It was pitch-black, the only light seeping through an occasional curtained window. He felt his way, climbed over succeeding fences, until he thought he had gone about sixty yards. When he made his way out to the street, he was no more than ten yards behind the large truck. A glance at the fresh gouge in its right front fender told him what he wanted to know.

Pitts moved up behind the truck, then inched along the passenger side, until he could hear voices inside the cab. He gave the side of the truck a solid whack with the lead pipe, then ducked down under its bed.

The passenger door opened immediately, and as it slammed shut Pitts saw two white-clad legs standing next to him. A grin flicked across his broad, flat face.

"Hola," he whispered as he drove the pipe up between the legs, feeling it crunch against the softness of the man's crotch.

The Abakua hit the ground with both knees and began to gag as Pitts emerged from under the truck and sent a second blow to the back of the man's head.

Keeping low, he circled the front of the truck and crouched again. The second door slammed, and another white-clad figure came around the front fender. This time Pitts used the lead pipe like a police baton, jabbing it forward into the second man's solar plexus. A knife clattered to the street as the man pitched forward, and Pitts grabbed the back of his head and drove his knee up into his face. The second Abakua sprawled on the street like a bag of white linen. Pitts picked up the knife, checked that both men were unconscious, relieved them of their wallets, then circled the truck, puncturing each of the four tires. He watched with satisfaction as the truck settled on its rims, then walked slowly back to the *palero*'s house.

"You wanna cuff those scumbags?" He was grinning at Martínez.

The major shook his head. "Are they alive?"

Pitts gave him a shrug. "Yeah, but they ain't gonna feel too good tomorrow."

Martínez nodded, and Devlin thought he detected a note of approval. "I would like to see them," the major said.

Martínez removed Adrianna's sketches from his pocket and walked to the fallen Abakua. When he returned he handed the sketches back to her. "They are the same men from this afternoon. The likenesses are excellent," he said.

A gleam came to Adrianna's eyes, and Devlin could tell she was pleased she was finally a part of their ragtag investigation. "It might be better if we just leave those clowns where they are," he told Martínez. "There's no point in tipping Cabrera that we're onto him. All those Abakua will be able to say is that they were run over by some elephant with a lead pipe." He turned to Pitts, shaking his head. "Did you get their IDs?"

Pitts handed over the wallets. Devlin opened the first, noted it was empty of any money, and eyed Pitts again.

"Hey," Pitts said. "It's a poor country."

Devlin handed the wallets to Martínez, who immediately withdrew two small books. "Their identity papers," he said. "I will have two of my most trusted men pick them up later tonight." He glanced at Pitts. "If they have recovered from the elephant attack, they will be taken someplace where Cabrera cannot find them. We will hold them as long as our law permits."

6

U.S. Senator Warren Burgess sat behind the dark mahogany desk. It was midnight and the only light came from a solitary banker's lamp, its luminous shade casting a green tint about the small study tucked into one corner of the senator's nine-room apartment in the Watergate.

The man seated across from Burgess seemed suited to the dim lighting. Everything about Michael DeForio was dark—his hair, his eyes, even the five-o'clock shadow that covered his cheeks and chin. Tonight, his clothing was dark as well, black jacket over black slacks and a black polo shirt.

Burgess could feel the sweat in his palms as he smiled at Mickey D, the street name given to DeForio by his bosses. It could stand for Mickey Dark, Burgess thought as he realized yet again just how unnerving it was to have this man in his home.

DeForio was forty years old, the youngest capo in the Gambino crime family. But he was a different breed of gangster. Unlike other mid-level mobsters, he did not head a crew of thieves and legbreakers and shakedown artists. He was a graduate of the Wharton School of Finance, with a master's degree in business administration, and for the past seven years he had worked as the Gambino family's "Washington liaison." It was something that gave the man weight. Especially for a U.S. senator who had been in the mob's pocket for the past fifteen years.

DeForio took a sip of the drink Burgess had given him. Single malt, just like the man who poured it. He studied the senator, took in the very patrician nose, the distinguished wings of white hair along the sides of his head, the slightly uplifted, slightly arrogant chin. The perfect WASP. The perfect candidate for the moneyed set. But the man was a cheap cardboard cutout. Very cheap. Still, with a little luck—for us—he might one day find himself sitting in a large white house on Pennsylvania Avenue.

Mickey D leaned forward, struggling to keep the amusement out of his eyes. It was time for business. Real business.

"Senator, I always enjoy drinking your scotch. But it's time for a little serious talk. We're very close to moving ahead with our Cuban plan. But we're a little disturbed by the rumblings we hear that the administration may lift the embargo after the November elections."

"I thought there were problems in New York," Burgess said. "I thought there was a war going on because of Rossi's little blunder."

DeForio waved his words away. "All settled," he said. "In fact, Rossi's going to Cuba to resolve that problem. I'll be there at the same time to finalize things with Cabrera. But we'll want assurances that the sanctions will remain in place."

Burgess twisted nervously in his chair. "I'll beat the drums. Where Castro's concerned, it doesn't take much to stir up the conservative wing of the party. But there are people in the administration who are especially adamant this time. We may have to call on the Miami Cubans again."

A smile flickered across DeForio's lips. The last time plans had been laid to lift the embargo, the Miami Cubans had come through like champs. They had set up a special flight for one of their planes, then had fed phony information to a known Castro spy that the plane would be dropping plastique to anti-Castro insurgents. Castro's boys had bitten like the chumps they so often were, and had shot the plane down. And the embargo had remained in place.

"I love those Miami Cubans," DeForio said. "They've made so much money, and gained so much political clout, the last thing they want is to see Castro gone. Christ, when the old bastard dies, they'll all be crying in their rum."

Burgess relaxed momentarily. "They have been helpful. And I'm sure they will be again if we need them."

DeForio let out a raucous laugh. "Helpful. Hell, their little Helms-Burton bill was a stroke of genius. Castro was in a box with no place to go. The Soviet Union had collapsed and the Cuban economy—what was left of it—was in the toilet. The people wanted changes and they were fed up with the Comandante's bullshit about remaining true to the revolution. They wanted trade with the U.S., and the money it would put in their pockets. They wanted freedom to travel, just like all the tourists who were flooding in from Europe and Canada and Mexico. They wanted the whole damn ball of wax, and they had Castro's back to the wall. It was either give in, quit, or face a rebellion. Then the Helms-Burton bill passes, and all the Cubans who want change are faced with a very sticky problem. Suddenly all the very real goodies they've gotten over the past forty years are being threatened. All the agricultural land, all the houses they've been given, all of it will be up for grabs if Fidel goes under. And, just that fast, remaining true to the revolution doesn't look so bad after all." DeForio threw back his head and laughed again. "It was the smartest political maneuver in this century, and it did the one thing we all wanted. It kept Fidel in power." He paused, gave Burgess a wide grin, then added: "For now."

Burgess offered his own weak version of a raucous laugh, joining in this small taste of revelry. Above all else he wanted to keep this man happy. Very happy. "And Helms-Burton isn't going anyplace. Not for a long time." He leaned forward, adding weight to his words. "The administration knows better than to step on Jesse Helms's toes. When it comes to communists and U.S. foreign policy, that old cracker is a law unto himself. And it goes even beyond communists." Burgess smiled, genuinely this time. "Hell, who else but Helms could suggest a naval blockade of Iraq—a country that's ninety-nine percent landlocked—and not get himself laughed out of Washington?"

"Who, indeed," DeForio said. He leaned forward, his dark eyes hard on Burgess. "So I can assure my people they won't get sandbagged? That three or four months from now they won't see the embargo flying off into space?"

Burgess twisted again. "You can tell them it's a very safe bet."

Mickey D crossed one leg over the other, adjusted the crease in his trousers, and kept his eyes hard. "Safe bets are nice," he said. "But right now we're in the final stages of a major development plan. We are buying up foreign companies that are licensed to do business with Cuba, and we're finalizing negotiations that will give us control of Cuba's major offshore island. These things will solidify our business position well into the next century." He paused so his next words would have full effect. "We are talking about a two-billion-dollar investment over the next ten years. An investment of"—he tapped his chest—"*our* money. And a collapse of the embargo would hurt us." He stopped and gave Burgess a blatantly false smile. "So we're not looking for a safe bet, Senator. We're looking for a sure thing. And we're expecting you to pull out all the stops."

Burgess swallowed a snappish answer, just as he had swallowed so much in the past fifteen years. "All stops are out," he said. "You can give your people my assurance."

When DeForio had left, Burgess stood at his study window, staring out at the beauty of Washington at night. God, he loved that view, loved this city, the sense of power he felt being an integral part of it. And, above all else, he wanted nothing, nothing to take it from him.

He snorted at the idea. He was baiting himself with the obvious, the first and only true rule of politics: the maintenance of power. He turned away from the window and returned to his desk, trying not to think about all he had done to maintain that power over the past fifteen years. And all because of that little gambling fiasco, all those many years ago. He drew a deep breath. And, since then, everything you've done that has added to it.

He leaned back in his chair and closed his eyes. God, how he hated these people. How he hated everything they stood for, everything they were. And most of all he hated that he was part of it, part of them, and always would be.

He placed his hands over his face and tried to console himself. At least it wasn't treasonous. He didn't care about the Cubans. He believed in his heart they deserved whatever they got. What stuck in his craw was the way he had allowed these Mafia bastards to entrap him. *Him*. All wrapped up in this insufferable web.

"Bastards," he hissed aloud. "Goddamn bastards."

7

You still don't trust him, do you?"

Adrianna was seated across from him at the small terrace table, their light continental breakfast only picked at. Behind her, Devlin watched the people hurrying along the Prado, the steady line of "camel" buses jammed with morning travelers on their way to work. Cuba was beautiful and sensual, just the way the tropics were supposed to be, he thought. And it was constant chaos, the very antithesis of everything he had been taught to expect. It was the sultry Caribbean with a touch of madness.

"No, I don't trust him," he said. "I feel like we're being manipulated into something, and I haven't got the slightest idea what it is."

Adrianna stared down into her coffee. "I don't care about any of that, Paul. I just want to find my aunt. Just find her body and see that she's buried."

"I know that. I want that, too."

She looked up at him, as if questioning the truthfulness of his words, then looked back into her coffee as if the answer might be there.

Devlin reached out and took her hand. "I love you. And I'll do anything to keep you from being hurt. I just have to know what's going on. And right now I don't."

"Maybe you never will. Maybe all this insane voodoo can't be understood. At least not by us."

"Maybe."

Devlin watched an old man moving past the hotel. The man had been there ever since they arrived on the terrace. He just walked back and forth along the sidewalk, an ancient thermos bottle cradled in his arm, as he called out the word *"café"* to prospective buyers—the same, solitary word, over and over in a monotonous, pleading voice. Behind him an old woman followed his trail, two worn, already read copies of *Granma* held out in each hand, calling out the newspaper's name; hoping someone would buy them and read them again. *"Café." "Granma."* Morning songs that might put food on their tables.

Martínez had told him that the highest pension a Cuban could get at retirement—no matter what his rank or position—was two hundred and fifty pesos a month. At the current rate of exchange, that translated into fourteen U.S. dollars.

He looked back at Adrianna. "There are a lot of things about this workers' paradise that I don't understand. And Martínez and your aunt, and everything they believed in, are at the head of my list." He glanced back at the street, at the old man and the old woman. "Until we understand those things, I don't think we'll get close to solving this mess."

A figure caught the corner of his eye and he looked up and found Martínez smiling down at him.

"Perhaps I can help," the major said.

"With what?" Devlin asked.

"The great mystery of Cuba that you were just discussing." He gave Adrianna a small bow, then turned back to Devlin. "People of your country have been trying to solve this mystery for years. But they have failed, because they have never asked the right question."

"What's the right question?"

Martínez gave him his Cuban shrug and sat down. He was still smiling. "The question is: Why do we love it so?"

"Okay. Why?"

Martínez glanced at Adrianna, then back at Devlin. "The people," he said. "All Cubans love each other. And this island is the heart of all of us. All the people. So we love it as if it was one of us. Because it is."

Devlin shook his head. The man was unbelievably exasperating. He even talked with a shrug. "And Castro?" he asked. "Does everybody love Fidel?"

Martínez nodded emphatically, smiling now at the edge in Devlin's voice. "Yes. Everyone loves Fidel. He is a great hero, who loves the people even more than we love each other. And if he had died ten years ago, Cuba would be a better place today."

Devlin was startled by the statement. "I see a prison cell with your name on it, Major."

Martínez laughed. "No, that will not happen. At least not for speaking ill of Fidel. He knows people are angry with him. He simply believes we are children, and he knows what is best for us. If I go to prison, it will be for other things."

"Like helping us?" Adrianna asked.

He looked at her and shrugged again. "*Sí*. Maybe that could be a problem. And, again, maybe it will be a problem for Colonel Cabrera." He turned back to Devlin. "There is an old joke about Cuba. It tells of God creating the world. In the north, He created beautiful mountains and valleys, wonderful lakes of clear, clean water. Then he told Saint Peter that he must put in something bad so it would not be perfect. So he added cold and snow and ice. Very bad, *muy malo, no*? Then he created the southern lands, with lush tropical forests, and wonderful food just growing from the trees. And Saint Peter said, 'God, this is perfect.' So God added dangerous animals and poisonous snakes. Again, very bad."

The smile on Martínez's face widened. "Then God created a magnificent island. A paradise with beautiful beaches and warm weather. Fruits that you could pick from the trees. No dangerous animals. No poisonous snakes. Perfect. And Saint Peter said, 'But, God, you have forgotten something bad. This island is too perfect.' And God said, 'No. It will not be perfect. On this island I will put Cubans.' "

Adrianna smiled for the first time that morning. "So you're telling us that Cubans are difficult."

Martínez nodded in mock gravity. "Very difficult. But also very loving, and very tolerant of each other. You see, we only want two things. We want to remain Cuban, and we want to live decently. Fidel gave us both." He paused. "For a time." His smile turned regretful. "After the revolution, for the first time in our history, we lived without two things that had always been part of Cuban history. Foreign domination and an oligarchy that kept the masses poor and sick and ignorant."

He waved away an objection he knew Devlin would make. "Oh, I know. You will say our socialist experiment was dominated by the Soviets. But to us, it was a matter of manipulating the Soviets into giving us what we needed." He laughed. "And, remember, my friend, at the time no one else, and certainly not the United States, wanted to give us anything at all. So we had little choice. We knew what the Soviets wanted, and we knew we would never give it to them. Instead we played the Soviet game, and they gave us everything we wanted. And today, we have the highest literacy rate in all of Latin America. Today, eighty percent of our people own their homes. Today, there is free medical care for everyone who needs it. And, in the end, I think you will agree that the Soviets"—he paused to give Devlin another Cuban shrug—"well, the Soviets, they got *nada,* nothing at all."

Devlin raised his chin toward the street. "This is not paradise, my friend."

Martínez shook his head. "No, it is not. The world has

changed, and Fidel has been unable to change with it. He is like an old horse who keeps returning to the same pasture because once there was grass there. But there is no more grass in this old pasture of ours. And the people know this, and realize that we must be part of this new and different world. But we must also keep what Fidel has given us, what Cuba has fought so hard to get. We must remain a Cuba for Cubans. And we must never again allow an oligarchy to oppress the one thing that makes Cuba worthy of existence—its people."

"Tell me what's wrong with your country," Devlin said.

"Ah, many things," Martínez answered. "First is repression, of course. We are not free to come and go as we would wish. Next is this dual economy that has been dropped on us like a stone. Today, we have a peso economy and a dollar economy. Two separate worlds." He waved his arm in a large circle. "I can take you to dollar stores, where everything must be purchased in U.S. currency. They are magnificent stores that are the same as stores in your country. Then I can take you to peso stores, where Cubans must buy in our currency. They are the poorest stores of the poor, where little is available."

Martínez raised a lecturing finger. "Now, in the past, Cubans could only hold pesos, never dollars. Dollars were only for tourists. The system was designed to bring money into our country, to prop up our failing economy. It was illegal for a Cuban to even have a dollar in his pocket. But the peso was worth nothing, and this created impossible hardships. It also told us that what we had, what was just for Cubans, was worthless."

Martínez's eyes seemed to fill with sadness, and he drew a long breath before he continued. "So the law was changed, and Cubans were allowed to have dollars. Now, of course, everything of value requires dollars. Everyone *needs* dollars to live decently, and they will do anything they can to get these dollars."

Devlin thought of the beautiful young prostitutes parading past the hotel each night, the flyers he had seen, advertising *paradores*, the private, dollar-only restaurants people ran in their homes, the young and the elderly, together, peddling anything they could on the streets—*café, Granma, a box of cigars, señor. Only thirty dollars.*

"Sounds like a rotten system," he said.

"*Sí.* As I said before in my little joke: Nothing is allowed to be perfect. There must be something *muy malo, no*? And it will remain so until we have a more open economy." Again, he raised his finger. "But before that can happen, there is the great trick we must learn to do. How to open our economy and still keep the good we have given to the people. If we cannot do this trick, perhaps it is better to suffer as we are."

Ollie Pitts walked toward the table. "Are we suffering this morning?" he asked.

Devlin glanced up at him, taking in the satisfied vision of a man well fed. Pitts had spent the last hour in the hotel restaurant, having declined to join them for a continental breakfast on the terrace, and there was little doubt he had eaten everything in sight. It was, after all, on the arm—Devlin's arm. A free meal. Irresistible to a cop. Something akin to bears and honey.

Martínez smiled up at him. "In Cuba, we accept suffering. It is an unfortunate part of our nature."

"Yeah, well, it ain't part of my nature," Pitts said. "Suffering sucks. Anybody makes you suffer, you should break something on their body."

Adrianna rolled her eyes. "Do you have any more words of wisdom, Detective?"

Pitts held his hands out at his sides, as if accepting adulation. "Maybe later," he said.

Adrianna shook her head. "I tingle in anticipation."

Martínez placed both palms on the table. "Well, we must go, in any event." He pushed himself up. "As you requested last night, I have made arrangements for all of us to fly to Santiago de Cuba at noon today. That will give us adequate time to meet with Colonel Cabrera at ten, as he requested. It will also give us time to do as Plante Firme advised."

"The cemetery," Devlin said.

"Sí. So we can gather soil from the would-be grave of our Red Angel."

The Necropolis de Colón befit its name, a city of the dead that occupied more than fifty square blocks in the heart of Havana. It was quite a sight to come upon, Devlin thought, especially in a communist country. It was surrounded by a high, ocher-colored wall, emblazoned with white crosses, and the entrance was a massive sixty-foot arch, topped with statues depicting the Virgin Mary and other Catholic saints.

Devlin took in the statues and white crosses, then turned to Martínez. "For a communist, your Comandante seems remarkably tolerant of religion."

Martínez gave his mustache a conspiratorial stroke. "Let us say he received a message from God."

"How so?" Adrianna asked.

"You have seen the great, seventy-foot statue of Christ that overlooks Havana harbor?"

"Yes. It's magnificent."

"Well, in 1959, one day after Fidel marched triumphantly into Havana, lightning struck the statue of Christ, knocking off its head." He began to laugh. "The leaders of the revolution, of course, were horrified. They were very aware of the people's superstitions, and they feared the country would rise up and beg Batista to return. Within a day, the statue was repaired, and there is now a lightning rod running up its back to prevent any further comment by the Almighty."

"No wonder he let the pope pay a visit," Pitts said.

"How could it be otherwise?" Martínez stroked his mustache again. There was an impish glint in his eyes. "After all, Fidel was educated in Catholic schools."

They entered the cemetery and made their way down a wide, stone walkway. Ahead stood a small, domed church in which religious funerals were conducted. To its right was a fifty-foot monument, topped by an angel, and dedicated to nine firefighters killed during a catastrophic blaze in 1890.

All about them there were elaborate tombs and above-ground burial vaults, many bearing the busts or photographs of the dead. It made Devlin wonder about the difficulties presented to Cuba's horde of grave robbers. When they entered the cemetery, they had passed through heavy iron gates, and guards appeared to be everywhere. He asked Martínez about it.

"Yes, there are many guards," the major said. "And at night the gates are closed and locked, and, as you see, the walls are quite high, and very visible from the street."

"Then how do they grab the stiffs?" Pitts asked.

"By means of an old Cuban tradition," the major answered.

"Bribery," Devlin suggested.

"Let us just say that many of our cemetery guardians are known to shop in our dollar stores."

They turned onto another walkway and passed a tomb shaped like an Egyptian pyramid.

"The tomb of José Mata," Martínez said. "One of Cuba's most renowned architects."

He continued on another fifty yards, when Adrianna reached out and stopped him. She pointed to a vault set behind several others. At its head was a statue of a woman, cradling a child in one arm, while her other supported a large, marble cross. Surrounding the vault were small inscribed tombstones, at least fifty in all, each one garnished with a bouquet of flowers.

"What is that?" she asked.

Martínez gently took her arm and led her to the flower-festooned vault. "This is the grave of Amelia Goyri de Adot, a much-beloved patron of Cuban mothers. Each of the small tombstones that you see is a tribute to a miracle that Amelia is supposed to have performed for a dying child."

Adrianna turned to him, her face openly curious.

"It is a rather grim story," Martínez said. "But it speaks clearly about Cuban beliefs, or perhaps more correctly, what Cubans are *wishing* to believe."

"Tell me the story," Adrianna said.

Martínez studied his shoes for a moment, then began. "Amelia, as you see on her vault, died in childbirth in 1901, and her bereaved husband buried her with the dead infant placed at her feet. Years later, when the husband died, the vault was uncovered to accept his body, and for some reason the casket of Amelia was opened at that time. What was discovered startled those who were present, because the infant was no longer at its mother's feet, but was cradled in the dead arms of Amelia."

Adrianna stared at him for a long moment. "So Amelia was buried alive. My God, how horrible."

Martínez looked at her with his soft eyes. "But that is not how it was seen," he said. "To the people it showed only that even in death, Amelia had comforted her child, and people began to come to this place, and to pray to her for their own dying children." He waved his hand, again taking in the small, inscribed tombstones. "And these miracles for these other children occurred. Or, at least, it is how our Cuban mothers would believe it to be."

Martínez pointed to another nearby walkway. "And ahead, only a short distance from the much-revered Amelia, are the vaults of the Mendez family, where the equally beloved Red Angel was to be buried."

Adrianna moved ahead of them now. It was, Devlin thought, as if she were moving into her ancestral past, discovering it for the first time. He moved up behind her as she stood before a low iron fence that surrounded a platform made of large marble blocks. Five vaults sat atop the platform, with room for several more. She studied the names, the most recent of which was that of her paternal grandmother, who had died several years before her father and grandfather had fled the island.

"Hard?" he asked.

She remained silent for several moments, then nodded. "I feel like such a stranger. It's as though my family has been ripped in half, and this was the half I was never allowed to know." She paused, thinking about what she had said. "It must have been very hard for my grandfather to leave." She leaned her head against Devlin's shoulder. "If you died, I don't think I could ever go so far from where you were buried, know I'd never be able to visit your grave, never be able to come and tell you I still remembered, still loved you."

Devlin tightened his arm around her shoulder. "We'll bring your aunt here," he said. "And we'll come back and visit her."

"I must show you something," Martínez said. He was standing with Pitts on the other side of the gravesite.

Adrianna and Devlin made their way to the back and looked to where Martínez was pointing. At the corner of the gravesite a divot of earth had been removed from the ground.

"It is the same at all the corners," Martínez said. He reached into his pocket and removed a cloth bag. "Now we must do as the Palo Monte have done. We must take earth from the same places and put with it the red feather that Plante Firme has given us."

"And then?" Adrianna asked.

"And then we must keep it with us at all times," Martínez said.

8

The State Security compound, known as the Villa Marista, takes up ten square blocks of a modest residential neighborhood in the city's Sevillano district. Even from the street it appears ominous, the exterior as forbidding as the notorious prison known to be housed within its grounds. A high wall, topped with razor wire, circles the entire area. Watchtowers stand at the corners, each manned by armed guards. There are television cameras mounted every fifty feet capable of following any vehicle or person moving along the perimeter.

The interior is visible through the heavily guarded gate that serves as the compound's sole entrance. Beyond the gate a wide, grass-covered parade ground precedes a row of cinderblock buildings. The buildings are painted a flat, dull green, and uniformed guards armed with automatic weapons protect each. It is not a friendly place, nor is it intended to be. It gives off both an aura of power and one of dread, a place that few enter willingly, and where those who leave do so only when permitted.

Cabrera's office was stark and decidedly military, and when they entered, Devlin and Adrianna were offered equally plain and uncomfortable chairs. Cabrera sat behind a metal desk. He was dressed in uniform, his tunic adorned with numerous ribbons, and aside from the colonel, himself, the only other decorative touch was a large personally inscribed photograph of Fidel in battle fatigues and field cap.

Devlin took in the room, noting its sense of sparse isolation. Martínez had been asked to wait in the outer office. The major had seemed unconcerned, and Devlin had not objected. Both men recognized it as a time-honored police technique. Strip away any hope of assistance, and leave the subjects of interrogation feeling helpless and alone. The only question now was whether Cabrera would play good cop or bad cop.

"I believe another person has joined you in Havana," Cabrera began. "A detective named Oliver Pitts?"

"That's right, he came in last night," Devlin said.

"I assume he is here to help you . . . make your own inquiries?"

Devlin forced a smile. "Would that be a problem?" he asked.

Cabrera returned the smile. "Yes. I am afraid it would be a serious problem. As I told you when you first arrived, a very thorough investigation is being conducted."

"We have no doubt about that, Colonel." Devlin decided to fall back on the cover story he and Martínez had worked out. "Actually, Detective Pitts brought me some papers from work that required my attention. He decided to combine that with a small vacation."

Cabrera nodded. "And where is he now?"

"We dropped him off at Major Martínez's office on the way here. He wanted to see a Cuban police station and the major was kind enough to oblige." Devlin gave Cabrera another smile. "Sort of a busman's holiday, as we say in the States. After that, I believe he plans to do some shopping."

Pitts was actually reading through the reports on María

Mendez's death and disappearance. Placing those documents in foreign hands was a direct violation of Cuban law, and Martínez had assured them that Cabrera would be aware of that illegality before the day ended.

But he would not act on it, Martínez had said. Not officially, at least. The situation was *politically awkward,* and to move openly against a member of the Red Angel's family—no matter how indirectly—might prove dangerous. Even for the head of the secret police.

Devlin decided to push that point now, to put Cabrera on the defensive.

"I was wondering if we could see your reports on the automobile accident, Ms. Mendez's death, and the subsequent theft of her body."

Cabrera rocked back in his chair. "I am afraid that is not permitted." He came forward and folded his hands. "I assure you all steps are being taken. I can tell you that several individuals are being questioned, and I believe it is only a matter of time before we learn the reasons behind this unfortunate act."

Adrianna leaned forward, drawing the colonel's eye. Except for an initial greeting, Cabrera had ignored her, preferring to direct his questions to a fellow male, a fellow cop, and Devlin could see from her body language that the colonel's little game had hit all the wrong buttons.

"Can you tell me why neither my aunt's death nor the theft of her body has been reported in the newspapers?" There was an angry edge in her voice and it seemed to surprise the colonel. He obviously wasn't accustomed to being challenged in his own office.

Cabrera raised his folded hands in front of his face. "You must understand that things are done differently in Cuba," he began. "We are not required to release information about investigations that are being conducted. We consider such a practice unwise, since it would interfere with our efforts, and also give assistance to those who have committed the crime." His eyes hardened. "We also do not allow foreigners to conduct their own investigations. I want you to be very clear about that."

Devlin saw Adrianna's back stiffen. "Colonel, you really surprise me."

Again, Cabrera seemed taken aback. "And why is that, Señorita Mendez?"

Adrianna held his eyes. "My aunt was a respected, perhaps even an honored member of your government."

"That is very true—"

Adrianna didn't allow him to finish. "But so far, not only have you refused to give me any meaningful information about her death or the theft of her body, but now you seem to be telling me—perhaps even *warning* me—not to inquire into how these things happened."

Cabrera held out both hands, as if warding off her words. "Señorita, please allow me to give all assurances—"

Again, Adrianna cut him off. "No, Colonel, let me assure *you* of a few things. First, that I intend to find out what happened to my aunt. Next, that I intend to see that her body is recovered. And, finally, that I intend to give her a decent burial." She continued to stare Cabrera down, but allowed her voice to soften. "One more thing, Colonel. I sincerely doubt that any responsible member of your government will object to these rather small intentions. So if you refuse to help me, be *assured* that I will find someone in your government who will."

Cabrera's face reddened, and Devlin could see him fighting for control. "You will have whatever assistance I can give you," he snapped. "Unfortunately, there is nothing I can do for you at this moment."

Adrianna stood, still holding his eyes. "Then I assume we are free to go."

"Of course," Cabrera said.

As Adrianna headed for the door, Devlin stood and nodded to the colonel. "Nice to see you again, Colonel," he said.

Martínez threw back his head and laughed as Devlin told him about the interview. They had just driven through the gate and were headed back to his office to collect Pitts.

"Señorita Mendez, you must pardon me, but I think you may have—how do you say it?—pissed the colonel off." He began to laugh again.

A hint of concern came to Adrianna's eyes, then disappeared. "Since he already tried to have us killed, that doesn't seem like much of a problem." She glanced out the rear window, expecting to see white-clad Abakua trailing behind them. "Are we still being followed?"

"No," Martínez said. "Not once this morning. I imagine the colonel is wondering what has happened to his Abakua."

"And what *has* happened to them?" Devlin asked.

"They are like Detective Pitts," Martínez said. "They are taking a small holiday."

Robert Cipriani entered Cabrera's office from a small adjoining room. A bug in the colonel's desk had allowed him to listen to the interview with Devlin and Adrianna.

"Tough lady," he said as he took the same chair Devlin had occupied. "And, unless there's been some change in plans, I thought she was supposed to be a dead lady."

"There is no change," Cabrera snapped. "Just an unexpected delay."

"The Abakua screwed up?"

"My Abakua have disappeared. But there are other Abakua. By tonight, Señorita Mendez and her friends will be dead."

Cipriani nodded. "I think that's wise. There's a great deal

of money involved, and as I said, I don't think our friends will appreciate problems this late in the game." He raised his eyebrows. "I've dealt with those gentlemen. They're not known for their tolerance."

Cabrera picked up an envelope from his desk and tossed it to Cipriani. "Since you are so concerned, I have decided to let you supervise the matter yourself. There is an airline ticket inside. It is for Santiago de Cuba, which, according to my informants at Cubana Airlines, is where our friends are now headed." He smiled at the surprise on Cipriani's face. "One of my men will go with you, of course, and some other Abakua friends will meet you in Santiago. You *will* return here, my friend. Whether or not you also return to your cell will depend on how well you do this little job."

"Wait a minute, Colonel. Killing people is not my line."

Cabrera stared at him, a small smile playing across his lips. "I understand your reluctance. You prefer to take people's lives with a pen and a checkbook, not a knife or a gun. But do not fear. You will have only to supervise. Besides, there is another gentleman arriving in Santiago today, and since other matters will keep me in Havana, I would like you to represent me with him. It is a person you know well."

"And who's that?" Cipriani asked.

"An old friend of yours. The old man who has caused these problems. Giovanni Rossi. He is here both on a matter of health and on a matter of business. He will be staying in a villa in the mountains near Cobre."

"And what do you want me to do with Rossi?" Cipriani asked.

Cabrera smiled again. "Allay his fears, my friend. Just as I will allay the fears of his associate, who arrives in Havana this evening."

9

The Sierra Maestra Mountains rose in the distance as their taxi raced along the winding road that led from Antonio Maceo Airport to the port city of Santiago de Cuba. The mountains were as majestic and as beautiful as any Devlin had ever seen. Sharp peaks, covered in lush green foliage, seemed to leap from the arid plain below, punctuated by steeply descending valleys carved dramatically into their sides. It was a forbidding range, Devlin thought, clearly inaccessible except by foot, a place suited more to goats than people, the place where all Cuba's revolutions had begun, the very place from which Fidel and his original eighty-six followers had fought their hit-and-run war with the forces of Fulgencio Batista, until the people of Cuba had risen up to join them.

And María Mendez was there with them. He glanced at Adrianna, and saw that she, too, was staring at the mountains. Undoubtedly thinking similar thoughts about the young woman, the young doctor who would later become Cuba's Red Angel. All those years ago. Fighting somewhere in those mountains against the men who had tortured and raped her, the men who had crushed her chance ever to have children of her own.

Martínez's voice broke Devlin's reverie.

"Santiago is like a different Cuba," he explained as they raced past a series of small cattle farms. "Where Havana is cosmopolitan, with people always rushing about, here it is very Caribbean, a slower, more gentle pace. But you must not be fooled. It is a place of great and deep feelings. If there is to be trouble in Cuba, it will begin here. This is where the first gun will be picked up." He gave them his Cuban shrug, as if to say it could not be helped.

"So why don't they rise up and throw you guys out?" Ollie Pitts asked. He was grinning at Martínez, trying to goad him into another defense of Fidel.

There was an impish glimmer in the major's eyes as he took up the challenge. "Fortunately, the people are devoted to the revolution," he said. He made an all-encompassing gesture with his hand. "Here, in the eastern part of our island, life was always poorer and more difficult. So it is here that the revolution has produced the most change. It is also mostly Negro in population, and Palo Monte and Santeria are very strong here, and the people know that Fidel has always been tolerant of their beliefs. Some even say he practices them himself."

"Does he?" Pitts asked.

Now it was time for Martínez to offer a goading grin. "It is said Fidel has two *paleros* working just for him, and that this is why your CIA's many attempts to kill him have always failed."

Pitts refused to give up. "Oh, yeah? How far away is the Guantánamo Naval Base?"

Martínez laughed. "From here, about one hundred kilometers of winding mountain roads. From the people, it is more than a million miles."

The taxi made its way through a series of narrow streets that skirted the port, coming to a stop at a large, tree-shaded central plaza. One end of the plaza was dominated by the sixteenth-century Catedral Ecclesia, its twin spires rising more than ten stories, its central stone angel gazing down upon the people who filled the park's benches and walkways.

To the right of the cathedral stood the Hotel Casa Grande, one of Santiago's oldest and most elegant hotels, its first-floor terrace looming ten feet above the street like some lingering patrician stronghold, its red-and-gray-striped awnings shading those within from the scorching afternoon sun.

Martínez left them at the hotel, explaining that men were already in place watching the hotel's entrances to ensure that the Abakua would not get inside. He, himself, would stay at a nearby police station, where he could also conduct some preliminary inquiries into the local Abakua and their corrupt *palero,* Baba Briyumbe. He promised to return in one hour, and suggested they use the time to rest and refresh themselves for the long night ahead.

Devlin, Adrianna, and Pitts climbed the wide marble stairs that led to the hotel terrace and its adjoining reception area. Here the elegance of colonial Cuba reasserted itself, with gleaming marble floors, wrought-iron chandeliers, and a mix of wicker settees and chairs surrounding a marble statue of a sea nymph.

Ahead, the terrace ended in an ornate mahogany bar, its scattering of small tables and chairs situated so patrons could look down upon the people who filled the adjacent plaza. A sign to their right advertised a second terrace on the hotel's rooftop, and Devlin wondered if the building's architect had rendered his plans with an eye toward condescending views of the populace, as some colonial sign of preeminence.

Reception proved friendly, efficient, and quick, and they were led to adjoining rooms on the third floor. Adrianna was delighted with what she found. Their room was surprisingly spacious, with twenty-foot ceilings and graceful, old mahogany furniture—two queen-size beds, an armoire, matching upholstered chairs, and an oversized desk. Behind heavy brocade drapes, twelve-foot louvered windows overlooked the cathedral and the plaza, and when she opened them she smiled at the sound of the salsa rhythms that drifted up from the park.

"I feel like I've gone back in time," she said, smiling at Devlin.

He inclined his head toward the bath. "Wait until you go in there. It's all marble with gold fixtures. There's even a bidet. It makes our hotel in Havana seem like a Times Square fleabag."

A knock on their door produced Ollie Pitts, dressed now in a pair of massive red Bermuda shorts and another Hawaiian shirt. Devlin took in his enormous legs and thought of two tree trunks protruding from a billowing red tent.

"Martínez said we should refresh ourselves, so I'm thinking of a beer or two," Pitts said. "Anybody interested?"

Adrianna turned back toward the bed. "I think he meant a shower or a nap," she said. "I'm going to opt for a shower, then go down to the terrace with my sketch pad."

Devlin encircled her with his arms and kissed the back of her head. "Sounds good. Maybe you'll come up with another sketch we can use. I'm going to give my daughter a call and check in with the office. Then I'll go with Ollie. I want to get a look around, myself, just to see if any of Cabrera's boys have the hotel staked out."

She turned to face him. "You think he knows we're here? I thought that's why we didn't check out of our hotel in Havana. To throw him off. Isn't that what Martínez said?"

Devlin winked at her. "Maybe it worked. Maybe not. But Cabrera's the number two man in State Security, and Martínez claims he's also the head of the secret police. If that's true, I suspect the colonel knows just about everything that goes on in this country."

"Then why would Martínez lead us on like that? Why does he want us to think we can get away from him?"

"Good questions. Unfortunately, like everything else on this infuriating island, I don't have answers for those either."

"So what's happening at the office?" Pitts asked as they stepped into the elevator.

"Sounds like the mob settled their little war," Devlin said. "Cavanaugh tailed Rossi to Kennedy Airport. Seems like John the Boss hopped a flight to the Bahamas."

"You think the other families made him an offer he couldn't refuse?" Pitts finished the sentence with an evil cackle.

"Looks that way. Cavanaugh said there was a sit-down at Rossi's house a couple of days ago, and the old Bathrobe left town the next morning. Red wanted to know if he should follow him to the Bahamas."

"So what did you tell him?"

"I told him to forget it."

Pitts laughed again. "Hey, Cavanaugh ain't stupid. It never hurts to ask."

Despite Ollie's protests, the beer he wanted was put on hold. Instead Devlin led him on a quick tour of the surrounding area, then up onto a wide stone piazza that ran along one side of the cathedral some thirty feet above the street. They did not enter the church, but took up positions behind one of two stone lions that guarded the staircase to the street.

"Watch for nasty boys dressed in white," Devlin said. "If they're watching us, they should start to move when we don't come down."

Twenty minutes later two men wearing white shirts and matching skullcaps exited a store across the street and took up a position in the park where they could watch the staircase that led up to the cathedral.

"Bingo," Pitts said. "These Abakua must all be twins. Somebody should tell their mama to dress them a little less conspicuously. Those white costumes play hell on a good surveillance."

Devlin raised his chin toward the park benches that had suddenly emptied with the appearance of the Abakua. "Martínez claims it's a religious thing with this particular sect. It's also supposed to be a type of intimidation. People know if they mess with an Abakua, the whole cult will be out to get them. The white outfits are supposed to be a warning."

Pitts snorted at the idea. "Some fucking warning," he said. "The two outside the witch doctor's shack last night were a pair of pussies. They wouldn't make it across the Port Authority Bus Terminal without getting sliced, diced, and fucking hung out to dry."

Devlin smiled at Pitts's bravado. It was exactly why he had brought him to Cuba. It was what Ollie Pitts was for.

Martínez arrived on the hotel terrace one hour later, as promised. He found Devlin and Pitts sipping orange juice and beer, respectively, their eyes fixed on the people milling about the plaza.

"Your Abakua are back," Devlin said as Martínez seated himself at their table. He handed him a sketch of the men he had seen. Adrianna had also spotted them from the hotel terrace, and had produced a quick drawing before returning to their room.

"This is excellent," Martínez said as he studied the drawing. "My men saw them as well, but could only give a general description." He ran a finger along his mustache. "We also have another visitor to Santiago. Are you familiar with the name Robert Cipriani?"

"The fugitive financier?" Devlin asked. "The one my government has been trying to extradite for the past ten or fifteen years? I thought I read the Cubans had busted him and sentenced him to a long stretch in prison."

"That is exactly so," Martínez said. "At last report he was being held in one of Cabrera's very exclusive cells at State

Security headquarters. It would seem he has either escaped or has been given some special mission."

"Us?" Pitts asked.

"It is possible. But I doubt that is the only reason he is here. Cipriani is not a killer. He is a financial gangster."

"How do you know all this?" Devlin asked.

"Our police here work very closely with the immigration police at the airport. Just to be aware of who is coming into their territory. It would appear that Mr. Cipriani and another gentleman—who I suspect is one of Cabrera's men—arrived on the flight following ours. They were met by two Abakua, who drove them to El Cobre."

"What's El Cobre?" Devlin asked.

"A small mountain village to the west. It is the site of a church that houses the shrine to the Virgin of Caridad."

"Maybe they just wanna say a little prayer?" Pitts said.

Martínez smiled across the table. "Perhaps that is so. It is a very famous shrine. Your novelist, and Cuba's great friend, Ernest Hemingway, presented his Nobel medal to the virgin shortly before his death." He shifted his gaze to Devlin. "But I suspect Señor Cipriani is here for other than prayerful reasons."

"I think we should find out," Devlin said.

"Yes, we should." He reached into a pocket and removed the small pouch containing the earth from the Red Angel's burial site. He laid it on the table. The red feather Plante Firme had given them protruded from the top. "But first I think we must confront Baba Briyumbe. Just to stir the pot a bit." He tapped his fingers on the table. "Perhaps it would be better if we do this without Señorita Mendez. It could prove to be . . . difficult."

"She's resting in our room," Devlin said. "I'll leave her a note that we had some errands to run."

"Good," Martínez said. "My men will continue to watch all entrances to the hotel. No Abakua will be allowed inside."

"What about State Security?" Pitts asked.

"No one from State Security will harm the niece of the Red Angel," Martínez said. "They will have others do that for them."

Baba Briyumbe's house was located on Maximo Gomez Street, only a few blocks from the waterfront. It was a moderate walk from the hotel, along a twisting route of narrow streets, filled with the occasional sounds of barking dogs and crowing roosters. Before one house, two men busied themselves gutting a pig. A score of children had gathered to watch, and they let out squeals of delight and disgust as the entrails spilled to the ground.

"Jesus Christ, ain't you guys ever heard of butcher shops?" Ollie Pitts groaned.

"Ah, but it is cheaper this way," Martínez said. "And what they do not eat, they can sell. Hopefully for dollars."

They waited at a corner for a battered truck to make its way past, its bed filled with people standing and sitting. It was followed by a horse-drawn wagon also filled with people.

"Our bus service from outlying neighborhoods and from the countryside," Martínez said. "One of the many private enterprises the revolution now allows. This second one with the horse also confronts our great gasoline shortages. It is ingenious, eh?"

Pitts shook his head. "If you're fucking Wyatt Earp," he muttered.

They moved halfway down the next block. The street ran at a moderate downward pitch, and from this upper point they could see the harbor some three hundred yards distant. Martínez stopped them and raised his chin toward a dilapidated row of attached houses across the street. The houses were all two stories, but the one they faced had only a blank wall at its lower level, with narrow, steep stone stairs leading to a gallery above. On the side of the street where they stood, the stucco wall of another building bore a painted portrait of Fidel in profile. The words SOCIALISMO O MUERTE were written beneath it.

"The *palero* must get a lot of business," Martínez said.

"Why is that?" Devlin asked.

Martínez turned to face the portrait. "The government only puts its propaganda in places where there is the movement of many people." He smiled at the two Americans. "To maximize its efficiency. Is it not so for politicians in your country?"

"Only when there are elections," Pitts said. "Then the politicians are running scared, because some other hacks are trying to take their jobs away, so we see their faces and their slogans everywhere."

Martínez nodded. "So it is the same. Except here we have only one political party, so the politicians must seek support all the time, because they never know when or from where opposition will come." He made a gun out of his index finger and thumb. "In such a system, change can be quick without great support of the people."

Devlin raised his chin toward the *palero*'s house. "The civics lesson is very interesting, Major. Now what about Baba Briyumbe?"

Martínez looked down the street, then back the way they had come. Devlin followed his gaze and saw two men in each direction—two in civilian clothes, two in uniform.

"Your people?" he asked.

Martínez nodded. "When we enter the *palero*'s house, they will move toward us. If there is trouble they have been told to force their way inside."

"That's very good cooperation from another city's cops."

"We are all the same, a national police, and the senior officer here is a captain, so he is at my orders." He smiled. "Also, he dislikes Baba Briyumbe, who was once suspected of telling a follower to kill his uncle so a *nganga* could be made from his bones."

"Did the follower do it?" Devlin asked.

"Oh yes." Martínez paused, as if deciding whether to say more. "The follower was a member of the police," he finally added. "A young man who was a secret member of the Abakua." He shook his head. "His crime was never officially made known to the people. But of course they knew. The captain arrested the man, and he was sentenced to be shot. In reprisal, Baba Briyumbe put a curse on the captain's family."

"What happened to the captain?" Pitts asked. His voice sounded just a bit nervous.

"To him, nothing," Martínez said. "But his child became very sick, and he was forced to go to another *palero* to have the curse removed."

"Jesus Christ," Pitts said. "I want a fucking piece. This Baba guy gives me any mumbo-jumbo shit, I wanna stick it up his nose."

Martínez reached into his pocket and removed the bag containing the cemetery earth and the feather. He held it out to Pitts. "Take this," he said. "It will give you more power over Baba Briyumbe than any other weapon."

The door to Baba Briyumbe's house was opened by a tall, slender man dressed all in white, another Abakua. There was an old knife wound running along his jawline, and his unbuttoned shirt revealed a crudely executed tattoo. To Devlin it appeared to be a solid red sphere the size of a grapefruit, bisected by five black arrows and a series of small crosses and circles. Behind the man, Devlin could see a tile-floored room, empty except for one thronelike chair facing five others. It reminded him of Plante Firme's courtyard.

Martínez displayed his credentials. He spoke to the man in a soft voice, but his eyes were cold steel. What Devlin caught from his rapid-fire Spanish was a request to see Baba Briyumbe.

The Abakua eyed Martínez, then Pitts and Devlin. He appeared to be in his early thirties, but the sneer that broke out on his face added an easy ten years in street time. He raised his chin toward the major and uttered one word: *"Irse."*

"The fuck is tellin' us to scram," Pitts said.

Martínez stepped through the door, bumping the man back with his shoulder, followed quickly by Devlin and Pitts. The man's hand went to his pocket, but it wasn't fast enough. The speed with which Martínez moved caught Devlin by surprise. The rigid fingers of one hand struck out, catching the man at the base of the throat. He staggered to one side, gagging, and Devlin quickly pinned his hand in his pocket. Not to be left out, Pitts took a step forward and drove his hamlike fist squarely into the man's face. The Abakua bounced off the tile floor like someone hit by a fast-moving train.

Devlin pulled the hand from the man's pocket and removed a six-inch gravity knife. He flicked it open and showed Martínez the razor-sharp edge.

"He thought you needed a shave," Pitts said.

Martínez stared down at the man, his eyes still steel. The Abakua stirred and Martínez drove the point of his shoe into his temple. Then he bent down, turned the now unconscious man over, and cuffed him.

"Now, that's definitely police brutality," Pitts said. "You could definitely lose your pension."

Martínez glanced up at him and Pitts shrugged. "Hell, it's only fourteen bucks a month. I think you should kick the skinny asshole again."

Martínez removed a nine-millimeter Beretta from his waistband and smiled when he saw both Devlin and Pitts stiffen. He inclined his head toward a door on the opposite side of the nearly empty room.

"I will shoot him later," he said. "Now we must find Baba Briyumbe and search his house. The captain tells me that his ceremonial room is down on the first level."

He led Devlin and Pitts to the door, his automatic held along his right leg. They entered a dark narrow stairwell and descended quietly. Ahead, they could hear the rapid jabber of two female voices. They slipped through another doorway, and into another tile-floored room. A *nganga,* almost as large as Plante Firme's, stood in one corner, surrounded by numerous vases and statues, one a hideous depiction of a man whose face and body were covered with sores. An older black man sat in a folding beach chair, his eyes glued to a portable black-and-white television set tuned to a Spanish soap opera.

Martínez snapped out a command, and Baba Briyumbe jumped from the chair.

"*Days of Our* fucking *Lives,*" Pitts said. "The fucking witch doctor watches *Days of Our* fucking *Lives.*" He let out a snorting cackle.

Baba Briyumbe glared at them with pitch-black eyes. He was well into his sixties, his head shaved to a shiny, gleaming brown. His face was grizzled and lined by years in the sun. He was of medium height with a large belly that pushed out against a white Miami Dolphins T-shirt, which he wore over baggy white cotton slacks and bare feet.

Martínez snapped out another command, which seemed to have no effect on the Abakua *palero.* He grabbed the man's arm and spun him around, then quickly patted him down.

Pitts had walked over to the statue that stood beside Baba Briyumbe's *nganga.* He pointed to the hideous figure covered in festering sores. "This is the ugliest fucker I've seen in a long time. It looks like it's got a terminal case of crud."

Martínez had pushed Baba Briyumbe back into his beach chair and shut off the television. "It is BabaluAye, the god of sickness and death. One of the most powerful and feared of the *orishas.*"

"Yeah, well, he don't look too fucking scary to me."

"That is because you are a son of Chango, who plays tricks on all the other gods."

"Yeah, that's me," Pitts said. "I'm a regular fucking jokester."

"Over here," Devlin said. He was standing over a small *nganga* that had been covered by a white drop cloth. "Looks like one of those baby *ngangas* the other *palero* was growing in his courtyard."

The others crowded around. Baba Briyumbe began to shout at them in rapid Spanish.

Martínez leveled his pistol at the *palero*'s head. *"Silencio,"* he snapped.

The *palero* stared at the bore opening of the pistol and snapped his jaw shut.

Devlin pointed down into the cast-iron pot, which was two feet in diameter and, like Plante Firme's, had a ring of small bones tied around its lip. The interior was filled with sticks, herbs, and old bandages, mixed in with clusters of bird feathers. Beneath the mass, they could see a glimmer of white bone.

"If we find bone and body parts, you're capable of running DNA tests, right?" Devlin asked.

Martínez nodded uncomfortably, and Devlin glanced at Pitts.

"My pleasure," Pitts said. He lifted one foot and kicked the pot over, sending the contents scattering across the tile floor.

Baba Briyumbe jumped from his chair and began shouting in a mix of Spanish and Bantu. Again, Martínez leveled the pistol at his head, but this time it had no effect.

"What's he saying?" Devlin asked.

"He is placing a curse on Detective Pitts," he answered.

Devlin looked over at Ollie, who was smirking. "In three days your dick will fall off," he said.

Pitts narrowed his eyes, and Devlin could see that catching the witch doctor tuned in to a soap opera had dispelled any voodoo threat.

"Yeah, well, you tell old mumbo jumbo that if it does, I come back here and shove it down his fucking throat."

Baba Briyumbe took three steps toward them, waving his arms and chanting. Pitts reached into his pocket and withdrew the pouch Martínez had given him outside. He held it up so the *palero* could see the red feather protruding from its top.

"Plante Firme," he growled. "Ooga booga." He pulled the pouch open, dipped two fingers inside, and withdrew a small portion of earth, which he then smeared across his forehead. He took two steps toward the *palero* and let out a lionlike roar.

Baba Briyumbe shrank back, eyes wide.

"Hey, I like this fucking mojo." Pitts's lips were spread in a wide grin. "Next time I go to the South Bronx, I'm gonna take this mother with me."

Devlin jabbed a finger at the *palero*. "Sit," he snapped.

Martínez repeated the order in Spanish. The *palero*, now ashen-faced, obeyed.

They knelt before the contents of the small *nganga*. A human skull lay in a mix of smaller bones. Devlin removed a pen from his pocket, fitted it into an eye socket, and lifted it so they could see it more clearly.

"It is an old skull," Martínez said. "It is not the Red Angel."

Devlin nodded. He turned the skull so he could see inside the cranial cavity. "You're right. This one's been in the ground for a while. If it was fresh, there'd still be bits of dried flesh attached somewhere. Even acid wouldn't get it all."

Martínez pointed to the other bones. "Feet and hands," he said. "Large ones. More likely from a man." Another small skull lay off to one side. It appeared canine. Then the bones of a bird, mixed among the black feathers. "We will search the house," Martínez said. "Then we will take Baba Briyumbe somewhere where we can question him in privacy."

Pitts raised his eyebrows and gave them a fast flutter. "I like your style. You get any openings on the Havana PD, you give old Ollie a call."

"You'll have to become a communist," Devlin said.

"Hey, communist, right-wing Republican, what's the difference? So long as I get to use my rubber hose."

Baba Briyumbe sat in a straight-backed, wooden chair, his hands cuffed behind his back. They were in a front second-floor room on Calle Aguilera, diagonally across the street from Santiago de Cuba's provincial palace. It was the "private place" Martínez had chosen to question the Abakua witch doctor.

Devlin stood at the window, watching people mount the high marble stairs to enter one of three arched portals guarded by provincial police. A large Cuban flag hung from an upper balcony. Beside it, a banner proclaimed EL PODER DEL PUEBLO. ESE SI ES PODER. Devlin gave it a rough translation: "The Power of the People. That Is Real Power."

He glanced back at Martínez. He was standing in front of the *palero*, peppering him with questions. Devlin drew a long breath. Something in this whole scenario just didn't jibe with what he'd been told. In the States, if a cop found a "private place" to interrogate a subject, he'd be on a one-way ride to the unemployment line, perhaps worse. Still, this wasn't the States, and Martínez didn't seem at all concerned. Yet Martínez had told him that Cubans weren't lacking in civil rights. Police powers were certainly greater, but strict rules existed. Suspects in a crime, for example, could be held only for seventy-two hours before evidence had to be presented to a grand jury, which would then either indict or release them. Civil libertarians would howl, but it was a far cry from a police state.

He motioned to Pitts and led him into a hall outside the room. "What's your take on this?" he asked.

"On the witch doctor?"

"No. On Martínez."

Pitts pursed his lips. "At first I didn't trust the little fuck."

"Why?"

"He was too fucking nice. You can't trust a nice cop."

Devlin shook the argument off. "What else?"

"Well, now he's suddenly Mr. Hard-ass, which I like. But it's like he's onto something he hasn't told us about. I get the feeling we're only seeing half of his game here."

"Your Spanish is better than mine. What are you getting out of this interrogation?"

"Hey, my Spanish is only good enough to get me arrested," Pitts said. He grinned at Devlin. "But he seems to be asking a lot of questions about Cabrera, about people maybe this witch doctor is supposed to meet. I'm not getting a sense that finding this Red Angel's body is a big thing for him. Not unless he can link it to Cabrera."

Devlin shook his head. "The last thing we need is to get dragged into some political game."

Pitts laughed at the comment. "Hey, back in the Apple our whole life is a political game. Ever since the mayor decided he wanted his own special squad, we've been drowning in fucking politics."

"Forget New York. Talk to me about here. What did you find out about Martínez while you were going through files at his office?"

"He's something called a *jefe de sector,* which means he's responsible for one section of Havana, sort of like a precinct commander, fairly mid-level in the command structure. I got pretty friendly with his second in command, a captain named Julio Pedroso. This Pedroso's main job seems to be working as a liaison with something they call the Committee for the Defense of the Revolution, or CDR, which is some kind of neighborhood watch that was set up after Fidel and his boys took over. To sort of keep an eye out for counterrevolutionaries. These CDR cats exist on just about every block. According to Pedroso, people on the block actually elect them every two years or so."

"Political spies for the police?"

Pitts shook his head. "Not according to Pedroso. He claims they're not used so much politically anymore. Now they pretty much keep an eye out for any criminal activity—burglary, street crime, even renting out rooms and not paying taxes on the profits. All kinds of shit like that. Pedroso says they report in every day, and it lets the cops know what's going on in every neighborhood, every day of the week. It also lets them know who's in that neighborhood when maybe he's not supposed to be." Pitts paused a moment. "What bothers you about the little dude?" he asked.

Devlin stared at his shoes. "I can't quite pin it down." He looked up at Pitts. "But you're right. He's too nice. He's like some Spanish Columbo, and there's no question he knows a helluva lot more than he's letting on. He also seems to throw a lot of weight here in Santiago, especially for a precinct commander from a city that's nine hundred kilometers away."

"He says it's because they're all part of the national police."

Devlin nodded. "Yeah, I got that part." He gave Pitts a long stare. "You ever know a cop who didn't guard his own turf? Who let some cop from another area just waltz in and take over."

"Not unless word came down from pretty high up," Pitts said. He grinned again. "I told you we shouldn't trust the little fuck."

Devlin nodded. "Maybe, maybe not. But it does make me wonder who Martínez has for a rabbi. Especially when he seems to be going up against a top dog in State Security, maybe even the secret police."

Baba Briyumbe glared at them when they returned to the room. But he was sweating now, and it wasn't from the heat.

"You get anything from our boy here?" Devlin asked.

Martínez reached out and lifted the *palero's* chin, forcing him to look him in the eye. Devlin noted that the glare Baba Briyumbe had given them disappeared quickly when he was forced to face Martínez.

"Baba Briyumbe is an unpleasant man, much impressed with his power," Martínez said. "But he has seen the wisdom in speaking to me." He gave them his innocent Cuban shrug. "It seems he was brought a body that was badly burned, and he performed a ritual, preparing it for a *nganga* dedicated to BabaluAye. It is to heal someone of great importance, he said. The ritual is a changing of heads, or changing of lives, which is a way of taking an illness from one person and giving it to another. There are many ways to do this ritual. *Paleros* have been known to go to hospitals and, through certain incantations, to take the sickness of a person in one room and give it to the person in another. It is a practice much feared in our hospitals. But when this is not possible, there is a second way." Another shrug. "This involves the use of a dead one, who was once a great healer."

"Yeah, that's great mumbo jumbo," Devlin said. "But where's the body now?"

Martínez smiled. "It is not mumbo jumbo, my friend. I have seen this evil work with my own eyes. But, as to the body. He says it is in the hands of his disciple, a young *palero* named Siete Rayos, which means Seven Thunderbolts." He smiled at the name. "He says the Abakua have taken both the *palero* and the body to Cobre."

Devlin hesitated, as if he didn't want to know the answer to the question he was going to ask. "Is the body . . . whole?"

"Baba Briyumbe would not say, but I suspect it is now part of a *nganga*. He would not leave such a task to a disciple."

"And it's in Cobre, the same place our friend Cipriani went."

"*Exacto.*"

"So we go to Cobre."

"Tonight," Martínez said. "After I make some preparations."

"What preparations?" Devlin asked.

Martínez simply held up one hand in a wait-and-see gesture.

10

Michael DeForio sipped his rum and smiled across the room at Antonio Cabrera. The rum, like the two prostitutes now jabbering quietly in an adjoining bedroom, had been a welcoming gift when the colonel arrived at DeForio's suite in the Capri Hotel.

"Excellent rum," DeForio said.

Cabrera nodded, accepting the praise. "It is the finest in all Cuba. Perhaps the finest in the world."

DeForio inclined his head toward the bedroom. "If the *putas* are equally superior, I will be a very happy man." He paused. "Providing our business also goes well."

Cabrera glanced toward the bedroom. He had little concern the two young women would eavesdrop on his conversation. Neither spoke English, which was the language he and DeForio would use. They were country women from Santa Clara, young and hungry and ambitious, women like so many others who had poured into Havana to become whores, to earn all-powerful dollars by offering tourists the same gifts their boyfriends had enjoyed for free. To Cabrera, the women were nothing but an amusing fact of life, one that also made them inconsequential. Still, he preferred to be safe.

Cabrera rose from his chair and closed the bedroom door, taking in the women's frightened eyes as he shut them away. They were greedy young women, eager to fill their pockets. They also were terrified to find themselves in the hands of State Security. He smiled at the thought. DeForio would indeed enjoy his stay in Havana.

Cabrera returned to his chair. "Now to business."

"Yes," DeForio said. "Let's begin with the Isle of Youth, and how we can best use Public Law Seventy-seven. Later we'll order up some dinner. Perhaps some champagne if our discussion proves successful."

Giovanni "John the Boss" Rossi sat in a cushioned planter's chair. There was a bottle of oxygen by his side with tubing that ran to a clear plastic mask held in his right hand. He stared across the room at Robert Cipriani and the two sullen Abakua who hovered behind him. Cabrera's man, a major named Cepedes, sat off to one side cleaning his fingernails.

"So they sent you to assure me that Mickey D and Cabrera know what they're talking about, eh?"

Cipriani raised his hands, then let them fall back. He was standing before a wall of glass that offered a view of the Shrine of the Virgin of Caridad, nestled against a rising peak of the Sierra Maestras.

"You ever notice the way the shrine seems to float on the side of the mountain?" Rossi asked. "You should see it when the sun sets. It's magic."

Cipriani turned and glanced out the window, more as a courtesy than from any real interest. It was six in the evening, and the sun was still hours away from setting.

"You're getting romantic in your old age, Don Giovanni." Cipriani turned back and smiled.

"I was always romantic," John the Boss said. "When I was a young button, back in the fifties, I worked here for

Meyer Lansky, and I fell in love with this island. As fucked up as it was then, it was a paradise. Hell, as fucked up as it is today under that nigger lover Castro, it's still a paradise."

Cipriani glanced nervously over his shoulder at the two Abakua.

"Don't worry about them. They do what they're told." Mattie "the Knife" Ippolito came up behind him and placed a hand on Rossi's shoulder. "Besides, I've got Mattie. Those two eggplants would wake up dead if they got within ten feet of me."

"Did you ever meet Castro back in the fifties?" Cipriani asked. He wanted to change the subject before he found himself in the middle of a bloodbath.

"I met him. Meyer left a handful of us here to see if we could bargain with that bearded prick. You know Meyer actually gave him money and weapons when his army was still up in the mountains. Meyer was just playing both sides, laying off a little of his bet, just in case Batista couldn't pull it together." He snorted at the name of the former dictator. "Shit, the only thing Batista could pull was his prick." He sat forward, his hand tightening on the oxygen mask. "But you think Fidel was grateful? The bastard personally put us on a boat, and told us we'd be shot if we ever came back." He sat back and glared at Cipriani. "Well, we're back. And the only thing I don't like about it is that we're gonna keep that sonovabitch in power."

Cipriani walked across the room and took a chair opposite Rossi. "It works better that way. For you. Not just for Castro." He spread his arms. "Look, Castro's fucked. The socialist camp that fed his economy no longer exists. He's back in the real world, and thanks to his enemies in the U.S., he's finding it a very unfriendly place."

Rossi waved his left hand, and used his right to take a deep breath of oxygen. "I know all that."

Cipriani leaned forward. "Okay. You also know he changed the laws on foreign investment back in 1992. He knew, even then, that foreign capital was the only thing that was going to save his revolution. I was consulted on that. I know how the thinking went."

Rossi chuckled. "Yeah, and it didn't work. And when they found out about the little side deals you were making, they threw you in a stinking cell and let you rot."

Cipriani raised his hands in another expansive gesture, then let them fall back. "That was only part of it. A very small part. If everything else had worked, the side deals wouldn't have mattered." He leaned forward, giving weight to his words. "I told them they had to deal with the U.S. Hell, I even had my bags packed and was ready to move to Brazil, just in case they decided to let the U.S. extradite me as part of any deal. But the deal never happened. Clinton was all set to lift the embargo—shit, American business was clamoring to get in here so they could milk the Cuban cow. But then the Miami Cubans"—he paused and smiled—"and your people . . . Well, you both just pulled the rug out, didn't you?"

"That was DeForio's idea. He sold it to everybody." Rossi hesitated a beat. "Everybody except me. Me, I wanted Castro out."

"Yes, I know. But with all respect, you were wrong on that one." Cipriani sat back and crossed one leg over the other. "Look. Castro did what he had to do. He changed the foreign investment laws. Joint ventures with the Cuban government are now permitted. Foreign corporations and economic associations are even allowed to own the facilities they build, providing those facilities benefit the country's development. And that means hotels, refineries, manufacturing plants, whatever. The Cuban government keeps its hands on the throttle, but we both know it's only a matter of time—and a little money spread in the right places—before that hand loses its grip."

"So who needs Castro?"

"Nobody," Cipriani said. "Except you." He leaned forward again. "Look. The changes in the law worked, to a point. Investment capital rolled in from Canada and Mexico and Europe. Even the Helms-Burton law didn't stop it. The Canadians and Mexicans and Europeans laughed at it. There was money to be made."

Cipriani leaned back and recrossed his legs. "But it still wasn't enough capital. Nowhere near what Castro needs. First, the markets aren't there, especially for sugar. Second, the Canadians and the Mexicans just aren't big enough players. They don't have the kind of ready capital that's needed to really put this country on its feet. And finally, the guys who do, the Europeans, aren't willing to risk that much on a country that's still run by communists. They've lived with communists at their back door for half a century, and they know they can't trust them. They've also seen what happens when a communist country goes under. Christ, the West Germans—the biggest players in the new European community—saw what happened to their economy when they reunified with East Germany.

"No, what Castro needs is the U.S. That's Cuba's natural market. And it's also where the big corporate investors are—the moneymen who are willing to gamble on Cuba's future." Cipriani seemed to drift for a moment, as if recalling his own days as a financial player. He brought himself back with a shake of his head. "There's no question that U.S. business wants the action. They know Castro will be dead in ten years, and they know the young guys standing behind him are champing at the bit to bring capitalism here big time. But as willing as they are, they also want to do it in a way that lets the people hang on to what they have—the homes they live in, the educational system, the health care. And that's okay. Big business understands why they want it. It's not because these young turks are good little communists. It's because they *know* if the people lose those things, it's only a matter of time before they'll have another band of rebels sitting up in these mountains." He gestured toward the

Sierra Maestras behind him. "Except this time the rebels will be shooting at them."

Cipriani stood and walked to the window and his Abakua guards. He turned back and smiled. "And that's the problem. The one your people have to overcome. Big business sees that the people behind Castro were willing to play ball, and they want to sell that idea to Washington. Hell, they wanted the embargo lifted two years ago, because there was a shitload of money to be made. Now, for you guys, this is a serious problem. If the embargo ends and big U.S. capital starts flowing in, any chance you guys have of making a major move will be greatly diminished. Those companies are just too big to muscle. And if it comes down to up-and-up competition, you'll never get everything you need to make your plan work. But if the embargo stays in force, and Cuba stays on the ropes, you're the only big game in town. And the Cubans are in no position to say no." He smiled. "Not as long as you use enough dummy corporations to hide who's really behind it."

"So why is Cabrera willing to play along? He knows who he's dealing with."

Cipriani glanced at the chair Major Cepedes had occupied.

"He went to the bathroom," Mattie the Knife said.

Cipriani lowered his voice. "Cabrera is one of the young turks waiting in the wings. He wants all the same things the other young turks want. But he also wants something else."

Rossi chuckled. "He wants to be the don, the king, when Castro bites the big one."

"Good bet," Cipriani said. "That's also why he was willing to do this little Palo Monte favor you asked for. You've been the opposition. Until now. So he wants to keep you happy." He paused, deciding if he should continue.

"Tell me, with all respect, did you ask for this favor because you knew it might kill the whole deal, or do you really believe in this Cuban voodoo?"

Rossi stared at him, a small smile forming at the corners

of his mouth. "What I believe in is none of your fucking business."

Cipriani raised his hands as if preparing to ward off a blow. "I'm just trying to cover my own back this time. I do *not* want to go back to one of Cabrera's cells in the Villa Marista, or worse, to one of this country's stinking prisons. And that's just where I'll go if I tell Cabrera you're on board, and then find out you never were." He shook his head. "I want out this time, Don Giovanni. That's all I want. My money is already in Brazil, and I want to visit it as soon as possible."

Rossi sucked in another lungful of oxygen. "Let's just say I have some personal reasons for wanting this little favor. And they have nothing to do with DeForio's plan." He waved a dismissive hand. "I'm the same age as Castro. This plan of DeForio's, it's a long-range thing. Oh, we'll make money in the short term. But the big money will come when we control this fucking country again. And that won't happen until Castro is dead and buried." He took another drag of oxygen. "And where do you think I'll be then, Mr. Moneyman? I'll tell you where. If I'm lucky, I'll be eating my fucking dinner through a straw." He gave another dismissive wave. "DeForio's plan means nothing to me. If it helps my friends, that's all to the good. If not, any money I lose won't mean a thing to me. So you tell your tin-pot colonel that John the Boss doesn't give a shit. He has my blessing. And my thanks for this little favor."

Cipriani nodded. "When would you like this, ah, ritual performed?"

"Tomorrow. In Havana. You tell them to take everything to Havana. I haven't seen that city in forty years, and I wanna go there again."

"The Abakua will have to go by car," Cipriani said. "They have to take their thing with them."

"In two days, then," Rossi said. "But no longer than that. You tell them what I said. Two days. No more."

Cipriani hesitated, not sure how he wanted to continue.

"There's also the question about the niece and the New York cop," he finally said.

Rossi glared at him. "What about it?"

A pained look crossed Cipriani's face. "Cabrera said they'd be dealt with here. He told me I should supervise."

Rossi continued to stare at him, then he started to laugh. "Cabrera thinks I need help?"

"I . . . I . . ."

Rossi waved the man's stuttering words away. "Get the fuck out of here," he snapped. "If I wanna kill the man with an adding machine, I'll call you."

When Cipriani and the others had gone, Mattie the Knife helped Rossi up from his chair.

"Time for a rest, boss?"

"Is the private jet ready to take us to Havana?"

"We're scheduled to leave at nine."

"Is Devlin on his way?"

"I made a call a few minutes ago." He glanced at his watch. "They should be leaving the hotel anytime now."

Rossi gripped Mattie's arm, his fingers digging in like a claw. "I want him dead. I want him dead before I leave. And, when we get back to New York, I want his kid dead, too."

Mattie patted his hand. The consequences of the man's plans chilled him. "Maybe you should think about this. This could be a bad thing. I know Cabrera has given the okay, but it could still hurt the deal DeForio's got goin', and that could upset some people back home." He let his hand rest on Rossi's, hoping it would be soothing. "A New York police inspector getting whacked in Cuba. It ain't good. The Cuban cops are gonna have to take a serious look at that. And if they look hard, they're gonna find Cabrera. And if they find him, they find DeForio."

Rossi glared at him. "Fuck Cabrera *and* DeForio. And fuck their deal. Devlin's a dead man. And before I leave this place, I wanna spit in his dead eyes."

11

They drove through the outskirts of the city, following the shoreline of Santiago's sprawling harbor. They passed a cigar factory, a rum distillery, and a brewery, all positioned to send their cargoes out to sea—mostly to customers that no longer existed. Poor houses, no more than two- or three-room shacks, were jammed into narrow adjoining streets, all surprisingly clean despite the obvious poverty. Young boys, barefoot and shirtless, played in vacant lots and along sidewalks, as young girls stood watching them. Other children sat with women in front yards, some weaving baskets, or mending clothing, or washing dinner dishes in large tubs. On nearly every street, fathers and husbands gathered in small groups, trying to breathe life into beaten old cars and trucks.

Adrianna, seated next to Devlin in the rear seat, let out a long sigh. "Everything is so damned poor here," she said.

The words didn't seem to be directed at anyone, and Devlin wondered if she was just speaking to herself, just wondering aloud about this strange, impoverished country that was part of her heritage.

She turned and spoke again, this time to the back of Martínez's head. "It's because of the embargo, isn't it?" she asked. "That's what's keeping everyone so poor."

Martínez let out a sigh that matched her own. "It is a large part of it. But it is also too simple an answer." He glanced back and gave her a regretful half smile. "An end to the embargo would make life easier. More tolerable. But Cuba must make changes, too. We survive the embargo. If anything, it gives us strength. It also gives us an excuse, an enemy at which we can point. If the embargo did not exist, changes would still have to be made. Now the government can simply make slogans about preserving the revolution."

"And that's still important to the people?" Adrianna asked. "Preserving the revolution?"

"Yes. Especially for the older ones, who knew the life Batista gave them. For the younger ones, not so much. They only remember the things they had before the East crumbled, and that these things they still want are no longer available to them." He made a gesture with one hand like the flapping wing of a bird. "Many would fly to Miami tomorrow, if they could. They see the Miami Cubans who visit, and they see American movies and television, and that is their new paradise." He glanced back and gave her another half smile. "There is a popular Cuban joke. A young child is asked what he wants to be when he grows up. The child says, 'I want to be a tourist.' " He paused and glanced out the window, as if the joke was painful to him. "But these children who want to be tourists, I am afraid some of them are twenty and thirty years old."

"So why doesn't your government make the changes?" Devlin asked.

Martínez let out a small, bitter laugh. "Fidel will not allow it." He glanced at Devlin, then Adrianna, his eyes harder now. "Fidel is like a monk. He sits in his cell and he worships his god, his revolution. And every small change he is forced to make causes him pain, and he fights it as long as he can."

"Sounds like Cuba needs a new revolution," Pitts said. He made a pistol with his hand. "Knock, knock, Fidel. Time to smell the coffee."

"Ah, yes, that is one solution." Martínez gave him a sad smile. "But what would we get, my friend? A puppet for U.S. business? The Miami Cubans and their old oligarchy?" He shook his head. "At least Fidel is for the people. He is wrong in many ways. But he wants only good for Cuba." Again he turned his hand into the wing of a bird. "Unfortunately, that good has also flown away."

They left the city and turned onto a narrow, winding road that rose into the Sierra Maestra Mountains. Here, in the lowlands, the earth was red clay, spotted with scrub pines and stunted brush. They passed soldiers walking along the road, then the small military base to which they were headed. A training ground on one side of the road was little more than a few rusted trucks and crumbling concrete fortifications, each pocked with bullet holes served up in training exercises.

"That's a military base?" Pitts asked.

Martínez nodded. "It is the major one for this region."

"Jesus Christ, I've seen better training facilities at small-town PDs. How come all the troops are walking?"

Martínez seemed mildly annoyed. Pitts was digging at his national pride. "There are no parts for their trucks, and those that run have little petrol."

Pitts glanced back at Devlin. "And this is the big threat to national security that those assholes in Congress are always ranting and raving about?" he asked. "Shit, the NYPD could take this island."

Martínez glared at him. "If you could find us in the mountains," he snapped.

"Ollie?"

Pitts turned to Devlin. "Yeah?"

"Shut up, Ollie. Not another goddamn word."

The road continued to climb, the vegetation becoming thicker and more lush. Goats and the odd cow wandered the roadside. Their car was forced to stop when a large pig blocked their way. It eyed them curiously, sniffed the air as if they might be food, then ambled into the brush. They passed horse-drawn carts and open trucks—the *autobuses particulares* that plied Santiago's streets—now carrying people home from their jobs in the city. Small cattle ranches appeared and disappeared, dotted with scrawny cows and men on horseback.

As they approached the village of Cobre, people appeared on the roadside selling floral wreaths and homemade candles. Several ventured into the road, waving their products as they drove past.

"For the shrine," Martínez explained. "As an offering to the Virgin of Caridad."

"Who is this virgin?" Pitts asked.

"Actually, it was a statue," Martínez said. "Many, many years ago, some sailors were out to sea in a small boat. There was a great storm, and it was certain they would be drowned. Then a wooden statue came floating to them—a statue of the Virgin. They took it into the boat, and the sea became calm. The people said it was a miracle, and the shrine was built to the Virgin. Now people come and ask for her intercession in many matters."

"It was a fucking piece of wood?" Pitts asked.

Martínez gave him a sly smile. "A wooden statue. It is religion, my friend. Just as Lenin said, the opiate of the people, no?"

The car turned into a side road, marked by a barely identifiable sign. A church appeared in the distance. It seemed to float on a canopy of green foliage, a peak of the Sierra Maestras providing a dramatic backdrop. There was a central spire, flanked by two smaller ones. Here more people lined the roads, offering their wreaths and candles for sale.

Devlin leaned forward to better see the church. High above the central spire two vultures soared in ever-widening circles. He glanced at his watch. It was almost eight. "Is the shrine still open?" he asked.

"It is open until dark," Martínez said. "So people may come after work. We are meeting someone there. There will, perhaps, be time for you to look inside."

"Who are we meeting?" Adrianna asked.

"A member of the local CDR."

"One of the spies you guys have on every block?" Pitts asked.

Martínez ground his teeth. "They are not spies. They are chosen by the people to help the police in their duty."

"Yeah," Pitts said. "We got 'em, too. We call 'em snitches."

"Ollie."

Pitts raised his hands. He gave Devlin an innocent look. "Okay. Okay. Not another word."

The shrine was on a high bluff above the village. Its entrance, Martínez explained, was in the church apse, facing the mountain that rose behind it. There was a steep circular drive that led to the rear of the church, ending in a large dirt parking area. Martínez pulled the car between two others, each holding six men. He excused himself, then went to speak to the men in each car.

Pitts raised himself up and peered into the car beside him. "I see at least two shotguns," he said. He glanced back and forth between the cars. "Twelve guys. Looks like the major doesn't fool around when he calls for backup."

"I'd like to see the shrine," Adrianna said.

Devlin gave her a quizzical look.

"If there's time," she added.

"I'll check with Martínez."

* * *

"Certainly," Martínez said. "I was actually going to ask the señorita to remain here with two of my men. The house we will be going to is a big question mark."

"What do you mean?"

"Only that I do not know what we will find. I would like to keep from placing the señorita in danger."

"Where's the house?"

"That is another question mark. The CDR man has not yet arrived."

Devlin stared up at the sky. The vultures were still circling. When he lowered his eyes, he saw that Martínez was now studying them.

"Let us hope it is not an omen," the major said.

A steady stream of people moved along the walkway that led to the entrance of the shrine. Young men and small boys lined both sides, offering bits of stone and postcard-sized pictures of the Virgin. Devlin took a piece of stone that appeared to be granite and handed two dollars to a small boy with hungry eyes. The child quickly rattled off something in Spanish and gave Devlin a picture as well.

"They're a dollar each," Adrianna said. "He doesn't want to cheat you."

Devlin ruffled the boy's hair, then reached in his pocket and handed the child two more dollars.

"The kid would never make it in New York," he said as he led Adrianna toward the entrance.

"Why?"

"Too honest."

Adrianna slipped her arm into his and squeezed it against her side. "But cute and clever," she said. "Clever enough to get two extra bucks out of you."

Devlin stopped and turned her to face him. "You think I've been had?"

"Oh yes."

His face broke into a wide grin. "The little bugger," he said.

They passed through a gate in the low iron fence that surrounded the shrine, then through a high arched doorway. Inside, they found themselves in a modest room, no more than twenty by thirty feet. Directly opposite, facing the entrance, was an ornate altar of Gothic arches and marble pillars. Set in its center was a statue of the Virgin of Caridad. The statue was dressed in satin robes of gold and ocher, and had a smaller statue of the infant Jesus cradled in its arms. On each side of the altar, and hanging in display cases on all the walls, were gifts of thanks to the Virgin, intermingled with pleas for help. A framed notice explained that there were thousands of these gifts and pleas, with many thousands more locked away in storage vaults, Hemingway's Nobel medal among them.

Devlin and Adrianna moved among the offerings. There were hundreds of military and sports medals, baseballs, soccer balls, small dolls, several full military uniforms, numerous passports and identity cards, even one membership card in the Cuban Communist Party. Most touching were the photographs and accompanying letters, each asking the Virgin to intercede on behalf of the person pictured. Some of the photos were of persons who were gravely ill, but most were alleged to be political prisoners, others, people who had simply disappeared. One photograph, Devlin noted, was draped with both a rosary and a red-and-white-beaded bracelet representing the Afro-Cuban god Chango.

Adrianna read one of the letters that lay beside the photograph of a young man.

"It's from this man's mother," she said. "It says he was a soldier in the army, and that he was taken away at night and accused of spying. His mother says he was innocent, but was never given a lawyer until the day of the trial, that he was convicted after only an hour of testimony, and has spent the last ten years locked in a cell with seven other men. She says he is very sick, and will die unless he is freed, and that she has appealed to the government, even to Fidel, himself, but that no one will help. Now she is turning to the Virgin as the only hope for her son, who she says is a good Catholic."

Devlin studied the photograph. It showed a young man, dressed in the uniform of a baseball team. He was no more than nineteen or twenty when the photo was taken, and had dark, bright, happy eyes.

"Do you think that's true? That he was never given a lawyer until the day of the trial, then convicted within an hour?"

Devlin nodded. "Martínez explained the different court systems here. Civilians have to be given a lawyer within ten days of being charged. From that point on, it's pretty much as it is back home. Bail. House arrest if you're sick or old. Innocent unless the state can prove otherwise. Martínez says the military isn't bound by those rules. There, you can be held indefinitely, and you're guilty unless you can prove them wrong. And you get one day in court to do that, with a lawyer you've never met, or even spoken to, going up against a panel of five judges, three of whom are military officers who approved the charges in the first place."

"God."

"I don't imagine it makes for very high morale, but it doesn't seem to matter. They aren't doing much soldiering anymore."

"What do you mean?"

"Every Cuban man has to spend two years in the army. He gets his basic training, but then he's usually sent to work on a farm. That's the army's main function now. Providing cheap agricultural labor. It also runs a chain of hotels for the tourist industry. Martínez said the government gave them that job almost ten years ago, because they didn't have anything else to do."

Devlin took her arm and led her back toward the door. "We better check with Martínez and see if his block watcher showed up."

Adrianna put a hand on his arm, stopping him. "Do you think we'll find her, Paul? Find her body?"

Devlin shook his head. "I don't know, babe. I think we're getting close. But there's too much going on that I still don't understand. I have no idea how the game is played here. Hell, it's worse than that. I don't even know the name of the game we're playing."

Outside, they found Martínez just inside the low iron gate. He was speaking with a smallish man, about fifty years old, dressed in rumpled trousers and a work-stained T-shirt. He had a full head of salt-and-pepper hair and matching three-day growth of stubble on his cheeks.

"This is Señor Miguel Caputo," Martínez said. "He works as a foreman on a nearby pineapple farm, and also as one of our CDR officers here in Cobre."

Devlin sighed inwardly. The man didn't exactly inspire confidence.

Martínez rattled off a quick explanation of who Devlin and Adrianna were, and it was met with a broad, almost toothless grin. Caputo turned to Adrianna and jabbered away in rapid-fire Spanish.

"He says he is honored to be of service, and that his entire neighborhood will be honored to have helped the police in this way."

Devlin nodded and smiled at the man. He turned to Martínez. "That's great," he said. "I'm happy he's honored. But what has he got for us?"

Ollie Pitts wandered through the gate. "Who's honored?" he asked.

"Señor Caputo," Devlin said. "The CDR guy."

"So what's the little snitch got to say?"

Martínez gestured with his hands, urging patience. "He has just arrived this very moment. Allow me to question him."

Martínez began with the man as Adrianna translated for Devlin.

"Martínez is reminding him that he filed a report about strangers coming to the village. Caputo is saying yes, that's true, that at first two strangers came to stay in a large house that sits on a hillside over there."

Devlin and Adrianna turned to where the CDR man was pointing, but apparently the church blocked the hillside in question. Devlin shook his head in frustration. Adrianna continued to translate.

"He says one of the strangers is an old man, who seemed to be sickly. The man with him is younger, but not too young, and is bigger and more robust. He says there were four Abakua with them. Then more men came today. A small man, who could be a gringo, and a Cuban who looked like a policeman. They had two Abakua with them as well. He says the second group of men left by car about an hour ago."

Devlin turned to Martínez. "The gringo? You think, maybe, Cipriani?"

Martínez questioned the CDR man again, then turned back to Devlin. "The description is fitted to him. But right now I am more interested in the one who seems to be sick. I have already left instructions that Cipriani is to be stopped if he tries to take a plane from the airport."

"What if he leaves by car?" Devlin asked.

Martínez shrugged. "There is a main road that takes twelve hours to reach Havana. On this road we would find them. But there are also many small roads through the mountains, and few police to patrol them. If they choose this way, then it will be difficult for us. But I doubt he will travel that way, unless he suspects we are pursuing him. It would take him two days to reach Havana, and Cabrera will want his information more quickly. And if this involves the death of the Red Angel, he will not want it discussed on the telephone." He raised a finger. "But this other man. He is a mystery. And he is apparently ill, and has at least four Abakua with him. This we must investigate."

"Who's watching the house now?" Devlin asked.

A group of worshipers was moving past and Martínez lowered his voice. "Señor Caputo says his wife is being of service in his absence."

"Jesus."

Martínez's eyes glittered with amusement. "Is this not how you would conduct a surveillance in New York?"

Before Devlin could answer, Caputo let out a shout and threw himself forward. Devlin spun around just as a man in a white shirt sent a knife slashing toward the little pineapple foreman's throat. Caputo moved just in time, and the knife cut across his shoulder. Devlin pushed Adrianna behind him, his hand instinctively reaching for a nonexistent pistol, as Caputo staggered and fell to one knee. The assailant advanced, his knife low, his eyes fixed on Devlin. Behind him, a knife flashed in the hand of a second man. Devlin concentrated on the first man, his attention fixed on the knife, his own hands held slightly above the blade so he could ward off any upward thrust.

The first man feinted to his left, then took a quick step forward. Just as he was about to hook his knife upward in a killing thrust toward Devlin's heart, Caputo threw his body into the man's knees. The assailant staggered, still lunging forward, but Devlin grabbed his wrist, twisting it away. His other hand shot out, slapping the back of the man's head, then pushing down as his knee smashed into the attacker's face.

The man hit the ground and his knife spun away. Devlin's eyes snapped up, searching for the second man. That fight was already over. The man lay on the ground, Martínez's pistol only inches from his face, Ollie Pitts's size-twelve shoe pressed against his throat.

Adrianna came into Devlin's arms and hugged him. Her entire body was trembling.

"Abakua?" Devlin asked, over her shoulder.

Martínez's men raced in from the parking lot. Martínez turned away from the fallen attacker and holstered his automatic.

"Yes, they are Abakua," he said. His face filled with rage as he stared at the fallen CDR man. Blood poured from a wound only inches from the small man's throat.

Martínez snapped out a command, and one of his men raced back toward the parking lot. Then he knelt next to the fallen man and spoke soothing words in Spanish.

"He's telling him that his man is going for a medical kit and to radio for an ambulance," Adrianna said. She watched as Martínez took a handkerchief from his pocket and pressed it against the wound. "I think he's worried the knife may have hit an artery."

Devlin pulled away and knelt down next to Caputo. The little man's color had faded badly, and he seemed about to go into shock. Devlin turned back to Adrianna and asked for the shawl she was wearing, then covered Caputo's body as best he could.

"How's he doing?" Devlin asked.

Martínez's head snapped up. "Who, this unimportant little pineapple farmer? This . . . snitch?"

"He's a brave man."

Martínez looked down again, and ran a hand along Caputo's forehead. "When he was just a small boy, he fought in these mountains with Fidel. He was twice wounded. When the revolution ended, the Comandante personally awarded him a medal for his courage." He looked up again.

Devlin chewed his lip. "I owe him," he said.

The major's eyes did not soften. "Yes, señor, you do."

* * *

They hit the house half an hour later. Martínez's men moved in quickly and professionally. Doors were smashed open, and the house was searched room to room. It was empty.

Caputo's wife arrived and told them that a car had left with six men and headed for the shrine. She said she followed it to the foot of the drive that led to the parking area and saw it leave quickly. That was almost a half hour ago, she said. And, when it left, the car held only four men.

Martínez told her what had happened and ordered one of his men to take her to her husband. Adrianna and three of Martínez's officers had remained with the fallen CDR man to await the ambulance that had been summoned from Santiago.

Devlin glanced at his watch. "The four who took off could be at the airport by now," he said.

"I will radio ahead," Martínez said. He gave Devlin a steady look. "Whoever they are, they were waiting to see you dead."

12

I give to you several choices," Martínez said. "I have available to me a very fast boat that can get you to Key West in a matter of hours. I believe a telephone call can also have American police waiting there when you arrive.

"Next is our own court system, a choice that will undoubtedly lead to one of the many prisons that are even less pleasant than the Villa Marista.

"Finally, you may choose to help the police in their duties, and when all is finished, you may find yourself sitting on one of the lovely beaches of Brazil."

Robert Cipriani stared at his shoes and said nothing. He was seated in the same room where Baba Briyumbe had been questioned. Cabrera's man, Major Cepedes, was under guard in an adjoining room. The two Abakua, who had accompanied them to the airport, were now sharing a cell with the pair arrested in Cobre after the attempt on Devlin's life. Much to Martínez's displeasure, the four men who had fled the shrine by car were still at large.

Cipriani looked up at the major. His eyes were devoid of

any hope. "I've already answered your questions. I want to be returned to the Villa Marista."

Martínez turned to Devlin and Pitts. "This is the first time in my experience that anyone has volunteered for a cell in the Villa Marista. State Security must have greatly improved the accommodations." He spun around and brought his face within inches of Cipriani's. "This is your last chance. If you continue to tell me you were released, under guard, so you could visit an anonymous friend, you will be held incommunicado for ten days, as our law allows. Then you will be placed on trial for conspiracy to commit murder. I suspect Colonel Cabrera will also charge you with escape, and Major Cepedes will be given a medal for achieving your capture. If you are found innocent of these charges, you will be placed on the fast boat I spoke of, and returned to the United States, where a long prison term awaits you. Now speak, or prepare yourself for everything I have told you."

Cipriani closed his eyes. "What is it you want to know?"

Martínez rubbed his hands over his face. "The same thing I have asked you for the past hour. The names of the persons you visited in Cobre, the purpose of your visit, and whether or not you were sent there by Colonel Cabrera, as the presence of Major Cepedes would seem to indicate."

"You're not offering me anything but a prison cell or a death warrant," Cipriani said.

"I am offering you a beach in a country that does not have an extradition treaty with the United States. If my information is correct, you were preparing to go to that country when you were arrested by Colonel Cabrera."

Cipriani shook his head. "I understand they've also got nice cemeteries in Rio."

"If you are afraid of Colonel Cabrera, I assure you he will present no problem for you."

Cipriani gave him a mirthless laugh. "I'm not worried

about Cabrera. If you get what you want, he'll be too busy trying to avoid a firing squad."

"Who are you afraid of?" It was Devlin this time. "Are we talking narcotics? Like maybe your visitor flew in from Medellín, and our poking around is screwing up some drug deal Cabrera has working?"

Cipriani shook his head. "I'll take my chances with Cabrera. When Cepedes and I don't show up, he's going to start looking." He let his eyes fall hard on Martínez. "You ready to take on State Security, Major?"

Martínez gave him a cold smile. "It would appear I already have, señor."

They sat at a large table on the Casa Grande's rooftop terrace. It was after midnight and a rumba band provided the rhythm for several dozen swaying hips. Devlin, Adrianna, and Pitts showed no interest in the music. Neither did the three men at the next table. They were Martínez's men, sent to play bodyguard while the major put the finishing touches on the arrests he had made.

Adrianna stared out over the waist-high terrace wall. There, appearing almost close enough to touch, the twin spires of the cathedral hovered in the darkness, the large granite angel set between them like some avenging specter. Beyond the cathedral, even the lights of the harbor seemed ominous, as if their normally romantic glow were hiding some new and yet-to-be-revealed threat.

Adrianna turned away from the view. "I don't like this city. It looks so small and peaceful, but it's not."

Pitts grinned at her. "Hey, it's hard to like a place where witch doctors put curses on you and a bunch of 'yoms try to slice you up with shivs."

"Watch the racist crap," Devlin warned.

Pitts raised his hands. "Okay, okay. A bunch of Abakua.

The same group of loonies who tried to do us in with a truck in Havana." He glanced at Adrianna and grinned again. "So how do you feel about Havana?"

Adrianna ignored him. She turned to Devlin. "Maybe we should forget everything and go home. My aunt's dead. Let the Cubans find her and bury her. She wouldn't want this. Not if it meant having you killed, too."

Devlin reached out and covered her hand. "Your aunt didn't even know me."

"No, she didn't. But I wrote to her, and told her how much I love you."

Pitts raised his chin. "I hate to break up this moment we got going here, but I think I see our little major headed this way."

They turned and watched Martínez weave his way through the dancers. As he reached the table, he placed a hand on his midsection and gave his hips a small rumba sway.

"Ah, the music is wonderful," he said as he took an empty chair.

"You seem very jolly," Pitts said. "Cipriani finally spill his guts? Or maybe your major from State Security?"

"I am afraid not. Señor Cipriani and Major Cepedes both remain very unhelpful. They are now on their way back to Havana by car. Under guard. My men will use back roads, so it will take them two days, but that will also make it difficult for Colonel Cabrera to find them, no?" He smiled. "It will also make them available to us if we need them. I have made arrangements for us to return to Havana tomorrow morning. We will fly to Varadero, where a car will meet us and drive us the last one hundred and forty kilometers." He gave them his Cuban shrug. "This will also present some difficulties for the colonel."

"Why are we going back?" Devlin asked. "I thought Plante Firme said we'd find the body here?"

Martínez nodded. "But I believe the body is being taken back to Havana by Baba Briyumbe's disciple."

"This Seven Thunderbolts guy?" Pitts asked.

"Yes, by Siete Rayos."

"Why do you think that?" Adrianna asked.

"Some new information has come to me." Martínez leaned forward and lowered his voice so it could just be heard over the music. "The men who fled the shrine—the old, sickly man and his companion, along with the two Abakua—left Santiago on a private jet, which is why my men at the airport failed to observe them. A later check of flight records showed that they arrived in Havana three hours ago."

"Did customs get their names?" Devlin asked.

"Unfortunately, there are no customs for internal flights, so there was no report filed in Havana. I did check on the flight's initial arrival in Cuba. It flew in yesterday with two passengers: a Señor John Smith and a Señor Matthew Jones. Both had Canadian passports that I believe to be false. One of the men required assistance getting off the aircraft, and both seemed to receive special consideration going through customs and immigration. Their entry forms indicated they were businessmen."

"Where did they fly in from?" Devlin asked.

"From Nassau in the Bahamas," Martínez said.

Devlin and Pitts exchanged looks, but remained silent.

Devlin decided to stick with the missing body. "What makes you think this changing-of-heads ritual hasn't already been done?" he asked.

"I am sure that it has not," Martínez said.

"Why?" Adrianna asked.

"Because the house in which the men stayed was being watched at all times. By either Señor Caputo or his wife. There were no visitors until Señor Cipriani arrived. And, most important, there was no *nganga*. In Cuba, the arrival of a *nganga* would not go unnoticed."

"And you're sure this sickly man is the reason my aunt's body was stolen?"

Martínez nodded. "Everything points in that direction. And now everything points back to Havana. I suspect the *nganga* is on its way there now. And that it will arrive within days."

"You think it's going by car?" Adrianna asked.

Martínez smiled. "It would make strange baggage on an airline, no? Even if it were loaded on a private jet, it would not go unnoticed or unchallenged by the immigration police."

"What about roadblocks?" Pitts asked. "Maybe you can find it before it gets to Havana."

"I am afraid there are too many small roads, and too few people to blockade them. It is exactly why Señor Cipriani and Major Cepedes are now traveling this way." He shook his head. "No, we must get to Havana and find this sickly man. Then the *nganga* holding the Red Angel's bones will come to us."

"We're thinking about going home," Adrianna said. "It's just—"

Devlin cut her off. "No, we're not." He reached out and covered her hand again. "I think it might be a good idea if you went home," he said. "But Ollie and I are going to stay."

Adrianna stared at him. "Like hell," she said. "If you're staying, so am I."

"I think it would be best if you all stayed," Martínez said. "But not at the Inglaterra. I am presently having some of your clothing removed and taken to a location where Colonel Cabrera will not think to look."

"Where?" Devlin asked.

Martínez smiled again, a bit coyly, Devlin thought.

"You will stay in the house of the Red Angel. Not the ancestral home her sister now occupies, but the one in Miramar, the one Fidel, himself, has given her." The smile widened. "We will hide under Cabrera's nose. His own house, also a gift of Fidel, is only a few blocks away."

13

Devlin put Adrianna to bed. When she was asleep, he entered Pitts's room through the connecting door.

"John the Boss?" Pitts asked.

"Could be. If it is, at least we know who we're looking for." He went to the telephone. "I'm gonna call a friend in our organized-crime bureau. He knows everything about Rossi, right down to the size of his dick."

"You think there's a Cuban connection we don't know about?"

"If there is, he'll know about it."

Devlin hung up the phone ten minutes later and let out a long breath.

"You got something?" Pitts asked.

Devlin nodded. "Back in the fifties, Rossi worked here with Meyer Lansky. He was small potatoes, just a button doing odd jobs, but apparently he made an impression. When Castro tossed them out, he went back to New York and started to move up in the organization. And that's when the NYPD started paying attention."

"So you think it's him." There was no hint of a question in Pitts's voice. He obviously thought so, too.

"It fits," Devlin said. "The old Cuban connection. The sick, old man, who maybe got introduced to Palo Monte back in the old days. The flight from the Bahamas, where Rossi and his goon, Mattie the Knife, just happened to be. The phony passports that used the same first names: John and Matthew." Devlin shook his head. "This thing walks like a duck and says quack, Ollie. Plus, you're forgettin' a few other things."

"Like what?"

"Like it was the body of Adrianna's aunt that got snatched. And that was something that just might bring *me, here*." Devlin tapped the side of his nose. "Like the fact that this sick old man waited around to see somebody get iced, and only took off when that didn't happen. And sending me to the boneyard has been somethin' John the Boss has wanted to do for a long time. He tried once, and it didn't work. But he's not the kind of guy who changes his mind. He just knew he couldn't try again in New York."

"And you think he set it up here?" Pitts's voice was incredulous. He shook his head. "That would mean he had Adrianna's aunt killed just to get you down here. That doesn't make sense. He can't have that kind of clout here."

"No, but maybe he has friends who do." Devlin waved his hand, as if dismissing his own argument. "Look, I think he knows everything about me. And everything about anybody I'm close to. It's the kind of mean old bastard he is." He waved his hand again. "But no, I don't think he set it up that way. That's too Byzantine even for an old Mafia bastard like him. I wouldn't put it past him, but I think he fell into this. I think he and his gumbas had something else going, and the situation just presented itself. And the old Bathrobe jumped on it with both feet. Look, if he believes in this crazy voodoo nonsense, and is looking for a cure, what better than the body of Cuba's most famous doctor. If Martínez is right, Cuba's Red Angel got rubbed out by Cabrera. And what a nice little bonus that she happens to be Adrianna's aunt. Because that just about guarantees that my ass is headed for Cuba. And that's something that will put me right in his sights. Right where everybody's been leading us, ever since we got here. And you know what else that means. That means Martínez could be involved right up to his rumba-shaking little ass."

Pitts thought about it. "I don't buy it. It doesn't play." He hesitated, forming his reasons. "Martínez is the one who tipped us that it might be John the Boss. If he was part of it, he would have known we'd tumble to that. It would have been a dumb move, and Martínez is too sharp for that."

Devlin nodded, acknowledging the point. "He is sharp. No question about it. But it's either that, or he's being played for a stooge, too. Or maybe he's got his own little game. And we just haven't figured it out yet."

"Okay, I'll buy that. But if you're right, we better find out what it is." Pitts hesitated, then asked, "So whadda we do now?"

Devlin walked back toward the connecting door that led to his room. He looked back at Pitts. "Now we stop being tourists, and we start being cops," he said.

14

The Red Angel's house was on Fortieth Street, two doors in from Avenue Five in a seemingly prosperous area of Havana known as Miramar. It was a neighborhood dotted with foreign embassies and the occasional upscale restaurant. There were several small hotels catering to visiting foreign officials and businessmen, and along the nearby coast there were discreet private clubs—once a bastion of Batista's oligarchy—that now served high-ranking Cuban officials who had modified their brand of socialism.

Mixed in were ordinary Cubans, just as poor and struggling as compatriots in more meager neighborhoods, many living on inadequate government pensions that forced them to seek out dollars wherever they could find them. Yet the homes of those in power showed none of that financial strain. They were large and well tended, with no battered automobiles parked out front awaiting repair. They were like the homes one would find in any affluent American neighborhood, and they seemed just as removed from everyday life.

"Your aunt lived well," Devlin said as they looked up at

the large modern stucco home that sat behind a high hedge. Devlin thought about José Tamayo, the "successful" writer they had visited only days ago. This was a far cry from the impoverished, firetrap apartment that housed his extended family.

"You are thinking, perhaps, there are contradictions in our socialism," Martínez said.

"You read my mind, Major," Devlin said.

Martínez made a helpless gesture with his hands. "You are right. Cuba has become a nation of contradictions. The government is dedicated to serving the people, but some in the government—those at its highest levels—live much better than the people they serve." He removed a key from his pocket and opened a locked iron gate. "This was not always so, and it is something our Red Angel argued against. But come, I will show you."

They entered the first floor and found themselves in a well-equipped clinic. The main rooms had been divided into a waiting room and four small examination cubicles. The large kitchen, in addition to a stove, refrigerator, and sink, also housed a laboratory.

Martínez turned to Adrianna and smiled. "Your aunt lived on the second floor, where you will find her private office, a sitting room, and two bedrooms. I have had blackout curtains installed over the louvered windows. It will be hot, but if you keep the curtains drawn, no one will know you are here. When the lights are out, you may open the curtains."

"What about the neighborhood CDR man?" Devlin asked.

"He has been alerted," Martínez said. "He will not mention your presence. Like many of our CDR officers, he was a close friend of our Red Angel, and is pleased to serve her visiting niece."

"Why was my aunt close to the CDR?" Adrianna asked.

Martínez waved his hand, taking in the makeshift clinic.

"Some in our government did not approve of her private activities. They felt it was critical of the overall system." He raised his eyebrows, indicating another contradiction. "Many in our poorer neighborhoods are neglectful about the need to have their children inoculated against illness. And our hospitals are too large to keep track of them. Some of these people are simply suspicious, and others prefer to seek help from the Afro-Cuban religions. The Red Angel worked with Santeria priests and Palo Monte *paleros* to convince them this was unwise, but she also worked with the CDR to identify those who had neglected these inoculations. Those, she ordered to come to her home in the evenings, and she personally made sure their children were cared for." A twinkle came to his eye. "The nightly line of people, coming to her home, did not please some others who live in this neighborhood."

"And when she was told to stop?" Adrianna asked.

"She laughed at them," Martínez answered. "It is said Fidel, himself, questioned these activities, and was told to mind his own business." Amusement came to his eyes. "There are not many in our government who do this, and in recent years their friendship became very strained. Mainly because of the embargo, and its effect on needed medical supplies."

Adrianna wandered about the first floor, picking up various items—a stethoscope, a blood-pressure cuff, an occasional medical book—holding them as though they might impart something of her aunt, then returning them to their proper places, as if her aunt might need them when she returned.

Devlin took Martínez aside. "We need two cars," he said. "Inconspicuous ones, nothing shiny and new that will attract attention. Rentals are fine, but I'll want to rent them under phony names so Cabrera can't trace them."

"I can arrange this," Martínez said. "Many individuals rent their cars. Some even serve as drivers. I will find two that are reliable."

"I don't want drivers," Devlin said.

"I understand. There is a small park across from my headquarters. If you meet me there at three, I will have them for you." He paused and gave Devlin a steady look. "You have something you are planning?" he asked.

Devlin inclined his head to one side. "We're detectives. We're going to detect."

Martínez's headquarters was located on Calle Zapata, only a few blocks from the cluster of government buildings that surrounded Fidel's compound and the towering monument to José Martí. It was a large white two-story building that resembled a small castle, with four turrets, battlements along its flat roof, and a high arched entrance that lacked only a portcullis. Pitts had described the interior as "a typical cop shop" with an elevated front desk and waiting area, off which lay a rabbit warren of smaller squad rooms and offices. The basement housed individual cells and a large holding pen.

Devlin and Pitts found Martínez seated on a small bench, reading a battered paperback novel. There was a paper lunch bag next to him. He smiled as they approached and held up the cover of the book.

"One of Tamayo's mysteries," he said. He raised his chin toward his headquarters. "His detective is much smarter than any who work for me."

"It's the same with our mystery novels," Devlin said. "Writers don't like cops who wander around trying to figure out which end is up."

Martínez laughed and tossed Devlin two sets of car keys. He raised his chin again, indicating two dust-covered cars parked in tandem, a tan Russian Lada, at least ten years old, and a dull blue Nissan Sentra of the same vintage.

"Good surveillance cars, no?" he said. "Very inconspicuous, very Cuban. Unfortunately, neither have air-conditioning. But all the windows open, which is not true of many Cuban cars." He shrugged. "Used parts and the embargo do not accommodate each other."

Devlin tossed the keys for the Lada to Pitts, who grimaced at the idea of driving a Russian car.

"Make believe you are a good socialist," Martínez said. "The Lada belongs to one of my men, and he has assured me it is reliable. Then there is the Russian engineering. If the car fails to start at first, you need only to beat it with a large stick."

Pitts reached into a pocket and withdrew a leather-covered sap. "I'll use this," he said. "Customs never found it in my suitcase."

Martínez arched his brows. "It is not legal here. Even for police." He let out a long breath. "Is this what you used on the Abakua outside Plante Firme's house?"

"Nah. I didn't have it with me then. Everybody kept telling me what a gentle city this is. I used that lead pipe I found in Plante Firme's yard."

"Promise me you will use it only on the Abakua," Martínez said. A small smile flickered across his lips. "Or Cabrera's men."

Pitts winked at him.

Devlin rolled his eyes. "Keep it in your pocket," he said. "Use that ham hock you call a fist."

"I'd still like some heat," Pitts said. "Just in case."

Martínez turned back to the bench and picked up a paper bag that Devlin had assumed was his lunch. He handed it to Devlin. "If you are found with these, I cannot help you," he said.

Devlin looked inside. The bag held two snub-nosed .38 revolvers. He slipped one into his waistband under his shirt and handed the bag to Pitts.

"They are loaded, but there are no extra cartridges," Martínez said. "I do not propose warfare, only self-defense."

"It's like fucking Mayberry," Pitts said. "Maybe I should keep my bullet in my pocket like Don Knotts."

Martínez glanced at Devlin. "It is very hard to make this man happy," he said.

"Indeed," Devlin said. "You should talk to his sergeant someday. She has some very strong opinions about his level of gratitude."

Devlin took a step toward his car, but Martínez held up a hand. He gave Devlin a no-nonsense look. "I want to know what you are planning."

Devlin drew a long breath. He had known this was coming. "I'm going to check some of the hotels to see if I can kick up anything on our sick old man. I assume your CDR men are keeping watch in their neighborhoods."

Martínez nodded. "And Detective Pitts?"

"Ollie is going to run a tail on Cabrera."

Martínez raised his eyebrows.

"Cabrera's never seen Ollie, so I think he has a shot at tailing him. If Cabrera meets with anyone suspicious, he'll drop off Cabrera and follow that person. If that proves productive, we'll run a second tail tomorrow. Ollie will stay with the colonel, and I'll pick up on the new target."

"And Señorita Adrianna?"

"She's going through her aunt's papers to see if there are any leads there. They're in Spanish, and she's the only Spanish speaker I have."

Martínez stared at Devlin, letting him know his rather blatant exclusion had been noted. He held Devlin's eyes. "Today, I will go with you, my friend." There was no question about refusal in his voice. He turned to Pitts. "We shall meet outside El Floridita at ten. It is a restaurant not far from your old hotel. Very famous. If you park in the area, anyone can direct you there."

* * *

Cabrera's car pulled out of the Villa Marista compound shortly after five. Pitts's Lada was tucked into a side street and he dropped in behind, fifty yards back.

The colonel's car moved slowly through the city streets, past the ferry terminal and onto Avenida del Puerto, which ran along the edge of the harbor at the tip of Old Havana. As they approached the Castillo de San Salvador fortress, the car entered the tunnel that ran under the harbor to Casablanca. Emerging on the opposite shore, it turned onto a winding drive that circled the Castillo del Morro, the sister fortress that together with the Castillo de San Salvador had guarded Havana harbor for more than two centuries. At a sign marked LOS 12 APOSTOLES, Cabrera's car entered a steep drive that led back to the water.

Pitts dropped back, waited, then followed Cabrera's car down the drive.

Los 12 Apostoles turned out to be an ancient gun emplacement, twelve two-hundred-year-old cannons, set in a long line and pointed toward the entrance of the harbor, each one bearing the name of one of Christ's apostles. Behind the gun battery stood the very tony Restaurant of the Twelve Apostles.

Pitts spotted Cabrera's car in the large dirt parking lot. The driver was leaning against a fender, smoking a cigarette, as he stared out at a passing car ferry. Pitts drove by unnoticed, and parked as far away as he could. Then he sauntered toward the restaurant, just another tourist looking for an expensive meal.

Cabrera was seated alone at an outside terrace table, facing the city. Pitts asked the maître d' for a similar table and was seated no more than twenty feet away. A few minutes later Cabrera was joined by another man. He was average height, about forty, Pitts guessed, with dark hair and dark eyes and a heavy five-o'clock shadow. He was dressed in black slacks, a pale blue shirt with the top two buttons undone, and a tan sport jacket. There was a gold Rolex on his wrist and a gold crucifix hanging from his neck. He looked like a flashy European businessman on vacation. Except he greeted Cabrera in American-accented English. The sound of his voice made Pitts smile.

"There is a problem," Cabrera said.

DeForio's eyes hardened. "This is a bad time for problems. We've already transferred a sizable amount of money to the bank in Panama. We're ready to move ahead quickly."

Cabrera nodded. "This difficulty will not stop our plans."

Mickey D stared at him. "You let me be the judge of that. Tell me about your problem."

The waiter came, gave them menus, and took their drink orders. When he had left, Cabrera leaned forward and lowered his voice.

"Robert Cipriani has disappeared," he began. "I sent him to Santiago de Cuba to meet with our friend, together with one of my men. Neither has returned."

"Have you checked with our friend?"

"He is in Havana now. I spoke with him this afternoon. He said Cipriani and my man left his villa in Cobre two hours before he left there himself. They were to return on a Cubana flight. Our friend traveled on his private jet."

"And Cipriani and your man never got here."

"They checked in for the flight, but they never boarded the plane. I checked with the local police and with the immigration police, but they knew nothing."

"That doesn't sound right."

"No." Cabrera shook his head for emphasis as he tried to decide how much more to say. DeForio was unaware of the assassination attempt on this New York police inspector and his woman, either here in Havana or in Cobre. This was a private arrangement with Rossi, just as the theft of the Red Angel's body had been. That second arrangement had produced an upheaval among the Mafia investors that had only recently been settled. Knowledge of the assassination attempt might produce yet another. Still, DeForio had to be told something.

"The major of the national police that I told you about, the one who is investigating the disappearance of the body . . ." He paused.

DeForio stared at him. "Yeah, what about him?"

"He was in Santiago at the same time."

DeForio's eyes widened. "You are joking with me, right? This crap with this old woman's body, tell me it's not coming back to haunt us again."

"I am not certain," Cabrera said. "I am attempting to discover the truth."

Mickey D covered his face with both hands and slowly drew them down. "Where is that fucking body now?"

"It is on its way to Havana, in the *nganga* that has been prepared. The ritual will be performed here, tomorrow, or the following day."

"Where?"

"I am not certain. Señor Rossi is hidden in an Abakua stronghold in Guanabacoa. I assume the ritual will take place there, or somewhere nearby."

"Where the hell is this Guanabacoa?"

"It is only a short drive from where we sit."

"Do you think this major knows about this?"

Cabrera shook his head. "It is not possible that he does. Only Señor Rossi, myself, and the Abakua *palero* know this place."

DeForio's face darkened, and his lips formed a hard line. "I want to see Rossi, and I want this fucking ritual over with. We gave in to Rossi on this voodoo crap. Now it's coming back to bite us on the ass again." He ground his teeth. "And I still don't know how you're going to resolve the disappearance of this big-shot doctor." He pointed a finger at Cabrera and lowered his voice to a whisper. "If this brings the government down, we could all be fucked. We *need* the Comandante in power if the embargo is going to hold."

"It is arranged," Cabrera said. "It will be done tomorrow."

"How?"

Cabrera leaned forward, bringing his own voice down to a whisper. "We have the body of another woman. The same age and size, and so badly burned and deteriorated a positive identification will be impossible."

"What about her fucking dental records?" DeForio hissed.

Cabrera smiled. "Her head is missing. It will be found in a *nganga* at the house of a *palero* named Plante Firme. But only a portion of it. Without teeth, of course. It would seem this *palero* may have been in league with antigovernment insurgents." Cabrera lowered his voice even further, and his eyes hardened. "This appears to be the course the investigation is following. This way, the evidence Martínez has gathered will not be contradicted."

"And what if the *palero* denies all this crap?"

"That will be difficult," Cabrera said. "Plante Firme will be dead tomorrow."

When they left the restaurant, Pitts dropped off Cabrera and followed the second man to the Capri Hotel. Inside the lobby, DeForio veered off to the bar. Pitts quickly latched onto a young prostitute, who surprised him by speaking semifluent English. He took a fifty-dollar bill from his wallet, her normal fee for an evening of pleasure, ripped it in half, and told her if she returned with the man's name and room number, she would get the other half.

"Geev me twenty dollars more," she said. Pitts was about to snatch the torn fifty from her hand, when she began nodding vigorously and assured him she would return with the name and room number in only a minute.

He handed her a twenty and watched as she approached a tall, slender young man, dressed in tan slacks and a white shirt and tie, one of several stationed around the lobby as security guards. She led the man to the entrance of the bar and whispered in his ear. When he whispered back, she handed him the twenty and returned to Pitts.

"Hees es called Miguel De-Four-e-o. Hees chamber es a berry es-pensive suite. Nombre Siete-zero-dos, how you say, Seben-o-two." She reached out and plucked the second half of the fifty from Pitts's hand. A wide smile spread across her beautiful face. "Now I tink I go and fuck heem."

Devlin and Martínez stood on Calle Obrapia as a milling crowd of tourists waited to push their way into El Floridita, the so-called cradle of the daiquiri made famous by Ernest Hemingway's patronage. A crazy man stood guard in front of the door, "protecting" the tourists and accepting tips. He refused to move despite warnings from the restaurant's official doorman, who repeatedly stuck his head out to utter harsh Spanish threats.

The crazy man was at least six-foot-three, rail thin, and well into his fifties. He had a gentle brown face and was dressed in dirty red shorts and a dirty striped shirt, with a chain of beer-can tabs draped across his chest like a bandolier. He had a wooden stick, tied at both ends with twine, and slung from his shoulder like a rifle. Flip-flops, a battered bicycle helmet, and a full gray beard completed his costume. When Pitts arrived at ten-fifteen, the "guard" saluted him and held out his hand for a reward.

"I already gave in Times Square," Pitts snarled.

"You're late," Devlin snapped, frustrated by his own unproductive day.

"Yeah," Pitts said. "But I come bearing gold."

They pushed their way inside and Martínez flashed his ID to the real doorman, who immediately made room for them at the crowded bar.

Pitts grinned. "Just like the Apple. A flash of tin works just like a double sawbuck."

Martínez shook his head. "Is he speaking English?" he asked Devlin.

Devlin ignored him and eyed the crowded mahogany bar with displeasure. Two young women with Canadian accents, obviously alone and on the prowl, gave them appraising looks. El Floridita was a tourist trap, a beautiful one, but still a tourist trap. There was a mural on the back bar, depicting three-masted sailing ships entering Havana harbor. In front of it was a bronze statue of a man giving water to a child, and to either side, iron baskets filled with fruit. To the left was a bust of Hemingway, along with seven photos showing the author with various American luminaries. The only ones Devlin recognized were the actors Errol Flynn and Gary Cooper. Two other photos were of Hemingway with a young Fidel Castro.

He turned to Martínez. "Why the hell are we talking in here?" he asked.

Martínez's soft eyes became infuriatingly tolerant. "Tourists have no interest in anything but pleasure," he said. "We will be ignored when we offer none. And there is a convenient side door onto another street if we must leave quickly." He added a gentle smile. "Besides, one of my men is outside. He will warn us if State Security put their noses in." The answer didn't satisfy Devlin, and Martínez placed a hand on his shoulder. "Trust me, my friend. I know how best to hide in my own city."

Devlin turned to Pitts as Martínez ordered them each a frozen daiquiri. "What did you get?"

Pitts told him, making a point of the seventy dollars he had given the Capri Hotel hooker. He grinned. "I hope it's worth seventy bucks in *expense money,*" he said.

Devlin stared at him. "Me, too, Ollie. Since it's my seventy bucks." He turned to Martínez. "The name mean anything to you?"

Devlin thought he saw a flicker in the major's eyes.

"No," he said. "But I will check our files, and also with the immigration police." He turned to Pitts. "Did you get the number of the car?"

Pitts handed him a slip of paper.

"I can tell from this license-plate number it is a rental car," Martínez said. "I will check that, also."

"I want to do more than check it," Devlin said. He took the slip of paper and copied the plate number in a notebook. "I'll get on this guy tomorrow morning," he said. "Ollie, I want you to follow Cabrera again. This time from his home. According to the major, he only lives a couple of blocks from the Red Angel's house."

"I will give you the address," Martínez said. His eyes lost their gentleness. "And I will accompany you to the Capri Hotel. I want very much to see this man with my own eyes."

When they left El Floridita, the crazy man was still on guard. As they moved past, he nodded to Martínez.

"Buenas noches, jefe," he said.

Devlin stopped short and stared at the man, then at Martínez. "Your man?" His voice was both amused and incredulous.

Martínez fought off a smile. "A good disguise, no?"

15

Cabrera telephoned my office this morning. He says his men have found your aunt's body."

Adrianna sat at the kitchen table stunned into silence.

Devlin placed a hand on top of hers, then asked Martínez, "Do you think that's possible?"

"No, I do not."

Adrianna stared at Martínez. She seemed torn between hope and doubt. "Why? Why can't they have found her?"

The major's face softened, his entire demeanor seeming to offer consolation. Devlin thought he would have made a great funeral director.

"It is possible, of course. But very unlikely. I am convinced that Plante Firme is right, that the body, or at least portions of it, were taken by the Abakua to Santiago to prepare for a changing-of-heads ritual. If this is true, the rest of the body would have been destroyed to keep anyone else from using it to . . ." He waved his hand in the air, searching for the proper word. "To interfere with this ritual."

"You mean there was never any hope of finding *all* of my aunt's body?"

Martínez's eyes filled with a genuine sadness. "I am afraid not. Once we learned that Palo Monte was involved, I felt certain we would find only certain parts needed for the ritual."

"What would they have done with the rest?" Devlin asked.

Martínez seemed to regret his next words. He glanced at Adrianna, as if to apologize. "I am afraid the rest of the body would have been burned, and its ashes scattered so they could not be of use to another *palero* who might work in opposition to the ritual."

"Why didn't you tell me this?" Adrianna demanded.

Martínez stared down at his hands. "There seemed no purpose to burden you with this unpleasant fact, unless we found . . ." He let the rest of the sentence die.

"What did Cabrera say about this body he supposedly recovered?" Devlin asked.

Martínez glanced at Adrianna again. "It is missing a head, its hands, and its feet."

"Then it could be her. Even if what you say is true, it could be." Adrianna stared at him, as if trying to force him to agree. "What if they messed up, and didn't destroy the body yet? It's possible, isn't it?"

Martínez nodded. "There is no way I can say for certain it is not. I do not believe it is so, but I cannot prove it at this time. The body Cabrera has found is said to be badly decomposed." He glanced down at his hands again. "Here, in the tropics, this is something that happens quickly. Also the head and hands are missing, along with the feet, making any forensic identification impossible. There is, of course, DNA, which takes a considerable amount of time—several weeks, even. And those results, of course, only give probabilities, something Cabrera could easily have worded to suit his needs."

Adrianna stiffened. "Why are you so determined to prove it isn't her?"

"Because I believe it was Cabrera who arranged your aunt's assassination, and also the theft of her body. And that he gave the body to the Abakua so their *palero,* Baba Briyumbe, could create a *nganga* for the ritual."

Devlin slipped his arm around Adrianna. "He's right. It fits."

"Why?" Her voice was challenging and angry.

"Because of what we found out in Santiago." He tightened his grip on her shoulders. "This *palero,* Baba Briyumbe, told us he was brought a body that was badly burned like your aunt's had been. He said it was prepared for a *nganga,* then turned over to a disciple named Siete Rayos, Seven Thunderbolts. That would mean the body was there in Santiago."

"Maybe they brought it back," Adrianna insisted.

"It is unlikely, but it is possible," Martínez said. "But that would mean that Cabrera's men found it during its journey back to Havana." He paused, regret again filling his eyes. "But this is even more unlikely. State Security does not have a great number of its forces spread throughout the countryside. Certainly not enough to conduct roadblocks or any routine surveillance of the many routes through the mountains. Like your own FBI, for these things they use the police."

"So if such a seizure had been made, your people would have been involved, and would have filed a report," Devlin offered.

"Yes," Martínez said. "And I have checked. No such report was filed." He brought his hands together, as if preparing to pray. "There is also the question of the man in Cobre. He was visited by Señor Cipriani in the company of one of Cabrera's men. I think we must assume that he was sent by Cabrera for some purpose. Baba Briyumbe told us the ritual was intended for this man in Cobre. But we know from Señor Caputo and his wife that it was not performed, and we know this man has returned to Havana, although we are uncertain exactly where he is." He raised his clasped hands in front of his face and shook them. "So the changing-of-heads ritual will be performed here. And I believe Cabrera, and this new man we have discovered, this Señor DeForio, will lead us to both the man from Cobre and the *nganga* that holds the Red Angel's remains."

"And what should we do about this . . . body Cabrera says he found?" Adrianna asked.

"For now, I would like you to ignore it. Later it may serve our purpose to oblige the colonel." He gave Adrianna a soft smile. "Colonel Cabrera does not know where you are, which is as we planned. It is why he called me with this news. He is concerned about this, and I assured him I would do all in my power to find you. If you agree, I will regretfully inform the colonel that I have failed."

Adrianna stared at the tabletop. "I don't know," she said. "I don't know what I should do."

"Let us be patient," Martínez said. "For now we must continue to follow Cabrera and this new man from the Capri Hotel. When the rabbit gets nervous, it runs. And I believe if Cabrera cannot find you, he will become a rabbit." His eyes glittered with the idea. "I very much want to see this rabbit run. It will tell us some things that are important."

"And what is that?" Adrianna asked.

Martínez smiled. "It will tell us what is behind your aunt's assassination. But to reach that truth we must see what Cabrera will do next."

Plante Firme entered the courtyard of his home at ten A.M., his eyes still heavy with sleep. He had worked late into the previous night, sitting with a dying man, and performing the rituals that would return the man's spirit to his guardian *orisha,* Oggun.

He gestured to his grandson, indicating he should feed

the pig, which was squealing loudly in its pen. Then he went to the outdoor kitchen and poured himself a cup of strong Cuban coffee.

He noticed there was no fresh bread and shook his head. His grandson was supposed to go to the bakery early each morning to get the government's daily ration of bread, something he seemed to forget with growing regularity. The boy was fourteen and forgetting seemed to be a great part of his life.

Plante Firme smiled as he glanced over at the boy tending the pig. It was as it should be at fourteen, he thought. Much on the mind as the body changed to manhood. He felt a deep love for his grandson, and knew that soon—in only a few years—the boy would begin the long learning process that would one day allow him to become a great *palero* himself. Plante Firme prayed each day to Oggun that his grandson would be worthy of his duties, and that he, himself, would live to help him achieve that goal.

He put on a stern face and called to the boy. "There is no bread," he growled in Spanish.

The boy lowered his eyes. "I forgot," he said.

Plante Firme folded his arms across his chest. He was naked, except for the wrinkled cotton trousers he had slept in and the *mpaca* that hung by a leather thong from his neck. To the boy, he looked like a large, brown bear.

As the boy passed, Plante Firme threw an arm around his shoulders and pulled him close, then began walking him toward the gate. It pleased him that the boy had grown so tall. His head was already past his grandfather's shoulder.

"Next year, when you begin your studies, your memory must be stronger," he said.

The boy nodded, but said nothing. To become a *palero* he would first endure the initiation of *hacerse el santo,* a spiritual rebirth that would require him to become a child again. During that time he would be allowed to do nothing, and would even be carried from room to room, as if he were incapable of walking. He would be fed and bathed like an infant, thereby repeating the entire process of growth as if he had been born again. He would even wear a diaper. It would go on for an entire week, and he was certain he could never bear the humiliation.

Plante Firme squeezed his shoulder as they reached the courtyard's solid iron gate. "Get the good bread," he said. "If they say the bread ration is all gone, tell them it is for me. If they know this, I am certain they will find some."

Plante Firme was smiling at the boy when he opened the gate. The shotgun blast threw them both back, and the *palero*'s final vision of his grandson's face was of an exploding mass of torn flesh.

When he hit the ground, he turned immediately toward the child. Ignoring the wound in his own shoulder, he ripped the *mpaca* from his neck and pressed it against his grandson's chest. The boy's body was still convulsing, then it seemed to stiffen and go suddenly limp, and the *palero* knew with certainty that nothing in his, or anyone's, power would save his grandson. Slowly, his hand closed on the *mpaca,* then he threw back his head and let out a bellowing, anguished roar.

Across the street, the car from which the shot had been fired sped away. Neighbors would report later that the faces of the two men inside were pale with fear.

When the call came in, Devlin and Martínez were seated in the front seat of the rental car, just outside the entrance of the Capri Hotel's parking garage. Martínez barked an order into the handheld radio, then stared out the rear window. Devlin turned with him and saw two men jump from a car fifty yards back.

"What's going on?"

"There has been a shooting at Plante Firme's house. The *palero* was wounded, and his grandson was killed."

"I didn't know you had men behind us," Devlin said.

Martínez stared at him. His eyes were like two black coals. "I always have men behind us," he said.

Earlier, before Martínez arrived that morning, Devlin had spoken to his organized-crime contact in New York. He now knew who DeForio was. What he didn't know was whether Martínez knew it as well. The backup in the car behind them made him think that Martínez did. If so, they were both playing the same cat-and-mouse game, and Devlin wanted to know why Martínez was playing *his*.

"Are you going to the crime scene?" Devlin asked.

"Yes. One of my men will stay with you."

"You think this shooting is connected to us?"

"I am certain of it."

"Then I'll go with you," Devlin said. "Have your men follow DeForio and we can catch up with them later." He saw the uncertainty in Martínez's eyes. "I'm a good homicide cop, Major. Maybe I can help."

A large crowd had gathered outside the *palero*'s home, well over one hundred, Devlin estimated. They were not the usual collection he had seen so many times in New York, people drawn by the morbid need to view the destruction of another human, as if being there somehow reaffirmed their own escape from mayhem. Here, the faces—almost entirely black—were filled with grief. Men and women chanted prayers he did not understand. Even the children were subdued.

"Are they praying for the *palero*?" he asked.

"And for his grandson," Martínez said. "The boy was destined to replace his grandfather. He had been chosen by the *orisha* in Plante Firme's *nganga*. This made him a holy child, not unlike someone the Catholics might consider a saint."

Devlin shook his head. "I hate to tell you this, but you've got to move those people out of there. Your men have to search the perimeter of the house for evidence."

"I know. My men should have done this, but I think they fear offending the *palero*. A great vengeance will follow this killing."

"You mean from these people, his followers?"

Martínez shook his head. "No. From Plante Firme. All his powers will be used against the persons responsible. And I assure you, my friend, that is something to be feared."

The people were moved back, and the search conducted. The shotgun-shell casing was found opposite the gate. It had been stepped on by people in the crowd, but Devlin felt certain its plastic coating would still yield at least a partial fingerprint from the person who had loaded the weapon.

Neighbors were questioned and reported seeing two men speed away. They had not been dressed in white, Devlin noted, not the sect of Abakua Cabrera had used against them.

"Cabrera would not trust this to the Abakua," Martínez explained. "They would fear Plante Firme. As you saw, even Baba Briyumbe feared this *palero*."

"And Cabrera's men wouldn't?" Devlin asked.

"Oh yes. They would fear him," Martínez said. "That is why they shot him from afar, and why they ran when they saw they had not killed him."

"But they still did it."

"Reluctantly, my friend. And only because they also fear Cabrera." He tapped the side of his nose. "They will still be running, afraid now that Plante Firme will find them, or that Cabrera will. When we find out who among Cabrera's men is missing, then we will know who the assassins were."

"And then you can pick them up."

"Perhaps," Martínez said. "If it is necessary. If not, I will simply tell Plante Firme who they are. His punishment will be more severe than any Cuba could give them."

"What would Cuba's punishment be?"

"Death," Martínez said. "But a much kinder death than the one Plante Firme will devise."

When they entered the courtyard they found the boy's body covered by a blood-soaked sheet. Devlin pulled it back and stared at the child's butchered face. He had seen many bodies during his years as a cop, many far worse than this, and he had become immune to most. But the body of a child still had impact. There was something obscene about it, something akin to the destruction of hope.

Plante Firme was in his sacred room, seated before his *nganga,* his wounded shoulder swathed in heavy bandages. He had refused offers of hospital treatment, and his wounds had been tended to here. There were smaller wounds on his face, where stray shotgun pellets had grazed his cheek. Devlin knew from experience that he would be feeling intense, steady pain, but he showed none of it. Instead he cast the coconuts and chanted in a low, rumbling baritone.

As they stepped into the room, the *palero*'s eyes shot up, filled with anger at the interruption. When he saw Martínez his eyes softened, and the two men began to speak to each other. After a few minutes Devlin heard Cabrera's name mentioned, and saw Plante Firme's eyes harden with hate.

The *palero* began to chant in a mix of Spanish and Bantu. Again, Devlin heard Cabrera's name as Plante Firme cast the coconuts. They rolled to a stop, showing two concave and two convex sides pointing up.

Plante Firme stared at them, his fists clenched in his lap, as he hissed the word *"Eyife."*

When they left the room, Devlin took Martínez by the arm, stopping him. "Sounds like you dropped a dime on the colonel in there."

Martínez was momentarily confused by the phrase, then seemed to grasp it. He nodded. "Yes, a dime has very much been dropped."

"And?"

Martínez started walking again, moving toward the gate and the street beyond. "The *palero* consulted the *nganga*. He asked if it was Cabrera who ordered the murder of his grandson. The answer was *eyife,* a conclusive yes."

"So what happens now?"

Martínez stepped through the gate and into the street. "I think the colonel's life is about to take a very unfortunate turn."

Martínez's men had followed DeForio to the Calle de los Oficios, a street in Old Havana that had once housed its most prosperous merchants. There, he had entered the Casa de los Arabes, a three-story building of Moorish design with massive wooden doors that were several centuries old.

When Devlin and Martínez arrived, they found Ollie Pitts stuffed into a narrow doorway halfway down the block.

"Cabrera showed up fifteen minutes ago," he said. "I gather DeForio's already inside."

"Did Cabrera go anywhere else first?" Devlin asked.

Pitts shook his head. "Just his office at the Villa Marista. He stayed there all morning, then left around one and came straight here." He inclined his head toward the other end of the street. "His car and driver are in San Francisco Plaza, over by the docks, near some big church."

"The Convent of San Francisco," Martínez said. "For years it was Havana's central post office. Now Fidel has allowed it to become a church again. But not for religion. The church and the convent have become a museum for tourists." He smiled at Pitts. "Perhaps it was sentimentality on Fidel's part. As a boy he studied under the Jesuits."

"Hey, that's great," Pitts said. "Interesting as fucking hell." He rolled his eyes. The major's tour-guide act was becoming a pain in the ass. "Anyway, I saw the driver buy a ticket for the car ferry. Now, maybe he's doin' this for himself, but it seemed to happen right after Cabrera snapped some orders at him, so the detective in me suspects they might be taking a little boat ride."

"Did you get a ticket?" Devlin asked.

"Of course," Pitts said.

Devlin turned to Martínez. "Okay, this is the way I'd like to play this." He pointed at Pitts. "We'll let Ollie stick with Cabrera and keep your men on DeForio. You and I will head to wherever this ferry goes and try and get ahead of them. If they all get on the ferry together, your men can radio us and we'll stay put. If not, if DeForio heads somewhere else when he leaves here, they can radio us and we'll catch up with them. Sound good?"

Martínez nodded. "It will keep the only people Cabrera might recognize out of sight. It is best when the rabbit cannot see the hunter."

"Where does the ferry go?" Devlin asked.

"One goes to Casablanca, the other to Regla." He glanced at Pitts. "Your ticket will be good for both places, but it is unlikely they will go to Casablanca, unless they seek another expensive meal at the Battery of the Twelve Apostles." He turned back to Devlin. "Regla, however, and the nearby town of Guanabacoa are strongholds of the Abakua."

16

The Iglesia de la Virgen de Regla faced Havana harbor and offered a clear view of the ferry landing only a few hundred yards away. Standing beside it, an ancient ceiba tree seemed to dwarf the small church in its wide-spreading limbs.

Martínez explained that the presence of the tree, considered sacred in the Afro-Cuban religions, was not a coincidence.

"All Catholicism in Cuba is tied to the *orishas,* the Afro-Cuban gods," he said as they entered the church and started down the center aisle.

"Many years ago, when slavery still existed on our island, both Palo Monte and Santeria were banned, and their practitioners greatly persecuted. Because of this, believers began using the Catholic Church to hide their religions. They did this by identifying their gods with various Catholic saints."

Martínez pointed to the statues of saints that lined the walls of the church interior. "Chango became Santa Barbara because of her traditional red robes, which is also Chango's color. Oshun, always dressed in gold and white, became the Virgin of Caridad. Eleggua came to be represented by Saint Martin, Oggun by John the Baptist, and so on."

He stopped in front of the altar and pointed to the statue of a black Virgin dressed in blue and white, the traditional colors of Mary, the mother of Christ. "And, of course, Yemaya, the goddess of the sea and the protector of sailors, the great mother of all the people."

They started back up the aisle. Worshipers, mostly black, knelt before the plaster replicas of various saints. A second statue of the black Virgin stood near the main entrance, and attracted the largest number of worshipers. Bouquets of flowers had been left at the statue's feet, along with an assortment of offerings and pleas for help—photographs of loved ones, a scrap of cloth with feathers sewn to it, a bowl of fruit, another of water, a small glass holding a dark liquid that appeared to be rum.

"At first the Catholic Church resisted this syncretism with the African religions." Martínez stopped and waved his hand in a wide circle. "But the people kept flooding into their churches, and the church saw it was more practical to ignore it. Now it has grown so common some priests actually encourage it. I have even heard priests give sermons in predominantly Negro churches in which the names of the African gods were invoked."

"I didn't know you were a churchgoing man," Devlin said.

Martínez offered a faint smile. "There was a time when the government feared that these priests might try to use these African religions against the revolution. So the police paid very close attention to what was being said. Those fears proved unjustified, but in those days, because of this fear, Sunday became a day when many of us went to mass." He raised a finger. "But we did not put our pesos in the collection basket."

Devlin laughed. "I'm sure you didn't. Marx would have spun in his grave."

They left the church and headed for the expansive shade

of the ceiba tree. From there they could see a car ferry headed toward the landing.

"They will not be on this ferry," Martínez said. "My men will radio us when they board."

"I just hope they come, and we don't find ourselves chasing back to Havana, playing catch-up."

Martínez stared out into the harbor. "They will come," he said. "This is where the Abakua *palero* will perform the ritual of the changing of heads."

"You seem very certain."

"I am, my friend. I can feel it."

DeForio and Cabrera stood on the dock, waiting to board the ferry. Cabrera's car idled beside them in a long line inching toward the loading bay. DeForio's Spanish was more than adequate, but at Cabrera's insistence they spoke only in English, a language the driver did not understand. Cabrera had risen in a system where listeners were everywhere. It was a system he knew better than most, and he saw no reason to take chances.

"So, you have no idea where this niece and these two New York cops are," DeForio said.

Cabrera glanced out at the water. The car pulled ahead three feet, then stopped again. Still, he lowered his voice. "They will be found. And, when they are, the men searching for them have orders to take them into custody."

"What happens then?" DeForio asked.

"That depends on how they react to the body we have found for them." Cabrera glanced at the American. He was lying to him, but that could not be helped. One way or another, the Americans would disappear. He had a secondary understanding with the old man—what Rossi had called a side deal—and it was far too profitable to ignore. "Hopefully, they will accept our findings. If not, I will see to it that they leave the country. It is only important that the government accept the body as that of our Red Angel." He gave DeForio what he hoped was a confident smile. "And that has already been arranged."

"Well, you better find them before they stumble across the real body," DeForio warned.

"It is impossible," Cabrera said. "Only parts of the body remain, and they are in a *nganga* under the control of the Abakua. Even if these people somehow overcame the Abakua, which is most unlikely, certain tests would have to be performed on the remains." He shook his head and smiled. "I assure you, if they find the *nganga,* no one will survive long enough to order those tests."

"It would be better if they just accepted the phony body, buried it, and went home. It would be cleaner."

Cabrera nodded his agreement. DeForio was right. It would be much cleaner. But unfortunately, such a scenario was impossible. The old man had made that very clear. No matter the outcome, the Americans were going to disappear—permanently. He smiled at DeForio.

"I am certain that they will," Cabrera said. "Then, I assure you, I will personally put them on the plane."

Cabrera's driver called to him through the open car window, and the colonel excused himself. DeForio watched as he spoke on the car's radio. When he returned, DeForio thought the colonel looked agitated, even a bit nervous.

"Another problem?" he asked.

"Plante Firme survived our attack." His voice was a low hiss. "His grandson was killed."

"What about your men?"

Cabrera drew a breath. "They escaped." He let the subject die there. He had no intention of telling DeForio that his men were missing, presumably running in fear—from both the *palero* and himself.

"What does this do to your plan? The rest of this phony body was supposed to be found at this guy's house?" DeForio's eyes had hardened. It was clear these repeated reversals were eroding his confidence.

Cabrera waved away DeForio's concern. He needed to make the problem seem less significant. "The man is only a Negro witch doctor, a superstitious old fool. We will do as we wish with him, and no one will take seriously anything he says, or does." Cabrera felt a tingle of fear as he spoke the words. He attributed it to the superstitions of his own youth and pushed it aside. There was too much at stake to allow old, childhood fears to intrude on what had to be done.

He gave DeForio a false smile. "This old *palero* knows what can be done to him now. It would not surprise me if he disappeared into the countryside. There, he can shake his rattle and issue curses on those who killed his grandson."

DeForio found logic in Cabrera's words. "Jesus, what the hell does Rossi see in all this shit? No wonder those old-timers got thrown out of here fifty years ago. They were all probably listening to these goddamn witch doctors." He shook his head. "Fucking old Sicilians. Thank God Rossi's one of the last of them." He looked at Cabrera and smiled. "Can you imagine, a man like that, one of the heads of the five families, believing in this shit?"

Cabrera returned the smile, fighting to ignore the fear that gnawed at him. Yes, he could believe it, he thought. He could believe it all too well, no matter how much he told himself he did not.

"Señor Rossi is an old man," he said. "We must be indulgent."

The crowd pressed in, surrounding the dancers. Bodies swayed and heads bobbed as the beat of the drums provided a steady, undulating rhythm. From the rear of the crowd,

Devlin could see only two of the dancers. Both were men, standing on high stilts, both dressed in costumes of bright yellow and red, colors worn to honor Chango, a much-favored *orisha* among the Abakua.

They had followed DeForio and Cabrera from the ferry, and now found themselves in the subcity of Guanabacoa, a small, independent municipality that still fell under the overall jurisdiction of Havana. But only technically, Martínez had explained. Guanabacoa was truly controlled by the Abakua. It was their stronghold, and few in the government sought to challenge it.

"This little festival," Martínez said, "it has been proclaimed only by the Abakua. The government does not recognize it." He waved his finger in a small circle. "But you see how many people are here. They are supposed to be at work. But the Abakua have declared a holiday, so for them it is a holiday."

Pitts and Martínez's men were ahead of them, staying close to Cabrera and DeForio, who had abandoned their car because of the crowd. Martínez and Devlin had remained as far back as possible.

"Keep your wallet and your pistol under guard," Martínez said. "Our friends dressed in white are Cuba's only danger to tourists."

Along the edge of the crowd, standing like sentries, Devlin could see a ring of white-clad Abakua guarding the ceremony. As they drew closer to the center of the circle, he could see the other dancers, men and women, each dressed in an elaborate costume, the women's bodies writhing to the beat of the drums, the men swaying beneath long poles, the tops of which were decorated in brightly colored cloth woven into intricate patterns to represent the *orishas* who were being honored that day.

The crowd seemed alive, like a single organism, and Devlin realized it would not take much to turn these people against a perceived enemy. Martínez had been right when he had used the term “stronghold.” And the people who controlled it, the Abakua, belonged to Cabrera.

He leaned into Martínez. “How are you going to stop this changing-of-heads ritual if it happens here?” he asked.

“I am not going to stop it, my friend,” Martínez said. “The ritual will take place. But after it does, the *nganga* will be taken away to safety. Then, I will seize it.”

“And the Americans, and Cabrera?”

“They, too, will not go far. But first we must locate this man from Cobre and the *nganga* that has been made for him. Then we will close the lid of our little box.”

When they cleared the crowd, one of Martínez’s men was waiting for them at the corner of a narrow side street. He reported in rapid Spanish.

“They have gone into a house on this street,” Martínez said. “There is a rental car parked in the driveway. The license plates tell us it comes from a rental agency that operates out of the domestic terminal at Havana airport—the same terminal where the plane used by the man in Cobre landed. I suspect we have found his hiding place.”

“We need to be sure.”

Martínez nodded. “Yes, my friend, you are right. As soon as Cabrera and Señor DeForio leave, we will execute a little plan that I have.”

“What do you mean, tomorrow night?” Rossi glared at Cabrera. “It was supposed to be tonight. You think I wanna stay in this nigger-infested shithole another day?”

Cabrera held out his hands in an expression of regret. “The *palero* will not come tonight,” he said. “Siete Rayos has cast the coconuts, and has been told by the dead one that he must wait.”

Rossi considered this, then let out a long breath. “All right, all right. Tomorrow night.”

DeForio couldn't believe what he was seeing. John the Boss Rossi, one of the most powerful figures in organized crime, giving in to the mumbo jumbo of a goddamn witch doctor. He stared at Rossi. The man was old and sick, but still someone to be feared. And he believed in this shit. He actually *believed* in it. DeForio ground his teeth. This had to stop. He had to talk to his people back home. A two-billion-dollar investment, and it was all hanging on some goddamn nigger rolling coconut shells on the fucking floor. And all of it right under the noses of the government. If the woman's body was found . . . If the two things were ever connected . . . He closed his eyes and pressed a thumb and index finger against them. He had to do something to lower the risk. At the very least get this thing moved out into the countryside. He turned a false smile on Rossi.

"Don Giovanni, with all respect, I have to move ahead with the business we're here to conduct."

Rossi turned his glare on DeForio. "The two things got nothin' to do with each other. You do what you think is best."

DeForio tried to phrase the next words in his mind before saying them aloud.

"This woman's body. It's causing some complications." He gave Rossi a helpless shrug. "Before, when this thing was being done so far away, it didn't present much of a problem." He spread his arms to take in the room. "But here, so close to Havana, it's right under *everybody's* nose. I just think it's dangerous." He placed one hand against his chest. "To all of us. To what we're trying to do."

Rossi jerked his chin toward Cabrera. "The colonel's got that under control." He stared at Cabrera. "Am I right?"

Cabrera nodded. "*Sí,* señor. It is all under control."

"With all respect again," DeForio began. "But it doesn't seem that way to me. We got a lot of exposure here that we don't need."

Mattie the Knife Ippolito stepped out from behind

Rossi's chair. "Hey, you heard what he said. It's under control. You just watch your fucking mouth."

"I'm just trying—"

Rossi cut him off. "You don't try nothin'. You're a fucking errand boy here. You do what you're here to do, and you keep your mouth shut. The heads of the other families agreed to this little thing I'm doing here. You don't like it, you take it up with them. But I warn you. You go up against me, they'll bury you with your fancy college diplomas sticking out of your ass. You got that?"

DeForio felt a chill. He shook his head. "I'm not going up against—"

Again, Rossi cut him off. "You bet your fucking life you won't." He gave DeForio a cold smile. "Because that's just what you're betting if you try."

Adrianna sat at the small, cluttered desk, her aunt's papers and correspondence spread out before her. It was clear that someone had gone through these same papers. The woman's meticulousness was amazing, yet many of the papers had been stuffed back into folders or the drawers of her desk with little care. Something clumsy and rushed, as if the papers had been found useless and were being cast aside.

The apparent search did not surprise her. Certainly, the disappearance of her aunt's body would have prompted police to investigate any possible threats from, or contacts with, groups or individuals who might be responsible. But it also bolstered Martínez's belief that her aunt had been murdered after she stumbled on information that endangered someone in the government. In either case, a search might then have been conducted either by Martínez himself or by someone looking for that information.

Adrianna sat back in the hard wooden chair her aunt had chosen for her desk. It was useless to speculate, and she doubted Martínez would tell her if it was he who had ordered the search. She glanced about the room. It was austere and simple, lacking even a single luxury. She recalled Martínez's claim that Fidel Castro lived and thought like a monk, and she wondered if many of those who had brought about Cuba's revolution had chosen that personal lifestyle.

Martínez had told her another story, this one about Che Guevara. Shortly after the new government had taken power, Guevara learned that he and other top officials were receiving compensation that was disproportionately high, and had ordered an immediate readjustment. Later, Martínez claimed, Guevara found he was unable to pay the family's electric bill. Fearing the power would be turned off, he had his wife telephone the appropriate official to ask for additional time. Martínez had insisted such an action never would have been taken against Che, but that he and Señora Guevara had obviously believed they were subject to that penalty.

She smiled at the story, perhaps true, perhaps only part of the Guevara legend. Still, she recognized that the country had changed from those idealistic days. Now there were private clubs for high government officials. There were comfortable homes and lifestyles that far exceeded those of the average Cuban. And there were men like Cabrera, who, if Martínez was right, were corrupting everything her aunt and the other founders of the revolution had struggled to achieve.

She wondered if she was really offended by that corruption, and found that she was. It was strange, since she did not believe in the core principles of the revolution itself. Still, it was there. A recognition that some effort for good, however naive or misguided, had been tainted by the same self-serving class who always seem to emerge at the end of every struggle—the people who always view an opportunity to give as a chance to take even more for themselves.

Adrianna stared at the papers spread across the desk. Her search had lasted three hours and had produced little more than a picture of her aunt's persistent idealism. She pushed herself back and began to rise when her knee struck the corner of the desk's middle drawer. Wincing in pain, she reached down to rub it, and found her hand brushing against something that had not been there before.

Adrianna pushed the chair back and peered into the desk's kneehole. The bottom of the middle drawer had fallen away, revealing a false bottom that held a single sheet of paper. She pulled the paper free and began to read. It was a simple message, and she translated it as she read.

"In the event of my death or disappearance, I direct investigators to my cottage in Guanabo. There, under the floor, you will find a safe. It may be opened with the following combination: 17 L; 32 R; 6 L; 27 R; 9 L. Documents within support my belief that corruption exists in our government that threatens the very fabric of the revolution."

It was signed simply María Mendez, M.D.

Adrianna copied the message in English, then returned the original to the hidden compartment. She stared at the copy. "My cottage in Guanabo."

Earlier she had come across a map of Cuba. She went quickly through the desk drawers and found it again. Guanabo appeared to be a small seaside village no more than fifteen or twenty kilometers from Havana.

But where? There was no address. Nothing to indicate where the cottage was located. Certainly, if investigators, or others who had searched her house, had known about the cottage, they would already have searched there as well. But what if they hadn't? Then the evidence her aunt had written about would still be there. She could think of only one person who might know about the cottage. Her aunt Amelia.

The taxi dropped Adrianna in front of her aunt's house fifteen minutes later. She crossed the crumbling sidewalk, then hesitated as her hand reached for the front gate. She wondered how her aunt would react to yet another unannounced visit. She had assured Devlin that her aunt Amelia had been overwhelmed by their earlier invasion of her home, perhaps even frightened by the presence of so many strange men. But even then she had doubted that was true. Amelia Mendez de Pedroso did not strike her as a frightened old woman. Her main concern had been that someone—specifically Adrianna—might want to take something from the home she had wrested from her "communist sister." Now Adrianna was coming back to ask about a cottage that might have been another bone of contention between the two women.

Adrianna took a deep breath and pushed the gate open, just as a hand reached out and took her arm. She twisted around and found herself facing two men. The one holding her arm had a thin mustache and a self-satisfied smile on his face. The other, standing directly behind the first, was taller and heavier and stared at her with open hostility. Both were in their early thirties and both wore civilian clothes, but there was no question in Adrianna's mind that she was facing two of Cabrera's men.

Adrianna pulled her arm free and glared at the man who had grabbed her.

"How dare you place your hands on me?" she snapped in Spanish.

At first the man seemed surprised, then his satisfied smile returned.

"I beg your forgiveness, Señorita Mendez," he said in Spanish.

Adrianna noted there was no regret in his voice.

"Colonel Cabrera wishes to speak with you. State Security has located the remains of your aunt, and it is necessary that you make a formal identification."

The second man had moved closer so he, too, could grab

her if she attempted to run. Adrianna struggled to appear unconcerned.

"I see," she said. "That is very good news. Please tell Colonel Cabrera that I will come to the Villa Marista later this afternoon. Right now I must see my other aunt, who has been taken ill."

The first man smirked at her. "I think your aunt has recovered from her illness. She left her home more than an hour ago." A car pulled to the curb behind him, and he gestured toward it. "I think we will go now," he said.

Adrianna shook her head. "No. I will wait for my aunt."

The second man stepped forward and took her wrist. His hand felt like a vise, and as she tried to pull away, he quickly slapped her elbow forward and twisted her arm up behind her back. Adrianna closed her eyes against the pain.

"Do not make us hurt you, señorita," the first man said. He reached out and stroked her cheek. "Beautiful women should be given pleasure, not pain."

Adrianna pulled her head away and glared at him. Her anger produced another smile.

"Now I think we will go," he said. "The colonel has been searching for you for more than a day. And he is a man who does not like to be kept waiting."

17

Devlin stood in the apartment window, staring out at the house in Guanabacoa. Cabrera and DeForio had left fifteen minutes earlier, followed by Pitts and two of Martínez's men.

The owner of the apartment stood behind Devlin muttering in Spanish. Two more of Martínez's men stood next to the man, whose home had been invaded and temporarily seized with a flash of Martínez's credentials. Now Devlin watched as Martínez approached the front door of the house across the street.

He knocked and waited until the door was opened by Mattie the Knife Ippolito. He could see the major bobbing his head submissively as he gestured toward the car parked in the driveway. Ippolito simply glared at him, then shut the door in his face.

"A very unpleasant gentleman," Martínez said when he returned to the apartment. "I simply informed him that I was a mechanic who would be happy to serve him if he had difficulty with his car." The major smiled. "He was very rude. From his accent I would say he is an American, perhaps even from your own city."

"You've been to New York?" Devlin asked.

"Oh yes," Martínez said. "I have traveled extensively in your country."

Devlin stared at him. "Who the fuck are you, Martínez?"

The major made a helpless gesture. "I am a humble police officer. Like yourself, my friend."

Devlin stared at his shoes. "Okay, Major. From one humble police officer to another, what now?"

"Now we go back to Havana and resume our surveillance. My men will remain here to watch the house. There are also several more watching the rear. They will notify me when we should return."

"What about the ritual and the *nganga*?"

"It will arrive at night, my friend. Perhaps tonight, perhaps tomorrow night. The Abakua *palero* will not want to draw attention to it. As I told you before, a *nganga* is not something that goes unnoticed in Cuba." He placed his hands together and rubbed them vigorously. "When the *nganga* arrives, or when our gentleman from Cobre leaves to go to it, we shall be there. Be assured, my friend. We are coming to the end of this mystery."

Adrianna sat in a chair in the middle of an empty room. The two men who had taken her from her aunt's house leaned against the wall watching her. The house they had brought her to was near the Marina Hemingway, and through an open window she could smell the sea and hear the sound of fishing boats returning to port.

Cabrera did not arrive until seven o'clock. He placed himself in front of her, arms folded across his chest.

"Where are you and your friends staying now, señorita?" he asked.

"You know where we're staying," Adrianna said.

"Oh yes. The Hotel Inglaterra. I know that much of your

clothing is still there. But the hotel informs me that the rooms do not appear to be occupied. Why is that?"

"The hotel is wrong."

"Ah, I see. And the absence of any shaving implements, or cosmetics, or a simple toothbrush, is undoubtedly another mistake our hotel employees have made, no?"

"Undoubtedly."

Cabrera stroked his well-trimmed beard and sighed. "It would be so much easier—for *you*—if you chose to answer my questions honestly. You are unaware, perhaps, that it is against our laws to give false answers to an officer of State Security."

Adrianna stared at him. "Then I think you should arrest me, and contact the American Interests Section at the Swiss embassy."

Cabrera threw back his head and laughed. "Perhaps in ten days, señorita." His face hardened. "If you survive ten days." He took a step toward her. "I want to know where I can find Señor Devlin and this Señor Pitts I am yet to meet. Then we can bring this matter to a conclusion. As I'm sure you know, it is also unlawful for foreigners to stay in our country without notifying the government of their living arrangements."

"I don't know where they are."

Cabrera raised one hand and the two men left their positions against the wall. Adrianna could feel her legs trembling, and she fought to control them.

"If you refuse to cooperate with me, I will be forced to turn our interrogation over to my men." He shook his head. "It is something I would regret very much. So, once more, señorita. Where are Señor Devlin and Señor Pitts?"

The door flew open behind Cabrera, and Ollie Pitts filled the frame. He was in a shooter's stance, and the barrel of his pistol was leveled at Cabrera's head.

"Your men go for their guns, and you're a dead man, Colonel."

Cabrera barked an order in Spanish and the two men froze.

"Who are you?" Cabrera snapped.

"I'm fucking Santa Claus," Pitts said through a grin. "Merry fucking Christmas."

Adrianna hurried across the room and placed herself behind Pitts. "How did you find me?" she asked.

"I'll tell you later. Tell those two wahoos to take their pistols out with two fingers, and to lay them gently on the floor. Then they should kick them over here."

When the two men had followed Adrianna's directions, Pitts turned his attention back to Cabrera. "You armed, Colonel?" he asked.

Cabrera shook his head.

Pitts smiled. "When I search you, Colonel, if I find out you're lying, I'm gonna kick you in the nuts." He reached down and grabbed his crotch. "*Comprende?* It's gonna hurt like hell."

Cabrera glared at him, then reached inside his jacket and withdrew a medium-sized automatic. He laid it on the floor and kicked it to Pitts.

Pitts glanced at it, and smiled. "Now don't you feel better that you did that, Colonel?" His eyes hardened. "Now handcuffs and keys, plus the keys to both your cars. Tell your men to kick it all over here."

Pitts collected the weapons and keys, then told Adrianna to cuff the three men together.

When she had finished, he gave Cabrera another grin. "You come out before we're gone, and I'll put small holes in your fucking heads, you got that, Colonel?"

Cabrera glared at him and nodded, and Pitts slowly backed himself and Adrianna out of the room.

Outside, he stepped over the unconscious body of Cabrera's driver, reached through the open window of his car, and ripped the microphone from his radio. Then he did the same to the second car.

"That should give us time to get the hell out of here," he said as he took Adrianna's arm and led her to his own car.

"How did you find me?" she asked as she slid into the passenger seat.

Pitts started the engine and pressed the gas pedal to the floor. "I've been tailing Cabrera. His driver went behind the bushes to take a leak, and I decided I'd take a little look around. When I heard your voice through that open window, I gave his driver a little taste of my sap and went in."

Adrianna leaned her head back against the seat and closed her eyes. "He wanted me to tell him where you and Paul were. Once he knew that, I think he was going to kill me, Ollie. And then I think he was going to kill you and Paul." She opened her eyes and looked at the hulking man she could barely stand to be in the same room with. "If you hadn't gotten there . . ." Her voice began to tremble as everything caught up with her. She drew a deep breath. "Thank you," she said.

Pitts winked at her. "Hey, forget it. Besides, we're not out of this yet. When Cabrera gets loose, he's gonna turn this city inside out. So we better find Paul and that sneaky little major. If we don't wrap this mother up soon, we could end up in one of those goddamn voodoo pots."

18

Devlin stared at Martínez. "This was a little too close, Major."

"You are right, of course." Martínez pressed an index finger against his lips, thought for a moment, then seemed to come to a decision. "I had hoped to keep our activities more hidden, but that now seems unwise. From this point Señorita Mendez will stay here unless she is with us. While she is here—and while we are elsewhere—two of my men will be inside the house with her, and two more will be stationed across the street. I will have to arrange for them to be out of sight, but that does not concern you."

Devlin studied him a moment. "These things seem pretty easy for you to arrange. Why is that, Major?"

Martínez resisted a smile. "Ah, not so easy, my friend. Nothing in Cuba is easy. Sometimes it is simply necessary."

Cabrera arrived at his home shortly after ten that evening. He lived in a two-story stucco house similar to the one occupied by Adrianna's aunt, and only four blocks distant. Like the Red Angel, he was unmarried, a man who had dedicated his life to his career, and his personal goals for the future.

His driver pulled the car to the curb. Cabrera waited as a second car pulled up behind him and disgorged four men, who immediately moved into positions at the front and both sides of the house. Then Cabrera climbed out and studied the placement of his men. The security was unusual, but after the incident at Marina Hemingway, the colonel had decided not to underestimate the audacity of his American opponents.

Fifty yards down the street, Martínez and Devlin watched Cabrera's men deploy. They were in Devlin's rental car, parked in the driveway of an unoccupied house, to which Martínez also had a key. Two of his men were already inside. Again, the major seemed to have come up with just what he needed on very short notice. When questioned about it, he had only smiled.

"Our chess game takes an interesting turn," Martínez said. "It would seem the colonel has decided the black king needs protection."

"What's your next move?" Devlin asked. "I assume you're playing white in this game."

"Ah, white has already made its move, my friend. Now a discovered check will be revealed. Watch."

Satisfied that the men were positioned properly, Cabrera started for the front door. Unlike the Red Angel's house, his was not hidden behind a high hedge. There had been one initially, but the colonel had ordered it removed to provide a clear view of anyone approaching his home. Floodlights, not presently engaged, also had been installed to illuminate the front and rear yards.

Cabrera climbed the front stairs. Three feet from the darkened front door, he came to an abrupt stop. A circle of cloth hung from the center of the door. There were five black feathers pinned to its surface and arranged in a circle around the skull of a bird.

The colonel felt a sudden chill. He understood the Palo Monte message. A curse had been placed on him, and the *mayimbe*—the spirit of the dead bird pinned to his door—would follow him everywhere until it was fulfilled.

Cabrera struggled against the fear. It was something instilled in him from his days as a child in the small rural city of Trinidad on Cuba's southern coast. He felt frozen in place, and had to will himself to move. Slowly, he began to back down the stairs. Then panic set in and he whirled around and ran back toward his still-waiting car, shouting out orders to his men as he fled.

Martínez and Devlin watched Cabrera's car race away, followed by the car holding his bodyguards.

"Are we going to follow him?" Devlin asked.

Martínez shook his head. "Another of my men will do so." A small smile played across his lips. "But I suspect he is returning to the safety of the Villa Marista. Perhaps later, when he has calmed himself, he will begin to move again. But, unknown to the colonel, we have people waiting for him. We have the very efficient Detective Pitts at the Hotel Capri, equipped with a radio. And my men are watching the house in Guanabacoa should he later go to the man from Cobre. The lid on our box is closing, my friend."

"What panicked him?" Devlin asked.

Martínez's smile became full. "Let us drive down and see."

Devlin stared at the warning pinned to Cabrera's door. He turned to Martínez. "You put this here?"

Martínez shook his head. "One of my men saw it earlier and informed me."

"Plante Firme?"

Martínez nodded.

"And this witch doctor just happened to have the colonel's home address?"

Martínez took Devlin's arm and started back to their car. "We must never underestimate powers we do not understand."

In the dark, Devlin could not tell if the major was smiling again. He suspected he was.

"I think we oughta roust this guy DeForio," Pitts said. "Put his feet to the fire. Maybe get this witch doctor to plant one of those little curses on his ass."

Devlin and Martínez had joined Pitts outside the Capri Hotel and had told him about Cabrera's run-in with the *mayimbe*.

"It is too early to take Señor DeForio out of play," Martínez said. "He is here for some purpose we do not yet know."

"But it doesn't have anything to do with the disappearance of María Mendez's body," Devlin said. He was speculating, but at the same time trying to draw Martínez out.

"I suspect you are correct," Martínez said. "But I know he is connected to Colonel Cabrera, and somehow to the man from Cobre. I want to know what this second connection is."

"What about this cottage in Guanabo. The one the Red Angel mentioned in the letter Adrianna found?"

"Unfortunately, this cottage remains a mystery," Martínez said. "I suspect it once belonged to our Red Angel's father. In the days of Batista, it was common for members of the oligarchy to have such places by the sea. Guanabo is such a village, with hundreds of small houses facing the beach. Most have been turned over to the people living in that region, and some have been awarded to members of the government."

"Then there should be records of her getting one," Devlin said.

"Yes, if it was handled that way," Martínez said. "It does not appear that it was. However, she could have simply kept it as part of her father's estate. Those records are kept by the Ministry of Interior. They are quite old. Most date to the early days of our government, and have been stored away. Regrettably, they predate our use of computers, so I have arranged for a physical search."

"How long?" Devlin asked. He wasn't sure he bought the story. The NYPD had similar problems locating old cases and department records. But it struck him as another convenient excuse that allowed Martínez to keep his cards close to his vest.

"Tomorrow, perhaps. Certainly by the following day. Then we will go to this cottage and see what the Red Angel has hidden away."

John the Boss shuffled across the tiled floor and slowly eased himself into the battered old sofa. The house they had given him was a shithole, he told himself. In the old days, when Meyer Lansky ran the country, they had lived like kings. Now everything was crap, and he was even forced to hide in a rat's nest surrounded by goddamn niggers.

He reached out and picked up the oxygen mask that rested on the arm of the sofa. He took three long breaths, then looked up at the young woman who stood nervously before him. She had been provided by Cabrera as a translator, and he knew Mattie had been fucking her late at night.

When he thought you were asleep, Rossi told himself. Except now you don't sleep so good anymore.

Rossi studied the young woman. She was young. Maybe twenty. No more than that. She was wearing a thin dress with nothing on underneath, showing off the shape of her tits. He wondered if she was wearing pants, but he couldn't tell. She had long legs, nice legs, the kind he had liked years ago.

But those days were past. Now he was too old, and too sick. Maybe when this change of heads was done. Maybe then. He really didn't care. He wanted to live, that was all. The doctor had given him a year, maybe two if he was careful. Careful. His mind snorted at the idea. Who the hell wasn't careful in his business? You were careful some sonovabitch traitor didn't stick a knife in your neck didn't come up behind you and put your brains on the street. How could you be careful when your own heart turned out to be the traitor, or some cancer started eating your guts.

No, a young woman wasn't what he wanted. He just wanted to live. And he wanted one other thing. He wanted that bastard Devlin dead.

Rossi waved his hand in a circle, getting the young woman's attention. "A man is coming, an Abakua. He's in the next room now, and when he comes in here I want you to translate for me." He watched the young woman nod her understanding. "You tell him exactly what I say. And then you tell me what he says, understand?"

"*Sí,* I understand, señor."

She's got a high, girlish voice, Rossi thought, a pretty voice, like a real young kid. Christ, the people you gotta depend on in this fucked-up country.

He raised his hand to Mattie, who was standing by the door. "Get him in here. Let's get this thing over with."

Mattie hesitated. "You sure you don't want to leave this with Cabrera? He said—"

Rossi cut him off. "Fuck Cabrera. He tells me he's gonna take care of this, but nothing happens. Maybe he's listening to this prick DeForio. Maybe he's double-crossing me. I want it done. And I want it done now."

Mattie raised his hands, as if warding off the verbal assault. "Okay. I just thought—"

"Don't think. Just do what I say," Rossi snapped, cutting

him off again. "I want that sonovabitch cop dead. And I want him dead before this change-of-heads thing happens."

The Abakua was in his early forties. He was medium height, but heavily muscled, and his shirt was opened to mid-chest, revealing a pattern of ritual scars from his induction into the sect.

"You have news for me?" Rossi asked.

When the young woman had translated, the Abakua nodded, then shot back a reply in rapid Spanish.

"He says the ceremony will be tomorrow night in Cojimar," the young woman said. "It is a village by the sea. He says the *palero* will send someone for you when everything, it is all ready." She nodded rapidly, trying to confirm that Rossi had understood her translation.

"You tell him that's good. You also tell him I have another job for him, and I'll give him ten thousand U.S. dollars if he does it before this ceremony happens."

Rossi listened to the translation and saw the Abakua's eyes widen when the amount was mentioned. In a country where a sizable pension was fourteen dollars a month, he was being offered a fortune.

"He says he will be happy to do anything you want," the young woman translated. There was a wildly hopeful look in her eyes, as if she were calculating some way to receive such a payment herself.

"All right," Rossi said. "You tell him this is what I want him to do."

When the Abakua had left, Rossi sent the young woman out of the room. Then he beckoned Mattie to him.

"This woman." He raised his chin toward the door

through which the young woman had exited. "I don't want witnesses to this agreement we made. You take her on a little walk. Tell her you wanna take her to some cantina." He raised a bony finger. "But she don't come back, *capisce*?"

Mattie let out an unhappy breath.

Rossi smirked at him. "Don't worry. We'll get you somebody else to fuck. Call Cabrera and tell him we need a new translator for this ceremony." He gave Ippolito a cold smile. "You can tell him just what kind of translator you want."

Mattie stared at his boss. After all these years he should have known better than to try to put one over on him. "What about the nigger?" he asked.

"When he does his job, we get rid of him, too."

"What if he fucks it up?"

"Then we don't have to worry about him." He waved his arm, taking in everything—the room, the neighborhood, Cuba itself. "The kind of money I offered that Abakua bastard . . ." He paused to let the cold smile return. "The only way he's gonna quit is if Devlin kills him."

Devlin lay in bed, Adrianna nestled against his shoulder. They had just made love, slowly, tenderly, and he hoped it had helped drain away the fear she had felt throughout most of the day. He stroked her arm, thinking she was asleep, hoping to provide comfort to her dreams.

She ran her hand across his chest.

"I thought you had already dozed off," he said.

He felt her cheek press harder against his shoulder. "Not yet. I was just thinking about everything that's happened since we came here, and how sorry I am I dragged everyone into this."

"You didn't drag us in."

It was Martínez. Devlin thought about that. It was the only thing that made sense. He knew he still didn't have an indisputable fix on the time line. But he was getting a feel for it. He thought about Martínez's call: Your aunt is dying, and you must come at once if you wish to see her. Then the Red Angel's death, and the theft of her body. But when they arrived they had learned that she had actually died earlier, even before Martínez's call. The major claimed he hadn't known, that the hospital had failed to notify him. It was a lame tale, and it wouldn't surprise him to learn the order of events were actually the reverse, that the major had played them just like Cabrera had—because he, too, wanted them in Cuba. But why? That was the big question, and only one thing made sense. Martínez had known Rossi was involved, and their presence would draw him out. It was all part of some elaborate game he was playing. But Devlin also knew he'd never prove it, probably never get close to the real answer. The Cuban cop hadn't come clean on anything yet.

"If we hadn't come . . . If I hadn't been such a wimp . . . If I hadn't jumped at the chance for you to come with me . . ."

Devlin pulled Adrianna closer. He didn't want to tell her about his suspicions. She didn't need the added burden of knowing her dead aunt was being used in some political game.

"We're getting close," he said instead. "Martínez thinks we'll wrap it up in the next day or two. Then we can bury your aunt and get the hell out of here."

"What about Cabrera? Ollie pulled a gun on him today. Then he handcuffed him."

Devlin turned and enfolded her in both arms. "I don't think Cabrera is going to be a factor when this is over. I think he's in this thing up to his neck. And Martínez thinks so, too. Don't forget, he's got Cipriani under lock and key, along with one of Cabrera's goons. So Cabrera's gotta think the major has a shot at proving it. But even if he can't, I think Cabrera is going to be happy to see us on a plane. He tried to get rid of us—gave it his best shot, and he loused it up. Once Martínez makes his move, I don't think he'll try again. He'll just want us gone. At that point we'll be a complication he doesn't need."

Adrianna was quiet, and Devlin knew she was thinking it through. "I hope you're right," she finally said.

So do I, Devlin thought. Because if I'm not . . .

19

The call came in to the Red Angel's house shortly after ten the next morning. With Martínez's men watching Cabrera, Ollie spent the night staking out the Capri Hotel. When Cabrera and another man arrived, he went immediately to a phone.

Fifteen minutes later Martínez was at the Red Angel's house with two men ready to stand guard inside. As he hurried Devlin to his car, he explained that his own men had already notified him about the activity at the Capri Hotel.

They rode the service elevator to the Capri's ninth floor, where Martínez produced a key to a room directly above the one occupied by DeForio. When they entered, Devlin found two more of Martínez's men surrounded by high-tech surveillance equipment. The men were monitoring two TV screens attached to VCR recorders. Next to each were video cameras fitted with coaxial tubes that ran down into the floor.

Devlin shook his head. "How long have you had this setup?"

Martínez gave him a boyish grin. "It was a gift of our

long-departed Russian friends. Ingenious, no? The lenses of the cameras are actually in the ceiling of the room below, and the image runs up through the tube. I believe your FBI used something similar in their famous ABSCAM investigation."

"Cut the crap, Martínez. I mean, how long have you had this *here*?" He was getting a little weary of the major's bumbling-cop routine.

Martínez stroked his mustache, fighting off a smile. He had known exactly what Devlin had meant. "For several days, my friend. Unfortunately, until this morning, we have learned little." The smile came out now, and he waved one hand in a circle. "Except for Señor DeForio's sexual habits. My men tell me they are extensive."

Martínez pointed to one of the VCR recorders, and one of his men removed his earphones and began to rewind it.

"We will watch what has transpired so far, then we will see what is going on now." He held one palm out, then brought the other on top of it as if slamming a lid down. "The box, my friend. It is turning into a very nice one, I think."

Cabrera extended his hand toward the third man. "You, of course, remember our deputy minister, Herman Francisco Sauri." He spoke in English, a signal that DeForio should do the same, both men aware that the deputy minister prided himself on his fluency.

DeForio stepped forward and took Sauri's hand. "It's been too long, Minister. Six months at least, I think."

Sauri extended his hands to his sides in an expression of regret. "I had hoped to get to New York earlier this year, but pressing matters here made that impossible."

Sauri was tall and slender, in his mid-forties, with distinguished touches of gray in his jet-black hair. He was clean-shaven and would have been considered handsome except for an unusually large nose that hooked sharply at its end. He wore a lightweight business suit that had the look of foreign tailoring, and an equally expensive silk necktie, all part of the image he chose to project. As the ranking first deputy of the Ministry of the Interior, he was among the most powerful of Cuba's younger cadre of rising politicians, and he was often touted as a reflection of the new Cuba, even as a possible future head of state.

DeForio gestured toward a side table that held an assortment of breakfast rolls, coffee, and freshly squeezed juices. "Please help yourself to any refreshments," he said.

Sauri waved away the offer. "Perhaps coffee, later. I think it best we get down to business."

They went to the suite's dining table, where DeForio had already arranged a series of maps and financial projections. The maps included an overall depiction of Cuba, a second of Havana and its environs, another of the resort community of Veradaro, and a final detailed rendering of a large island off Cuba's southern coast, the Isle of Youth.

DeForio pointed at the final map. "This of course will be our initial thrust, the Isla de la Juventud, the Isle of Youth. At present we're planning resorts in Los Colonos and Playa Bibilagua in the north, and another at Playa Roja on the southwestern coast. There are already hotels in these locations that we can buy and then expand to suit our needs. We would like, of course, to offer gambling at these locations as soon as we begin operating." DeForio pointed to the maps of Havana and Veradaro. "We also want the right to purchase or build hotels in both Havana and Veradaro over the next five years. These, of course, would remain free of gambling, subject to renegotiations later, when the present leaders of the revolution are no longer in power. With all those points in mind, my principals have agreed to your demand that five hundred million U.S. dollars, which is one quarter of our anticipated investment, be turned over to the government at this time, to be used in site development by government engineers, and to pay workers for the first phase of construction. It's understood that ten percent of that amount, or fifty million, will be used to cover costs incurred by the government." He looked up and smiled. It was a nice way to describe an official government bribe. DeForio brought his hands together. "Now, we're prepared to transfer this good-faith money—all five hundred million—as soon as the final agreement is signed." He pushed the financial projections across the table. "As you will see, this is one quarter of the two billion we expect to invest in Cuba, the percentage you requested to show our resolve in this matter."

"And the percentage of profits?" Sauri asked.

"As we agreed earlier," DeForio said. "Fifteen percent of all gambling revenues off the top, paid as a tax to the government, providing we also have use of several small keys off the island's coast, particularly Cayo Largo to the west."

Sauri drummed his fingers on the table. "And these *cayos* will be used to transport narcotics to the United States?"

DeForio looked down at the table. "That is not part of our formal plan, as you know. Let's just say the *cayos* will be used to defer some of the costs of the project."

Sauri smiled at the choice of words. The smile didn't carry to his eyes. "This of course is a great personal danger to us." He nodded toward Cabrera. "In the past, the government has taken a hard line with those involved in drug traffic. You recall the trial of certain military leaders in 1989, and their subsequent execution. One of those men, Alexis Lago Arocha, lived only a few houses from my own. His children were friends of my children, so it is a very vivid memory in my mind."

DeForio's face became solemn. "It is a danger, but one I am sure we can overcome. Nothing in the agreement reflects any questionable activities on the various keys, only the storage of construction materials."

Sauri held up a hand. "Cayo Largo is of particular concern. It is more than one hundred kilometers to the east of Isla de la Juventud, an unlikely choice for such an activity. It is something that might be questioned."

"It also has an existing airport, capable of handling reasonably large aircraft," DeForio said. "We would argue that building such a facility on another key would add considerable expense to our overall plan—an expense that would be reflected in our ability to purchase other facilities in Havana and Veradaro. I think any *reasonable* government official will accept this. Especially if there is a strong suggestion from the Ministry of the Interior." He raised his hands in a helpless gesture. "After all, it's not a lie, my friend. Even we have financial limitations."

DeForio walked around the table so he was standing next to Sauri and Cabrera. "As you know, any other activities we engage in on these keys will not be part of our formal agreement with the government. Or any *informal* agreement. They will strictly involve you and Colonel Cabrera, and anyone else you choose to involve out of necessity. We will, however, compensate you both—as agreed. When the documents are signed, we are prepared to make initial payments of five million dollars to the accounts you specify. That's five million for each of you, with the understanding that you will handle payments to others as you see fit." He raised his hands again. "Nothing on paper, no questions asked. As far as we are concerned, it's nothing more than a finder's fee."

"And future payments?" Cabrera asked.

"As agreed. A two percent royalty on all product shipped from Cuban soil."

"And we will have men present to assure the accuracy of the count?" Cabrera asked.

"Definitely. Nothing leaves any of the keys without first passing your people. Sort of an *unofficial* State Security inspection." He smiled at the two men. "I estimate your compensation at around ten million a year. For *each* of you."

"Payable in installments at the time of each shipment," Sauri added.

"To whatever foreign account you specify." DeForio hesitated a beat. "This, of course, is contingent on your assurance that no attempt will be made to alter the present government for at least five years."

Sauri laughed softly. "And this to assure the U.S. economic sanctions remain in place."

DeForio nodded. "It's the only way we can limit big-money competition for the properties we want. We don't want to find ourselves bidding against well-financed hotel chains. We already lived through that in Vegas and Atlantic City."

Sauri rubbed his hands together. He glanced at Cabrera. "Fidel would be amused, no? If he knew. Imagine, the Mafia keeping the revolution in power so they could eliminate capitalist competition. Of course he does not know it is the Mafia. He believes he is dealing with an unscrupulous foreign corporation operating out of the Bahamas—one that is simply trying to subvert the American embargo." He laughed more heartily this time.

"But he *has* signed on to our initial plan. Resort gambling on the Isle of Youth." DeForio intentionally formulated his words as a statement, not a question.

"Yes, yes," Sauri said. "It was difficult to convince him, but finally he agreed. The country is in economic crisis, and the revenues this will generate could equal our present losses in sugar, which we once hoped would carry our economy through difficult times. The fact that this gambling would be limited to the Isla de la Juventud made it palatable. It spares the people of the mainland, and will not appear to be a return to the days of Batista."

"Five years from now it may be different," DeForio said. "At least that's our hope."

Sauri laughed again. "And your power then will be such that your hopes will undoubtedly become reality. But it will not matter then. In five years Fidel's life will be closing in on eighty years. If he has not already retired, steps can then be taken."

"That, of course, we will leave to you," DeForio said. "By then, our investment plan will be completed, and the sanctions will no longer be a concern. In fact, it would benefit us if they were lifted."

"Something I am sure you will arrange," Cabrera said.

DeForio smiled. "You never know." He raised a finger. "But we'll always be grateful to the Comandante." He brought the finger to his nose and tapped lightly. "Hey, who can tell? Maybe we'll be so grateful, we'll contribute to Fidel's pension." He paused for effect. "Or a little something for the monument on his grave."

Martínez removed his earphones and dropped them in his lap. Devlin did the same. He was seated across from the major, and he took time to study his face. The man did not look pleased. Not like a cop who had just busted a major case. You son of a bitch, Devlin thought, certain now that this was what Martínez had been after all along, the game he had been using them to play.

"I'd expect you to look happier," he said.

Martínez raised his eyes and expelled a long breath. "Hearing that your government has agreed to play the whore to criminals is not pleasant news, my friend."

Devlin stared him down. "What about using innocent tourists and a bereaved young woman? How does that play for you, Major?"

Martínez placed his hands on the arms of his chair and pushed himself up. "It is time to go now, my friend. We have an endgame to conduct before our chess match is finished."

"And what exactly do you have in mind?"

Martínez started toward the door, followed by Devlin and Pitts. "Before he reaches the comfort of his car, our deputy minister, Señor Sauri, will be taken into custody by my men. He will be placed under house arrest in his own home until I have presented our evidence to his superiors. Other of my men will arrest Colonel Cabrera. He, too, will be taken to his home, where I will interrogate him. It is an action which I invite you to attend. Perhaps we will learn more about the Red Angel's disappearance."

"What about that scumbag DeForio?" Pitts asked.

"He will be placed in one of our detention cells, the same place were Señor Cipriani is now housed." He gave them his Cuban shrug. "Unfortunately, in time, we must avail him of the right to contact the American Interests Section at the Swiss embassy. But I doubt he will be treated sympathetically."

"And then?" Devlin asked.

"Then we will attend to Señor Rossi."

Devlin took the major's arm, stopping him. "It's nice to see you know his name."

Martínez gave Devlin a wistful look. "*Sí*, señor. I know his name. I have always known his name. But let us delay your questions until this endgame is finished."

20

Juan Domingo Argudin, the Abakua who had accepted Rossi's contract, smiled as he watched Devlin leave the Capri Hotel. The old man had been right. The man he wanted killed had been found just as he had said—by following this Cuban major who had been helping him from the start.

It had not been easy. This major was no fool, but the old man's plan had been a good one. He and his fellow Abakua had used three cars, and they had abandoned their customary white clothing. Then fate had intervened as well. Something had happened, and the major and his men had suddenly begun rushing about, all precautions abandoned. Now, he was certain, they would take this American to a place where the kill could be accomplished in a way that would permit his own escape.

Argudin signaled to his men in the second car. One of them had just been released by the police. He had driven the truck in their first attempt to kill the Americans, and Argudin had promised him he could kill the big American who had beaten him outside Plante Firme's home. He knew the man would do everything in his power not to lose them.

Following in his own car, Argudin thought about the money he would be paid. It was more than he had ever dreamed of having at one time. Enough to take him to Miami, where friends who had been part of Castro's Mariel Boatlift were now growing rich in the Cuban-American underworld. He momentarily wondered if his men, who would actually do the killing, would escape as well. He decided it did not matter. He had no intention of sharing the money with them. Once it was done, he alone would get the ten thousand U.S. dollars. And he would be one step closer to a new and prosperous life in Miami.

They returned to the Red Angel's house, where Martínez busied himself on the telephone.

Devlin took Adrianna aside and explained what had happened. As she listened he watched her face darken and her hands close into tight fists.

"I'm struggling to give him the benefit of the doubt," she said. "I'm struggling, but it is so hard."

Devlin stroked her arm. "Martínez says he'll explain everything—even answer our questions for a change—just as soon as this thing is wrapped up." He inclined his head toward the room where Martínez was using the telephone. "That includes interrogating Cabrera about your aunt, and nailing Rossi at this change-of-heads ceremony. I think he's setting those things up now. He's still positive we'll end up with your aunt's body after we do those things."

Adrianna looked away. "Or what's left of it," she said.

"I don't think we can hang that one on Martínez."

Adrianna's head snapped up. "Are you sure? After all this, don't you think it's possible he let them take the body so they'd lead him to the rest of it?"

Devlin stroked her arm again, trying to soothe away the anger. "No, I don't," he said. "Oh, he played us into it very neatly. There's no question about that. And he shouldn't have done it, because it put us at risk. But I saw the setup at the hotel. He had the business part of this thing cold, with us or without us. I think he needed us to help prove that Cabrera had your aunt killed, either because she had found out what he was up to, or because the colonel had cut a little side deal with John the Boss."

Adrianna stared at him. "You think Rossi might have set this up? Just to get you here?"

"To get *us* here," Devlin said. He placed his hands on both of her arms. "Look, I can't prove it. Maybe I'll never be able to prove it. If John the Boss set this up, it's something he'd play very close. Even his Mafia partners wouldn't know the real reasons behind what he was doing. He wouldn't tell anybody he didn't have to. It's the way he operates. But if it's true, it was very clever, exactly the way Rossi's twisted mind works."

He tried to soften his next words. "It's no secret that old bastard wants me dead. You were there the first time he tried. But he knows he can't try again. At least not in New York. If he did, the NYPD would bring the world down on his head." He looked away, wondering how she'd take what he was about to tell her. "I saw Rossi before we left. I didn't tell you about it because it was just a routine thing. Then, later, we got all wrapped up with what happened to your aunt." He gave her a cold, mirthless smile. "It happened the day before we left, and the old bastard was cocky as hell. He told me he knew everything about me." He shook his head in grudging admiration. "You know what? I believe it. I think he's made it his business to find out everything he could—everything about me that makes me vulnerable. And that means finding out about the people I love."

"So you think he found out about my aunt, and how close we were."

"It wouldn't be hard. You're a well-known artist, babe, and your Cuban ancestry has been written about pretty extensively. Your aunt was also a well-known figure in Cuba."

"And it would make sense that I'd come here if anything happened to her."

"Yes, it would," Devlin said. "Especially if you were told she was hurt and dying. And that old bastard was right. He knows me. He knows I wouldn't let you waltz into Cuba alone, or slip in illegally through Canada or Mexico. Not with all the hoopla the U.S. government spreads about it being unsafe to travel here."

"And you think Martínez found all that out?"

"At least some of it. And when he realized that Rossi was trying to set me up, I think he decided to get us both here and use us to force DeForio's hand. And Cabrera's. Remember, Cabrera's supposed to be the head of the secret police, as well as the number two guy in State Security. He's got a lot more power than a major in the national police. But Martínez has *us*. Suddenly we're here, and Cabrera can't get to us, and neither can Rossi, and now we're involved in the investigation of your aunt's disappearance. That had to put pressure on Cabrera. But more importantly, it had to make DeForio think that things were starting to unravel. It made the whole thing a threat to what he was trying to do, and all because of your aunt and Rossi, and this crazy change-of-heads ritual."

"That is a very good theory, and very close to the truth."

They turned and saw Martínez in the doorway.

"What part is wrong?" Devlin asked.

Martínez smiled at him. "Later, my friend. I promise you. Later you will have all the answers you need. But first, I must do something else. I must go to Cabrera's house and conduct my interrogation. There are some answers I need, before I can provide answers for you. Are you interested in accompanying me?"

"You bet your ass I am," Devlin said.

* * *

Juan Domingo Argudin was becoming frustrated. Everywhere the American went he was surrounded by Cuban police. His men had followed the gringo to this neighborhood where all the big shots lived, only to find police surrounding the house he had entered.

The police seemed unusually alert, so Argudin decided to be cautious. He stationed his men at both ends of the block, far enough away to avoid suspicion, but positioned so at least one car could follow the American when he left again. His own car was a block and a half away, just close enough to detect any activity at the house. He knew an attack here was impossible. There were simply too many police. He also knew the American would not stay here indefinitely. When he left, they would follow, and sooner or later there would be fewer police. Then, he thought, they would have their chance, and the American would die. Then, finally, his pockets would be filled with ten thousand American dollars.

Martínez left his men behind to guard Adrianna when he escorted Devlin and Pitts to his waiting Chevrolet. He drove the four blocks to Cabrera's house with the pedal pressed to the floor, the engine of the ancient Chevrolet whining like an angry cat. He was a madman on a mission, Devlin thought.

He turned to Pitts. "You think the major might be anxious to get this done?"

"I dunno," Pitts said. He leaned over the rear seat. "You anxious, Major? You warming up your rubber hose?"

"It is a pleasure I have been looking forward to for many months," Martínez said.

"Could cause a bit of a scandal, couldn't it?" Pitts asked. "I mean two top guys mobbed up like this? A little government plan to let the wiseguys open a casino? A little side deal on narcotics?" Pitts tried to catch Martínez's eyes in the rearview mirror. He wanted to give him an evil grin.

Martínez stared straight ahead. "It is possible, of course. It is also possible it will never be known here in Cuba." He glanced at Devlin, a small smile playing on his lips. "It is different here, you see. Trials need only be public when it serves a greater purpose. Some matters that involve our government officials and our military can be handled more discreetly. It is a question of the nation's morale."

Devlin laughed. "That's a great line, Martínez. I suppose you'll want to swear us to secrecy."

"But of course, my friend. That is exactly my hope. You may disagree, of course, in which case I am sure the government will decide that a public trial is necessary. But then you will all have to remain here as witnesses for the state. And these trials can take a very long time. There is also an additional problem. As you know, you have broken many laws in my country, which I am willing to overlook. But if others begin to investigate, this may not be possible—"

"Enough. Enough," Devlin said. "I don't care how you handle this. I just want to wrap this thing up, bury what's left of Adrianna's aunt, and get the hell out of here."

Martínez stared straight ahead again, and Devlin thought the Cuban major was trying not to laugh.

"Ah, I hope I have not given a poor impression of my country," he said. "The office of tourism would be very upset if that were the case. I am sure they would like you to remain and enjoy the many pleasures we have to offer."

"Yeah, I'm sure they would," Devlin said. "But I think I'll get back to New York. People only try to kill me there about once a year."

Martínez pulled his car to a stop in front of Cabrera's house. Two of his men were waiting outside. He spoke to them briefly, then sent them away.

"No witnesses?" Pitts asked.

Martínez raised his eyebrows, feigning offense. "You are too suspicious, my friend. There are other men inside. I have sent these men to Guanabacoa, to make sure our forces are adequate to watch Señor Rossi."

"Hey, that's just what I thought you were doing," Pitts said. He turned to Devlin. "Isn't that what you thought, Inspector?"

"What I think is that we should get this thing over with." He took Martínez by the arm. "But if you're going to rough Cabrera up, do it when we're not around. All I want is some answers, and whatever's left of this woman's body. Okay, Major?"

Martínez nodded. "It is understood. I promise you will have what you want. I also promise that you will not see my men and me touch even a hair on the colonel's head."

When they reached the front door, Devlin noticed that the mojo, or whatever it was, no longer hung from Cabrera's door. He asked Martínez what had happened to it.

"It had to be removed," Martínez said. "It was a very potent Palo Monte curse. Even my own men would not dare enter such a cursed house."

"You gotta be kidding me," Pitts said.

Martínez let out a long, tired breath. "No, my friend. I do not joke. Perhaps, before you leave Cuba, you will understand."

They followed Martínez across the foyer and into a well-appointed living room. A young man stood next to a paneled door with a Russian assault rifle cradled in his arms. He was dressed in civilian clothes, but immediately snapped to attention as the major approached. Martínez spoke to him briefly, then turned to Devlin and Pitts.

"The colonel is in his study, contemplating his fate. Another of my men is watching him do this. I think we should join them and help the colonel understand exactly what his fate is."

"Let's do it," Devlin said.

Martínez spoke to the guard in Spanish. Devlin couldn't understand what was being said, but it seemed he was giving the guard detailed instructions. Then he opened the door. A second guard, also armed with an assault rifle, stood just inside. Martínez issued another set of instructions, and the second guard joined the first outside.

Cabrera was seated in a leather chair. He glared at the major, then launched into a diatribe in Spanish.

Martínez held up his hand. When he spoke his voice seemed unnaturally calm.

"You will speak in English, Colonel. As a courtesy to our American guests."

Again, Cabrera rattled off harsh words in Spanish.

Martínez let out an exasperated breath. "I have assured these men that you will not be harmed in their presence. So you have a choice, Colonel. You may speak English now, or we will leave this room and send in the two men outside, who will convince you of the wisdom of following my orders. Then we will return, and you will speak English. Which do you prefer?"

"You dare to threaten me?" Cabrera spoke the words in English.

"That is very good, Colonel," Martínez said. "And yes, I do dare to threaten you. As of this moment you are relieved of your duties. You may consider yourself under arrest, and whatever authority you enjoyed under the revolution is suspended indefinitely."

Cabrera snapped out in Spanish.

"English, Colonel." Martínez inclined his head toward the door, indicating his men outside. "I will not warn you again."

"I said you have no right to suspend my authority," Cabrera snapped.

Martínez walked to Cabrera's desk and perched himself on its edge. "That is an argument you can make at a later date, Colonel. For the present, you will simply answer my questions, or you will suffer the consequences."

"What crimes are you charging me with?"

Cabrera's face was red with anger, and Devlin realized he was not frightened. The man had a lot of power, and he knew it, and Devlin wondered if what Martínez had on him would be enough, or if the major was overplaying his hand. This wasn't the United States. It was a country that operated under a different set of rules, and Devlin had no idea what those rules were.

Martínez ignored Cabrera's question. He looked around the room.

Devlin did the same. The study was richly furnished. The sofa, like the chair in which Cabrera sat, was covered in glove-soft leather. There was a wall of books, almost all of which appeared to be rare and presumably valuable. The desk also appeared to be an antique, as did several side tables, one of which held an array of small figures that Devlin recognized as pre-Columbian.

"You live well, Colonel," Martínez finally said. "But I imagine you would have lived an even richer life once Señor DeForio had deposited five million American dollars into your foreign bank account."

Cabrera stared at him. The color seemed to have drained from his face. "It is a lie."

"Then it is a lie that we have on videotape, Colonel." He paused, letting the words sink in, then nodded. "Yes, the suite at the Capri Hotel was wired." He waved his hand in a circle. "But, perhaps you and Deputy Minister Sauri were only luring Señor DeForio into a well-laid trap. Perhaps this trap also involved the assassination of María Mendez, and the later theft of her body at the request of the American gangster Señor Rossi." He raised his hands, then let them fall back. "Of course, some might consider this theft of our Red Angel's body an extreme technique of entrapment, but it would indeed be an interesting defense, would it not?"

Cabrera seemed to pull himself together. Again, his eyes took on a hard glint. "You believe you will defeat me this way, Martínez?"

Martínez stroked his mustache, as if considering the question. "You are already defeated, Colonel. You will receive a *military* trial for your crimes, and, as you know, the rules are quite different under those circumstances." He turned to Pitts. "As I explained earlier to the inspector, in our military courts, evidence is presented by the state and is presumed to be correct by those who sit in judgment. The defendant is then required to prove his innocence." He gave them his Cuban shrug. "He is not helpless, of course. He is given an attorney. But unfortunately, the attorney is not assigned until the very day the case is presented to the court, so the defense has a difficult task."

"I like it," Pitts said. "Who's the judge, a kangaroo?"

Martínez smiled. "There are five judges. Three military officers and two civilians."

"Hey, three kangaroos out of five. That's not bad." He turned to Cabrera and shook his head. "Sounds like you're fucked, Colonel."

Cabrera glared at him, then turned back to Martínez. "These American fools seem to have emboldened you, Martínez. Perhaps you should explain what will happen when your political frailties are exposed."

"I doubt such exposure will occur."

Cabrera let out a derisive snort. His eyes filled with contempt. He turned back to Devlin and Pitts. "Since you are so fond of Martínez, and his great powers, I will see to it that you all share the same cell."

The major shook his head. "It is embarrassing to see you debase yourself in this way," he said. "I hope you will show more dignity when you are brought before the military court."

Cabrera straightened in his chair, his entire body filled with defiance. "And who will bring me before this court? You, Martínez?" His mouth twisted into a sneer. "And under what authority, if I may ask?"

Martínez leaned in close, so his face was only inches from Cabrera's. He spoke softly—this time in Spanish. Devlin only caught a few words—*presentar, jefe, departamento, técnico*, and *investigación*—but the effect on Cabrera was instantaneous.

The colonel paled, and his lips and his hands began to tremble. Martínez sat back and folded his hands in his lap. "As you now realize, your trial is assured. But, perhaps, you can spare yourself the ultimate penalty, your execution. That, of course, will depend on your level of cooperation."

Cabrera's voice came out in a croak. "What is it you want to know?"

Martínez withdrew a voice-activated tape recorder from his pocket, placed it on the desk, and pressed the start button. He gave the time, place, date, and Cabrera's name. Then he stood and began pacing back and forth. "First, let us begin with Dr. Mendez," he said. "Who ordered her assassination?"

"I did." Cabrera's voice was barely audible.

"Please speak louder, Colonel Cabrera."

"I did."

"Was this at the direction of an American gangster named John Rossi?"

Cabrera let out a shuddering breath. "In part, yes."

"Did it also involve certain information that Dr. Mendez had uncovered?"

"Yes."

Martínez stopped pacing and again folded his hands. "Tell us about this."

Cabrera's arms were trembling now, and he clenched his fists to fight it off. "Dr. Mendez learned of the plan to permit gambling on the Isla de la Juventud. She went to the Ministry of Interior to express her opposition."

"Was she also aware of the plan to allow narcotics to be shipped from Cayo Largo?"

Cabrera shook his head. "We did not know. She said nothing of it to Deputy Minister Sauri."

"But you feared she might also discover this?"

"No." He hesitated. "We did not know. We feared . . . Minister Sauri feared she would take the matter to the Comandante himself, and that further inquiries would be ordered, and that it might expose who the American investors really were."

"So you decided she must be killed." Martínez said it as fact, not a question.

"That she be silenced in some way, yes."

"And is this the same reason you *silenced* Manuel Pineiro, our former spymaster?"

Cabrera became agitated. "That was on Sauri's order, not mine."

Martínez shook his head. "Very well, we will concentrate on what *you* did. How did Señor Rossi fit into this plan to kill the Red Angel?"

Cabrera placed his hands on his face and slowly drew them down. He looked up at Martínez. His eyes seemed to be begging him to stop.

"Answer my question," Martínez snapped.

Cabrera stared down at his lap. "It came about at the same time," he began. "Señor Rossi sent a messenger to Cuba, suggesting that Dr. Mendez be used in a change-of-heads ritual. He is a believer in Palo Monte. It is an old belief, from many years ago when he lived in Havana. The messenger said he wished to save himself from a grave illness."

"And did he offer you money to do this?"

Cabrera nodded.

"Say the words, Cabrera. Do not nod your head."

"Yes, he offered me money."

"How much?"

"Half a million dollars." Again, Cabrera's voice came out in a whisper.

"Louder, please," Martínez snapped.

"Half a million dollars."

"And this was all that was required of you. That you arrange for Dr. Mendez's death, and the theft of her corpse."

Cabrera shook his head, then realized he should answer aloud. "No. He also wanted me to contact Señorita Mendez in New York, and to tell her of the accident in such a way that she would come to her aunt."

"And then?"

Cabrera swallowed. "The messenger said an American man would undoubtedly accompany her, and that he was to be killed, along with the woman."

"Both were to be killed?"

"*Sí*. Yes, both."

"And were you to be paid for this as well?"

Cabrera nodded again, then caught himself. "Yes. I was to be paid another half a million."

Pitts let out a whistle.

Martínez held up a hand, warning him to be quiet. He began pacing again.

"So first you arranged the assassination of Dr. Mendez?"

"Yes."

"And who did you give this assignment?"

"The Abakua who have worked for me in the past."

"Their names?"

Cabrera rattled off a series of names.

"And these men, they used a truck to cause a car accident involving Dr. Mendez?"

"Yes."

"And were these the same men who arranged the theft of our Red Angel's body?"

"Yes. Together with a *palero* named Siete Rayos."

"And they then took that body to Santiago de Cuba?"

"Yes."

"Were you paid when that body was delivered?"

"Yes."

Martínez went to the desk and picked up a piece of paper and a pen. He handed them to Cabrera. "You will write down the name and location of the bank, and the number of the account to which the money was sent."

He waited while Cabrera complied, then continued.

"And were these same men who attacked Dr. Mendez, and who later took the corpse, the ones who later tried to kill Dr. Mendez's niece, and the Americans accompanying her?" He paused. "And who attempted to kill me, as well?"

"Yes."

Martínez stopped pacing. "You have done well, Colonel. There are but a few more questions."

Cabrera looked up, a faint glimmer of hope in his eyes. Martínez ignored it.

"Now we must turn to the attempt on the life of the *palero* Plante Firme," Martínez began again. "Was this ordered by you?"

"Yes."

"And why was that, Colonel?"

"Minister Sauri wanted the Americans gone, even if it angered Señor Rossi. He was afraid our plans were being placed in danger." He looked away, then forced himself to continue. "Another body was located. A woman of the same age and physical size as Dr. Mendez. The body was stolen from a cemetery and burned to conform with Dr. Mendez's injuries, and the head and hands and one foot were removed. These were to be found later in a *nganga* placed in Plante Firme's home . . ." He paused. "After his death."

"So he could not contradict your finding?"

"Yes."

"And this assassination was attempted by two of your men, who have since disappeared." Martínez gave him the names of two men.

"Yes. Those were the men. We have not been able to locate them."

"But the assassination failed, did it not?"

"Yes, it failed."

"And Plante Firme's grandson was murdered in his place."

"Yes."

Martínez turned to Devlin. "Are your questions answered, my friend?"

Devlin nodded. "Except for the location of Dr. Mendez's body."

Martínez turned back to Cabrera. "You can answer this question?"

"Yes."

"Do so."

"The body, or what remains of it, has been made part of a *nganga* now under the control of the *palero* Siete Rayos."

"And the remaining parts of the body?"

"Destroyed, the ashes scattered at the direction of the *palero* Baba Briyumbe, who prepared the *nganga*."

"And the change-of-heads ritual for Señor Rossi is still to take place."

"That is my understanding."

"When?"

"Tonight. After dark."

"And where will this happen?"

"At a house in Cojimar."

"You have the address?"

Cabrera nodded, and Martínez did not correct him this time.

"Write it on the paper I have given you."

As Cabrera did so, Martínez turned back to Devlin. "Is there anything else?"

"No. No more questions," Devlin said. "I just want to get my hands on Rossi. Around his throat would be nice."

Martínez smiled at him. "I take it you did not know that the lovely Señorita Mendez was always to be part of this killing that Señor Rossi paid so generously to arrange."

"No. But I do now."

Martínez raised his hands in a gesture of helplessness. "I am afraid I cannot allow you to give him the death he deserves." He raised one finger. "But I believe I can help you give him even greater misery."

"How?" Devlin's eyes were cold, blue steel, and the scar on his cheek, the gift of an old knife wound, had turned a vivid white.

"In time, my friend," Martínez said. "But well before you take your leave of my country."

He turned back to Cabrera, and noticed that the colonel had succeeded in regaining some composure. "Do you have something more to say, Colonel?"

Cabrera straightened his back. "I wish the privilege of an officer," he said. His voice broke as he spoke the words. "I wish a pistol, and time alone in this room."

Martínez walked back to the desk and turned off the tape recorder.

"I am afraid I cannot accommodate you."

Martínez went to the door and rapped lightly three times, then stepped back. The door swung back slowly to reveal Plante Firme.

Devlin heard Cabrera gasp. The old *palero* was naked to the waist. He wore a straw hat with several large multicolored feathers protruding from the brim. In his left hand he held the long staff Devlin had seen at his home. It was nothing more than the straight limb of a tree, denuded of bark, the top forking into five separate branches, six to eight inches in length, each holding an individual white feather. Plante Firme's *mpaca* hung from his neck on a leather thong, and in his right hand he held a crudely fashioned rattle, also covered in white feathers.

He stepped into the room and began to chant in a mixture of Spanish and Bantu as Cabrera shrank back in his chair, his eyes frozen with fear.

Martínez took Devlin and Pitts by the arm. "Perhaps you would like to leave now," he said.

Devlin shook his head. "No, I'd like to stay."

"As you wish, my friend."

They watched as Plante Firme advanced. His steps were slow and methodical, each bare foot planted with an audible slap on the polished tile floor.

Cabrera's eyes widened and his entire body shook. He pressed back in the chair as if hoping it would swallow him.

Plante Firme stood before him now, the feather-festooned rattle held high above Cabrera's head. His low, rumbling voice rose until it seemed to shake the walls of the room. Then he lowered the rattle and thrust it against Cabrera's chest.

The colonel's body stiffened with the blow. He let out a high-pitched scream; his eyes bulged in his head, and his body began to jerk uncontrollably. His face twisted in agony, then collapsed with the rest of him into a limp mass.

Devlin stepped forward and placed two fingers against his neck. There was no pulse. He looked at Plante Firme. The *palero*'s face was expressionless, except for a fading glint of hatred in his eyes.

Devlin turned to Martínez. "He's dead."

Martínez nodded, and Devlin turned back to look at Cabrera's lips, waiting for a blue tinge to appear. Nothing happened.

"It wasn't cyanide," he said. "Maybe curare." He turned to Martínez. "What's your guess, Major?"

"I make no guess," Martínez said. "Many would say it was magic."

"You think if I opened Cabrera's shirt, I'd find a small puncture wound near his heart?" He inclined his head toward Plante Firme. "Maybe from a needle embedded in his rattle?"

"I would not know," Martínez said. "I do know that it would offend the *palero* if you were to do so. I must insist that you do not offend him."

Devlin turned away from the body. Plante Firme took his arm and spoke. The words sounded urgent.

"The *palero* says you will be in great danger when you leave this house. He asks that you take great care."

"What does that mean?"

"It means we should listen." Martínez went to the door and snapped out an order to his two men, and they immediately ran toward the rear of the house. Devlin heard a door open as the men headed into the rear yard.

Martínez glanced quickly at Devlin and Pitts. "To the front door," he said. "With caution."

All three had their weapons drawn as Martínez reached for the knob of the front door. He eased it back, then moved quickly across the open frame. The move drew immediate fire, only a second too late. Martínez flattened against the wall and shouted out a command. From each side of the house steady bursts of automatic-weapon fire erupted as the major's men fired toward the street. Martínez leaned out and emptied the clip of his automatic.

Pitts swung into the door frame, crouched low, his weapon out in front. Devlin spun in behind, slightly higher, his own pistol leveled at the street. They fired, then jumped back. Another burst of automatic-rifle fire came from the sides of the house. There was no return fire.

Pitts jumped back into the door frame, ready to fire again. Devlin followed.

"Shit," Pitts said. "It's over, and I didn't get off one clean fucking shot."

Devlin pulled him back from the door. "Wait for Martínez's boys to confirm the kills," he ordered.

A few minutes later words were shouted in Spanish, and Martínez stepped out onto the front stairs, followed by Devlin and Pitts.

They eased their way to the street, weapons held down along their legs. Three men lay scattered on the roadway, two near one car, the third sprawled next to another. A fourth man was slumped against the steering wheel of the second car. Martínez's men stood to each side of the cars, their weapons pointed toward the ground.

"Dead?" Devlin asked.

Martínez nodded.

"Cabrera's people?" It was Pitts this time.

"No, I do not think so," Martínez said. He glanced at Devlin. "I think Señor Rossi has not yet given up on his plans for you."

Plante Firme stepped past them. He had followed them from the house unnoticed. He used his staff to turn one of the bodies, then reached down and tore open the man's shirt, revealing a series of ritual scars.

"Abakua," he said.

"Hey, we owe you," Pitts said. He turned to Martínez. "The old boy must have seen them when he came in."

"You discount magic?" Martínez said.

"Hey, magic is fine," Pitts said. "As long as these scumbags are dead."

Martínez turned to Devlin. "I detect skepticism in your detective," he said. "I wonder what he would think if I told him that Plante Firme has been in this house since before we arrived. Or that he was kept in a room at the rear of the house on my orders."

"Are you shitting me?" Pitts said.

Martínez smiled at both men. "No, my friends. I am not *sheeting* you. Even so, it seems the *palero* still knew about the Abakua. It is curious, no?"

Devlin pushed it aside. It was more than he wanted to deal with. "There's something else that's curious," he said.

Martínez's eyes glittered. "And what is that?"

"When you were grilling Cabrera, you said something in Spanish. It seemed to change everything. He was like a whipped dog after that. Now, I only caught a few words. *Presentar* was one. Then *jefe,* and *técnico* and *investigación.* What did you tell him, Martínez?"

The major stroked his mustache. "Your Spanish, it is improving," he said. He looked down and studied the toe of his shoe. "It is quite simple," he said. "I merely introduced myself to the colonel."

"As what?" Devlin asked.

"As *jefe de Departamento Técnico de Investigación.* Chief of the secret police." He offered Devlin a small bow. "General Arnaldo Martínez, at your orders, my friend."

"I thought you said Cabrera held that job."

Martínez shrugged. "A small lie, I am afraid. What the politicians would call a matter of convenience."

21

You're a sneak, General."

Martínez smiled at Adrianna. "Yes, I am afraid it is so. Your beloved aunt has told me this many times in the past."

"So now it's Cojimar, is it?" Devlin asked.

They were seated in the kitchen of the Red Angel's house, drinking strong Cuban coffee. Martínez studied his cup for a minute, then looked up at Adrianna.

"It is Cojimar," he said. "But I must ask that the señorita does not accompany us."

Adrianna started to object. Martínez held up a hand.

"Please," he said. "There are good reasons that I ask this."

"Tell me your reasons." Adrianna's voice was cold and hard and unhappy.

"First is the *nganga,*" Martínez said. "We will be finding the remains of the body it holds, and this is not something I wish to inflict on you. Next is the question of the Abakua who attacked us outside Cabrera's home. I cannot be certain all were killed. It is possible there are others who we did not see. So I must insist that you remain here under the watch of my men. To do otherwise would be foolish, both to the memory of your beloved aunt and to your safety."

"He's right," Devlin said.

Adrianna turned on him, eyes sharp, voice snappish. "But it's okay for you and Ollie. For the two *big guys*."

"Let's just say it's important for me. I want to be there when Rossi gets his."

Adrianna turned away. "And they talk about Spanish machismo. Christ."

Devlin took her hand, but she pulled it away.

"The general has the final say. I'll go along with whatever he decides," Devlin said. "I won't like it if he says you can go, but I won't try to change your mind."

Adrianna's eyes locked on Martínez. "Well?"

Martínez rolled his eyes. "*Madre de Dios*." He looked at Devlin. "May Lenin forgive me."

Devlin laughed. "That's all right. She has that effect on everybody. You mess with her, you pay."

Martínez drew a heavy breath. "A compromise," he said. "You will come with us, but you will wait at a distance under the protection of my men."

"But then I come in later," Adrianna said.

"Yes, yes. You may come in later." He turned to Devlin again. "She is always this way?" He watched Devlin nod. "*Madre de Dios, señor. Madre de Dios*."

They went in three cars, passing through the tunnel to Casablanca, then on to a nearly deserted highway for the ten-kilometer drive to the small fishing village of Cojimar. Everything changed quickly upon leaving Havana. The rural landscape took over, offering broad plains dotted with farmlands. Along the coast, quiet, unfettered pleasures of the seaside ruled, the beaches left mostly undeveloped and open to those who drove or hitchhiked out each morning.

Above the beaches, small pockets of well-tended houses sat in suburban clusters. Closer to the sea the houses were older and smaller and poorer, many little more than shacks. Martínez explained they were the homes of fishermen, not unlike the ones Hemingway had written about in his novella *The Old Man and the Sea*.

"Hemingway kept his sport-fishing boat here," Martínez said. "Tourists think he kept it at the marina to the west of Havana that bears his name."

They passed a restaurant, La Terraza, and Martínez explained that it was one of the author's favorites. "He came to eat and drink here after fishing. It was cheap then. Now, because they have put his picture on the walls, the prices are those only tourists can afford."

"What is this?" Pitts asked from the rear seat. "Everywhere I go, it's Hemingway slept here, or ate here, or farted here. He's like fucking George Washington."

Martínez laughed. "You are offended we honor an American? He gave us our pride by praising our culture. Even when we lived under Batista's heel. We do not forget such a gift."

"And it brings in bucks from the tourists," Devlin countered.

"Indeed," Martínez said. "It is an enduring legacy. And a profitable one for the revolution."

Devlin glanced out the rear window. Adrianna was in the next car, surrounded by Martínez's men. A second car of armed men followed. He wondered if she was enjoying the scenery, or simply fuming at being treated like a helpless woman.

"How many men have you got assigned to this little caper?" he asked Martínez.

"There are nine with us, then we three, of course. I have four men watching the house, and three more who have followed Señor Rossi."

"How many Abakua will we have to deal with?"

"My men say there are four at the house, plus the *palero,* Siete Rayos. Two more have picked up Señor Rossi and his man."

"Has Rossi gotten to the house yet?"

Martínez picked up his handheld radio. "I will check," he said.

He spoke briefly, listened to the response, then glanced across the front seat at Devlin. "He has just arrived. The ceremony should begin quickly now."

Devlin calculated the odds. Six Abakua, plus the *palero,* Rossi, and Mattie the Knife. Nine in all, against the nineteen they would throw against them. But they held the house, and at least two or three of the men would be left to guard Adrianna. The odds might look good on paper, but he still didn't like it. "You think it's enough?" he asked.

"The ceremony will occupy their attention. We will take the men outside quietly, then move quickly on the house. It is safe to attack them here. Cojimar is not an Abakua stronghold." He tapped on the steering wheel playfully. "Our force will be sufficient. Remember, the great English poet Robert Browning once said that less is more. It is a principle I have often found to be correct."

Christ, Devlin thought, now I'm getting quotes from another dead writer. "I think the man was talking about poetry, not police work," he said.

Martínez laughed again. "It is the art of police work."

Devlin ground his teeth. "Just please make sure Adrianna is kept as far back as possible."

"Do not fear," Martínez said. "It is all arranged. You are in the very capable hands of the secret police."

"Yeah, that's what I'm afraid of," Devlin said.

Juan Domingo Argudin had followed the three cars from Havana. The assault at Cabrera's house had been a disaster; all his men had been killed. He had escaped, having been far enough back to avoid detection, but it was a hollow consolation.

He had returned to the house that he believed was the American's base of operations, and had been proven correct. But the police also had been there in force, and his hopes for the wealth he had been promised had again been thwarted.

Now, as he followed the caravan of cars traveling east, his despair deepened. As they approached the outskirts of Cojimar, there was little question where the American and his police bodyguards were headed. His only hope was to get there first. Perhaps the old man would even pay for the warning. And then, if the old man escaped, there might be still another chance to kill his target.

Siete Rayos raised his arms toward the ceiling. The *nganga* he had brought from Santiago de Cuba sat before him, four lighted candles placed about it, marking the major points of the compass. The *palero*'s voice rumbled with a prayer, largely in Bantu, the words running together so they were barely distinguishable, one from the other.

John the Boss sat across from the *palero,* the *nganga* between them. He studied the man's face. It was painted with slashing lines of white chalk. He was naked, except for a pair of tattered shorts, and his chest was covered with ritual scars, which on his dark brown body appeared even darker, almost black.

Rossi leaned in toward the woman who had been sent as his new interpreter. She was short and fat and homely, and so far Mattie had not tried to fuck her.

"This *palero,* he seems young," he whispered. "What's he doing?"

"He prays to BabaluAye," the woman whispered. "He

asks the dead one be permitted to perform a change of lives. Yours for another."

As the woman finished explaining, the *palero* lowered his arms, withdrew a long-bladed knife from his belt, and extended it across the *nganga*. He spoke to Rossi in Spanish.

"Now you must feed the *nganga* with your blood," the woman whispered.

Rossi winced at the idea. All the *paleros* he had known in the past had been old men. This one was no more than forty, forty-five tops. He believed in the rituals, had even seen them work in the old days, but they had all been performed by men well into their sixties, even older.

He placed his arm over the *nganga* and watched as the *palero* made a small cut in the heel of his hand, then turned it so the blood would drip into the iron pot.

Rossi watched the trail of his own blood. It dripped onto a mixture of sticks and herbs, beneath which he could just make out a faint glimmer of white that had to be the woman's skull. There would be other bones, too. He knew that, but he could not make them out. Her hands, cleaned of all flesh, would be there, and the bones of at least one foot. There would also be the bones of a dog to carry messages for the dead one, and those of the night bird to help the dead one see through the darkness of death.

"You okay, boss?"

Mattie had leaned down to whisper in his ear, but Rossi made a quick gesture with his free hand, telling him to move away.

The *palero* filled his mouth with rum and spit it into the pot. He began to chant.

"BabaluAye erikunde. BabaluAye binkome. BabaluAye nfumbe. Nikise."

He picked up a handful of small, fragile seashells, no larger than peas, that sat next to him on the floor. He placed the shells in a mortar, then began grinding them with a pestle until they were transformed into a fine, white powder.

"You must place both hands over the *nganga* so you may receive the powder," the woman whispered.

Rossi did as he was told, and the *palero* emptied the mortar into his cupped palms. Then he took Rossi's hands and turned them over so the fine, white dust fell into the *nganga*.

He reached across the pot and opened Rossi's shirt, revealing his pale, bony, old man's chest. He dipped one finger into the pot and gathered some of the white powder, then rubbed the finger into the still-leaking wound on Rossi's palm. Reaching out again, he used the mixture to draw three lines on Rossi's chest.

Rossi felt a surge of warmth fill his chest, almost as if some power were forcing its way beneath his skin. The *palero* began to chant.

"Angel Roja, nfumbe. Opiapa. BabaluAye binkome."

One of the Abakua, who had been standing in the shadows, moved forward now, leading a tethered black goat. The goat's head had been covered with a hood, and the animal moved hesitantly, its hooves clicking erratically on the tiled floor.

When he reached the *palero,* the Abakua forced the animal down, pulled the hood from its head, then grabbed its horns, and forced the head back so the neck was exposed.

The *palero* slashed quickly with his knife and the animal bucked violently. The goat's mouth opened in a bleat of pain and surprise, but only a gurgling hiss of air escaped the gaping wound in its throat. Blood poured into a bowl beneath it.

The thrashing animal became still, and the *palero* picked up the bowl of blood and began to mumble an unintelligible prayer. Finished, he extended the bowl across the *nganga*.

"Now you must drink," the woman whispered.

Rossi's hands trembled slightly as he took the bowl. Behind him, he heard Mattie suck in a sharp breath as he brought the bowl to his lips.

"You must drink half, then what is left must be fed to the *nganga,*" the woman whispered.

Rossi held his breath and drank. The blood was warm and surpassingly sweet in his mouth, but he still felt his stomach wrench violently as he swallowed. He fought it off, then tipped the bowl, pouring what was left into the *nganga.*

The *palero* raised his arms above his head and began rotating his head. His eyes closed as a second Abakua began a rhythmic beat on a drum. The woman next to Rossi folded her arms across her chest, then lowered her upper body in a deep bow and began to sway back and forth.

Rossi wiped the blood from his lips with the back of his hand. He was certain he could feel strength returning to his body, strength he had not felt in years. He straightened his back and drew a long, deep breath.

Juan Domingo Argudin parked his car at the top of a hill that overlooked the house. It was nine-fifteen, but a half-moon cast enough light that he could see at least two men hidden in the brush below, their presence unknown to the four Abakua who guarded the front of the house.

The rear of the house faced the sea, a place from which there could be no escape. He calculated the odds of reaching the rear door unseen. There was an overturned skiff not far from the final bit of cover, then only ten meters or so of open sand to the corner of the house. He studied the rear of the house for other watchers, but saw none. One man might do it, he decided, providing his movement was very slow, using every bit of cover, every shadow that offered concealment. But only one. For more it would be impossible. He picked up a large rock and hurled it into the heavy foliage between the two police watchers he had spotted. He hoped the sound would draw the attention of the two Abakua guards and concentrate the police on any movements they made. From the height of the hill he could see the lights of three cars approaching along the road, about half a kilometer away, and he knew it was the caravan he had followed from Havana.

Argudin slipped into the heavy brush and began to make his way down the hill. There was little time now. Almost none at all.

"How do you feel, boss?"

Mattie Ippolito helped Rossi to his feet. The old man's legs were cramped, and he held tightly to Mattie's arm.

He stood and stretched. He shook one leg, then the other, forcing the flow of blood back into each limb.

"I feel good. Good, Mattie. It's unbelievable how good I feel."

"I thought I'd puke when I saw you drinking that goat's blood," Ippolito said.

Rossi chuckled. "I thought I would, too. But, you know, it didn't taste bad at all. Like a warm, sweet wine."

Mattie shuddered and shook his head. "Hey, I'll stick to Chianti. You know what I mean?"

Rossi reached up and gave his cheek a sharp pat. "When those bastards in the other families see me like this, they'll shit their pants," he said. "They already had the stinking lilies ordered for my funeral."

The rear door opened and Argudin slipped inside. He hissed a warning at the two Abakua inside, and they immediately went for the rifles that lay on the floor at their feet.

Argudin hurried across the room and began babbling at Rossi.

"What the fuck is he talkin' about?" Rossi snapped. He grabbed the woman by the arm. "Tell me what the fuck he's saying."

"He says the police are outside. He says they will be here in minutes." The woman's eyes were wide with fear.

Rossi pushed her toward Argudin. "Ask him if Devlin is with them. The American. Ask if the American is with them."

The woman did as she was told. Argudin nodded vigorously at Rossi, then used some of the few English words he knew.

"Outside. He come. Berry soon."

Rossi moved across the room, more quickly than Mattie had seen him move in years. He grabbed a rifle from one of the Abakua and thrust it toward Argudin. He turned to the woman. "You tell him to get outside and kill the American. I want him dead. No matter what happens I want that son of a bitch dead."

22

On Martínez's orders, the drivers killed their lights and coasted to a stop fifty meters from the house. A bend in the road provided concealment, and Martínez dispersed his men in two teams, one along the rock-strewn beach, a second through the heavy foliage at the base of a small hill that rose above the sea. Two men remained behind with Adrianna. Their orders were to hold that position, even if the others came under heavy fire.

Devlin, Martínez, and Pitts moved down the road, keeping to the edge that offered the most cover. They would be the first to draw fire, Devlin realized, and while he admired Martínez's chutzpah as a leader of men, he felt a sudden longing for an NYPD SWAT team.

Martínez raised a hand, stopping them near a banana tree. A cluster of the green fruit hung just above their heads, and Pitts reached up and picked one.

"You taking a meal break?" Devlin hissed.

Pitts ignored him, peeled and bit into the undersized banana, then spit it out. "Tastes like shit," he whispered.

Martínez shook his head. "It is a plantain. It is better

cooked." He inched closer to Devlin. "Is he always like this?" he asked.

"Always," Devlin said.

Martínez pointed toward the house. It was little more than a shack built on pilings. Narrow stairs led to a porch that ran along the entire front. Two Abakua stood at the bottom of the stairs, two above on the porch. All were dressed in white, all easy targets for the rifles and shotguns carried by Martínez's men.

Devlin estimated the distance to the house at thirty yards, and he knew Martínez's men would be even closer.

"They have to know we're here," Devlin said. "If they're going to resist, they should have at least taken cover by now. I can see two more at the windows. They haven't even killed the lights behind them."

"Señor Rossi may be counting on Cabrera to protect him if he is taken."

"What about the rear of the house? Any chance of a boat coming in to pick Rossi up?"

"It is low tide, and it is shallow near the beach. He would have to wade out at least fifty meters. Such a plan would be suicidal."

Martínez brought his handheld radio to his lips and whispered orders to his men.

"I am sending three men to the rear of the house, and the others will begin closing in on the front from both flanks. Let us go forward, slowly." He began to move down the road again, staying low and close to the heavy foliage. Devlin and Pitts followed.

Argudin slipped out the rear door and flattened himself against the sand. He crawled the ten meters to the overturned skiff, keeping the rifle parallel to his body, then rolled into the thick brush at the edge of the sandy strip. He waited, listening for movement, then crawled again to the heavy foliage at the base of the hill. Just as he reached it, two men came out of the thick growth ten meters ahead and ran low to the ground to the rear of the house. Both carried automatic assault rifles.

Argudin let out a relieved breath. He touched the red-and-white beaded necklace at his throat and thanked Chango for watching over him. Had he left ten seconds later, he would have been trapped on the sand with no chance of escape.

He waited and watched as the two men were joined by a third, who had come from the other side of the house. When they took up positions outside the rear door, he began to inch his way up the hill. He wanted a shooting position that provided a clear field of fire at the front door, and close enough to his waiting car to provide a quick escape.

Rossi looked out the window and smiled. Twenty yards out he could make out three figures moving at the edge of the road. They were staying close to cover, but sooner or later, he knew, they would have to enter the house. With the lights from the windows and the open door, the Abakua on the hillside should have a clear shot at that son of a bitch Devlin.

He turned back to Mattie. "Tell the woman I want the Abakua to get rid of the weapons. Then I want them outside. Tell her they should have the others ditch their weapons, too. No resistance, tell her. Our friends will get us out of this later."

"What about Devlin?" Mattie asked.

"I think he's gonna have an accident," Rossi said. "But we'll be in here with our hands up. We won't be part of it, *capisce*?"

Martínez lowered his radio. "My men say the Abakua have thrown their weapons into the brush."

"Don't trust it," Devlin warned.

"Yeah," Pitts added. "Where that old bastard's concerned, don't trust anything."

Devlin studied the house, now only twenty yards distant. The front door was open, and together with the windows to each side, it threw a heavy beam of light on the front porch and stairs. Too much light.

"I suggest we keep to the side of the road, then get inside as fast as we can when your men hit the door."

"The light," Martínez said. "Yes, I have noticed it, too."

They moved up until they were only ten yards from the stairs. Martínez's men had herded the Abakua to one side, searched them, and forced them to the ground with their fingers locked behind their heads. A second team had moved through the front door, weapons ready, and Devlin was certain those at the rear of the house had also closed in.

At Martínez's order they moved quickly, low to the ground, up the stairs and in, pistols held low against their legs. High up on the hillside Argudin scrambled to a position just below his car. He saw the Americans follow the Cubans into the house too late to line up a shot. He touched the beads about his neck. When they came out, with the help of Chango, he would be ready.

Rossi sat in a chair in the center of the room, his eyes fixed on Devlin. His shirt was still unbuttoned, and beneath it the marks of the ritual were still visible. Mattie Ippolito stood slightly behind him, and to his left the *palero* knelt before the *nganga*.

"Bathrobe," Pitts said. "What are you doin' here? They got good cannoli in Cuba?"

Devlin walked across the room and looked down into the *nganga*.

"He must be makin' minestrone," Pitts said. "Maybe a little pasta fagioli." He moved next to Devlin and looked inside. Blood and white powder were splattered across the wood and herbs. "Don't look too appetizin'." He used the barrel of his pistol to spread open Rossi's shirt, revealing the ritual paste of blood and powder that marked his skinny, old man's chest. "Not too nice, Bathrobe. I see you missed your Saturday bath again."

The *palero* began babbling in Spanish, and Pitts reached into his open-necked shirt and removed the pouch containing the dirt from the cemetery, topped by the red feather. He waved it at the *palero* and saw the man shrink back.

"Ooga booga," he said, grinning.

"You still have that thing. And you're wearing it." Devlin couldn't hide his surprise.

Pitts seemed momentarily embarrassed, then recovered his bravado. "Hey, after I saw old Plante Firme in action this afternoon, I figured what the hell."

Devlin looked down at Rossi. Throughout it all, the old man had remained silent. Devlin bent down and stared into his hate-filled eyes. "What's the matter, Bathrobe? *Nganga* got your tongue?"

Rossi gave him a cold smile. "Nice to see you, Devlin. What more could an old man ask than to see an old friend one last time?"

"You going somewhere, Bathrobe?"

Rossi let out a cold laugh. "Me? Sure. I'm goin' back to New York. You plan on goin' somewhere, Devlin?"

"I'm on vacation," Devlin said.

"Hey, it's always nice to take one last vacation."

Devlin returned the laugh. It was as biting and as cold as Rossi's had been. He nodded toward the *nganga*. "You take the cure, Bathrobe?"

"Hey, it's wonderful. You should try it. I feel a hundred percent. I may live another fifty years." He laughed again. "Now, wouldn't that piss some people off?"

"Don't count on it," Devlin said. He held Rossi's eyes. "Dr. Mendez might not have worked her powers for somebody who tried to ice her niece."

Momentary concern—maybe even fear, Devlin thought—flickered across Rossi's face, then disappeared. The old bastard really believes in this stuff, he thought. Martínez had come up beside him, and Devlin held out an arm, keeping him back. He turned to Pitts. "Kick that fucking thing over," he snapped.

Pitts placed his foot against the lip and pushed. The *nganga* tipped over, spilling its contents across the floor. The *palero* screamed, and Pitts grabbed the pouch around his neck and waved it again.

"Ooga fucking booga."

"Ah, my friend. It is sacrilege," Martínez moaned.

"Tough shit," Devlin snapped. He pointed down at the human skull, the bones of two hands and a foot, all the digits still held together by bits of cartilage. He turned back to Rossi. "You're screwed, Bathrobe. DNA is gonna put your skinny guinea ass in a Cuban jail."

Rossi threw back his head and laughed, with genuine pleasure this time. "Hey, Devlin, how you gonna arrange that?" He inclined his head toward the bones. "Let them run their tests. It's gonna show I was in New York when whoever that is croaked."

Martínez motioned to one of his men, who began gathering the bones and placing them in a large plastic bag.

He turned to Rossi. "You are under arrest, señor." Then to Mattie: "As are you. The American Interests Section will be notified at the end of ten days."

"What the fuck you mean, ten days?" Mattie growled.

"Cuban law, señor." He gave them his patented Cuban shrug. "Proper procedures must be followed."

A rustle of activity came from behind them, and Devlin

turned to see Adrianna coming through the front door, still guarded by the two Cuban cops.

Martínez growled at the men, and received a rapid and humble reply. He let out a long breath.

"It seems Señorita Adrianna would wait no longer." He looked at Devlin. *"Madre de Dios, señor."*

Devlin moved toward her, trying to block her view, but she quickly stepped to one side, her eyes riveted on the spilled *nganga* and the Cuban cop holding the clear plastic bag filled with bones.

"You know that bag of bones, lady?" Rossi called out. He let out another cold laugh. "My condolences."

Pitts's hand shot out and grabbed Rossi's face between his thumb and fingers. He squeezed until the old man's face was a mask of pain.

Mattie lunged forward, but Pitts struck out with his free hand, the fingers held rigid. The blow caught Ippolito at the base of the throat and he staggered back, then collapsed to one knee, gagging for breath.

"Let him go," Devlin said. "But if he says another word, break his goddamn jaw."

Devlin slipped his arm around Adrianna and walked her to the cop holding the bag.

"It's over," he said.

"Nothing's over," Rossi snapped.

Pitts sent the back of his hand smashing into the side of Rossi's head. The blow knocked him from his chair.

"It's over, babe," Devlin said. "Now we can bury her the way she would have wanted. Then we'll go home."

Adrianna turned and pressed her head against his chest and began to cry.

23

Devlin took Adrianna out on the porch while Martínez's men gathered evidence inside. Martínez followed with Pitts in tow.

"We must have no more violence on our prisoners," he said.

Devlin glanced at him and saw his eyes were filled with a mischievous mirth. He looked at Adrianna. Her hands were folded across her chest, as if holding herself intact, but she was no longer crying.

"We have one more place we must go, when Señorita Adrianna is ready," Martínez said.

"Where is that?" Devlin asked.

"To our Red Angel's house in Guanabo, some twenty kilometers to the east of here."

"You found the address," Devlin said.

Martínez nodded. "It was as I thought. It was the weekend house of her father, the señorita's grandfather. The records were old and difficult to find, as I feared they would be. But now we have the location, and we can go there and discover the meaning of her last message."

“I don’t know,” Devlin said. “I think Adrianna may have had enough—”

“No. I want to go,” Adrianna said. “There may not be time later, and I want to see it. The house. What she wrote.”

Devlin moved to Adrianna and pulled her toward him.

Martínez stepped forward and placed a hand on Devlin’s shoulder. “It will be best, I think—”

Martínez’s words were cut off by the unmistakable crack of a rifle. Wood splintered off the wall of the house, and Devlin instinctively pushed Adrianna to the floor of the porch. Below, Martínez’s men guarding the captured Abakua turned toward the hillside and returned fire.

“Get her inside,” Devlin growled. He jumped over the porch rail and hit the dirt road running for the hillside.

Pitts followed, his pistol barking two covering shots up into the hill.

“Go left, Ollie,” Devlin shouted. “I’ll take the right.”

Devlin hit the thick foliage and started a slow, weaving pattern up the hill. Two shots cracked over his head, cutting into covering vegetation ten feet above him. His mind registered the position of the shots, and he realized the shooter wasn’t aiming low enough, was failing to compensate for the sharp, downhill angle. He cut right, and moved up again. To his left, Ollie fired two more rounds, trying to draw return fire. Behind them, Martínez shouted an order, and the guns of the Cuban cops fell silent. Devlin was certain Martínez would be moving up behind them, and he called out a warning to Pitts.

Devlin crawled the final ten yards, using the thick vegetation for cover, then stopped three feet short of the roadway at the top of the hill. He could see a car parked ten feet to his left, and decided to gamble that it belonged to the shooter, and that the man would be closer to the car rather than farther away.

He rolled out into the road, then crawled behind the car and circled it. From the other side, he looked down the hill and saw a man, set in shooter's sitting position, four feet below. He caught movement to his right and saw Ollie climbing over a small hump in the terrain. The shooter saw him, too, and swung the rifle in that direction.

Devlin didn't wait; he scrambled to his feet, let out a warning shout to Pitts, then launched himself over the edge of the hill. The shooter was spinning to the sound of his shout as Devlin's body crashed into his side. The rifle flew off into the foliage as they both tumbled down the hill.

Devlin struggled to his feet, and found the man already up, about three feet below him. A long-bladed knife flashed in his hand.

Argudin feinted to his right, then lunged forward, the tip of his blade aimed at Devlin's solar plexus in an upward killing thrust.

Devlin's arm lashed out, knocking the blade aside, but not before it bit into his forearm, just above the wrist. He drove his knee into Argudin's face, then grabbed his knife hand and spun him to the ground.

They struggled to their knees, their bodies twisting for advantage. Argudin growled and grabbed for Devlin's throat. Devlin butted his forehead into the man's face, knocking the hand away.

Still holding fast to Argudin's knife hand, Devlin brought his free hand down, then up, slapping his palm into the man's groin. His fingers closed on his testicles and he yanked upward, bringing a long howl of pain. The knife fell to the ground, and Devlin released the man's wrist and drove the now free hand into his throat, then squeezed with both hands, using the man's throat and balls to pull him to his feet.

Argudin howled again as Devlin yanked up, lifting him

still higher, then propelled his body out and away, and threw him down the hill.

"Oooh. I bet that smarts."

Devlin turned and saw Pitts grinning at him.

"That dude's girlfriend sure ain't gonna be a happy lady *tonight*." Pitts was still grinning as he stepped forward and bent to look at Devlin's damaged arm. "Looks like he got in a lick, but not a very good one." He took a clean handkerchief from his pocket and began wrapping the wound.

Devlin turned and looked downhill. Argudin lay writhing on the ground ten feet below him.

"Don't worry," Pitts said. "That boy is *not* about to run off. Not with his balls all squished up like mashed peas." He let out a coarse laugh.

Below, Devlin saw Martínez and three of his men break through the foliage and reach the fallen shooter. Martínez placed his hands on his hips as he studied the man twisting in pain at his feet. Then he looked up at Devlin and gave him a nod of approval.

24

The half-moon sat above the sea, sending out a rippling beam of liquid gold. Water lapped gently against the shore no more than twenty yards from the road. Adrianna stared out the open car window and thought about the violence they had just witnessed and the soft, peaceful scene that lay before her now. It was as though the sea needed to exert calm, she thought, to bring everything back, to let everyone find their lives again.

She reached out and took Devlin's hand. "How's your arm?" she asked. "Does it hurt much?"

"It's fine." He glanced at the freshly bandaged wound, then smiled at her. "Knives," he said. "Whenever I get myself into something, there always seems to be somebody with a knife."

"You're going to look like a quilt if you don't retire," she said.

He grunted in reply, not wanting to deal with her unspoken question. "Are you okay?" he asked. "That wasn't very easy for you back there."

Martínez's car passed over a narrow, steel bridge that

spanned a small, tidal river. Children played near the road on the other side. Most looked ten, maybe twelve, a few younger. The smaller ones were probably little brothers and sisters, Adrianna thought. It was eleven at night, and they all still wore bathing suits.

They were in Guanabo now, the small seaside village where, years ago, her grandfather had taken his family to enjoy the sea. She wondered if her father and her two aunts had been like these children, laughing and playing late into the night.

"Those children are still out, still playing," Adrianna said, now avoiding *his* question. "It's as if they don't want to give up the day."

Devlin squeezed her hand. He thought he understood what was going through her mind, what she was feeling. He realized that talking about it wouldn't help her. Not now. They could do that later when she was ready.

He looked at Pitts and Martínez in the front seat. Ollie had his head back and seemed to be dozing. Martínez drove, glancing occasionally at the houses they passed.

"Tell me about this place," Devlin said. "Ever since we found out who you really are, your skills as a tour guide have fallen off."

"You are right," Martínez said. "My intention was to instruct you about my country." He paused. "And to distract you at times." He briefly took his hands from the wheel, holding them up in a "what can I say?" gesture. "But I found I also enjoyed it. Perhaps I have discovered a new vocation for my retirement years."

Pitts grunted, letting them know he was awake and listening. "Hey, that tour-guide business might work, Martínez. You and your boys could keep even better tabs on the tourists."

Martínez laughed. "You misunderstand the duties of the secret police, my friend. We do not watch foreign visitors.

There are others who have that duty. We watch the people who *watch* the foreigners. And we watch the other police and the government officials who might be serving their own interests instead of the revolution's. It is not unlike your own government and police agencies, I think. They all have their divisions of internal affairs, no?"

Pitts sat up in his seat as if someone had goosed him. "Jesus, Martínez. Don't say that. Don't tell me I've been working with the goddamn Cuban shooflies." He turned to Devlin. "Holy shit, you can't tell anybody about this, Inspector. God, I'll be ruined, anybody finds out."

Devlin waved him off. "Tell me about this place, Martínez."

Martínez put his arm out the window and pointed toward the houses they were passing. They were like beach houses in many seaside communities back in the States, almost all uniformly small, somewhat battered, and well worn by the sea.

"Guanabo has always been a place of escape. In the days before the revolution it was only the oligarchy who could do this. They would flee the pressures of Havana with their families and come here to rest and enjoy the pleasures of the ocean.

"When the new government took power, many of the houses were given to the people of the region. None were taken by the leaders of the revolution. It was something that was not done in those years." He cocked his head to one side, in what Devlin thought of as a gesture of regret. "Our ideals were more pure then," he added.

"And later?" Devlin asked.

"Later those attitudes changed. But mostly among those who held high posts below the leaders." He glanced back at Adrianna. "Of course there were those like your aunt, who kept houses that had been in their families for years. In her case, I know for a fact, it was more an act of sentiment, a way of remembering her family and what their life together had been like."

"So some of these beach houses belong to the big shots," Devlin said.

"Yes, some."

Devlin thought he detected a note of bitterness in his voice. "You are a purist, aren't you, Martínez?" he said.

"Yes, I am afraid you are right. There is little I would not do to preserve our revolution, or at least the good I believe it has done. But at times it seems a losing battle."

"But you still fight it," Adrianna said.

"*Sí.* Yes, still I fight." He glanced back again. "Your aunt often called me the Cuban Don Quixote. I am afraid, at times, she was right."

"But she was the same," Adrianna said. "Everything I've ever heard about her says so. You told me she even argued with Castro."

"Yes. Yes." He laughed. "But if I had called her *Doña* Quixote, she would have chased me down the street."

Adrianna looked toward the sea, her mind filled with her aunt. "I wish I could have seen her here. Here in Cuba. In her real element."

Martínez said nothing. He slowed the car. "Up ahead, on that small rise of beach, overlooking the sea. That is the house."

Adrianna stared out the window. The house was small and neat, with a cluster of coconut palms off to one side, the fronds swaying now in the soft breeze that came off the water. There was a porch that appeared to encircle the entire house, and as their car drew closer, she could see beach chairs placed about it, all of them arranged to face the sea.

There were lights on inside the house, and Adrianna saw shadows on the porch she thought were men. "Do you have people here?" she asked.

Devlin had been lost in his own thoughts, his weariness, and the pain that throbbed in his arm. Now his eyes snapped toward the house. He could see them, too, at least three men, posted well apart. Guards watching every approach.

"How long have you had them here?" he asked.

Martínez ignored him. He picked up his handheld radio. "Let me give a warning that it is only us," he said.

He spoke rapidly as he pulled the car into the sandy drive that cut into the front yard, then stepped out quickly as one of his men approached. Devlin noticed the man was carrying an Ingram M-10 submachine gun, fitted with a sionic suppressor. It was a small weapon, easily concealed, only ten inches long with the wire stock collapsed, but still capable of repelling a large force, spitting out seven hundred .45-caliber rounds per minute, the suppressor assuring that each round was no louder than a book lightly slapping against a table.

Devlin climbed out of the car, followed by Adrianna and Pitts. He nodded at the weapon. "Pretty heavy firepower, Martínez. And it won't even wake up the neighbors."

He could see a faint smile play across the man's lips as he turned and started toward the house. "Come," Martínez said. "It is time to finish our little adventure."

They climbed the front stairs. Another of Martínez's men opened the front door, then stepped aside to allow Adrianna to enter first. The others followed her into the house, then watched as she seemed to stagger, then come to an abrupt stop.

Across the room, a woman sat in a chair. She was in her early to mid sixties, and her right arm and shoulder were wrapped in heavy bandages.

Adrianna let out a gasp, then raced to her. She fell at the woman's feet, and Devlin could hear her voice, broken by sobs, begin a rapid, stuttering, disbelief-filled series of questions. The woman cupped the back of her head with one hand and pulled her against her breast and began to whisper soothingly against her cheek.

"Dr. María Mendez," Devlin said.

Martínez nodded. He was fighting off another smile. "*Sí*, my friend. You are about to meet our beloved Red Angel." He looked up, eyes twinkling. "When did you realize?"

"Not until I saw your men outside. Then it finally clicked. It was just too much firepower to guard a letter locked in a hidden safe." He shook his head. "You're a weasel, Martínez. You had me right up to the last minute. I knew something was phony all along, but I never suspected this."

Martínez let out a soft laugh. "What is this weasel you are calling me?"

"It's a sneaky, devious animal. It means you are a royal son of a bitch, Major—or General, or whatever the hell you are."

Martínez clapped Devlin lightly on the shoulder. "Ah, that is a weasel. Yes, I am all those things. But only when necessary. And this time I assure you it was very necessary to be such a weasel. I could not risk Cabrera finding out that his assassination attempt failed. Even the police officers who came upon the scene were transferred to duties outside the city to make sure the truth would not get back to him."

"So there *was* an attempt on her life. That part was real."

"Oh yes. And it came close to success. The Abakua forced her car from the road, and it burst into flames when it crashed. Fortunately, our Red Angel was thrown from the car. She was found later, still unconscious, when officers stumbled on the scene before the Abakua could finish the task Cabrera had given them."

"And the body?"

"A friend of our Red Angel. And a most fortuitous event. Except for the fact this woman was killed." He made an obligatory gesture of regret. "You see, this woman was close to our Red Angel in age and size, and she had no family of her own who might raise questions. Also her body was so badly burned, she could easily be mistaken for the owner of the car.

"When my men realized who the other, unconscious

woman was, I was called to the scene, and when I learned the Abakua were involved, I knew it had to be Cabrera's work, and I immediately ordered the deception."

"So she's been hidden here all the time."

"Yes."

"Did she know what you were doing? The way you were using her niece?"

Martínez looked horrified. "Oh no. Never." He glanced across the room. "But I suspect she is learning this now, and that soon I will pay for my sins."

Devlin turned to the two women. Adrianna was looking at him, tears glistening on her cheeks. He went to them, and knelt before the older woman.

"It's my aunt," Adrianna said, barely able to speak the words.

"I know. Martínez just told me what happened." He reached out and lightly touched the woman's unbandaged hand. "This is an unexpected pleasure," he said. "Very unexpected."

María Mendez's eyes glittered with pleasure. "I, too, am pleased," she said. "I have heard much about you, but only in letters." She looked down at his bandaged arm. "I see the intolerable Martínez has put you through much these past days. He is a scoundrel."

She looked past Devlin, and forced her eyes to harden, but Devlin could tell it was done with effort.

"You will pay for this, Martínez," she snapped. "Even generals are not immune to my wrath."

Martínez came across the room, drawing a heavy breath as he approached. "Ah, my beloved Red Angel. It was a necessary pragmatism, only intended to keep you safe."

María Mendez held his eyes in an unrelenting stare. "I have remained safe for sixty-four years without your help. I am sure I could have survived these few days as well. Even in the mountains, with Batista hunting me, I survived. And all of it, when you were sitting on your mother's knee." She wagged a finger at him. "You think you must protect me, Arnaldo? You think you are so powerful just because the revolution has made you a general? I think it is time you had a lesson, and learned about *my* powers."

"Get him," Pitts said from behind them. "The man's a shoofly."

Martínez ignored him. He raised his hands in a gesture of futility. "I assure you, I have great respect for your powers. We have been friends for many years, and I have watched in fascination as you have tormented members of our government." He stepped closer, a small smile starting to form. "But I am confident my actions to guarantee your safety will be approved at the highest levels. You are a treasure to our country, María."

María Mendez rolled her eyes. She turned to Adrianna. "Listen to this man. He is the father of all scoundrels."

"But a devoted scoundrel," Martínez said. "Both to you and to the revolution."

María Mendez reached out and pulled Adrianna to her again. "At least he was not able to kill you all," she said. "If I had known of his insane plan, I never would have allowed it."

She glanced past Adrianna's shoulder. Martínez was still standing before her, and Devlin thought he saw a small smile begin to form on her lips. "Thank you for your protection, Arnaldo. Even if it was unnecessary and overdone." She paused a moment. "And what have you done with Cabrera?"

Martínez inclined his head to one side. "I am afraid he is no longer with us."

A cold glint came to María Mendez's eyes, and Devlin realized he was not watching some helpless old woman.

"And that thief Sauri?" she asked.

"He is under house arrest," Martínez said. "We also have in custody Señor Cipriani, Señor DeForio, and the mafioso Rossi, who had hoped to make use of your body." He raised a finger. "Which reminds me. There is a certain service I believe you can perform for Señor Devlin. If you will permit me, I will arrange it for tomorrow morning."

"Is this another of your scoundrel's tricks?" the old woman asked.

"But of course," Martínez said. "But it is one I think you will enjoy."

An hour later they were seated in a semicircle about María Mendez, listening as she explained how she had learned of the plan to bring gambling to the Isle of Youth.

"I was told of this plan by Manuel Pineiro, who once ran our intelligence service. He was very concerned, and believed something very wrong, perhaps even corrupt, was happening." She shook her head. "But he was retired for many years, and no longer had strong contacts in the Ministry of Interior. He said they just brushed his concerns aside." Her eyes hardened. "And then, of course, he was killed. In an 'automobile accident.' " She shook her head. "I did not even suspect he had been murdered. So I went to Sauri, who I knew, and expressed *my* opposition."

"What did he do?" Adrianna asked.

"At first he tried to bribe me," she said, laughing. "He said the government would add a condition to the plan—a demand that the foreign developers build and endow a children's hospital on the Isla de la Juventud." She held up one hand like a traffic cop. "This made me suspicious. Sauri had always opposed all my efforts to draw money away from the revolution's grand projects." She waved her hand in a broad circle. "And to use that money for our deteriorating health programs." She wagged a finger. "Now, suddenly, the health needs of the people were important, and he wanted to include them in *his* plan. It was a miracle. And it smelled like old fish. That is when I went to Martínez and told him he must investigate."

"And that," Martínez added, "was when I learned that Cabrera's men had put our Red Angel under strict surveillance."

"And then you started to tumble to the rest of their plans," Devlin said.

"Yes," Martínez said. "But before I had adequate proof, they moved against her." He nodded toward María Mendez, momentary relief flooding his eyes. Then it was gone as he hardened himself against any display of sentiment. "The rest, of course, you know," he added.

One of Martínez's men entered the house and came to him. After a whispered conversation, Martínez excused himself and left.

Adrianna reached out and took her aunt's hand. "Have you known Martínez a long time?" she asked.

The old woman laughed. "For a hundred years," she said.

"And you trust him?"

María squeezed her niece's hand. "Completely." She rolled her eyes. "He is a scoundrel, of course. But it is his job to be a scoundrel." Her face became tender as she spoke about her friend. "And it is a thankless job. Of this there is no question. The secrecy of who he is, and what he does, denies him any recognition from the people, or even from his family and his friends. To those who know him personally, he is simply a police administrator who has risen so high and no more—a very modest success in life. For a proud man like Martínez, this is difficult, I think."

Their heads turned as the door of the cottage opened. Martínez stood holding the door back, his eyes filled with mischief. Adrianna let out a gasp as a second man entered.

Fidel Castro walked slowly across the room. He was dressed in his trademark fatigues, free of any decorations or distinctions of rank. His gray-streaked beard hung to mid-chest, and his gait reflected his seventy-three years. He was a tall man, easily six-three, and he had the bearing of a man used to deferential treatment.

Devlin and Pitts stood as he approached, but Castro ignored them. He went straight to María Mendez and began speaking to her in Spanish.

The old woman immediately cut him off. "Speak in English, Fidel. I have guests who do not understand our language."

Castro stiffened at the rebuke, then shook his head as if it were an indignity he should have expected.

"You know my English is bad," he said. "Why do you make me do this?"

"It is a courtesy," María snapped. "It is also my wish in my home."

Castro raised his hands and let them fall back. "I come to tell you I am happy you are safe, and you treat me this way." He looked down at Adrianna. "This is your niece?" he asked.

"My niece, Adrianna."

Fidel reached down and took her hand, then bent and kissed it. Devlin detected a slight flush come to Adrianna's cheeks.

"Your aunt torments her oldest friends," Castro said. He gave Adrianna a sly wink. "But we all still love her . . . in spite of herself."

"You do not love me enough to get me the medical supplies I need."

Castro raised his hand—in exasperation this time. "You no longer work for the government. You resigned in protest. How can I get you anything?"

"Of course I resigned," María snapped back. "You had abandoned the people's needs. Something was needed to bring you to your senses." She turned to Adrianna. "And do you know what he did? He had the government announce that I *retired*. Not that I resigned in protest, that I *retired*."

Castro waved his hand in the air. "Let me announce that you have *unretired*."

"Never."

Castro shook his head. "I will find a way to get you the medicines and equipment you need. I do not know how, but I will find it somewhere."

María stared at him for several long seconds. "And prostitution? Will you see to it that this disgusting practice that puts our young women on the streets—a practice *you* have permitted to return to our country—will you see to it that *this* is ended?"

Castro looked at the ceiling. "I will do everything in my power to see that the laws banning it are enforced," he said.

María Mendez gave a firm nod of her head. "If you do these things, I will *think* about returning to my post," she said.

Castro raised his hands, then let them fall back to his side in a surprising gesture of helplessness. "Torturer," he said. He looked at the others as if seeking support. "She was this way even in the mountains when we fought Batista. Never a word of respect. Only arguments."

María snorted, but said nothing.

With effort, Castro knelt before her. He took her hand. "You are a stubborn old woman," he said.

"And you are a stubborn old man."

"*Si*. We make a good pair," Castro said. He placed a second hand on top of hers and stroked it gently. "I am pleased you are well. Cuba would be a poorer place without you."

María reached up and stroked his beard. "Thank you for coming, Fidel."

Castro nodded. "You will truly consider my proposal?"

"I will truly consider it."

Again with effort, Castro pulled himself up. He nodded

to Adrianna, then glanced at Devlin and Pitts. “I have heard about you two,” he said. He raised a finger and shook it, then headed for the door.

“That’s it?” Pitts said as the door closed. He stared at Martínez. “No medals? No Lycra concession? That’s it?”

“Be thankful we’re not in jail,” Devlin said. He looked down at Adrianna. There was a broad grin spread across her face.

“Fidel Castro kissed my hand,” she said.

25

Giovanni "John the Boss" Rossi sat in the small cell he shared with Mattie Ippolito. The bottle of oxygen that had been at his side for months stood in the corner. The Cuban jailer had put it there, even after he had explained it wasn't necessary. He had not used oxygen since the ritual, and felt no need for it now. Or ever, he told himself.

What he did need was Cabrera, or Sauri, or somebody who could get him the hell out of this stinking cell. Then he could find a way out of the country. But this clown Martínez had kept him isolated. Not even a stinking phone call, or a lawyer. Nothing.

Rossi glanced around the cell. It was in the basement of a police station that resembled a small castle, and it had been obvious since they arrived that Martínez ran the show. Even his attempts to lay some serious money on his jailers had been ignored. A thousand bucks just to deliver a message. And these clowns had looked at him like he was crazy.

Rossi shook a finger at Ippolito. Mattie was seated on the opposite bunk, only three feet away. "We gotta find a way outta this shithole," he said.

Ippolito raised his hands an inch from his lap, then let them fall back. "The cop said ten days before we could contact anybody. I think he means it. I think he's gonna break our chops as long as he can."

"These fucking Cubans think I'm gonna sit here eating rice and beans for ten days, they're crazy." Rossi placed his hands on his knees and pushed himself up. "How much money you got?"

"A little over two grand," Ippolito said.

"Okay. I got at least a grand in my pocket. At least the Cubans didn't take our money away from us. So we'll up the ante to these guards. Offer them two large, wave the cash under their noses. That still leaves us with a grand for traveling money."

Ippolito reached into his pocket, then froze as the door to the cellblock opened. He withdrew his hand and leaned back against the wall as he watched Devlin and Pitts saunter in with the Cuban cop.

"Hey, Bathrobe. How's it hangin'?" Pitts called. He grabbed hold of the bars and let his eyes roam the cell. "What a shithole. Hey, Martínez, if this is the way you treat Americans, I gotta tell you, I think it's a fucking disgrace."

Martínez feigned embarrassment. "But, señor, these accommodations are among the best in Cuba. Our real prisons are truly horrible. But this . . ." He waved his hand at the cell. "This is luxury."

Rossi sneered at the trio. "Hey, a comedy act. This joint even has entertainment. Martin and Lewis. Abbott and Costello." He raised his chin, indicating Devlin. "Whassamatter, Inspector? You don't know any jokes? You join in, you guys could be the Three fucking Stooges."

"You're the only joke I know, Bathrobe." Devlin grinned at the old man. "How much bribe money did you lay on the guards today?" He shook his head. "Oh, yeah, the cell's bugged. But you knew that, right, Bathrobe?"

"Fuck you," Rossi snapped.

Devlin stepped up next to Pitts and placed his hands on the bars. "How you feeling, old man? How's your health today?"

Rossi sneered at him. "I'm a hundred percent, Devlin. It's like twenty years fell off me." He used both hands to slap his chest. "I'm like a young bull again."

Devlin glanced at Pitts. "Mind over matter?" he asked.

"Definitely," Pitts said. "I think the old Bathrobe really believes in all that ooga-booga crap. I think those mumbo-jumbo witch doctors coulda put a fucking bag lady in that pot, and old Bathrobe woulda believed in the fucking cure."

Rossi snorted, and Devlin turned to Martínez. "Show him the newspaper," he said.

Martínez held up an English-language edition of *Granma.* One of the lead stories above the fold carried a photograph of María Mendez. The headline read RED ANGEL SURVIVES CRASH. COMPANION KILLED. Next to it was a second story, detailing a nationwide crackdown on prostitution.

Ippolito got off his bunk and snatched the paper from Martínez. He read the story about the Red Angel, then turned to Rossi. "It says this doctor wasn't killed. It says a friend of hers was." He looked back at the paper to make sure he got the words right. "It says she'll be back at her job at the Ministry of Health by the end of the month."

Rossi took the newspaper from Ippolito's hands, looked at it, and snorted again. "I recognize the picture," he said. "But even if the picture's legit, the newspaper's a phony." He looked up at Ippolito. "It's all bullshit. Devlin and his Cuban buddy are just tryin' to turn the screws on me." He glanced through the bars. "Go away, Devlin. Go fuck your little girlfriend. Go have a nice life while you still got time." He slapped his old man's chest again. "Like a bull, Devlin. Like a fucking bull."

Devlin turned to Martínez. "He doesn't believe us." He turned to Pitts. "He thinks we're bullshitting him, Ollie."

"Hey, it's show-and-tell time," Pitts said. "Martínez, you gotta do your thing."

Martínez nodded, offered up his Cuban shrug, then walked back to the door. "I will do my best," he said.

María Mendez entered the cellblock with Adrianna at her side. She walked up to the bars and stared down at the old man seated on the bunk. She looked at the newspaper in his hands, then raised her face.

"Do you recognize me from my photograph, señor?"

Rossi stared at her. His lower lip trembled, almost imperceptibly, and his breathing was suddenly labored. He fought it as long as he could, then his hands began to shake. He stared across the cell at Ippolito. "It's a fake," he gasped. "The broad's . . . a fake."

He could barely get the words out. Mattie hurried across the cell and dragged the bottle of oxygen to Rossi's side.

Rossi grabbed the mask and placed it over his mouth. "She's a . . . fake," he said, his words barely audible through the mask.

Devlin took the Red Angel's arm and turned her toward the door. Halfway there, he stopped and looked back at Rossi.

"Hey, Bathrobe. Sorry to rush off. But we gotta get Ollie to the airport. He's got a flight back to New York."

"Yeah," Pitts said. "I gotta start spreadin' the word about the old Bathrobe bein' locked up in a Cuban jail."

Devlin shook his head. "I guess the boys will figure you're a goner, Bathrobe. Not right away, of course. A day or two might go by before they start dividing up your turf. Jesus, could be a helluva mess."

Devlin started away again, then stopped once more. He looked back over his shoulder. "Hey, Bathrobe," he called. "Have a nice life." A smile spread across his face. "How did you put it a little while ago? Oh, yeah." The smile widened. "While you still have time."

Outside the cellblock they waited while Martínez locked the ancient steel door.

María Mendez, Cuba's Red Angel, reached up and gave Devlin's cheek an affectionate pat. She turned to Adrianna. "This man," she said. "He reminds me of Martínez. He, too, is something of a scoundrel."

Adrianna looked at Devlin and smiled. "I know, Auntie. He's a terrible scoundrel. It's one of the things that makes him so lovable."

Please turn the page
for an early look at

UNHOLY ORDER

A Paul Devlin Mystery

by

William Heffernan

Available in hardcover from
William Morrow and Company

1

They followed the vested priest in long lines, two abreast, first the men, then the women, all of them young, all looking as though they had just stepped from steaming baths—every one so clean and fresh and seemingly innocent. Next came the nuns, also young, each one dressed in the black and white habits you seldom see anymore, large rosary beads wrapped around their waists, the crucifixes at the ends hanging to their knees. Brothers followed in black suits, each distinguishable from the handful of priests who brought up the rear only by the black neckties they wore in place of clerical collars.

Paul Devlin watched as the coffin was placed over the open grave. Watched as the young men and women divided, each sex moving to opposite sides of the bier; the nuns then stepping in front, closest to the coffin, the brothers and priests forming a rank at its foot.

Sharon Levy leaned in to Devlin and whispered. "God, all those kids. They look so freshly scrubbed. It's scary."

Devlin glanced at his tall, redheaded sergeant. "You have something against clean?" he asked.

"I love clean," Sharon said. "It's uniformed clean that makes me nervous."

She was right, of course. Devlin had noticed it, too. All those pink cheeked kids, all in their late teens or early twenties, all with faces that looked almost angelic. Every bit of it so out of place, considering the corpse.

The mutilated body of the young nun they were burying had been found three days ago, gutted and stuffed in the trunk of a car at Kennedy Airport. It was late summer, still oppressively warm, and the car had been abandoned in the long-term parking lot. There hadn't been much left by the time the nun was found—at least for forensic purposes. But there was enough to tell she had been carrying heroin in her body. A lot of heroin, packed in condoms she had swallowed.

The detectives who first caught the case initially speculated that the young woman had only been posing as a nun when she came through customs. It had proven a false assumption. The woman, Maria Escavera, was a second-generation U.S. citizen, whose parents had emigrated from Colombia. She was also a postulant in The Holy Order of Opus Christi, where she had chosen the religious name of Sister Manuela.

So far the media hadn't tumbled to the drugs. That part of the forensic report had been buried. They only knew that a nun had been viciously murdered, and that was how Mayor Howie Silver wanted it to remain.

We don't need a goddamn media circus, he had said, when he had handed Devlin the case.

Devlin looked down the long winding cemetery road all the way to the main gate. Uniformed cops were there now holding back the newspaper reporters and television crews.

It was already a circus, and would be an even bigger one once the newshounds got wind of the drug angle. Then it would become a full-scale three ringer. Of that Devlin had no doubt. There was no way to avoid it. Sooner or later word would leak out—a cop hoping to curry favor, or someone in the ME's office. He only hoped it came after they had found the killer. If it came before . . . He didn't even want to think about it. He shook his head, annoyed by his thoughts. Stop whining, he told himself. It's part of the job, the one you wanted, the one you agreed to do.

Devlin was inspector of detectives; a rank that had lain dormant for many years until the mayor had cajoled him into returning to the force from an early disability retirement. The promotion that went with the job gave him unusual power in the New York Police Department, a fact that he enjoyed more often than not. He worked directly for the mayor with the right to supersede even senior commanders under Howie Silver's umbrella of protection. It was Silver's way of escaping the political intrigue that permeated One Police Plaza, the headquarters building better known as "The Puzzle Palace" to working cops. It allowed the mayor to put Devlin in charge of the high profile, politically dangerous cases that so often battered, and occasionally broke, any man foolish enough to become mayor of New York.

But the power of the mayor might not be needed for this case. The NYPD brass seemed more than willing to step aside.

Devlin considered the gathering again. Everyone present was a member of Opus Christi—*The Holy Order*, as it was known to its members. It was one of the most influential factions within the Catholic Church; some said the most influential, even surpassing the Jesuits. The mayor had made his position clear. Devlin was to find the killer, and keep the press at bay—not only to cover Hizzoner, but also to avoid any embarrassment for the Archdiocese of New York. Devlin understood. He had already clashed with the archdiocese on an earlier case, and the mayor had borne the brunt of its wrath. It was with good reason that New York's Catholic prelature was known as *The Powerhouse* to the city's politicians, a distinction not lost on NYPD's senior commanders.

The priest began the final prayers, driving away Devlin's thoughts. The prayers were in Latin, something he had not heard since childhood when he spent every Sunday morning sitting with his sister and parents at St. Joseph's Church in Queens. During the intervening years, the long dead language had been abandoned by all but a few Catholic sects. Hearing it now he recalled how mysterious it had seemed to him all those years ago, a tongue known only to those initiated in the sacred rituals of *Holy Mother, the Church.* A faint smile flickered on his lips as he thought of that term and how the Dominican nuns who had ruled his earliest years of school had used it over and over again to elevate those in Rome who ruled the lives of every Catholic.

Again, he studied the gathering of young men and women, as they recited the Latin responses to the priest's prayers. He wondered if they understood the meaning of the words they mouthed, something he had never achieved himself. Perhaps they did. They seemed so intent. Many had their eyes closed; others had raised them to the heavens, all emulating a "Christ-like" attitude of devoutness that his own nuns had struggled but failed to achieve with their ragtag collection of New York street kids.

Devlin's gaze stopped on one young nun. Tears streamed down her cheeks and her entire body seemed to tremble. He leaned in close to Sharon Levy. "That nun in the first row, the one who's crying and shaking like a leaf . . ."

"Yeah, I already spotted her," Sharon whispered back. "Looks like somebody we should talk to. Find out what's got her so scared."

Devlin felt eyes burning into his back. He turned and

found that two suits had slipped in behind the priest. The older of the pair—a man who appeared close to Devlin's own age of thirty-eight—was staring at him intently.

The man started toward him immediately, stopping only a foot away. His voice was low and hushed to avoid disturbing the service; his words blunt to the point of being rude.

"If you're with the press, you don't belong here," he said.

Devlin reached into his jacket pocket and withdrew his badge and ID wallet. He opened it, flashing the tin. The man studied it intently. "And who are you?" Devlin asked.

The man ignored the question. "Are you investigating Sister Manuela's death, officer?" he asked instead. He was a few inches shorter than Devlin's six feet, and painfully slender except for a slight paunch. His eyes were a soft, pale brown, like his hair, and he had a long, thin nose and tight, narrow lips. His pale gray suit hung on him like a sack.

The man's tone had remained overbearing, and Devlin decided to put a quick end to it. "The rank is inspector, not officer," he said. He nodded toward Sharon. "And this is *Sergeant* Levy." He paused a beat. "I asked who you were?" He held the man's eyes, defying him to continue his self-important game.

The man broke eye contact and forced a smile. "I'm Matthew."

Devlin waited for more, but nothing came. It was like pulling teeth. "Matthew what?"

The insincere smile came again. "My last name is Moriarty. In Opus Christi we tend to use only our Christian names." He held the smile. "As the apostles of Our Lord did."

"You're here in some official capacity?" Devlin asked.

"Well, of course I'm here to celebrate sister's life in Christ, and her reunion with Our Lord and Savior. But otherwise, yes, I'm also here for a more official purpose." Matthew appeared ready to stop with that then seemed to realize that further reticence might be unwise. "I'm director of public information for The Holy Order," he said. "I'm here to deal with the media."

Or not deal with them, Devlin thought. "Good. Then maybe you can also expedite some interviews for us."

"Interviews? Who could you possibly want to interview?" Matthew waved his hand, dismissing the foolishness of his words. "What I mean is, that I can give you whatever information you need."

Devlin offered up his own insincere smile. "That's not how it works, Matthew. *We* decide who we want to talk to, and we talk to *them*."

"But the members of our order don't know anything about this tragic business."

Sharon Levy stepped forward, moving closer to Matthew. She was a tall, willowy redhead, strikingly beautiful. She also was an out-of-the-closet lesbian who had little tolerance for self-important male bullshit.

She patted Matthew's arm, instantly unnerving him. "Matthew, Matthew, Matthew. Let me explain. People in your holy order knew the victim, right?"

"Well, of course."

"Good. We need to talk to them." She hurried on before Matthew could object. "And if I'm right, nuns never travel alone—sort of a custom to go at least in pairs. Am I right there, too?"

"Well, yes, but . . ."

Sharon cut him off. "So, when Sister Manuela flew into Kennedy, there were probably one or more other nuns with her. Am I still on target there, Matthew?"

"Yes." Matthew's eyes had grown severe and suspicious.

"Then for starters, we need to talk to whoever was with her. Then we need to talk to anyone who knew her."

Sharon gave him a bright smile that almost made Devlin laugh.

"So, you see, even though you can probably tell us a great

deal, there are still a lot of people we need to talk to. And since some lowlife scumbag viciously murdered one of your brethren, I'm sure you want to do everything you can to help us do that. Am I right, again?"

Matthew had seemed jolted by Sharon's choice of words, the term *lowlife, scumbag* making him take an involuntary step back. But Sharon had achieved what she was after. Matthew's little game of who's running the show had come to a screeching halt.

He began haltingly. "You . . . must . . . understand . . . that life within The Holy Order is very insular . . . Very protected. This is done for the benefit of our members' immortal souls. Contact with the outside world . . . is limited."

Again, Sharon cut him off. "Hey, we understand. And I promise we'll be as gentle as possible."

Matthew eyed her suspiciously, clearly not believing a word she had said.

"Certainly you don't expect to have free run of our complex and all its members."

Now it was Devlin's turn. Sharon had set the tone. He was definitely "bad cop" to her good. "That's exactly what we expect," he said. "We can't find a killer if we're told who we can talk to, and who we can't."

Matthew shook his head. "I'll have to talk to my superiors."

"You do that," Devlin said. "And you explain that we're looking for cooperation. If we don't get voluntary cooperation, then we'll have to do it with a court order." He hurried on before Matthew could speak. "Now I'm running this investigation at the request of Mayor Silver. And the mayor has asked me to do everything in my power to keep the press deaf, dumb and blind about certain particulars of the case. Namely the heroin that was found in Sister Manuela's body, and the fact that she was smuggling it in condoms she had obviously swallowed, and that somebody gutted her to get that heroin back." Matthew's eyes had widened in horror. "Now I'll do my best to do what the mayor wants, and keep your group and the archdiocese from being embarrassed by all this." Now Devlin shook his head, imitating Matthew's earlier reaction. "But if I have to start getting court orders, and hauling people downtown to talk to them, it's going to make that part of the job very hard. The press isn't stupid. And they find out about court orders very quickly. You make sure your superiors understand that, okay?"

Matthew seemed stunned. "I'll do what I can," he said. He reached into his jacket pocket and withdrew a business card. "Call me at this number later."

"I'll do that," Devlin said. "By the way, what was Sister Manuela doing in Colombia?"

Matthew seemed momentarily flustered. "I'm told she was visiting her family," he said.

Devlin watched Matthew walk away, a slight slump to his shoulders. Then he turned back to the gathering around the grave, taking in the nuns who stood closest to the coffin, wondering which of them had been with the murdered nun on her family visit. It was a hot, humid day, steamy, and Devlin noticed that despite the heat all of the nuns seemed crisp and fresh. In all the years he had dealt with nuns, all the way back to his childhood, he had never seen one perspire. He wondered now, as he had many times, how they managed to do that.

Devlin sat behind the desk in his private office, Sharon Levy perched on its edge. Devlin only used the office for private conversations, preferring to use a vacant desk in the outer bullpen, so he could work more closely with his team of five detectives.

"How do you want to handle this?" Sharon asked.

"With speed." Devlin raised his hands and let them fall back to his desk. "There's no way we're going to keep the press in the dark no matter what the mayor thinks. They're already circling the carcass, and sooner or later they're going to be all over our collective ass. So first, I want two people handling the interviews at Opus Christi. Get as much as we can, as fast as we can. You head that up. I think those kids, especially the young women, might talk more openly to you." He grinned. "Besides, I think Matthew likes you."

Sharon rolled her eyes. "Who should I take with me?"

"Ollie Pitts."

"Oh, Christ."

"Exactly. But I think a dose of Ollie will keep Matthew and everybody else in line."

"Do I get combat pay?"

Devlin laughed. "Because of sweet, lovable Ollie? How can you even suggest such a thing."

The telephone interrupted them. It was the mayor. Devlin had been expecting the call. He listened for several long minutes as an unusually nervous Howie Silver rattled on. Sharon watched him. There was a scar on Devlin's cheek, a gift from an earlier case, and it whitened whenever he became angry. His team of detectives had learned to watch for it—a sign they had pushed the boss too far. Now, as Devlin listened to the mayor, Sharon saw the scar grow whiter with each passing second.

The mayor paused for breath and Devlin jumped in. "Howie, here's the bottom line. I can't promise you the press won't find out about the drugs, or that this nun was gutted to retrieve them. My people and I will do the best we can, but there are too many mouths, too many people who know what happened. Second, our best shot is to get this killer *before* they find out, and we sure as hell can't do that if you're telling me we have to tiptoe around these Opus Christi clowns. And finally, limiting our ability to investigate this case the way it *has* to be investigated defeats the whole purpose of having this squad. If you insist on it you have to accept the fact that it's a prescription for failure . . ."

Sharon could tell the mayor had cut him off, and she watched as Devlin listened and stewed. But he wouldn't have it any other way, she thought. She had worked for the man for two years now, and she had learned that he was a truly complex character. First he was a detective, deep down into his personal core. He loved the challenge of finding the answers to something that seemed unsolvable. But even that wasn't enough. He seemed to need more. He reveled when obstacles were thrown in his path by outside forces. She hadn't been with him on his last case in Cuba, where a combination of Castro's government, Afro-Cuban voodoo cults and a faction of the U.S. Mafia had been aligned against him. Ollie Pitts had been there and had told her about it. It was the type of case that brought out the best in the man. Just like the Roland Winter case. She had been at his side throughout that bit of madness, as the city's most powerful real estate magnate had tried to end Devlin's career, and when that had failed, his life.

Devlin's voice roared back as the mayor paused again. "Look Howie, you've got plenty of people at the Puzzle Palace who can handle this case. Pick one, and give them the scenario you're giving me. Then sit back and watch the walls come tumbling down. Because their chances of finding this killer are just about nil if they can't interview everyone they *need* to interview." Devlin listened again. When he resumed his own side of the conversation there was an even sharper edge in his voice. "It won't work. It's that simple. You have to start by investigating the nun and everybody who knew her. There is no other way. And when the press discovers what happened—and they will—and when they find out we don't have a killer in custody because we've run a half assed investigation—and they'll find that out, too—

then I can promise you that all our butts are going to be hung out to dry."

Again, Devlin listened. When he spoke again his voice was smoother, softer, but just barely. "What I need is for you to tell those Opus Christi people to cooperate with us. And I need you tell them if they don't, there is no way you can keep the press deaf, dumb and blind. You also have to tell them that I *will* get a court order if I have to, because if you take that ability away from me I can't do the job. It's obstruction, pure and simple, and we can't work that way. So, boss, I hate to say it, but if you insist on that, you might as well give the case to someone else right from the start. Because my people and I won't be able to do you a damn bit of good."

Again Devlin sat and listened. Finally, a small smile flickered across his lips. "We'll do our best," he said.

Sharon grinned at him as he hung up the phone. "So?" she asked.

"The mayor says find the killer before the press and the archdiocese have him for lunch."

"Do we have to tiptoe around everybody?"

Devlin shook his head. "But the mayor doesn't want us to break too many chops, either. These people like to make phone calls, and that gets Hizzoner jumpy."

"So Ollie's out?"

Devlin grinned at her. "Not a chance. Ollie's in."

Sharon rolled her eyes again. "Well, I tried. What about a court order if we need it?"

"Not a problem, but we should try to avoid it."

Sharon raised her eyebrows, feigning surprise. "So you got what you wanted."

Devlin stared up at her. "We'll see. They mayor's been known to change his mind when things get unpleasant. I do know that we better deliver. We better catch this guy *before* the press starts chewing on Hizzoner and these holy rollers.

Otherwise we might find ourselves working out of a squad room on Staten Island."

Sharon shrugged. "Hey, there's always a chance we'll get a nice view of the harbor," she said.

When Sharon and Ollie Pitts had left for Opus Christi's Manhattan headquarters, Devlin joined his remaining three detectives in the bullpen and handed out assignments.

Stan Samuels was a tall, thin, aesthetic looking forty-year old, who looked more like an accountant than a first grade detective. He was known as "the mole" to his fellow cops, because of his passion for digging through old records. Devlin told him to search every record he could ferret out; to find out everything he could about The Holy Order of Opus Christi, from the time the group was founded, through the opening of their new headquarters in New York.

Red Cunningham was a three hundred pound, baby-faced behemoth, who could plant a bug anywhere. He also had close contacts with NYPD's wire experts in narcotics and intelligence. Devlin told him to call in any favors he had in those divisions, and get whatever they had on major drug dealers who were importing heroin into the city from South America. He also was told to check city records for architectural drawings of the Opus Christi headquarters, and to figure out where best to plant wires if that proved necessary.

Ramon "Boom Boom" Rivera—the group's self-proclaimed Latin lover, and the squad's computer whiz—was given the assignment of a complete computer search of everything dealing with Opus Christi. He also was to find out the type of computer system the group used, and to determine if, and how that system could be hacked.

"Sounds like you think maybe this group might be involved in this drug deal," Boom Boom said, when he had finished.

"Not necessarily the group, itself," Devlin said. "But maybe somebody who's part of the group." He leaned back in his chair and glanced at each of the three detectives. "I just don't buy a young nun getting tied up in a drug deal all by herself."

"I read the DD-5's those homicide detectives filed. Said her parents were from Colombia," Boom Boom said. "Could have been a family thing. Maybe I should run a check on them."

"You do that," Devlin said. "I talked on the phone with the homicide dicks who caught the case. Now I want to talk to them in person. Get things they might not have put in their DD-5's and work back from there." He pushed himself up from the chair. "We don't have a lot of time. The mayor didn't hand us this thing until it was two days old, and that's very old for a homicide, so get cracking. One other thing. No comments to the press. You refer all questions to the deputy commissioner for public information. No exceptions."